THE END OF ALL FLESH

A STORY OF THE PROMISE TO NOAH
BASED ON GENESIS 5-9

By Robert Wetmore

The End of All Flesh

Scripture quotations are taken from the *Holy Bible,* New Living Translation, copyright© 1996. Used by permission of Tyndale House Publishers, Inc., Wheaton, Illinois, 60189. All Rights Reserved.

Some Scripture quotations are taken from the New American Standard Bible: 1995 update. 1995. LaHabra, CA: The Lockman Foundation. Used with permission. All Rights Reserved.

Cover Art by Christy Harner and Jeremy Sniatecki

ISBN 978-0-9849359-7-0
Printed in the United States of America

Published by

www.FindingChristBooks.com

To my father
E. George Wetmore

Introduction

Over the years, I've seen many children's books about Noah, usually picturing a big boat, lots of animals and a bright rainbow. It's almost always (if not always) a happy story, painted in pastels. The real story of Noah, however, is far from happy. It's a disturbing tale about violence, sin, rebellion and the most terrifying calamity ever to befall the human race. The scope of the story escapes us, even though in America, we should have a sense of what catastrophic disasters look like. We have witnessed the devastation inflicted by hurricane Katrina, the tsunami in Indonesia, the horrible earthquakes around the world, even the disaster wrought by Mount St. Helens. Imagine such catastrophes all rolled into one, multiplied a thousand fold, ravaging the entire globe and destroying all but eight humans and the animals they protected.

The End of All Flesh is about that historical disaster, although from the first paragraph to the last it is most obviously a work of fiction. No one should suppose these storylines, characters and dialogues are true. The fiction, however, is based upon the written facts recorded in the Bible. I have no doubt that Noah, his wife, Shem, Ham, Japheth and their wives were utterly real people, and they most certainly did build an enormous boat or barge and did survive a worldwide flood. Yet I do doubt if any of this story's events actually happened the way I write them. You might ask, why then invent a fictional account of their experience, when we have the reliable account already perfectly recorded in Genesis 5-11?

First and foremost, this story is about God's next step in fulfilling his promise to Eve. The entire Bible, Old Testament and New, is really one story, the chronicle of the Messiah's line of descent from Eve through Noah, Abraham, Isaac, Jacob, Judah and David. Every Scripture account drives forward the central theme of the Bible–God has promised a Savior to deliver us from the serpent. The End of All Flesh highlights the promise and the pathway God took to fulfill it through Noah.

The story also puts that pathway into various possible settings, all imagined, of course, but hopefully reasonable. Noah lived for five hundred years before he began building the barge. One can only guess what it would be like to have experienced centuries of gaining and honing skills and knowledge without losing one's intellectual edge. We treat Noah as if he were one of us, but we are a race sadly devolved from the glory days when the genetic pool was richer. This story guesses what life might have been like in those circumstances. It attempts to argue that these were real people, and they should be seen as real. This is why I have created a fictional account of a real event: to put flesh on the bones of Genesis.

I used several helpful resources in writing *The End of All Flesh*. John Woodmorappe's *Noah's Ark: A Feasibility Study* (Santee, CA: Institution for Creation Research, 1996) gives dozens of answers to questions about feeding, watering and caring for the animals on the ark. His book is not for the casual reader, but instead stands as an excellent source for anyone who needs possible solutions to problems with ventilation, waste removal and a hundred other problems. In addition, I found a superb site online http://www.worldwideflood.com. This site focuses especially on engineering questions for the barge/ship/boat. I stole lots of ideas from them, but in no way can blame them for what I have written below. Over the course of writing *The End of All Flesh*, lots of different sources helped me greatly, including the superb Keil and Delitsch Commentary on the Old Testament.

Dr. Michael Hildenbrand (Ph.D., U.C. Berkeley) continually made helpful suggestions and offered solutions to various biblical problems I encountered. My brother-in-law, Tom Robb, gave me some good ideas to move the story in a better direction. Joyce, my very encouraging wife, kept me writing and thinking. I bounced many ideas off of her, and she always gave me good advice. In addition, my daughter Christy Harner, owner of Binary Ventures, designed the original cover art. Time after time Matt Harner helped me plot my course through the story. Without Matt, this book probably would have lacked many of its most important themes. After the entire book was finished, my son Daniel read it carefully and made several invaluable suggestions, leading me to add what is now my favorite chapter and fix another chapter in desperate need of repair. The book is significantly better because of these two changes. An anonymous woman went through the book with a fine tooth comb and helped me clean up the final copy. I would also like to thank the great homeschoolers in my class on world-views. You guys are in this book. *The End of All Flesh* is dedicated to my father, E. George Wetmore, a man who came to a childlike faith in Jesus Christ during the last year of his life. In light of that unimaginable miracle, *The End of All Flesh* is especially dedicated to the gracious God who heard our many prayers over many years that my father would spend eternity with Jesus.

List of Characters

Achire–Woman who cared for Yakheed during his illness

Aidyl–Woman in tanning quarter who suggests arsenic as a solution to problem

Aleac–(A-lay-ac) As a girl, listened to stories of promise. Wife of Ham

Arpachshad–Oldest son of Shem and twelfth son of the Promise

Bur'el–Yakheed's trusted foreman and friend

Cram–Brother of Tam and farmer in town beside the river

Cush–Ham's oldest son

Darbe–Abused child in the town beside the river

Eelanna–Sister of Achire who died from plague

Eisse–First daughter and oldest child of Imas

Elizabeth–Little girl befriended by Noah outside the city of Mehujael

Emah–(Eh-mah) Daughter of Wehtam, Noah's wife

Enoch–Son of Jared, and seventh son of the Promise

Enosh–Son of Seth and second son of the Promise

Etena–(Eh-teh-na) Wife of Imas

Evol–Leatherworker in Prathar who had escaped from city of Mehujael

Ham–Middle son of Noah

Hannah–A friend of Aleac. Wife of Japheth

Han–Fifteen year old fieldhand working with Noah in Yenah's farm

Imas–(Ee-mas) Farm owner who helped Noah return to civilization

Japheth–(Jay-pheth) Youngest son of Noah

Jared–Son of Mahalalel and fifth son of the Promise

Kenan–Son of Enosh and third son of the Promise

Lamech–Son of Methuselah and ninth son of the Promise

Loree–Daughter of Sivitt, first to discover the plague

Mahalalel–Son of Kenan and fourth son of the Promise

Mehujael–A descendant of Cain and founder of a great city where Lamech lived

Methuselah–(Meh-thoo-ze-lah) Son of Enoch, and eighth son of the Promise

Neela–Arpachshad's wife

Noah–Son of Lamech, and tenth son of the Promise

Phranko–Son of Nod, elder of tanning quarter in city of Prathar

Prathar–Founder of the city of Prathar

Qanath–Sister of Lamech's first wife Katina, becoming his second wife after Katina's death

Rehtak–Second daughter of Imas

Seth–Son of Adam, first son of the Promise

Shelah–Arpachshad's son, thirteen son of the Promise

Shem–Oldest son of Noah, eleventh son of the Promise

Sister—(or Ayalah) Sister of Yakheed

Sivitt–Father of Loree, first to die from plague

Sredael–Brother of Han who worked with Noah in Yanah's farm

Tam–Brother of Cram and farmer in town beside the river

Tinith–(Ti-neeth) Daughter of Yakheed

Truk–Smith in Prathar

Tubal-cain–descendant of Cain, a forger of iron and bronze

Tyal–Brother of Han who worked with Noah in Yenah's farm

Wehtam–(Way-tamn) Father of Emah

Werd–Rich owner of most land outside the city of Yakheed

Yakheed–(Yakheed) Orphan child raised by Sister

YAHWEH–The Hebrew name for the Creator of the universe. This is the name by which He called himself all throughout the Old Testament. Christian Bibles usually write this name as "the LORD."

Yaneth–Shem's daughter

Yenah–(Yay-nah) Owner of farm where Noah worked after the disaster of Mehujael

What is a Cubit?

We can't know exactly the length of a cubit, but we can make a guess that it runs somewhere between 17.5 inches and about 22 inches. For this book, we're calling a cubit 18 inches, or .5 meters.

Cubits	Meters	Feet
1	0.5	1.5
10	5.5	15
20	10.9	30
30	16.4	45
40	21.9	60
50	27.4	75
60	32.8	90
70	38.3	105
80	43.8	120
90	49.2	135
100	54.7	150
110	60.2	165
120	65.6	180
130	71.1	195
140	76.6	210
150	82.1	225
160	87.5	240
170	93	255
180	98.5	270
190	103.9	285
200	109.4	300
210	114.9	315
220	120.3	330
230	125.8	345
240	131.3	360
250	136.8	375
260	142.2	390
270	147.7	405
280	153.2	420
290	158.6	435
300	164.1	450

Table of Contents

Chapter One

Year 1056

The girl opened her eyes and sat straight up. She looked around, but the room was black, and she could hear only the sounds from the dozen women and their children asleep on the floor. Something, not these women and not these children, had broken her sleep. At ten years old, the girl knew how to sense when danger was near. She sniffed the air, listening, tense and ready to run. All was silent except for the buzzing of flies and the murmur of sleeping women and children. A dog was barking in the distance, and the breeze was brushing the roof. But none of these sounds had awakened her.

In the last town, when the hunters came, she alone had escaped. Before any woman or child had stirred, she had already crawled across the floor to a small opening in the wall. By the time the first torch had been tossed onto the roof, the girl was outside and throwing herself across the road into the refuse ditch. Nobody saw her, because nobody expected a child to be so quick. But she was. She had dragged herself through discarded filth beside the road, listening for footsteps of running men, but none came her way. During that horrible night a year before, all she had heard was children inside the huts crying for their mothers. The girl had forced herself to keep crawling. *Hurry*, she had thought over and over. *Can't look back.*

It seemed to take forever before she finally came to woods, but when she did, she got up and ran. In the distance, she had heard men shouting and women screaming, and the girl hoped, as she raced past the trees, that no one would escape. Otherwise men might search the woods and stumble upon her. *Hurry!* she had urged herself, and she fled until her lungs ached and her legs felt heavy and useless. *Can't look back*, she had continually thought. *Keep on moving.* Only the watchful and clever stay alive. No one who looks back survives the night.

But she had survived that night a year or more before, and now, she again found herself preparing for danger. Her hand silently searched the dirt floor until she came upon her knife. The girl felt around for her water skin and rags. Quickly and quietly she placed them into her bag and stood, still listening and looking toward the faint outline of a door. *Not that way*, she reasoned. *They'll be there for sure. Get to the back.* She started to move.

That's when a woman's groan broke the silence of the night. The girl stopped in surprise. *Yes*, she suddenly realized; it was a woman's voice that had awakened her. *Someone outside in the road*, she thought. Not one of these women who slept here, but somebody younger. That meant a stranger was out there, hurt. Another cry came and then urgent sobbing. The girl stared at the faint outline of the door and wondered what to do. She probably should lie back down and try to sleep. One thing was for sure; she must not go out. Whatever had hurt this woman was probably still out there. Nobody could be stupid enough to go outside after the sun had set.

Nobody, that is, except the woman, whoever she was.

The girl, however, did not lie back down to sleep, but stood staring at the door. The moaning had aroused her curiosity. *Why would anyone be on the road in the middle of the night?* Listening to the sobs, which were starting to intensify, the girl wondered what kind of person she was. A prostitute who had been beaten and left to die? A cripple, dragging herself along the road to beg? A mother seeking her stolen child?

The girl's desire to know what was happening beyond the door continued to bother her until she decided, against all her better judgment, to go out and see for herself. She stepped over and around the sleeping bodies and made her way to the door. With stealth she lifted the three stout planks barring the entryway, one by one, and set them aside. The door swung open, and the girl stepped out into a moonlit road.

There, on other side of the lane, was a woman, half lying and half leaning against a tree stump, positioned as if she were giving birth. The girl now understood the groaning she had heard; it was the pain of labor. She stared at the woman with curiosity, wondering who she was, where she hailed from and how she had come to give birth in such a place as this. The woman looked awful, even in the moon-light.

Her pallid skin looked as though the sun itself had bleached away all of her color, so pale compared to the girl's own rich brown skin. Long greasy hair draped itself in tangled strands across her face. The rags she wore barely covered her emaciated body, and her hands, grasping her thighs, were more skeletal than human. The baby was already coming, but something was clearly wrong. The girl had seen child-birth several times before, but never had she seen one like this. The woman seemed to be weakening, her breathing jagged and her moans feeble.

Opening her eyes, she stared into the sky, tears running down her face. The girl, who moved closer, guessed the woman was almost entirely spent. Something in the woman's eyes seemed to say she had given up hope for herself. Even so, she seemed determined to make one last effort to bring this baby into the world. For a few short moments a look of sadness covered the woman's face. A tear streaked down her cheek, leaving its imprint like an unhealed scar. She closed her eyes and grimaced, began groaning, and then, as if summoning whatever strength she might still possess, she cried out with a long agonizing shout. The cry ended suddenly with a sharp intake of breath. The hands dropped, the legs slumped to the ground, and her face went blank.

At that moment, silence blanketed earth and sky. The girl stood transfixed, gazing at the woman who lay unmoving on the ground before her. She had never felt this sensation; as the woman had exhaled her last breath she became a lifeless body; all was cold and vacant, little more than skin stretched over gaunt bones, lying on the ground with death on its face. The girl shivered, not from the cold of the night air, but from a vague consciousness that she was like this woman, all alone with no one to care whether she lived or died.

A new sound broke the trance, and the girl looked down with a start. There on the ground, smeared in blood, lay a crying baby, arms and legs moving helplessly. *What a tiny thing,* she thought. *It's so helpless. It shouldn't be here on the ground.* She moved across the road and stooped down.

"You'd better leave it alone, girl," a gruff woman's voice said from behind her. "The mother's dead, and we can't take care of nothing here."

The girl stood and turned. She saw the Strong Woman in the doorway, holding a club in her hand. Three or four others stood behind, and the girl wondered how long they had been there. "It's too cold for a baby out here, Ma'am," she answered cautiously. After a moment, the girl added, "Perhaps I could wash it off and cover it and take care of it."

The Strong Woman scowled. "You've got no milk for it."

"Yes ma'am," the girl said meekly.

"Besides," the Strong Woman said, "you have weaving to do and no time for playing with babies."

"Yes ma'am." The girl thought for a moment. "Could I make a sling for it and wear it on my back?" The Strong Woman said nothing.

Another breeze ran through the streets, this time harsher and colder. The girl reached into her sack and pulled out her shawl, draping it over her head and shoulders. She shivered. The night was turning bitter, and she worried this baby might not survive until morning. She glanced at the other women, huddled in the doorstep. A guilty look on their faces said they didn't want to care for another baby, but neither did they want this child, lying in the moonlit road, to be abandoned.

The Strong Woman frowned. "You have no milk, girl. Babies don't eat gruel."

The tiny boy let out a lusty wail. The Strong Woman looked down, and the girl saw conflicting emotions in her eyes. The girl could say nothing more without the risk of angering the Strong Women and losing her living quarters. There was nowhere else to go, at least not here in this village. So she said nothing, bent over, picked up her sack, with the rags, water skin and knife, and took a hesitant step toward the doorway.

A raspy voice spoke. "What about the goats?" The girl looked up to see the woman with the raspy voice looking into her eyes. "She could feed it with goats' milk."

The Strong Woman scowled. "And who is going to feed us?"

Scowling back, the other woman answered, "We'll make do."

Moving halfway across the road, the Strong Woman stared at the baby for a long time, weighing her own desire to rescue it against the troubles it would bring them all. Finally she shook her head. "The thing probably won't last the night anyway." She turned toward the doorway. "Cut the cord, wash the baby and put something warm on it. You won't be able to feed it until morning when we milk the goats."

The girl nodded, "Yes ma'am." She waited until the Strong Woman walked back to the doorway and disappeared into the dark room. The girl watched for a moment longer, and then went to the crying baby. She dropped to her knees. Rummaging through her sack, she found the knife, her water skin and a rag. It was going to be a long night.

She gingerly took the cord in her left hand and made a loop. After her blade cut through the cord, she picked up her water skin and began sprinkling water over the baby lying before her in the dirt. Then, for the first time, she picked it up. It was so fragile, so vulnerable, and she felt pity for it. With gentle motions, she washed off as much blood as she could. Then carefully she dried the baby and wrapped it in her rags.

It was at this point she realized someone was standing beside her. Looking up, she discovered the woman with the raspy voice smiling. The woman's eyes were focused not on the baby, but on the girl herself. For a rare moment, the girl almost felt kindness in the woman's eyes, as if she cared about her. It made her feel wanted. The woman asked, "What's its name? It's got to have a name of its own."

The question surprised the girl. She didn't like learning people's names or telling anyone her own. It was safer that way. The woman, however, was right. This baby deserved a name. Even if it didn't survive the night, it still deserved a name. But how could she name him? A tiny crying boy, his mother dead, his father unknown. No one in the world would ever care if he lived or died. She paused for a bit, staring at his tiny feet and hands. He was helpless and, just like her, he was all alone.

She looked thoughtfully at the woman. "Yakheed," she finally answered. "I'll call him Yakheed."

In the moonlight, the girl almost imagined a tear in the Gaunt Woman's eye. "Yakheed... That means 'lonely,'" the woman muttered. She ran her hand through the girl's hair. "That's you, isn't it little one? It's a hard world for a woman, there's no mistaking that." She moved toward the house. When she reached the door, she turned to watch the girl, baby on her shoulder, picking up her knife and water skin and rags. The woman shook her head.

"You're not alone anymore, child. You've got your little Yakheed now."

The girl looked up, nodding. She rose and walked to the Gaunt Woman who was standing in the doorway. The baby was quiet now, lying on her shoulder. A breeze pushed through the streets and pierced her threadbare clothing. She hugged the baby tightly and entered the doorway. After she came in, the Gaunt Woman pulled the door shut and barred it tightly with the three planks. The girl stood for a moment in the pitch black room. She could hear the breathing of women and children who were spread out across the floor. She felt the warmth of the baby nestled under her shawl. Moving across the room, she found her spot and lay down and then pulled her ragged blanket over the baby on her chest. "Yakheed," she said. "It also means my only unique child. Goodnight, little Yakheed," she whispered almost voicelessly. Then she closed her eyes, feeling the baby's warmth upon her. The cold wind shook the roof, but neither the child nor the baby stirred. They were both asleep.

Qanath rushed through the fields past row after row of tall grasses. Her eyes kept glancing beyond the fields and woods to the billows of smoke pouring into the sky in the distance. She came to a wooden fence, frantically climbed over it and began racing toward the house now clearly in sight.

The house stood beneath three massive terebinth trees and was surrounded by an ancient wall almost the height of a man. Large rocks formed the wall, which had only one gate constructed of four sturdy timbers. The gate stood open: Qanath thanked Yahweh. The house itself was built with long logs which had been notched at their ends to join together with the lumber of the connecting wall. The roof above was thatched, woven with golden straw, carefully intertwined in a symmetric pattern. Although the house had a door, it had no real windows, beyond the slats cut in the logs below the roof line, which let in air and some light. On the western corner of the stone wall stood an animal pen, fenced in and large enough to hold a dozen domestic animals.

She reached the gate and quickly crossed the yard, calling out in an agitated voice, "Katina! Sister!" Reaching the door, she peered into the dark room, again calling out "Katina," but no one answered. After waiting a moment to adjust to the blackness, Qanath entered the shadowed room. "Katina!" she repeated, but this time she heard voices coming from the back room. "Why aren't they answering me?" she said to herself, stepping over a bedroll on the floor. She made her way across the floor to the doorway, pulling aside the curtain.

Lamps lit the room to reveal Qanath's sister, Katina, sitting on a cushion, leaning against the food chest. Her dark brown face was flushed and her eyes half closed, with beads of sweat forming on her forehead. Lamech was kneeling beside her, anxiety covering his face. He looked up at Qanath. "Her pains have begun."

Qanath shook her head in disbelief. "Of all the times. . ."

"What's wrong, sister?" Katina asked.

"There is smoke coming up from the village, lots of it, and it's filling the sky."

She crossed the room and began picking up clothing and blankets. Suddenly Katina gasped, and Lamech took her hands in his. "Squeeze my hands," he said quietly. The woman grasped as hard as she could, waiting for the pain to pass again. Several minutes passed before she relaxed her grip and laid back. Sighing relief, Lamech glanced over at her sister, who was tying cloth into a tight bundle. She, obviously, had decided what needed to be done. The bag she had carried in was already bulging with food.

Lamech looked up again. "What are you doing, sister-in-law?"

Qanath continued to work, rummaging through items on the shelf. "We're leaving, preferably in the next five minutes." She looked toward the front room. "Are your axes out there?" she asked anxiously.

Lamech nodded.

She grabbed a lamp and pushed by him toward the curtain. He glanced nervously at his wife. "We can't leave, sister-in-law," he called after her. "Her pains are closer now. It's almost time."

Lamech heard Qanath rummaging through the chest, then heard something being dragged across the floor, a piece of pottery breaking and the door slamming. Katina again moaned, and Lamech squeezed her hand. Once it passed, he looked around the tiny room. They had almost no hope at this point. He had axes and bows, yet only he and Qanath could wield them. The outside wall might slow invaders, but it could not keep them out. The house, as sturdy as it was, could not stand if they brought fire, for the thatched roof would ignite in a second, and they soon would be burned alive. Lamech and Qanath wouldn't last long against two dozen bloodthirsty marauders. The village was already burning; its inhabitants probably dead, so they could not count on help from there.

"Lamech," Katina said weakly. "I can't move. Not now."

Her husband took a deep breath. He stroked her hair, pondering what to do. Little time remained if they were to escape alive; it was probably already too late. Somehow Katina would have to hold on. He looked into her eyes and saw profound fear. In the calmest, gentlest voice he could muster, he explained to her, "They're coming this way. They will kill me and then you and the baby inside you. They'll leave your sister for last, and I very much doubt if she will keep her honor before she dies. I cannot let this happen, Katina."

She grabbed at his robe weakly, pain shooting across her face. "Please, husband, please don't move me. I don't think I can survive."

Her words troubled him. This first birth seemed to be taking a terrible toll on her already fragile body. He took hold of her hand and softly kissed it. "Pray with me, wife. God will hear us." Then, lifting his eyes, he prayed: "God of Seth and Enoch, I beg You, deliver my wife and my baby." Closing his eyes, he uttered a quiet "Amen."

He paused, holding her hand to his lips. Over the past 183 years, Lamech had faced numerous dangers and hardships, but never with a wife and baby. Whatever it took, he would not fail her. Tenderly he laid her hand back upon her womb and smiled. "Trust me, wife. Trust God."

Qanath was already outside when he emerged from the house. She had been piling blankets and food onto the two-wheeled oxcart and was now placing straw where Katina would lie. The cart, with large wooden wheels, was a simple platform with no sides and two long poles fashioned to attach it to the ox. Lamech paused for a moment, wondering how his wife would manage to stay on this small cart and then ran to the animal pen to fetch the ox.

"No," Qanath called from the cart. "Oxen are too slow."

He paused for a moment, thinking. She was right. They would never reach the forest in time with an ox. Instead, he led the mule to the cart. After placing the yoke on its neck, he tied the poles to it and then secured the mule to the fence. Pausing for a moment to scan the billows of smoke now filling the sky, he wondered how much time it would take before the Nephilim arrived. He nodded to Qanath, and the two entered the house.

Katina's cries greeted them. When they entered the room, they found her on her side in pain. Lamech motioned Qanath to the far side of her sister while he knelt beside her, kissing her forehead and speaking quietly to her. Then Qanath and Lamech slipped their arms beneath her legs at the knees and behind her back, putting her arms around their necks and rose carefully. Katina cried out. Lamech looked at Qanath, and they silently agreed that nothing must slow them at this point, not even Katina's screams.

They moved her across the room and brought her through the doorway. Every step seemed to intensify her pain, and Lamech had to keep whispering assurances that she would be alright, that he was protecting her, that their baby would enter the world safely

They laid Katina in the cart, leaning up against the blankets, her knees up and feet almost reaching the edge. After a moment, they set off across the fields toward the stream. The ground was level and the grasses, no higher than their knees, bent under the wheels and then quickly sprang back, leaving little trace to indicate they had passed by. Before them, about a thousand cubits away, stood a line of trees guarding the stream. It was this waterway they needed to reach.

Lamech hoped to pull the cart down the bank into the shadows of the willows which brooded over the waters. If they could make it to this spot, they might escape with their lives. Time, however, was against them. The village was close by, and it would not take the marauders long to march to Lamech's rich farmland. The route led straight east through the woods and continued east after it exited for about two hundred cubits before turning south to pass by Lamech's house.

The worried man kept glancing to the place, perhaps two thousand cubits away, where the road emerged from the forest. He would be able see the first soldier come out of the woods, but this was hardly a comfort, since the oxcart would be just as visible to people on the road as the road now was to him. He wanted to urge the mule forward, but also worried that any more jostling might overwhelm Katina, who was desperately trying to control her fear.

He glanced over at Qanath, walking beside her, hand on her shoulder, keeping her balanced as they rolled over grasses and soft dirt. She looked terrified, which Lamech guessed was more because of her sister and the baby than for her own safety. They continued on slowly toward the shelter which was still in front of them.

After journeying a long distance like this, Katina screamed. Qanath whipped around to the back of the cart and quickly examined her sister. "Mercy! The baby's head is almost out, Lamech. Stop the cart."

Lamech looked to the stream, which was still at least a hundred cubits away. Quickly, he turned to search where the road and forest met. What he saw stopped his heart: a lone figure had just come into sight from the forest, walking east along the road. It was a man, he thought, a man who even from this distance seemed at least a head taller than any villager he knew. This one was a Nephilim. Without a moment's hesitation, Lamech impelled the mule to move faster, and the cart began bounding toward the trees.

"Can't you hear, man? The baby's coming. Stop the cart," Qanath cried out angrily.

Lamech answered softly, but firmly, "Quiet woman. Look to the road."

Qanath, who was trying to keep up with the back of the cart, answered between gasps for breath, "I don't dare look, Lamech. I have a baby to catch."

Katina moaned, and Lamech silently asked the God of Seth to protect his wife. The cart bounced toward the tree line, while Lamech kept a watchful eye on the man far away. "I don't think he has seen us, yet. He's still walking. But when the road turns—"

A cry from Katina cut his sentence short. Lamech looked back to see the running Qanath, her hands cupped, reaching out in front of her, almost touching the platform. She looked as if she were trying to catch something. He prayed out loud Qanath would keep it safe. Yet he dared not stop until they reached the trees, where at least the branches of the willows could shelter them from unfriendly eyes. They traveled on for a few more moments, bringing them so close that Lamech thought they might make it.

A sharp groan from Katina in an entirely different voice, however, caused him to turn his head. Qanath, still running, was holding a baby in her outstretched hands. Grief covered her face, as if something was wrong. Still, the cart rolled on, Lamech's heart beating furiously as they closed in on their destination. Looking out over the fields, he saw another figure emerging onto the distant road. Without a doubt, more would shortly follow. He urged the mule onward and with a final spurt, they pushed through lush willow branches and disappeared into the shadows, much as a timid child retreats into his mother's skirts.

He stopped the mule and hurried to Qanath, who was holding a crying baby in her hands, the cord connected to a placenta lying in the straw. One glance from his sister-in-law, tears streaming down her face, told Lamech to look to his wife. There Katina lay on the straw, moaning in agony, her dark face ashen and eyes half opened. He moved around the wheel to the side of the cart to be closer to her. Leaning over, he kissed her on the forehead. She turned her head to look at him.

"It hurts," she whispered. "The baby. . . alright?"

He took her hand and held it gently. "The baby is perfect."

Struggling to speak, she asked, "Girl?"

"Boy," he answered, glancing at the child. "He is the child of the Promise."

She nodded, and a smile came over her face. For a moment, a glimmer of hope flickered into his mind, that this nightmare might be done and the worst might be behind them. Then came a sharp intake of breath and she winced. "Lamech, it hurts," she whispered again. She breathed in jagged gasps. Finally she muttered, "Hold it?"

He motioned to Qanath, who leaned over, handing him the child. Carefully laying it onto Katina's chest, he softly positioned her hand onto its back. His fingers lingered tenderly on her arm as she stroked the crying baby. He looked back at Qanath, faced buried in her hands, weeping silently. Then he saw a crimson color growing on Katina's dress and in the straw beneath her. She did not have long to live.

He looked back to his wife. The child, no longer crying, lay quietly upon her. Katina's light brown hair, soft and flowing with curls, was gently laid out on her shoulders as a mantle. Her perfect brown skin almost glowed in the shadows beneath the trees. *She is so beautiful,* he thought to himself. *Of all women, most beautiful.* Her eyes were closed, and she looked as if she were cherishing every beat of the baby's heart, every rise and fall of the baby's chest.

They stayed there, silently holding that moment. All around them, trees sighed as the wind breathed through their branches. The stream cascaded over rocks and swirling eddies, surrounding the family with gurgling whispers. Birds called to one another in gentle songs, and the light softened into evening dusk. The three of them, father, mother and child, did not hear or see any of this. For just this short time, they still had one another, and they savored every touch, every thought, every breath.

And then it ended. Katina's shallow breathing stopped, and her hand slipped down. The peacefulness of her face went blank. Lamech stared at her, scarcely believing she was gone. For the longest time, he did not speak. Finally, leaning forward, he silently said goodbye and then kissed her on the lips. He picked up the child and carried it to Qanath.

"We must find the nanny goat if this boy is to survive," he said quietly.

Qanath took the child and then pointed toward the fields. "Something is on fire out there, Lamech. I've been watching it for a long time."

Lamech turned around and stared for a moment, then crept out to the field. She was right; the farmhouse and storage shed were bright with flames. The Nephilim were destroying everything on his farm.

Qanath came out of the shadows carrying the child, now wrapped in a blanket. Lamech looked up at her. In her arms was the son, first promised to Eve. For nine generations the promise had been passed on from father to son, beginning with Seth. Nine generations of suffering and hardship.

When he was just a boy, his father Methuselah had brought him on a long journey to meet Seth, the son of Adam and Eve. Grandfather Seth had sat him down in his house beside the river and there taught him the story of the Creation and the Fall. Someday, he told Lamech, a descendant of Eve would crush the serpent's head and open the way to the tree of life. Lamech himself was a son of that promise, and he must therefore have a son and pass the story on to him.

"Who knows?" Grandfather Seth had said with a smile. "Perhaps your son will save us all."

For a long time, Lamech sat there, thinking on Seth's charge to him so long ago. Finally he stood and took the child from Qanath. "I will find the nanny goat," he said with determination. "This boy must not die. He is the son of the Promise."

She looked at the child and nodded. It would be a miracle if any of them survived the night, yet she found herself believing they would, because of this child. The air was turning colder, and in the morning they would need to scrounge for food to survive. Gazing out over the field, she saw the house continuing to burn. Shaking her head, she wondered how long it would take to rebuild what had been destroyed that evening, but she believed the promise and therefore believed they would find what they needed.

The Promise. . . This little child was the fulfillment of God's promise to Eve. For a long time, Qanath stared at the child, wondering if he was the chosen one.

"What is his name?" she finally asked.

Lamech looked surprised. She asked again, "What's the name of the boy?"

He thought for a moment, looking out over the fields. "Look at it, Qanath. Look at all of the grief we live through because of Adam's sin. I worked for years to build that house and storage shed. We worked for weeks harvesting our wheat, and now all of it is gone. All because of the curse on the ground."

He handed the boy to Qanath. "I call him Noah, for rest. From the ground on which the Lord put a curse, this child will bring us relief from all our hard work. He is the son of the promise."

Qanath watched Lamech set out across the fields toward the burning buildings. *Noah,* she thought; *Rest from all our hard work*. She hugged the child gently. "Well, Noah, we have a hard road ahead of us. A very hard road."

Chapter Two

Year 1066

Yakheed looked back. There she was, twenty or thirty cubits behind, trudging up the path, struggling as if she were carrying a heavy pack. "Come on!" he urged. Sister said nothing and kept plodding. The ten year old boy began racing up the hill, but then stopped and turned, looking thoughtfully at her. She did seem awfully tired. The year had been hard on both of them, but especially on Sister. Her dress, so pretty when she had sewn it five years ago, now only hinted of its original colors, its fabric lying wearily on her frame, pulled tight in the middle by thin rope. The sack she carried reflected her clothing--mended so often it was more darns than cloth.

When he called out again, "Come on, Sister!" she looked up and smiled, and he thought to himself, *She's happy*. Her green eyes glowed, her rosy lips and chestnut cheeks flushed with sassiness. Big wide curls of brown hair spilled out from under the cap, which roosted on her head like a hen on its brood. Somehow, when she smiled, Sister could make even that careworn dress of hers look pretty enough.

Normally, life's unending chores did not give her much time to smile. Every morning, before the sun rose, she would wake Yakheed. Together they hiked out to the fields beyond the village walls, where they farmed their share in the village plot. As soon as they arrived, the two went to work--weeding, picking bugs, culling leaves and harvesting any ripened vegetables or fruit. The garden supplied them with most of their food, beyond the wheat and other grain for which they would barter. It was hard labor, partly because they needed to work as quickly as they could, partly because they had to bend over the entire time, but also because (beyond Sister's well-worn knife) they did not possess metal tools for digging, hoeing, cutting and harvesting.

Well before the sun reached its zenith, they would return to their loom in the women's common house. This machine was Sister's prized possession. Somehow the Strong Woman had gotten hold of it when Yakheed was still a baby and had appointed Sister to work it. Once Sister got the hang of it, her dexterity convinced the Strong Woman to let the girl supervise all of the weaving for the entire group. Since Sister had been working it for almost ten years now, Yakheed had never known life without a loom, and he had been helping since he could remember.

Three years before, Sister announced to all that Yakheed would be her sole helper, and since then they had been a fast working team. Officially the loom belonged to the Strong Woman, who nevertheless had made it clear that if anything happened to her, Sister would become its new owner. Such a possession elevated Sister to a place of respect among the women. Although everyone worked hard to contribute to their overall success and survival, Sister's job was unique, because it required a skill level far above the other crafts and jobs in the common house. No one could weave as quickly or skillfully as she.

Today, however, the Strong Woman had forced Sister to let her loom sit still. "You look tired," she scolded. "Take the boy with you and get some rest. Find a quiet place outside the village and relax."

Hence the boy found himself outside, gardening done, weaving untouched, waiting for Sister on the path to Zillah's Watch. He had never been there, but others told him the Watch stood as the highest point in the land, and he longed to gaze out over the countryside from a soaring eagle's perspective. "Come on, Sister!" he called again. Before long she reached him.

"You walk too fast, boy," she said. "How can a sister keep up with a monkey like you?"

He smiled. "Sister, do you want me to carry you the rest of the way? You seem a bit slow today." He turned, looking up the path. "I don't think it's too far ahead. It's all grass up there. I'll bet you we have only another forty or fifty cubits to walk."

"Then let's get on with it," she said, tussling his hair. The boy winked at her and then shot ahead. Within moments he had disappeared from sight.

Sister resumed walking and before long reached the knee-high grass. Wading uphill through grasses for another twenty cubits or so, she spied the boy standing at the mountain's peak. When she finally reached him, the sight took her breath away. There from the mountainside, she saw their entire world laid out before them like a colorful tapestry. Yakheed could hardly contain himself in his exhilaration. He excitedly pointed out plots of farmland, scattered houses, the village and two meandering rivers.

"Look!" he almost shouted, motioning to the nearest river. "Behemoth are standing in the water. I've always wanted to see one and now I have!"

"Now you have," she said. "Two of them, no less." Gazing out over the landscape, she could hardly believe her eyes. The world before her was huge, and yet forests and villages and rivers alike appeared as tiny spots on the ground. They seemed unreal, so dreamlike that she wanted to leap off the mountainside and float over the whole world. Finally, after gazing for what seemed to be hours, she moved to a plot of soft grass and sat down, smelling the air. The breeze here was fresh, free from village smells--animals, sweat, rotting garbage and waste. Here flower blossoms and cedars perfumed the air, and she found herself inhaling deep drafts of aroma, savoring the fragrance, exhaling and then breathing it in again. For a long time, all she did was sample the scent of a world unspoiled by human beings.

She looked over to Yakheed. His eyes were closed, and his arms stood straight out from his sides as if he were flying. The breeze chased over his face and ran through his hair like deer bounding through meadow grasses. *He's in ecstasy*, she thought to herself. She had never seen him so happy. *Has he ever been outside of the village?* she wondered. *Away from farming and weaving?* Shaking her head, she said aloud, "This is all new to you, isn't it, boy?"

Yakheed said nothing, still drinking in his freedom.

Suddenly she gasped in shock, clutching her side. The sharp sound broke the boy's rapture. He turned to her in surprise.

Sister was on the ground, lying on her side, obviously in pain.

In a second, Yakheed was kneeling beside her. "Sister," he said urgently. "What's wrong?"

For a long time, pain stifled her reply. She held her side, as if trying to contain what seemed to be an explosion going on within her. The boy lay down, huddling against her back, gingerly holding her, hoping not to intensify her suffering. He whispered to her, stroked her arm, told her not to be afraid, reminded her he was there. In spite of all his efforts, her groaning deepened, and the boy began to wonder if she were about to die. *Not here*, he thought fervently. *Please, not here all alone with no one but me to care for you.* He couldn't go for help; no one would come. *Please, not here.*

Finally, Sister sighed and carefully turned over onto her back. Yakheed sat up and pushed the hair out of her eyes. "Sister, what happened?"

Shaking her head, she answered weakly, "I don't know. I've never felt anything like it. It was as if someone was stabbing me again and again."

The boy looked at her thoughtfully. "Is it over?"

She considered for a moment. "It's better, but I don't think I can move without it coming back."

Her words stunned him, because he knew for certain she had to move and must do it soon if they were to survive. They couldn't stay here on the mountain. It would be too cold at night, and animals might attack once the sun set. Besides, they would need water and food by morning.

Yakheed looked up and realized the sun had almost reached its zenith. They had taken at least half the morning to reach this spot, and it might take at least all day to get back to the village before dark if she continued in pain. Yakheed was strong, but he didn't think he could bear Sister, even though she wasn't much bigger than he. Even if he could carry her, he certainly could not transport her all the way back to the village.

Nonetheless, they had to leave immediately, or she would not survive the night.

Yakheed rose and began collecting their possessions. He drank several gulps from the water skin, took a few bites of bread and then put them in the sack, tying it tightly. Once everything was ready, he returned to Sister, who lay on her back, eyes closed, clearly trying to stay as still as possible. Kneeling beside her, he stroked her forehead. "Sister," he said confidently, "It's time to leave."

Sister's eyes opened. "I can't," she said. "If I move at all, the pain will knock me right off my feet."

The boy nodded. "It probably will, but even if it does, we still have to get off this mountain, and therefore you are going to have to get up."

Her eyes narrowed, and Yakheed saw trouble brewing. "Boy, you know better than to order me around. Who do you think I am? Who do you think you are?"

"I know who I am," he answered, smiling. "Yakheed. You are Sister, and I am ordering you to get up now."

"I am not Sister, boy! My name is Ayalah, and you are not moving me one cubit."

Yakheed looked at her in astonishment. "Your name is Ayalah? Deer? That's a beautiful name. Why have you kept it such a secret?"

Sister flushed. "Never you mind. Just leave me be."

The boy considered for a moment, then stooped down and slipped his arm behind her neck.

"Yakheed! Please stop!"

He paused, looking her in the eyes. "Sister Ayalah, you are all I have in the whole world. You saved me when I was a baby, and you have taught me and fed me, and I am not going to let you die here. Now," he said firmly, "put your arm around my neck, and let me help you get up."

Carefully, he raised her, holding his breath, dreading the chance she would collapse in pain again. Nothing, however, happened. Once Sister Ayalah was on her feet, he picked up the sack and slung it over his shoulder. "Are you okay?" he asked hopefully.

She nodded.

They began walking.

The journey down the mountain was difficult. Ayalah tired quickly and often needed to stop. After every pause, Yakheed would work carefully to stand her up again, but as time went on, her pain began to grow, and this made the process more difficult. Twice during their trip down the path, Ayalah collapsed to the ground in agony and could not move. Both times, the boy knelt beside her and spoke quiet assurances. The second time she almost went unconscious, but the boy did not give up, encouraging her to persevere. After that episode, getting Ayalah back up was especially delicate. She was becoming less coherent, almost unaware of Yakheed and their situation. From that point on, he half carried her, half supported her as they made their way through the forest to the fields outside the village walls.

The last leg of the journey was unbearable. By this point, Yakheed found it almost impossible to keep Sister from falling to the ground, which she did three or four times after walking only a few hundred steps. The last time she fell, he could not rouse her, no matter how fervently he begged her to awaken.

Kneeling beside her, he looked up to the sky, desperately assessing their situation. The sun was setting, and although he still saw the village walls across the fields, he knew unless they hurried, they would not reach them before dark. Sister would be stuck out here in the fields all night. Her only hope was reaching the village before the watchman shut the gates. He looked down at her, lying on the ground. He had to awaken her, and they had to make it there.

"Sister!" he said sharply. She moaned and moved slightly.

"Wake up!" he yelled, shaking her.

She opened her eyes vaguely and muttered, "No. Leave me alone."

Grabbing her shoulders, Yakheed violently shook her. "Get up! Now! Do not go to sleep! Get up!"

Her eyes opened wide, and even though he suspected she barely knew who he was or where they were, she said, "I can't."

"Yes, you can, and you will." He slipped his arm under her at the waist. "I'm going to pick you up, and you are going to lean on my back. Okay?"

Sister nodded weakly.

Somehow, the boy got her up sufficiently to position her on his back. She didn't weigh nearly as much as she should have and that helped, but she was still heavy enough that he couldn't bear all of her weight. They set off, her arms hanging over his shoulders, her feet touching the ground.

Yakheed's many years of lugging firewood had strengthened his legs and built into him physical endurance. He had never, however, experienced anything as overwhelming as this: half carrying, half dragging a grown woman across an open field. Nevertheless, he continued to convey her over the rough ground. Before long, he could barely move his legs, each step devouring what little strength still remained. Yakheed, however, refused to surrender and his feet kept moving forward.

About three quarters of the way to the gate, his foot caught a root, sending him sprawling. Ayalah landed on top of him, her weight smashing his face into the ground, causing pain to shoot through his body.

Instantly, fury rushed to the surface, and a roar exploded from his mouth, "No! You can't stop me! No!" he bellowed. He got up on his hands and knees, Sister resting on him. He then forced his legs to stand. For the last one hundred cubits, blood running down his face, Yakheed dragged Ayalah to the village gate. There, he saw the watchman run out from his post. The boy fell to his knees and as the watchman reached them, he collapsed to the ground.

All Yakheed could hear was the beater on the loom. He sat up and immediately pain shot through his face and head. Holding his head in his hands, he uselessly tried to focus his thoughts, but his brain wouldn't cooperate. Looking around, the boy realized he was sitting on the floor next to their loom. Two women were trying to feed the weft through the shed, but were doing it all wrong.

"What are you doing?" he asked disrespectfully.

They both looked down at him, surprised. Suddenly he remembered everything: the hike to Zillah's Watch, Ayalah's attack and the agony of the journey back. His eyes frantically began searching the area for a sign of Sister. When he discovered her, lying on the floor just beyond the loom, he immediately went to her. She was on her back, eyes closed, still as death. Scrapes cut across her dress, probably, he thought, from her many falls. Her face was badly bruised and her hair a nest of tangles. At first, Yakheed couldn't tell if she was breathing, but bending down close to her face, he could hear her barely exhaling. He looked up at the women, who were watching him with interest.

"Has she gotten up yet?" he asked.

The older of the two women shook her head. "She hasn't made a sound since they brought you two in last night." She looked at him curiously. "What happened?"

Yakheed told them the story. When he was done, the younger woman glanced to Sister and then to Yakheed. "You carried her?" she asked wondering. "All the way from Zillah's watch?"

"Not carried," he answered. "Sort of helped at first, then sort of carried and at the end mostly carried her. She couldn't do much across the fields, that's for sure."

The older woman smiled at Yakheed. "Well, boy, you should rest today. We'll find work for you tomorrow, I'm sure."

He looked confused. "I don't need work, Ma'am. I weave with Sister."

The woman gazed first at Ayalah and then at the boy kneeling beside her. She shook her head. "Sister here won't be doing any weaving for a long time, child, and we can't afford to wait until she's better."

"I'll do it myself, then."

The younger woman laughed, but the other had a serious expression on her face. "I don't doubt you could do it boy. You've got the courage and smarts. "We . . ." She waved a hand toward the loom. "We don't know much about this loom, and if we're going to learn to work it, we'll need someone to teach us."

Yakheed knew he had to be careful with his words. "I know it backwards and forward, but I don't think I could teach it well enough for anyone else to learn."

The older woman's eyes narrowed. "If you know it well enough to use it, then you should know it well enough to teach others."

"I'm sure you're right," he said, keeping his head down as a sign of respect. "It's just I might keep forgetting one thing or another, and then the whole cloth would be ruined."

Deep in thought, the woman stared at the boy as he nonchalantly rose, walked to the loom and began deftly feeding the weft through the warp. His hands moved quickly and with obvious skill. Within moments, he was already weaving fabric. His confidence and his determination caused her to shake her head in dismay. It would take months of training and practice, and she doubted if even then she could approach the level of his craftsmanship.

"Alright! You win, boy," she said quietly. "See what you can do about keeping this thing going. Even if we get half our cloth, it'll be more than I could produce."

Yakheed bowed his head to her. "Thank you, Ma'am."

The woman turned to leave and then stopped short. "Boy. . ."

He faced her.

"She probably won't live, you know. If she does, she may end up being weak. You understand?"

He nodded, understanding entirely. Women could live in the common house only as long as they continued to benefit the common house. If Sister didn't heal in the next couple of weeks, the two of them would be out on the street. He glanced down at Ayalah, sleeping on the floor. He wouldn't allow that happen to Sister. "I brought her down the mountain, Ma'am, all by myself. I carried her across the fields on my back." He looked up to the woman. "I'll take care of her. She'll make it. She and I, we take care of ourselves, by ourselves."

Smiling, the woman brushed hair out of his eyes. "I hope so, boy. You deserve better than being all alone. It's a hard enough life as it is."

The women left him, and the boy returned to running the loom. Fortunately, they had begun the cloth the day before their journey to Zillah's Watch, which saved him from having to string the warp, a job he could not do by himself. He took a deep breath and began to work, feeding the weft through the shed, pulling it firmly into place using the beater, and then feeding the weft back through.

As the hours passed, new rows of material began forming under his skillful fingers. Occasionally, he would stop only long enough to check on Ayalah, always immediately returning to his work. He had never labored so quickly, yet when he glanced down at the developing material, he saw far less fabric than he needed. It wasn't that he lacked skill; the problem instead was with the loom. It was built not for one, but for two or even three people, and using it any other way was awkward at best.

Yakheed recognized he could work only as fast as the loom could move. Yet also he understood how urgent it was for him to produce as much cloth as he and Sister had fashioned earlier as a team. As his hands continued to fly through the treads, the boy began mulling over ideas to change the way the loom worked. Suddenly a thought came to him, *Maybe I can pull the warp up and back down with my feet! If I could hook something to my foot. . .* The rest of the day, he pondered a new invention.

The light from the sun was mostly spent. Women and children were now preparing their bedding when Yakheed first heard Sister moaning. The voice was weak, but he needed no second notice. Immediately leaving his work, he came beside her. Although she had not yet opened her eyes, he could tell something was changing and Ayalah finally was waking. He neatened her blanket, laid out his bedding, then sat down beside her and watched. People passed by, and the boy could feel their glances, but he took no notice. His gaze could not leave her face, longing to see her eyes open once more. *Her color is better now*, he thought to himself. *She's breathing differently. She will live.*

When Sister finally woke, dusk had spread itself over the common room. The din of whispers and children's lullabies hardly noticed a conversation between a boy and his sister/mother. Those two talked of a journey down a mountain and a trek across a field. They shared their secret worries and hopes as long as they could, until darkness hushed the common room. Then she, still weary, slipped back into a tranquil sleep.

Before long, one could hear only breathing and the sounds of night. And, all by itself, the sound of someone crying as he lay beside his Sister. Tomorrow he would fashion cloth. Tomorrow he would plan his better loom. He would nurse his Ayalah to health. Tonight, however, he was just a boy, holding the hand of the only one who cared, and he was determined not to let her go.

Lamech glanced back. The boy was dragging behind again, staring off into space, barely moving forward. His annoyance boiled over into a shout. "Noah! Let's go!" he called angrily.

The boy's head shot up. Lamech watched his pace quicken, still upset that the boy wasn't yet moving as rapidly as he could. Why wouldn't he at least try to hurry? Last year when the cousins visited, Noah poured himself into every game they played. As soon as they left, the boy went back to his old ways, slow in the fields, slow cutting wood, slow building fences, slow in every task he tackled. Lamech glared impatiently as the child made his way toward him, no longer dawdling, but still not hurrying.

A fortnight ago, the two said goodbye to Qanath and set out on their expedition. Passing through their own country and then walking among the great hills, the two had slept every night in shelters known only to Lamech and his family. The journey was hard and wearing on both of them, but Noah's lingering came not from weariness, but rather inattentiveness.

Finally, the boy reached him, and his father unleashed his anger. "Don't you care about getting to shelter before night falls? Unless we hurry, we'll be stuck out here in the wilderness."

The boy looked up at his father. Lamech saw defeat in his son's face. He stopped for a moment, regretting his quick tongue. Reaching out and taking his son's hand, he sighed. "Come on, then, let's get going." They walked through the woods, hand in hand.

Throughout the rest of that morning, they talked about the sky, trees, animals, unusual birds and as many subjects as Noah might bring up. The boy's mind continually astonished his father. He might be only ten, yet he asked questions so probing, at times his father was simply unable even to guess how to answer.

Before long, Noah wanted to know why from a distance he could see his father strike a rock with his hammer before he heard the sound. "Father," he asked, curious. "When we're close, I see and hear the hammer hit the rock at the same time. How can the two be different?"

Lamech shook his head. "I have no idea, son."

The two continued walking down the path, the boy deep in thought. Finally, Noah said simply, "They travel."

Lamech looked at him, surprised. "What travel?"

Noah answered, "Sound and sight, and they travel at different speeds! Isn't it obvious? When they're close, they arrive at the same time, but when they are far away, sight arrives first because it moves more quickly." An excited look came over his face. "Think about it, Father. When two men race together, at first they stay pretty close to each other, but after a while, the faster man will get farther and farther ahead." He smiled. "When sight and sound race, at first, sight and sound are pretty close together. After a while, the sight leaves the sound behind."

"In one hundred and ninety two years, boy, I have never asked that question or heard that answer," Lamech said, shaking his head.

"Yes," the boy said, his eyes glistening. "But you know I'm right."

The man nodded his head. "I think it makes sense."

He looked at his son, already staring off into the forest. This boy was not only clever in thought, but was also the smartest builder in their region. Last year, Noah had gotten it into his head that the village needed a bridge over the river Ito. For the next two weeks, he devoted himself to creating, testing and redrawing his designs. He carried his plan on a piece of board to the village elders.

At first, they thought him arrogant, daring to teach two hundred year old men about rivers and buildings. The sketches, however, persuaded them at least to listen to the boy. When he answered every question they fired at him, with convincing numbers and sensible solutions to difficult problems, they decided to build a bridge. Amazingly, the bridge was a remarkable success, and now men, animals and carts were crossing the river without danger or difficulty. All because of a nine year old boy's audacious intelligence.

As they walked, Lamech mulled over this child's accomplishments. "You know, Noah," he finally said in a tone of respect. "That bridge you built helps a lot of people."

The boy nodded.

"I am very proud of what you did."

A strange look came over the boy's face. He walked beside his father in silence. Lamech could sense something wrong, yet couldn't guess what it might be. *His response wasn't unusual*, he thought. The boy was easily hurt and often grieved over seemingly innocent comments his father might make. He would grow quiet, sometimes go off by himself, sometimes not speak for hours.

As he glanced at the boy walking beside him, Lamech guessed Noah was struggling with guilt, since guilt often seemed to cloud his thoughts and actions. Indeed, the boy lived with guilt. Perhaps he simply hated failing his father, like today when he had walked so slowly. At that time, the father's rebukes had clearly wounded the boy's conscience, and the child had walked in hurt silence for over an hour.

Yet his self-reproaches didn't drive him to change his behavior. Even today Noah had been truly sorry for being so slow, but nevertheless walked only a bit faster after Lamech had rebuked him. That was not unusual for Noah; the boy's scruples tortured him, but rarely helped him change. Almost always, the boy simply let the moment choose his path. Whatever he felt at the moment, that's what Noah ended up doing. He might know it was not right or not the best, but he simply had no will to stand against the flow, and his father felt incapable of helping him to change.

They walked on in silence for at least an hour, and Lamech's thoughts continually wondered about his son. What would happen to Noah? Would the boy ever learn to stand on his own? *He's only ten*, the father reminded himself. *The boy has time to grow.*

He glanced again at his son, walking beside him, but his son would not return the gaze.

They continued on their journey throughout that day and the next. On the third day, they left the hill country and came to a woodland populated with enormous trees. This was the Behemoth Forest, named for trees whose pedestals stood broader than the most powerful behemoth and whose towers disappeared into the sky. As they entered this mighty timberland, their progress slowed to a crawl. The wood simply overshadowed any urgency they might have had up to now.

Lamech found himself, as he walked, gazing upward, imagining these columns stretching all the way into eternity and the boundless vision dizzied him. When he brought his sight back to earth, however, he discovered another eternity–tower after tower of massive trees extending as far as his eyes could see. Even the tree trunks overwhelmed him, with scraggly bark not unlike the bison's hide: stiff and wiry. Burls the size of a boar bulged from the trunk of the tree like brawny muscles. Thick roots delved deep into the earth. The trees stood as fortresses, powerful and impregnable.

The entire world beneath those pillars lay silent: no calls of birds, no animal cries, not even a breeze unsettled the quietude. The calm muted the two travelers' footfalls, and they floated rather than walked amidst the soaring foundations of the heavens. For a long time, neither felt able to speak, their voices stifled, their senses whelmed.

Lamech glanced at Noah, who was enthralled by the trees. He was walking blindly, his eyes pointed to the ceiling above them, trusting his father to direct his feet. Lamech smiled. Always Noah had loved trees and rivers and valleys and everything unspoiled by man. Often after the sun had set, Lamech would go searching for the child in the fields and find him lying on the ground, staring into the ocean of stars, completely unmindful of the dangers of night. He now had that same look on his face.

After many paces into the woods, Lamech dared to break the solitude. "What are you thinking, boy?"

"Father," the boy said in a quiet voice, "they're like stars, aren't they?"

Lamech looked above. "Like stars?"

Nodding, the child answered, "When you look straight above, the trees fill up everything in the world. It's as if the trees are real, and nothing else exists. Just like the stars at night. The whole world disappears into shadows as soon as the stars come out, and all you see are stars and stars and more stars."

Lamech gazed straight up. The boy was right. Above him loomed only trees, and the rest of the world around them indeed was faded into shadows. He turned to look at his son, whose face shone with excitement. *This is Noah's world*, he thought to himself. *He would rather be here by himself than anywhere else.*

For the rest of the day, they walked among the trees, absorbing the quiet, lost in thought. All of this territory was new to Noah, but not to Lamech. He was traveling home. Many times he had trekked beneath these trees since he first left home one hundred years ago. The quiet of the forest reminded him that he was nearing his father and mother, the great river and the great wall. In three days they would reach the rolling grasslands, and then two days later would bring them to the river itself. Just the thought of seeing his parents and family was enough to quicken his pace along the pathway. He could think of little else the rest of that day.

Five more days passed before the river finally came into sight. It was almost noon when they crested the final hill and saw seven or eight buildings in the distance. Lamech had to keep himself from running the rest of the journey--they still had a walk ahead of them. As they continued, he noted every familiar landmark, even though fifteen years had passed since his last visit. The fields were much the same, although the forest had reclaimed some land. A flock of sheep grazed in the distance, almost exactly where flocks had been pasturing since he was a boy. He pointed out across the grasses.

"Look at the fields, son." Noah's eyes followed his gesture. "Look how green the grass is. It's fresher here than anywhere we've ever been."

Noah suddenly pointed in excitement. "The river! I can't believe it. It's the river!"

Lamech smiled. "What about it, Noah?"

"Father," the boy answered exhilarated. "That's the river you told me about, the one in the Promise."

They continued down the path, the boy running ahead, talking, shouting and pointing. At one juncture, he stopped, waiting for his father to catch up. Lamech didn't take long, since his excitement was almost as intense as his son's. By this point, they could see the houses more clearly and could even distinguish sheep and cattle pens. When the father reached him, the boy took his hand and led him forward.

"Will we meet him?"

Lamech smiled. "Meet whom?"

"Adam, the father of men. Is he there by the river?"

Lamech shook his head. "No, son. Adam died over a hundred years ago."

The boy asked a second question. "Will she be there?"

The way the boy asked the question surprised his father. "You mean Eve? No, she died not long after Adam."

"What about Grandfather and Grandmother?"

Lamech smiled. "I hope they will be here, although some people may be in the fields when we arrive. We'll see."

They walked along in anticipation until the pathway led up over the final short hill. Before long, the footpath brought them down into a tiny village. The houses were fairly far apart from one another, so that several more could have been built in between them. All of them were stone, rather than wood and were built to last many decades of weather and toil. Six of the houses were perhaps fifteen cubits from the path, but two almost opened out onto the way itself. Each house was unique, some old and some fairly new.

The houses seemed almost as strong as the hills themselves, built of stones gathered from the river. Since Lamech himself had helped build the fourth and sixth houses in the village, he knew how sturdy they were, and he found himself wondering if even the Nephilim would be able to undo these defenses.

The village seemed deserted, but this did not surprise Lamech. They had arrived in the middle of the day, when every hand was needed in the fields to care for crops or tend animals. Yet Lamech hoped someone would be within the village. His hope was rewarded, for as they passed through the village, they could hear the sound of metal clanging.

The boy looked up excitedly to his father, who smiled and led him to the last house along the path. This dwelling was built of large stones, perfectly smooth and skillfully fitted together. The abode had a massive wooden door, with images of leaves and flowers carved into its thick red wood. On either side of the door stood two windows, shutters opened to welcome cool breezes.

Lamech smiled, remembering well each stone, each shutter, each carving in the door. When he looked up, however, he discovered a roof which was not thatched like his, but made somehow of thin cut shakes of wood that overlapped one another. This was new to him and looked much safer and sturdier than his own. He would have to ask how one constructed such a roof, or better yet, have Noah ask. He smiled. Of course Noah would ask. It was his nature to do so.

They followed the hammering sound around to the back of the house and came upon a shelter, also constructed of stone. The opening of the shelter faced toward the east, probably to admit the warmth of the morning sun while shading from afternoon heat. Within the shelter, Lamech found the object of his journey. There a smith, stripped to the waist, was pounding the share of a plow, his arms and chest glistening with sweat. He was tall and muscular, with light brown hair running almost to his shoulders. His skin, although lighter than that of Lamech or Noah, was still a rich chestnut. Lamech smiled.

"You are looking well, my father," he said loudly.

The man's head shot up. Surprise covered his face. "Lamech!" he cried. Dropping his hammer, he rushed to his son. "It's been so long!" For a long time he held his son, with clear affection. Then the man turned to the boy at his side. "Am I correct in guessing this is my grandson?"

"This, Father," Lamech said, "is my son, Noah."

The man dropped down to Noah's level and threw his arms around him. Lamech watched with pleasure as his father tightly embraced the boy. The man released the boy, who was obviously a bit uneasy, and gazed intently into his eyes. "Noah. . . 'rest.'" Curiosity came over his face. "Why did you choose this name, Son?"

"When he was born, I don't know why, but a feeling came over me, as if this child would be the one to bring us rest from our labors." Lamech glanced down at the boy standing beside him. "What it means, I'm not sure, but when I named him, the idea was so strong I could not resist it."

"Noah. . . interesting. I wonder what it means for the sons of Adam." He knelt there for a long time, deep in thought, gazing into the boy's face. A look of confusion gathered in Noah's eyes, causing the man to smile. He put his hands on his shoulders and said, "Well, Grandson. Do you know who I am?"

The boy nodded. "You are Methuselah, my father's father, seventh in the line of descent from Adam." Awe came over his face. "You knew Father Adam and Mother Eve."

Methuselah laughed. "Boy, your own father knew them well."

"Yes sir," Noah answered. "But Father said you grew up with them and lived with them for many years."

The man embraced the boy again. After a few moments, he released him and stood. "I most certainly did know them. They were as close to me as my own mother and father." Turning, he pointed toward the place where the footpath met the river. "Down there, boy, beside the river," Methuselah said, "that's where they lived." A wistful look came over his face. "Mother Eve always loved that river. We would sit beside it for hours, and she would tell me the story of our family."

"Grandfather Methuselah," the boy said excitedly. "Did Mother Eve ever talk of Eden?"

Methuselah put his hand on Noah's shoulder and smiled. "She told me about every animal and every tree and every stream. I must tell you the stories she told me of the first days, stories you must then tell your own children and grandchildren." He looked to Lamech, who was running his hand over the sharpened plowshare. "I'm assuming, Lamech, this is why you have come to me, that I could teach the boy." He paused, looking hopeful. "You're not moving here, are you?"

Lamech shook his head. "No Father, not yet. I hope to come here one day, but we must stay for a while in Cain's country. The boy's mother died in childbirth, and I took her sister, Qanath, as my wife. She has asked to stay there, nearer to her own family, and I have agreed to this until the boy is grown."

Methuselah nodded. "Has she born you other children?"

"Two sons and a daughter," he answered. "Which is why we cannot stay more than a fortnight. Qanath's brothers are caring for the farm until we return, but they can only do so much."

Methuselah smiled. "I entirely understand, my son." He looked down to discover Noah staring at him almost reverently. "So, Noah, Son of Rest. . . plowshares will have to wait. You and I need to do some talking."

He reached over to a tunic, thrown over a bench, pulled it over his head and then took the boy's hand. They began walking toward the footpath, Methuselah already talking. "Now, boy, tell me about the creation." Lamech, standing beside the shelter, heard Noah answering, "In the beginning, God created the heavens and the earth. . ."

He watched them make their way down toward the river. The boy already knew the story, but Lamech wanted him to hear it from one much closer to its source, one who had traveled year after year to the entrance of Eden, one who had sat at Mother Eve's feet as she described the earliest days. Whatever the boy's name meant to humankind, Lamech wanted him to devote himself to the Promise. He worried about Noah, who so often seemed complacent and uncaring. Perhaps Methuselah would instill into the boy a sense of how important he was to God's promise.

He shielded his eyes from the sun. There they were, standing on the riverbank. Methuselah was pointing down the water toward Eden, and Lamech could imagine the boy's excitement at being so close to what once was paradise. Down that river was the real meaning of hope, for in that garden stood the tree of life. All the rest, the farming, the building, the inventing, the raising of children, all of the rest was simply the echo of what happened in that garden so long ago.

Lamech watched the boy and his grandfather sit down beside the river where Lamech himself had sat with Mother Eve when he was a child. Hopefully the boy would listen not just to the words, but to the meaning behind them. Hopefully this boy would give them rest from the labor of their hands and from the curse on the ground.

Chapter Three

Year 1076

The stranger stood looking out over the crowded street. Lamech, standing among those in the assembly, watched the stranger carefully. Lamech frowned. Hundreds upon hundreds of farmers, shopkeepers and craftsmen had packed into the square to hear news from this visitor beyond the hill country. The summons had gone out only yesterday, but the dangers of the times gave people plenty of incentive to come out.

Lamech looked around the public gathering place. It stood in the middle of the central village, the oldest and most prominent section of Mehujael. Here, on neatly laid out streets, stood thirty or forty finely crafted stone buildings, some of them residences, but most of them workplaces for craftsmen and various trades. Six streets spanned out from there, much like spokes in a wheel traveling to the rim of the city's most ancient wall. Beyond this central district stood hundreds of other homes and places of work, most of ancient stonework.

The original village had been constructed by Mehujael, a great-great-grandson of Cain. For several hundred years the first town prospered and attracted farmers and craftsmen from other regions to settle in its streets or outskirts. Then, in the seven hundred and fifty third year after Adam's creation, a terrible fire burned the city to the ground. Over two hundred died, a horrible shock in a world where death came rarely. The wooden buildings, often crowded in close quarters, provided kindling for the flames which destroyed most of the city.

That experience led Mehujael, his offspring and the others who now lived with them to three important decisions about how they would rebuild their city. First, they decreed that stone would now serve as the primary building material. Second, they resolved to follow a definite plan for the placement of streets, trades, commerce, residences, water and waste. Third, they chose elders to organize rebuilding and to bring order to village life. The people carried out these wishes, and a magnificent city had stood the test of time. The original elders for the most part still continued to serve the city.

As Lamech looked over the crowd, he saw Mehujael and most of his sons (one had died in the great fire, two others from accidents, and one had moved far away). Many of these men had piercing minds. They possessed energy and physical strength and exercised skills honed by centuries of hard labor and thoughtful practice. The vibrancy of this enormous city was due in no little part to their wisdom. Yet, as Lamech glanced at their faces, he could see that rumors from far away villages had stirred a fear in them they had not known in many years.

An unsettled air hovered over the assembly and the people kept anxiously glancing at the stranger who stood before the crowd. Lamech turned to examine this man. The visitor towered over the men of the village. Light skinned, he had a massive head, the features of which seemed exaggerated, almost grotesque. Beads of sweat rolled down his shaved scalp, which was covered with intricate tattoos. His thick black beard hid most of his pale face, yet what could be seen beneath that beard was unnerving. His dark eyes bulged, his brows hanging over them like thick rock ledges hanging over deep caves. Hair covered his extensive chest, as well as his arms and legs. Everything about the man spoke of almost superhuman power. Perhaps just his presence was enough to worry those who stood before him.

Even if he weren't so enormous, his clothing would have identified him as a Nephilim. He wore a tight rhinoceros hauberk, embossed with iron studs on the front and back. A row of silver, gold and copper bracelets ran from his wrist to his elbow, and a thick copper ring encircled his neck.

Just their gear alone is enough to frighten every man in this assembly, Lamech thought to himself. *Of course, that's the whole point.* This was the way of the Nephilim, a people perhaps an entire cubit taller than any other son of Adam.

Lamech thought back to the stories his father had shared with him when he was a young boy. One afternoon they had been working together in the fields.

"Father, where did the Nephilim come from?"

Methuselah glanced down at his son. "No one knows for certain their origin, but it has been told that three centuries ago, one of Cain's offspring grew to be enormous, almost five cubits tall, with massive arms and legs and brawn to match. When his father Tubal-cain saw his son's strength and agility, he sought for wives suitable to match his son."

"You have told me about Tubal-cain before, haven't you? Didn't he discover something special?"

"Yes, my son. He discovered the process for forging iron and bronze. This made him very famous and men began to revere him and desire to have his amazing iron tools."

"Why couldn't they just make their own iron tools?"

Methuselah smiled. "Tubal-cain hid that secret so that no one except for those in his family knew the process. He also had much ore on his land. He and his sons began to mine the ore and develop specialty tools. These became so prized and coveted that soon many fathers brought their tallest and heftiest daughters as brides in exchange for iron implements. Tubal-cain's son ended up fathering a stable full of sons, and within a few decades a hundred of Tubal-cain's grandsons had grown into powerful fighters."

Lamech looked up at his father. "My friends and I were talking about the Nephilim the other day and how they call themselves 'the sons of God.' Where did that name come from?"

"When men become stronger than others, pride easily sets in. They saw themselves as superior to all of Adam's race and indeed they were superior. They fought viciously, with intelligence and agility, and many had almost savage strength and character. They began to consider themselves as the sons of God."

"But they are not like God at all. They are so vicious now. How did that happen?"

Methuselah thought for a moment. "With their pride, they wanted sons to pass on their might to the next generation. But they didn't have enough wives, so Tubal-cain commanded his sons to search for the tallest, strongest women in any village or farm they came upon."

"Didn't these women already have husbands?"

"Usually, yes. They would travel as a horde through many lands and take from the daughters of men any bride that suited their fancy. Generally, they simply killed the husbands or fathers who tried to stop them and burned to the ground all resistant villages."

"Why didn't the people try to stop them?"

"Remember that these sons of God, as they called themselves, were armed with their grandfather's iron weapons.   And they didn't just burn the villages, they would destroy the crops and slaughter anyone who attempted to oppose them."

"That is awful, Father."

Methuselah nodded. He paused for a moment. "They were really the first and most dreadful army in human history. Soon, every farm house and village feared the scourge of the sons of God. Tubal-cain continued to supervise and breed this new race. It was more like breeding animals than raising children. Within a century, he had raised a might army and now we know them as the Nephilim."

Lamech's thoughts came back to the present. The Nephilim were now a race of men more feared than the most violent of behemoths or predators. They still took whatever women they could find and dragged them back to their cities north of the River Gihon. The mightiest Nephilim might have a harem of a hundred wives, hoping to produce as many powerful sons as they possibly could. To fund their military exploits, they enslaved neighboring peoples, exacting huge tributes of grain and goods. Thus far, those cities and peoples on the western side of the River Gihon had been protected from the great armies. Only small bands of Nephilim raiders had attacked the smallest villages and farms on this side of the river. As Lamech looked at the man standing before them now, he wondered if this relative safety was about to end.

Lamech looked out over the crowd, trying to spot his son. As he scanned the faces, he recognized many of the people he had urged to come, but so far as he could tell, Noah was not here. Lamech sighed, shaking his head. *How could he be so irresponsible?* he wondered.

He mulled over where his son might be. Possibly in the shed smoothing down the model of his latest building project. Possibly he had gone out to the fields to weed the garden, which was terribly neglected. Possibly sleeping in his bed again! The father felt his anger rising inside. The boy–of course he was not a boy but a twenty year old man–knew how important it would have been to be here. Yet he chose his own lazy ways over the best interests of his city.

"People!"

The voice startled Lamech out of his thoughts. He looked up to discover that the stranger had climbed atop a wagon.

"People, listen to me!" The crowd stilled in apprehension.

The stranger spoke again, with an air of haughtiness. "I come from beyond the hills and beyond the great river Gihon. I am an officer in the army of the Nephilim."

A quiet murmur ran through the assembly.

He waited, looking impatient. The noise quickly subsided.

"You people are living in a dreamworld. It's time to wake up!"

Sweeping his hand before him, he said, "Fine stonework you have here. Your carved doors, your terebinth shutters, your orderly streets are remarkable. Even your sewers and running water have impressed me greatly."

He looked up and pointed. "These roofs! I have never seen a design like this!" Smiling, the man spread wide his arms and said dramatically, "Yes, indeed! This city of Mehujael rivals the finest cities north of the river."

He poignantly paused, letting his words sink into his audience's ears. No one spoke, although an occasional whisper barely broke the silence. It was clear the stranger was enjoying the effect he had created and did not want to spoil it quite yet. His style infuriated Lamech, but at this point the city was at the mercy of this Nephilim from beyond the River Gihon.

Finally the stranger continued. "Indeed, that's your problem. Your city is simply too attractive, people of Mehujael! It's like leaving a bucket of food out on the streets at night. It won't take long for the dogs to snatch it away from you and consume it all."

In a sweeping gesture, he said, "The Nephilim do not like successful cities, friends. They are coming, readying themselves to cross the river and when they come, they will destroy every house, every shop, everything you have."

He stopped speaking. The crowd, at first silent, slowly began to murmur, their agitated hum rising like dust stirred by panicked cattle. Lamech looked around him and sighed. This is why he had moved his children and Qanath to the city of Mehujael. The armies of the Nephilim had ravaged the countryside for the past thirty years, driving Qanath's father and brothers across the River Gihon.

The day the Nephilim burned his farm, the day his son was born and his wife had died, he vowed to move to a place of safety. When the boy was only six months old, Lamech led his family across the River Gihon to this city. He had hoped the river would bar Nephilim from harassing those living beyond the hill country. Now even that hope was gone.

A noble man stepped through the crowd, approaching the speaker. His clothing was simple, and he wore no insignia of authority, yet the people accorded to him respect fitting for a king or governor. This was Mehujael, founder of the city, and the people parted and bowed before him. He reached the speaker, who was still standing on the wagon. The Elder regarded him for several moments, his eyes undaunted by the speaker's powerful build.

Finally he spoke, loudly enough to be heard by his people. "Why would the Nephilim want to destroy our city? We don't have anything they want; we don't threaten them in any way!"

The stranger nodded. "I know. You do, however, have several very important features. First of all, people fleeing the Nephilim are coming to your gates, asking for asylum. Second, you are a wealthy city without enemies. They worry you will create an army, join with other cities and defeat them. Third, they do not like your traders, who are bringing your goods to other cities. Your commodities are of high quality and compete too freely with what the Nephilim's vassals' produce."

Mehujael considered this for a few moments. He looked up again. "When is this wave of Nephilim coming? How long do we have?"

"They are at this moment subjugating the last city states north of the river. Once they have completed this task, they'll begin building barges. I cannot guess how long it will take, but probably no longer than eight months."

Lamech's heart sank. That was hardly enough time to prepare. A murmur ran through the crowd. Mehujael turned to the assembly and raised his hand to silence them. His eldest son came forward, bowed and then whispered into his father's ear. The old man nodded and turned to the stranger.

"And why are you here? What possible gain do you have in warning us?"

The Nephilim opened his mouth to speak, but stopped. He gazed at the elder, seeming to weigh his options before answering. Finally he smiled.

"I might as well be honest with you, Elder," he answered. "My father is. . . was. . . a great leader among the Nephilim. He was called a 'son of God,' and only the greatest leaders are allowed this title. Our people adored him. Many assumed he would be our next ethnarch, but his popularity ended up provoking our rulers to stop him. My father now lives in impoverished exile."

"So, you come to us because you seek to overthrow your rulers?"

"I seek to overthrow them, yes."

Mehujael smiled. "Their armies will cross the River Gihon and march to our city. If we hold them off, that will give your troops time enough to destroy the barges and then take your capital by force."

"You, sir," answered the stranger with obvious admiration, "understand perfectly."

The Elder said to him, "And what can we do?"

"Your city is open for the taking." he said with intensity. "The walls would not withstand any serious attack. Even if they were adequate, you could never last a long siege. Your water supply is easily blocked. Too many people live here to keep supplied with food. Your soldiers are poorly trained and are too few. You have no horsemen and few iron weapons."

Mehujael's oldest son again whispered into his father's ear. "And how, sir, do you know all of these things? Have you been spying on our city?"

The stranger laughed. "Me? No, I have sat in on many counsels of war about the city of Mehujael. Our spies have been reporting on your city for many years now. You have few secrets we do not know."

The Elder looked into his eyes with an incisive glare. The stranger held his gaze with both arrogance and assurance. Mehujael nodded slowly. "You tell the truth. What are we to do?"

The Nephilim thought for a moment. "Find your brightest minds and build sturdy walls. Prepare your city with water and food. And... build an army."

At this, the crowd burst into spontaneous conversation. The elder turned now to view them, fear etched upon every face. Lamech watched the city's founder, obviously deep in thought. This man had guided this city for seven hundred years, through fires and dangers and many distresses. For him, defeat was unthinkable. Since the Nephilim had arisen, however, the world was changing and Mehujael would have to adapt or lose everything. He obviously realized this, for he stepped up onto the wagon and took his place beside the stranger.

He looked out over the assembly with a fiery expression. "People," he shouted. "We have little choice. I have worried about the Nephilim for many years, but I never dreamed their hordes would come this soon. If we expect to survive, all of us will have to surrender our own comfort and safety for the next six months in order to build sufficient walls, store sufficient water and food, fashion weapons and armor and man an army. We will need builders, craftsmen, farmers and soldiers– all."

He looked out over the crowd. "Lamech, you fetch your son and bring him to us. Tell him we need new city walls, new sources of water and weapons. Find him now."

Lamech bowed and turned to leave. His heart was sinking as he passed through the crowds. Mehujael remembered Noah's bridge, the city gates he designed, the new blueprint for roofs (learned in part from Methuselah) and his inventions in metallurgy. In such a great city as this, the young man had earned himself a prestigious reputation.

Clearly Mehujael, however, did not understand the way the boy worked. For Noah, creating bridges and roofs was a game, not a mission. Turning such tasks into a mission would cause the boy to wilt; the more pressure he felt, the slower he would function. Finally he would simply stop working altogether. Lamech, as he made his way out of the city to his farm beyond the walls, doubted if his son would survive the next six months.

The little girl was sitting on the banks of the creek when Noah saw her. She played in the water with her toes, watching it swirl, making it splash. Unaware of anything but the stream, the girl chatted as if she were sitting with a friend. As Noah watched her, he realized that the "friend" was a little doll, fashioned out of straw, with a simple white cloth serving as its dress.

"It's gonna be cold tonight. Go out and find some wood! Eliza-beth! Make sure you find that wood now. Yes Auntie. " At this the girl began a sing-song chant. "Yes Auntie, yes Auntie, yes Auntie, find the wood." She began splashing her feet in the water in cadence with the song, growing louder and louder until she was almost shouting. Suddenly she stopped and shook her finger at the doll. "Elizabeth! You haven't gathered any firewood, have you? You're in trouble!"

Noah decided it was time to interrupt this discussion. "So, are you Elizabeth or are you Auntie?" Noah asked from his vantage point.

The little girl started and turned around, her cheeks blushing and a look of embarrassment on her face. "Who are you?"

"Noah." He pointed across the fields. "My family lives on the farm over there."

Elizabeth nodded. "I am Elizabeth." She waved her hand in no particular direction. "We live over there somewhere."

Noah tried to look in the general direction she indicated. "There's a lot of 'over there' over there. Could you be a little more specific?"

"Nope," she answered, shaking her head. "Don't know what spelific means."

"Spe-ci-fic," he said. She shook her head again. "You know, accurate. . . exact. . . precise. . . particular. . ." She continued shaking her head.

Noah thought for a moment. "The word 'specific' means clearly defined or identified. It's about making sure you are accurate in some venture you are undertaking. You know, being rigorous in your conversation."

The little girl laughed. "You're funny, Mr. Noah."

"I'm not 'Mister Noah.'"

A mischievous looked flitted into her eye. "Okay, Miss Noah."

"No!"

"Madam Noah? Monster Noah? Marble-mouthed Noah? Moonchpa Noah?"

"No, just Noah will do," he said with exasperation.

The little girl thought for a moment, but then smiled. "No... I think you are Moonchpa Noah. That's your real name."

"But I've never heard of a Moonchpa before!"

She nodded, knowingly. "Neither had I. At least not until I met you, Moonchpa Noah. You are the first Moonchpa and therefore the best."

He started to open his mouth, but she interrupted again. "The best Moonchpa doesn't argue. He just accepts the truth."

A strange feeling came over Noah. This girl was smarter than he.

"Now," she said. "You'd better sit down next to this creek and talk with me, like a good Moonchpa."

And talk they did. They talked about trees and clouds and chores in the kitchen. Elizabeth told him all about her fireplace, her house (it was very small and messy), her garden (full of weeds), her age (she was seven), her friends (all imaginary). The experience was unique for Noah, who never had learned the trick of conversing with his brothers and sisters, all of whom were much younger than he and therefore were to him little more than nuisances.

This girl taught him how to listen. Much of it was nonsense, but whenever Noah tried to point that out (which at first was often) Elizabeth reminded him that the best Moonchpa doesn't argue, but simply accepts the truth. After a while, when he stopped arguing, he began to see the world with Elizabeth's eyes.

After they, really she, had talked for quite a long time, Elizabeth suddenly stopped, crossed her arms and said quite seriously, "Enough about me. Tell me, Moonchpa Noah, all about you."

Noah began explaining his life, how his mother had died when he was born, how his father had married his aunt (at this Elizabeth's eyes went narrow), how they had journeyed from the land of the Nephilim to Mehujael and were now working a farm here outside the city. He did not mention the bridge he had designed or any of his other projects, but did talk about how much he hated weeding the garden ("So do I!" she exclaimed), feeding the pigs and chickens ("We have none," she explained) and working in the fields ("Do you like anything?" she asked, a comment which unsettled Noah more than he would have admitted).

When Noah had finished, Elizabeth picked up a twig from the ground and began stripping the bark from it, asking in a distracted manner, "So, Moonchpa," (the "Noah" part of the name at this point forever disappeared) "does your Aunt Qanath lie in bed during the day?"

"No, of course not! She has three other children."

Still seemingly fascinated by the process of debarking the twig, she asked, "Does she beat you every day?"

He shook his head.

The twig, now denuded, began twirling in her fingers. "And…does she say all kinds of means things about you? That she hates you? That you're a bad person? That you should have died when your mother died?"

Elizabeth's questions confused Noah. Why on earth would she ask about his mother's sister, whom she had never seen? Elizabeth might be a bit on the imaginative side of life, yet these queries didn't sound like fantasies but nightmares. His aunt had told him once that he was socially awkward, which meant he didn't know how to interpret hidden meanings in what other people would say to him. So he had to use his logical mind to piece together the pattern in their conversation. What he deduced disturbed him deeply.

"Elizabeth, you have an aunt, don't you?"

She nodded quietly, still staring at the twig.

"Is your mother dead?"

Another nod.

"And your father?"

Again nodding.

"Do you live alone with your aunt?"

She looked down to the pond, for some reason in shame.

"And she beats you and calls you mean things and lies in the bed all day and makes you fetch the wood and clean the house and weed the garden…"

A 'yes' barely escaped her lips.

Noah's eyes filled with tears. "Are you supposed to be gathering wood right now?"

"Yes," she answered in a quavering voice.

"Then let's do that immediately, so you can bring it home. Then maybe she won't beat you."

The girl said in a dead voice, "It won't matter."

He didn't know what to say to that, so he got up and reached out his hand, smiling.

Elizabeth looked at Noah's hand and then into his eyes. "You won't ever hurt me, will you Moonchpa?"

His tears now ran freely, and he could barely speak. "No, Elizabeth, I promise."

She took his hand, he pulled her up and led her to the trees.

It did not take long for them to gather plenty enough wood for a fire. In fact, Noah made several piles of wood and hid them under some leaves.

"Remember now, Elizabeth," he said. "Find the great terebinth tree, and you'll find your woodpiles waiting for you."

She left him, arms full of wood, walking down the pathway, toward the area where Noah assumed she lived. For a while, he simply watched her as she walked, wondering if he could somehow help her, but not sure what he could do. Then he turned to the fields, which he had left unattended for far too long.

In the distance, near their large plot of land, a man stood, arms folded. Noah began walking toward the figure, wondering who it might be. After several minutes, he realized it was none other than his father, Lamech. His heart sank. Another lecture, consequence, another failure.

His father's face was grave as he reached him. "Noah," he said grimly, "something has happened."

The first two weeks were relatively easy. Noah spent the entirety of every day talking to builders and masons and craftsmen, to soldiers, to farmers, to those who quarried rocks. More than anything, he needed information about areas in which he had no personal experience.

Because Noah had designed the bridge, many roofs and the western city gate, the elders had put a heavy load on him. They expected him to help them prepare for almost certain disaster. First, the city needed a defensive wall system which could effectively repulse any enemy attacks. Second, they would have to develop a means for harvesting, transporting and storing vast amounts of food within the city to prepare for a potentially long siege. Third, they needed a way to divert water into the city and distribute it. The city had given Noah whatever he needed to accomplish the task, including a fine horse and saddle, to save time in his many travels.

The water turned out to be the easiest task. Running beneath the city of Mehujael were at least three underground rivers. Normally it was fairly easy to find these rivers in the countryside, for certain kinds of weeds or grasses often grew above the spots. Obviously in the city, they would have to guess at where to dig. In order to find water, Noah set apart forty workers who did nothing but dig into the ground along the most likely line.

For the sake of speed, he urged them to make rectangular wells large enough for two men to work side by side. As the workers delved into the earth, they supported the walls with rows of timbers. The real challenge, as always, came when they encountered rocks in the ground. Hitting the rocks with hopefully harder rocks was hardly useful, since the harder rocks continually split or broke.

Noah wanted smithies to forge iron stakes for breaking rock, but discovered from them that brittle iron would probably crack. The only way to make iron less brittle was to blow air into the iron as it melted and to melt it again and again in an exceedingly hot fire, such as that produced by coal. Noah told the council of elders that they needed to find coal and iron ore, so they sent a hundred workers to the hills beyond the River Dania, to search for both. Meanwhile, Mehujael called upon each smith to train a dozen men in the craft of fashioning weapons and tools.

Noah's contribution to food gathering and storage turned out to be small. After talking to shopkeepers, farmers and women of the city, he recommended the elders organize a council for storage of food. These workers then organized a massive effort to dry fruits and vegetables and to collect grains. Great storage bins were constructed in central locations of the city and were filled as the months went on.

One contribution Noah did make was to urge farmers to plant more grain. Normally, they could only harvest a small yield. This time, however, many from the city would join the harvest. This, of course, gave the smithies even more work, producing scythes for harvesting grain.

Noah's greatest task, the city walls, turned into an almost impossible battle. In order to repel the Nephilim, the walls had to be unscalable, unbreakable and easy to construct. They would have to provide a way for the city's soldiers to hide from enemy spears and arrows, while at the same time allowing them to repel siege ladders or platforms.

In addition, Noah early on was convinced the city needed two sets of walls, an inner wall and an outer wall, with a gulf of about fourteen cubits between them. Obviously the problems of having two walls doubled the building challenge, but it also more than doubled the defenses. If they had only one outer wall, as hard as the defenders would try to stop them, the enemy would eventually be able to bring their ladders and platforms right up to the wall. There they would continually attempt to throw up ladders and siege structures. Sooner or later, they might succeed and breech the defenses.

They could not do this, however, to an inner wall, for there would hardly be enough room to carry either their ladders or their platforms, especially if the inner wall were significantly taller. Noah quickly decided to make sure that the outer wall gates and the inner wall gates did not line up. If invaders broke through the first wall, they could not reach the inner gate except by running directly beneath the city's archers and defenders. Many, if not most, would die before they reached the next opening. Furthermore, the inner wall did not need to be constructed of stone, since it would hardly be exposed to the kind of continual attack faced by the outer wall.

After talking to builders, he devised a system for manufacturing the vast numbers of mud bricks they would need to construct the inner wall, using simple dirt and reeds. Unfortunately, the outer wall had to be heavy stone, which was difficult to quarry and transport.

The obvious problem, of course, was time. To build two complete walls in six months was almost impossible. For an entire week, Noah argued with the city elders, trying to make them see the benefits of having a two-walled defensive system. He almost gave up when a completely new approach to the outer wall hit him.

The idea came to him when he was filling several sacks with dirt. After three or so sacks, he noticed how much a difference the dirt made in the sack's strength. Without the dirt, the canvas material couldn't even stand up, but once it was filled, the sack could serve as an effective barrier. Why not do the same thing with the city's defenses? The walls needed to be strong enough to stop pickaxes from tearing them down and thick enough to withstand battering rams. Why not construct them in layers, with sturdy stones on the outside, with another simple wall of mud bricks constructed two cubits behind it and fill the empty space between the shells with rubble? The stones would repel axes, the rubble would absorb heavy blows and the mud bricks would hold them all together. With enough workers, the mud bricks would be relatively easy to construct and the rubble would be easy to dump into the shell.

Even so, they still had no time to quarry the number of stones they would need to build such an outer defense. Here, however, Noah had seen a solution, albeit a horrible solution. Over a thousand stone houses stood on the plains outside the city walls. When the invaders came, those houses would probably be destroyed anyway. Why not dismantle them now and use their stones as building material for the city walls?

The idea had first come to him in the early days of that first week, but he had purposely kept silent about it. The only way this plan would work was if thousands of people lost their homes. Of course, his own home would be destroyed, but that did not concern him. He worried instead about the many farmers on the flat plains and the many poor whose hamlets lay within the shadows of the city's prosperity. These were people who survived from day to day on the gleanings from the fields, or depended on what they could grow in their own gardens. The only realistic solution carried with it an impossible dilemma: to save thousands upon thousands of lives in the great city, he would have to destroy the homes and livelihoods of those who lived beyond its walls.

Late in the second week, Noah took an early morning horse ride through the villages in order to count the number of stone houses available. As he rode, he surreptitiously recorded the approximate size of each house and guessed how many stones it might yield. The morning wore on, and his board became full with numbers and computations.

During the two weeks since he had first conceived it, this theory had bothered his conscience, but he had tried to ignore its implications. Riding along the road, however, changed everything. Mothers in tattered clothing were already out in their fields, hoeing the dirt with sharp stones or sticks. Children were walking on the road carrying impossibly heavy buckets of water from a stream or community well. In one place, he came upon four men using sticks, stones and one iron shovel to dig an irrigation ditch. Everywhere he went, he came upon people. A few of the farms seemed prosperous, but these were the exceptions. It was clear the majority of the people he encountered were poor.

Although he had gone out to take stock of available stones from houses, instead everywhere, Noah saw people. Whether they were working, walking, or talking to one another, they were still people. He especially noted the many children running, carrying, digging, weeding, often laughing, sometimes crying. These were the families his perfect plan needed to use if it was to succeed: an entire culture of human existence.

Some of these homes had been here for centuries, probably passed down from family to family. Fathers almost certainly identified themselves by their land, their houses, their traditions and their family inheritance, all of which must become disposable if the city were to survive. He and his father were newcomers to this world. What right had he to destroy an entire existence to save another, albeit a much more populous one?

On his return home, he tried desperately to consolidate all of his facts and figures to determine if they could find enough stone to build their wall. His instinct, however, almost always right, said they could. No matter how hard he tried, however, faces kept crowding out the numbers and computations. He found himself weeping as he rode, weeping for what had to happen, weeping for those whose lives were about to change forever.

On the way home, he saw Elizabeth running along a pathway into a nearby hamlet. She nimbly wove through the many people who were walking along the path through the grain. He called out to her, but she was running so quickly and he was far enough away that she didn't hear. It would have been wonderful to stop and talk with her, but he couldn't dare postpone what he needed to do. Making a mental note, however, he determined to go back as soon as the opportunity presented itself.

When he finally reached his own farm, two answers had formed in his mind, but both were impossible. Either he must remain silent about the stone houses and allow everyone in the city to die, or else present his "plan," and let all of those outside lose everything.

Noah climbed down from his horse, tying it to a tree. He slowly walked along the furrows to where he saw his father Lamech broadcasting his seed. As he walked, he looked over the fields. In a few months, all of this would be burned. The houses would be rubble. Whether his plan worked or not, the entire world would simply cease to exist, because a group of people, the Nephilim, had an insatiable greed for power. His eyes returned to his father, standing there, watching him. Here was a man who understood what it meant to lose everything. Lamech would know what to do. "Father," he called to him. "I need to talk."

Lamech nodded. They made their way to the stream, where the father sat down on the bank. Noah began picking up firewood and stacking in it piles around a large terebinth tree. After a few minutes, he spoke. "You know, if we want to fight off the Nephilim, we're going to have to build the outer wall of stone. Mud bricks won't stop them in the end."

"I've always agreed with you on that, Son," the father said. "But we don't have enough stones to build anything. It would take us years to quarry that much rock. We don't have years."

Noah carried a bundle of wood to the terebinth tree and dropped it on the ground. He sighed, sat down beside it, tears in his eyes. "Father, we do have stone, but not in the quarries and not in the hills. We have plenty enough, but . . ." His voice trailed off.

As his father waited, Noah sat in silence. He knew the solution, but could not bring himself to say it. This was a weight too heavy to bear on his own.

After a few minutes of silence, his father came and knelt beside him. "Son, if you have an answer to the problem, no matter how difficult it may be, you must tell us."

Burning with guilt, Noah divulged his secret plan of action. He described a scheme for dismantling the houses and transporting the stone to the building site. He explained the manufacture of mud bricks on the plains beyond the walls, the period of drying them, the process for laying them, his program for constructing the double-rimmed outer wall. He outlined how they would gather the rubble left over from destroying the villages and convey that to the site, where they would fill the shell of the outer wall. But the people, for them he had no blueprint, no perfect design to restore their lost income, their stolen homes, their abandoned family heritage.

"It's the only way to save Mehujael, but not those outside. The city could hardly take them in, Father. There simply won't be enough food or water for everyone."

For a long time, the two kept silent, neither wishing to admit what was obvious to both.

Lamech finally spoke. "If you do not take down their homes, son, the Nephilim will do it for you, and they will not stop with the villages and the farms, but will keep on destroying and looting until nothing is left but a hill of rubble and a plain full of rotting corpses. By building that wall, you are at least giving those people a chance that after all this is over, they can live long and fruitful lives."

Noah shook his head in disgust. "I do not have the right to take anything from anyone, Father. This isn't my duty. I'm just a boy who likes to build things."

Lamech rose and walked across the ground to the water's edge. "No, son," he said, looking away from him, out over the stream. "You are not just a boy. You are Noah, the son of the promise."

The young man looked up sharply at his father. "What?"

Lamech turned to his son. "You are the seed promised to Eve in the Garden of Eden. Didn't my father tell you?"

A sick look passed over the young man's face. He weakly shook his head, but said nothing.

"When you were born, God gave me your name 'Noah,' which means 'rest.'" Lamech paused. He looked into his son's eyes, but his son turned away in confusion. "You are the one, Noah, the one who will give us rest from our work and from the toil of our hands arising from the ground which the Lord has cursed."

Lamech did not say aloud what he hoped in his heart, that perhaps Noah might be the promised son who would crush the serpent's head and open the path to the tree of life. This, however, he could not know. All he could say with confidence was that the boy would give them rest from their hard labor. He thought about this promise and what it meant for humanity. Without the promise, there was no hope for anyone. For a long time, they sat without speaking.

Finally, the young man stood.

"No," he muttered, looking down to the ground, brooding.

"You have no choice, son. This is God's doing, not yours. You cannot deny God's calling on your life." He stepped toward his son, but Noah retreated.

"I am not the son of the promise, Father. I will not bear that weight, and I will not bear the burden of moving all of these people from their homes."

Lamech spoke quietly. "So, you will let them all die? And all of the people of the city? Will they all die too?"

"Yes...no...I don't know. It's not my burden."

Lamech stood in silence, gazing at his son, wanting to hold him, to help him do what was right, but he could say nothing. The young man turned and began walking toward the farmhouse in the distance. For a long time, Lamech stared, and then took the horse's reigns. He had a duty to perform. He mounted the horse and headed toward the city gates.

Within two weeks, the procedure for dismantling the houses began. Surprisingly few families resisted. Most simply took what possessions would fit on a cart or a donkey's back and began making their way along the road toward whatever towns might receive them. Some left quickly, while others hung on, hoping perhaps the process would halt before city soldiers reached their tiny villages. The demand, however, was so great, no hamlet could be spared destruction. Soon the road was filled with carts, animals and sorrowful people journeying to find a home.

One evening, Noah left his father's farm to find Elizabeth. He brought with him gold given to him by the village elders. He was hoping Elizabeth's aunt would be willing to part with her for a bag of gold. As he walked along the road, he saw a small family ahead: a father, mother and three young children. Two children sat on the back of a mule, which the mother led along the road. The father carried the youngest on his shoulders. They had no shoes, little clothing, and the bundles tied onto the mule's back would hardly sustain them long. Noah shook his head in despair, but what could he do?

He turned at the path where two weeks before he had seen Elizabeth running home. Surprisingly, no one was on the pathway, even though the last time he had been here, dozens of pedestrians were making their way back and forth toward the hamlet. At first, he wondered if perhaps it was dinner time, but doubted that, since the sun was still somewhat above the horizon. Surely someone would have been here. That thought began to worry him, and his pace quickened. Why would no one be on the pathway? And where would they be? He began jogging down the path. "Elizabeth!" he called out, but no one answered.

The hamlet was one of many he had surveyed several weeks before. Except now, it could hardly be described as a hamlet. Where ancient stone houses had stood only days before, piles of rubble lay in random heaps on the ground. The village of thatched roofed houses, which once all opened unto a quaint cobbled street had been reduced to broken beams of wood and door frames, lying haphazardly beside mounds of thatching, straw and other materials. Where Noah stood, he could gaze straight across the village square to distant fields, now open before his eyes. It was as if a wall of water had rushed through the streets, burying the dead and sweeping away the living.

Wind whistled urgently over remnants of a village that never again would hear children laughing, women bargaining, never again know the touch of human life. Except for wind, the scene stood silently fixed and cold. It was not his fault, he understood. The Nephilim had done this, had betrayed them all. This street witnessed to their cruelty. Yet he, Noah, had a part in this destruction.

Something across the square fluttered, a piece of white cloth. He gingerly clambered over piles of wood and stone to reach a little doll, snagged on a post. It was fashioned out of straw, with a simple white cloth serving as its dress. He reached out and gingerly removed the doll from the post, folded it and placed it in his pocket. He sighed. Elizabeth had been here, but for some reason had left her precious doll behind. He would never have a chance to help her now because she had been dragged away like all of the rest of the people. He could not be a part of such an undertaking. It was then he knew he could not stay.

The next morning, Lamech came out of his house to find his son standing beside his horse, two saddle bags slung over its back. He had suspected Noah would not remain in the city, even though the Elders had entreated him to stay. To remain would somehow make him responsible for what had happened to the people, and this Noah would not do. As Lamech gazed at his son, who looked both frightened and defeated, he realized it was useless to try to hold him here.

"Where are you going?" he asked.

Shaking his head and looking down, Noah answered, "I don't know. I can't get away from the Nephilim, and I can't stay here knowing what I've done to these people. Perhaps I'll find a village somewhere quiet, out of the way. It doesn't really matter, as long as I don't have to answer for anyone else but myself." He turned to leave.

Lamech ached. "Noah," he said in a quiet voice.

The young man stopped, but did not turn.

"Anywhere you go, you will still be Noah, the son of the Promise, the one who will give us rest."

The son shook his head.

Lamech said urgently, "At least assure me that you will tell your sons the story of the Promise."

Turning slowly, Noah looked at his father with bitterness. "I will have no sons, Lamech son of Methuselah. This burden will not pass on to any other human being. If I am the son of the Promise, then the Promise dies with me."

Many months later, a ragged young man leading a horse made his way up the lane toward a large farm house. The house overlooked a complex of fields, barns, animal pens and scattered small dwellings. The setting sun cast long shadows, and the owner of the house had to squint to see the young man clearly. It was not until he reached him that the owner saw the sadness etched into his features. The man asked for a place to sleep, perhaps with the animals and a place to keep his horse for the night. Against his better judgment, the owner led the youth to a stable, to a bed of hay and offered him food, which the young man appreciatively devoured.

In the morning, the owner, assuming the youth would be gone, instead found him cleaning out the stalls and turning the hay. The youth's hard work impressed him, which led the owner to offer him a deal: free food and a place to live in exchange for hard labor. Eagerly, the youth accepted his offer. Within a short time, he had made for himself a home in one of the shacks on the property and found a stall for his horse and was busy at work caring for the many animals on the farm. When the owner asked the boy for his name, he answered Noah, son of Lamech, son of Methuselah. The owner, Yenah, grunted, having heard none of these names before.

Three years passed. Noah proved an invaluable help to the farmer. He had great ability in many areas, both physically and especially mentally. Some of his ideas about improving their techniques for working and building, had already proved invaluable. The problem came, more often than not, in Noah's inability or seeming unwillingness to fulfill his promises or sometimes to bring a job to its completion. His inventiveness contributed to the farm, and he worked hard most of the time.

One day, a stranger and his family approached the main house, and the owner asked Noah to give them food, water and temporary shelter. The youth led them to a hut beside his own small dwelling and brought them food for the day, with enough provision to last them an additional week on the road. After a while, the owner himself came by to exchange news. After giving him profound thanks, the stranger began telling them about their journeys and recent encounters. In the course of conversation, the man asked about the youth's name who had been so generous in helping them. When the owner gave it, a dark look clouded the stranger's face. "Noah, eh? That's an unpopular name where I come from."

Surprised, the owner asked the man why, furtively glancing over at his silent worker, who was suddenly busying himself wrapping the additional food in cloth. The stranger grunted.

"Have you heard of the great city of Mehujael?" Yenah shook his head. "No? Well, in that city, the name Noah means disaster."

"That's for certain!" the wife said with a scowl. "A day doesn't go by without me pronouncing a curse on that evil man."

Nodding, the husband continued. "You see, this Noah was a clever sort of fellow. He built our bridge, he built our gates and lots of other things. Everyone talked about him as if he was the greatest human being since Cain. Now, a few years ago, the city elders had a problem. You see, the Nephilim were coming, and our city didn't have any defenses to hold them back. So they went to this Noah, and he told them to take the stones from all of our houses and land to build their stinking walls."

The wife cut in. "And he makes sure they don't let all of us poor farmers move into the city where it's safe. No sir! We simply give up everything and have to fend for ourselves."

"That's about the long and the short of it," the husband said. "This Noah fellow, he gets up and leaves before they even finished the walls."

The wife nodded. "We camped out in front of the gates, hoping they'll have pity on us when the armies of the Nephilim arrived."

"Did they arrive?" Yenah asked with curiosity.

"Oh, they arrived, alright," answered the man. "Armies such as like you've never seen, carrying battering rams, towers and all the rest, and the city let us in at the last second."

"Good thing, too. They were as big as giants and as strong as behemoths. Our troops tried to fight them, but couldn't do much. They were just too big."

Yenah glanced at Noah and saw tears running down his face.

"And what happened to the city?" he asked the man.

"It was hard," the man answered bitterly. "This Noah fellow had planned things all wrong. He didn't dig near enough wells, so people would stand in line all day just to get enough water."

"And the food," chimed in the wife. "Tell him about the food."

"Rotted in the storage houses," the husband said. "Everyone knows you just can't throw food in a pile and expect it not to rot. It got so bad they were eating their own animals, if you can believe it."

"And he didn't even think about the sewage! The Nephilim stopped up the canals, and human and animal filth choked the streets until you could hardly breathe."

A look of profound sorrow overtook the man's angry expression. "That's when the sickness started."

"Sickness?" Noah asked.

The stranger nodded. "Like when a person drinks fetid water in a swamp and ends up retching his insides out. You know, they get weak and nauseated? Before this, I had heard one time of someone dying from it. Well, in the last months of the siege, it happened to a thousand people."

His wife nodded. "Oh, at least." .

Yenah, noticing his youthful worker's horrified expression, asked the man, "Why did it happen?"

Shaking his head, the stranger answered, "I don't know. Could be the water, though. All those animals and their waste so close to the wells. Could have been the human waste too, for that matter. All I know is the water smelled like death."

"Tasted like death too," the woman added. "I think it was the food."

"Could have been," the stranger said, glancing at his wife. "Could have been the food, I suppose. Whatever it was, people died." He paused for a moment, tears filling his eyes and then started to say, "My own…" but could not finish his sentence. He began to cry.

The wife put her arms around her weeping husband. "Our own boys, Jared and Emeth. Their skin was burning, they were so hot. The poor little things just wasted away."

For a long time, no one said anything. Yenah scanned the room. The couple's seven children sat quietly, looking at their parents and each other. The experience had obviously been horrendous, and they looked gaunt and tired. The husband, wiping his tears on the sleeve of his tunic, looked shamefacedly at Noah and his employer. Noah stood by the open window. His shoulders were slumped, and a look of self-reproach dominated his face. Yenah felt sorry for the young man. This was a heavy burden for one so young to bear. Finally Noah broke the gloomy silence.

"What happened to the Nephilim?" he asked quietly.

The man looked at him in surprise. "Them? After a year, they left! How do you think we got here? Some kind of revolution happened in their capital city or something, and they gave up the battle and went home."

The woman added bitterly, "But not before killing most of our soldiers, burning all our fields and forests and leaving us with nothing."

The man nodded. "And no sooner did the stench of their rotten soldiers leave the city walls, than the elders gave us the boot, and put us out on our own. My ancestors have lived on that plain for five hundred years. Why, both my great-great-grandfather and his grandfather died on the battlefield right before the city gates. That didn't mean nothing to them. They just sent us on our way."

"And Noah's father?" the young man asked.

"Who?"

Yenah glanced at Noah and then turned to the stranger. "The father and family of Noah, the one who built the walls."

Shaking his head, the stranger said, "I wouldn't know. Didn't ever hear anything about him." He looked up with a bitter smile. "Probably dead. Would serve them right."

Yenah walked over to the door. "I think you're being hard on this Noah fellow. It sounds like the Nephilim were the real culprits."

The stranger stared at him for a moment, thinking. Finally he spoke. "You can't understand, out here in the wild, what it was like there in the city. Before last year, I'd never seen much death. I mean, my great-grandfather's great-great-grandfather died in our house when I was a boy, and my neighbor was killed by wolves one spring, but nothing more than that."

"That's right," his wife said. "Even if someone's leg gets cut off, it heals up, and I've never seen anyone in my whole life get the sickness, let alone die from it."

"We saw nothing but death, week after week," the man said grimly. "It changes ya, to watch your neighbors carrying out their loved ones and throwing them into an open pit. This Noah, fellow, it may not be all his fault, but a lot of it is. He was a mite too arrogant in my mind."

"He was that," agreed the woman.

"Well," Yenah said quietly. "You are welcome to stay here overnight, but I'm afraid no longer."

The stranger looked up. "You wouldn't happen to have a bit of work for me to do, would you sir?"

Shaking his head, Yenah said, "I'm sorry, but no. This young man here works solely for food and a place to sleep. We could not support anyone else."

Early the next morning, Noah slipped into the stable. Slung over his shoulder was a large canvas sack. As he approached his horse, a voice broke the morning quiet.

"Why are you leaving, Noah?"

He swirled around to see Yenah, fully dressed, standing in the corner. "I...I..." Noah stammered.

Yenah walked to him slowly, smiling gently. "You've done nothing to me. It's hard for me to imagine that you did anything wrong to anyone else."

The young man dropped his head. "You heard them. It turned out worse than my worst nightmares."

Nodding, the older man put his hand on his shoulder. "So, now we know each other, don't we? You'll never have to worry about your dark secret getting out from me, Noah. How much safer could you be than that?"

The youth looked into the man's eyes. "If you can promise me, sir, that you will never discuss this again, then I will stay."

Yenah smiled. "I promise not to mention this again. Now, put your things away, get to work on that fence in the pen. You've been putting it off for a whole week."

Noah smiled weakly. He made his way back to his dwelling and threw all his earthly possessions on the floor. He looked around the room and then went out to mend a broken fence.

Chapter Four

Year 1096

Bur'el quietly entered the council room. Immediately he saw his good friend and master Yakheed, standing before a group of seven city elders. They sat in leather-covered chairs fixed behind an ornately carved table. The elders wore deep red robes, symbols of their authority over the city and its inhabitants. The look on their faces was far from amiable; *a bad sign*, Bur'el thought, *for his friend's petition*.

He looked around the room. The council room was large enough to accommodate two or three hundred citizens and in the past had heard appeals brought by large assemblies of people. The dome ceiling had carefully designed openings to allow light in without admitting rain. That light fell upon intricate murals that populated the vaulted ceilings with panoramas of the Great River, horses, behemoth, farms, a city, and—of all things—looms. Bur'el smiled. Those looms were actually Yakheed's invention and craft. Through his skills in invention and trading, weaving had become this city's greatest industry. Traders traveled far and wide plying fabrics from Prathar, the city of weavers.

Now, however, Yakheed the weaver was unable to convince the elders of Prathar to abandon their latest project. "Please!" he passionately pleaded. "I beg you not to build ramparts around this city!"

Seven elders sat around the table, glancing at each other. Flickering light of candles exposed discomfort on their faces. The meeting had already run for hours. The sun had set, the gates were barred, and the city readied itself for sleep. They had debated back and forth. The elders were convinced the city needed a defensive wall to protect from Nephilim invasion. Yakheed passionately disagreed, but his arguments seemed to be making little headway.

After a long silence, the tall man sitting directly across from him smiled. "Yes, of course, Yakheed, we understand your position. It's just that—"

"It's just that you don't understand my position!" Yakheed said. "If you grasped the mind of the Nephilim, you'd realize that putting up a defensive wall is announcing to the world you choose to defy them. It forces them to respond, or else every village in the land will do exactly what we are doing."

"And when they do, the Nephilim will be helpless to stop us," answered an elder, seated all the way at the far left end of the table. "They'll have a hundred battles, all at once."

Bur'el carefully watched Yakheed's reaction. This was Prathar, the father of the city and, therefore, the most influential council member. Most of the time, Yakheed maintained a cordial relationship with him, recognizing his influence and working hard to keep him as a friend. Bur'el had never known Yakheed to jeopardize his relationship with city leaders through rash actions, but this time, he suspected his friend needed to face the problem head on.

Yakheed answered respectfully, "Master Prathar, they will not have one hundred battles all at once. We'll be the first to oppose them, so we'll be the first to be destroyed. The moment the Nephilim hear that our stone masons are cutting rocks for the wall, they'll don their armor, cross the river and march across the plains. This city will be ashes before the wall is half built."

"Of course, it would almost certainly happen anyway if we don't build the wall," Prathar said with a condescending smile. "Don't let the quiet lull you to sleep. They'll be here sooner or later. At least we may be able to stop them if we have a wall. We must do what we can to resist."

Bur'el saw an inkling of unease fleet across Yakheed's face, as if the man sensed his delicate position. He softened his manner. "Maybe they will. But maybe they won't. I have thirty women who do nothing but weave fabric as gifts to the Nephilim. They value our cloth above anyone else's. So far, it's worked, hasn't it?"

Although several elders nodded, their expressions were hardened, as if Yakheed's answer meant nothing to them. Bur'el glanced around the room. A suspicion in the back of his consciousness began to clarify; before this meeting had been convened, Prathar had convinced the elders into building the wall. The die was already cast. Bur'el recognized this from the way the others kept glancing at Prathar, waiting for him to take control of the meeting, deferring to his replies, approving his every comment. The founder might appear nonchalant, but it was obvious he was guiding the meeting to a foregone conclusion.

For several minutes, no one spoke. The elders seemed to be anxiously waiting for Yakheed to answer them, but he said nothing, his mind apparently racing through perplexing questions about Prathar. Bur'el couldn't imagine why Prathar would put the city at such risk. Was he trying to undermine Yakheed's influence in the city? Yakheed employed over one hundred and fifty women and men in weaving cloth. He had arrangements with farmers from miles around to bring him flax, wool and other fibers. Even though many others also produced fabric, it was Yakheed's reputation and expertise that guided the industry. This could be the real reason Prathar would take such a gamble. He saw his city slipping over under Yakheed's influence, and he wanted to bring it back. A war would return Prathar to his rightful prominence.

Yakheed grunted, as if he were displeased. "All right, you win. Build your invitation to Nephilim retribution."

A look of surprise brightened the faces around the table.

"But. . ." he added.

A wary look flitted into Prathar's eyes. "But what?"

"I want. . ." he said slowly, as he looked around the table, "to be in charge of the project."

Prathar slowly stood up straight. "What do you mean?" he asked quietly. "Building city walls is a task for masons, not weavers!"

Yakheed picked up a small patch of cloth, lying on the table. He ran his fingers over it, sensing its weave, noting its pattern. It was purple, a difficult color to procure, a color especially favored by the Nephilim. "Do you see this cloth? In order to keep the city safe from invasion, I pay twelve bags of gold for enough purple dye for the Nephilim royalty. I have merchants who spend six months finding the shells to make it, I pay craftsmen to process the shells, farmers to grow the flax, shepherds to shear the sheep, teamsters to carry the raw materials, children to card it, young women to spin it, artisans to weave it, seamstresses to sew it, traders to transport it. All of those people are my livelihood. When the Nephilim armies cross the rivers, every man and woman is free to leave this city and find refuge, all except me. If I leave, I lose my workers, my farmers, my looms and my trade. I may never be able to rebuild what I could lose. If this city is to have a wall, I want it to be a mighty wall, strong enough to stop any army. And. . ." He looked around the table with a piercing gaze, "I want it to be completed before the first Nephilim soldiers reach the river."

Bur'el silently gasped. Even though Yakheed's move made sense, it was risky. If the elders accepted his offer, then if the defense failed, only Yakheed would be blamed. If, on the other hand, he succeeded, the city would almost belong to him. Prathar stared at him with a mixture of respect and caution, but he did not deny Yakheed's logic. Of all the men in the city, this was a man who knew how to get whatever he needed. The elders requested Yakheed and Bur'el to leave the room while they debated his request. In less than a quarter of an hour, they summoned Bur'el and the weaver back into their presence and appointed him as overseer of the city's defenses. For another exhausting hour, they discussed their approach to protecting the city. Finally, Prathar stood.

"Well then," he said confidently, "Do we have any other questions for Yakheed?"

The men looked among themselves, shaking their heads.

He looked at the weaver. "Do you have any questions for us?"

Yakheed shook his head.

"We have an agreement, then. Yakheed, we are at your disposal."

The elders rose, talking quietly among themselves, making their way out the door. Yakheed, however, stayed seated at the table, deep in thought. The men filed out, leaving him alone at the table. Prathar, the last to leave, turned in curiosity.

"Is something wrong?" he asked.

Yakheed rose from the table slowly. "Wrong?" he answered, frowning. "The whole thing, building a wall, fighting a war, surviving a siege–it frightens me. That's all."

Prathar regarded him for a moment, a questioning look on his face. "You, Yakheed, afraid? I doubt if you have ever been afraid in your entire life!" he said. Prathar turned to leave, but stopped. He stood for a long time without speaking.

Finally, he spoke, his back still to Yakheed. "You must understand, weaver. The Nephilim will win in the end. Every year we wait, they conquer more and more. No one can stop them."

Prathar slowly turned. Bur'el could see the pain etched into his features, as if all hope was gone. The founder glanced over at him and nodded. "Both of you must understand; we can hardly hope to succeed in what we do, but if we wait until they have subjugated every town and village in every land on earth, they will conquer us anyway. Even if they don't, we still will have no one left to buy our wares."

Yakheed looked at the founder with surprise. He stood slowly, his eyes fixed on the city's founder. "My father, I did not understand. Now you have my assurance; if any human can stop the Nephilim, it will be done here at the gates of the city of Prathar."

Prathar bowed to the weaver and then turned to the door. Slowly, he exited out the door, clearly burdened with the task before them. Bur'el watched the closed door for a long time, wondering. He glanced around the room. The candle light played fluttering shadows on the murals on the ceiling. Yakheed sat silently, obviously overwhelmed by the nearness of the future. Finally, he laughed. "Well, Bur'el my friend and foreman—what a trap we lay for ourselves! If we do nothing, they will swallow us like an ocean wave, but if we resist, they will crush us without mercy. What can we do?"

Bur'el shook his head in perplexity. "I suppose our only recourse is to start building the walls, my friend."

The two men rose and left the council hall together. Dusk had settled on buildings and shops, with shadows gently brushing across the cobbled streets. Distant sounds of children's laughter, the calls of venders, a woman singing, seemed muffled by the blanket of evening. The air washed around them like a gentle whisper, warning them to quiet their voices, to soften their steps. Bur'el, as he walked beside Yakheed, almost closed his eyes to soak in the world around him.

"This is the last night, you know," Yakheed spoke quietly. "It's the last night we can see these sights this way. Tomorrow, this city will become our fortress. We will no longer see these people as vendors, shopkeepers, weavers, tradesmen. We'll count their heads as our soldier ranks. We'll measure their shops as storage bins. We'll rank their crafts as supplies for war. We'll value their women as weapon makers."

"And the children?"

Yakheed shook his head, a sadness in his eyes. "As mouths to feed."

He put his hand on Bur'el's shoulder. "Tonight, my friend, let's enjoy our city." The two walked down the lane toward the weavers' street.

The elders had agreed that their decision must be secret until the work actually began. Three weeks later, however, they had made almost no headway on their still secret project. Yakheed would not build a wall unless it could withstand the full onslaught of Nephilim soldiers. Furthermore, it had to hold out against siege towers, fire, battering rams, ladders and any other trick the Nephilim might throw against it.

The elders urged speed, not perfection, but both Bur'el and his master refused to back down. This wasn't like building a new loom, which would cause little damage if it wasn't quite right; unless these walls did their job perfectly, they would never survive. The few who knew about the undertaking had no experience in the art of warfare. Neither Yakheed nor his foreman had ever faced an enemy in battle. Any information they might find had to come from someone who had experienced war. As far as they knew, only one city had withstood the Nephilim: the city Mehujael. Therefore they needed to find someone who had survived that infamous siege.

The two men began visiting every shop in the city, casually inquiring about the former lives of the city's inhabitants. Since they didn't want their secret plan exposed until absolutely necessary, they told people they were looking for new trade opportunities and wanted to find people who had lived in great cities. Eventually, after an entire precious week of probing, Yakheed heard a rumor about a man and woman, tanners, who lived on the outskirts of the city, refugees from Mehujael. As soon as he learned directions to their shop, Yak-heed made his way through the streets to the tanners' quarter. He needed no signs to tell him he was close. The entire area reeked of the foul-smelling stench of saffron, green, indigo and black dyes mixed with cow's urine. Yakheed could hardly imagine how humans could survive living in such a loathsome place. His head was almost dizzy from the stench, but before long he came to the shop he sought. A wooden sign above the door said, Evol, son of Mattew. Bright leather covered the doorway, studded with brass rivets arranged in intricate patterns. *Even in the midst of pungent odors, here was an artist*, he thought to himself.

He pulled a bell string, and in the distance he heard a bell ringing. "Come in!" came a shout from within. Yakheed entered. Laid out before him was an enormous courtyard, carefully organized with perhaps fourteen vats, so large that a bull could have been completely submerged in them. Each vat had its own color, such as indigo or green. A rugged man, standing over one of the vats, was fishing with a long pole for a large piece of leather soaking in the tub of yellow liquid. He looked up and spying Yakheed, bowed, laid down his pole and deftly walked along the planks to an area shaded by a thatched roof. There at a large stone table sat a woman, expertly sewing a leather jacket.

Yakheed bowed, introducing himself. Then, according to the custom of the city, he inquired about their family, health and prosperity. Finally, after covering all formalities, he asked the one question that had brought him there: had they been in Mehujael? A suspicious look washed over Evol's face, and Yakheed wondered if the man had already guessed the real purpose of the visit. Nevertheless, both Evol and his wife freely answered his questions.

Yes, they had been in Mehujael during the Nephilim siege from beginning to end. It was only twenty years ago, and they remembered everything with piercing detail. They described the system of the outer wall and the inner wall with its alternating gates. Evol had worked for six months on the two-layered outer wall.

"Mud bricks on the inside and stone outside with rubble within! Ingenious!" said Yakheed.

The man explained the process of dismantling houses and transporting the stones to the wall, the work of fashioning sturdy gates and the approximate heights of each bulwark. The woman described the failures of the water systems, food storage, waste disposal and animal husbandry. Yakheed was certain their own city's much smaller size was an advantage in a siege and thought they could survive, but the couple adamantly disagreed.

Evol stroked his beard. "A small population means you don't have enough soldiers to hold them back. They come on you like ocean waves, you know. Hard to stop that kind of onslaught."

"It's not just the battle, either. You've also got the suffering behind the gates," the woman added darkly. "Especially when the illness came. It went through the city like a fire through a dry field. It was horrible: the sickness, the starvation, the foul smell, the dead bodies. After a while, every morning I woke up wondering if we'd be next. It was awfully hard to face another day. It went on for months and months like that, until we could barely drag ourselves out of bed to stand in line for water. The people lost the will to fight."

Evol nodded, and Yakheed saw in his eyes vivid memories of horror. "I'll never go through that again, I can tell you for sure. Standing on the walls when ladders are thrown up on either side of you is enough to haunt your dreams forever. With all our might we'd push the ladder off with long poles and then another cursed ladder would drop into its place. Hour after hour we fought and kept wondering if it would ever end. Twenty years, and it still haunts my dreams.

"But you did beat them," Yakheed said.

The man shook his head, irony in his smile. "No, they beat themselves. Some kind of revolution in their capital city sent them on their way in a hurry. No one can beat them. They're more animal than human. If the Nephilim ever march on this city, no matter what it costs us, we will get as far away as we can."

They talked on for the rest of the morning, the couple answering each one of Yakheed's penetrating questions with helpful observations. At the end of their discussion, Yakheed finally gave in to his curiosity.

"Tell me," he asked them. "Who dreamed up your defenses? I've designed more machines than anyone I know, but I couldn't invent defenses like you had in Mehujael!"

Evol shook his head. "A young man. Actually, just a boy. He designed our bridge, our roofs, our gates and then our entire defense."

Yakheed bent forward eagerly. "And his name?"

"He was the son of Lamech, son of Methuselah. His name was Noah."

Eight hard months passed. Massive walls, impenetrable gates, complex systems for storing food and channeling water all grew into place. While the work of seizing homes for stone had been relatively easy in Mehujael, here the task was much harder. No one could prove that the Nephilim were threatening the city, and no one could guarantee the walls would hold them back. The settlers outside the city gates knew this. In the end, the city's newly formed legion marched out upon the plain and slaughtered all who resisted. Yakheed had opposed Prathar and the city elders in this decision, but had too much at stake to fight against it vigorously.

Anyone who worked full time on the building projects was promised a place in the city. Farmers who provided their harvests to be stored as food were rewarded with quarters built within the city walls. The problem of food storage plagued Yakheed, for no one had a good solution to inevitable dangers of spoilage. Water also worried him, because at first, they had a difficult time finding good enough sources. A fast-moving river lay not far beyond the city's southern wall, and until this point the city procured its water from channels redirected into the city. Yakheed suspected, however, that the Nephilim would quickly block these channels to cut off the city's water supply. Therefore, they needed to discover a new source of water in the ground. Until this point, no one had ever searched for underground water. After several months, however, excavators had dug enough wells to sustain the population if the river was cut off from them.

In most cities, enemies have the option of attacking from any direction. The river on the city's south side made access to the southern walls difficult, forcing an attack most likely from the north. In addition, almost immediately beyond the river sat a mountain, which made it difficult for an enemy to carry supplies and equipment from the south. The mountain, less than a half day's journey to the summit, was a curiosity to those who visited the city. Most mountains were simply large hills, but Halftop rose perhaps fifteen hundred cubits above the plain. The first settlers of the region had christened it Halftop because it looked as if at one time something had cut half of the mountain's peak clean off. Those who hiked to the area often commented that once they reached the top, they had to hike down tree lined slopes to reach the deep blue lake which lay in the center of the crater. Much of the city's iron came from this mountain, making it valuable to the community.

The people of the city worked frantically to finish their preparations for the coming battle. Every day a constant stream of wagons brought grain into the city to be stored in towering silos. By the end, they had stored enough food to feed them for two years of siege and had a water supply sufficient to sustain them indefinitely. They had forged arrows, spears, axes and knives to defend the city walls. Prathar was prepared as it could be for the coming invasion.

In the end, however, they weren't ready enough.

Messengers stationed near the river sounded the first warning. An enormous army, towing siege towers, wagons of supplies and armaments, crossed in mass at Gruber Ford. As the days went on, the thousands upon thousands of fierce looking soldiers plundered the countryside, taking whatever they needed and destroying whatever was left. The reports came back with scattered news of slaughter and destruction. Within days, dozens of villages lying between the river and the city had simply ceased to exist.

That information terrorized almost everyone behind the massive city walls. Many chose to leave rather than stand against certain destruction, fleeing into the hills or deep forest. The flight unnerved even the most hardened soldiers. Yakheed, on the other hand, saw this as great news, promising more food for those who stayed. Once the attack began, no one would worry about the cowards who left. They wouldn't have time.

In this, however, Yakheed's naiveté could have proved fatal. In the midst of battle, they might have rued every lost hand and every missed shoulder. The steady train of exiles, who piled their belongings onto two wheeled carts or the back of a mule, carried away much of the city's stamina and strength. When wave after wave scaled the walls, many a defender died not for lack of courage, but for paucity of reinforcements.

Finally the exodus stopped and the road emptied. Throughout the next six days, scouts brought reports of an enemy host numbered beyond imagination marching toward their land. They described enormous towers hauled by teams of oxen and a seemingly endless stream of carts carrying provisions, as if the soldiers were preparing for a drawn out siege. The scouts depicted the Nephilim as massive, possibly a head taller than anyone in the city

"The shafts of their spears," warned the chief of the scouts, "are as thick as a man's arm, but they carry them as if they were kindling wood. No one could stand against such men in battle."

On the seventh day, watchmen descried smoke on the horizon, and the mighty gates were shut and barred. The stone masons completed their work of blocking the eastern gate with mammoth stones they had prepared. Iron bars reinforced the massive beams which now barred the enemy from the city. Then all the work was completed, and the people gathered in the streets, nervously looking toward the north and waiting.

A foreboding silence settled uneasily over the city. By late afternoon, the advance regiment, a company of about two hundred warriors, marched along the road. The city residents, standing on the walls, silently moaned in despair, many of whom had never seen Nephilim men-at-arms in their full array. At this point, the elders commanded all but soldiers to abandon the walls.

Yakheed stood on the bulwarks, first looking out over the fields at the soldiers and then surveying their own defenses. He had copied the walls of Mehujael, following the plans of this man named Noah. The outer walls were three cubits deep, giving defenders plenty of room for maneuvering. A half cubit thick outer shell rose up another three cubits above this platform, providing protection from arrows and spears. This shell had breaks in it, sometimes every cubit, sometimes every half cubit or a distance in between. From a distance, the breaks made the wall look like a set of teeth with large gaps between each incisor. The breaks were about a half cubit wide, big enough to enable defenders to hurl rocks, throw spears, brandish axes at any Nephilim who attempted to scale the walls using ladders or siege towers. Even as ladders came up onto the tower, the outer shell would protect the defenders, and the gaps would allow them to use long poles to send the ladders off the wall and back to the ground. Much of their defense would be against such ladders and siege towers. Yakheed silently thanked the couple, long gone, who had described this aspect of siege warfare.

Defenders could access the outer wall in two ways. Three massive gates on the inner wall gave entry to the space between the inner and outer defenses. A detachment always guarded these gates and shut them at first warning of a serious attack against the outer walls. Soldiers could also reach to the outer wall by way of reinforced gangplanks which spanned the fourteen cubit gap between the inner and outer defenses. This was the main pathway between the city and the outer wall and critical to their success. In the pitch of battle, they would need to send fresh troops as instant reinforcements. Yakheed appointed four guards to watch each gangplank from the inner wall, ready at a moment's warning to draw the plank. This he also copied from the man named Noah. Whatever defenses they had raised over the past six months were largely due to him. He hoped they would be enough.

Yakheed looked back over the plain and inwardly groaned. The Nephilim were without a doubt terrifying to behold. The men were mostly pale skinned with night black hair. A bright red streak slashed across their black helmets, and they put the same streak on their shields. They wore tough armor, studded with iron rivets on the front and back. Each man bore a hefty spear, a short bow and a broad bladed sword. They set up camp about five hundred cubits from the city gate and waited.

Yakheed gazed at them with amazement. He had seen a few Nephilim before this, but never a whole fighting band. Even by themselves this vanguard of two hundred men looked invincible.

Yakheed shook his head in despair. How could he ever have imagined they could defeat an entire host of such warriors? Any thought of engaging an enemy like this on the battlefield was ludicrous. Their own soldiers had never fought a real foe, yet this enemy had not only fought gruesome battles, but had rarely been repulsed. Now that he saw them, he doubted if his soldiers would effectively repel these warriors from scaling the city walls. They were simply too strong, too experienced and far too warlike.

Grimly smiling, Yakheed at least could find comfort in knowing Sister was far away, safely hidden in mountain caves and cared for by his people. As for himself, he now faced the inescapable realization he was about to die, and everyone in the city would die along with him.

Within three days the entire force established itself out of the range of archers, but close enough to crush any hope the people might have had. For two months, Yakheed had attempted to train thousands of men and women to man the outer walls. As best as they could, they had practiced repelling ladders, destroying siege towers. Now these soldiers stood silently dreading the horrible attack about to break loose upon them.

The first attack came on the fifth day. Yakheed was supervising the smiths, who were frantically fashioning iron arrow heads, when Bur'el burst into the shop. "Come!" he said. "It's begun."

Yakheed grabbed two axes, slipped them into his belt and slid two knives into their sheaths. In a moment he and Bur'el were charging through the crowded streets. In the distance, they heard the ungodly roar of savage men, pounding drums, braying horns and the fearful cries of the farmers, shopkeepers and tradesmen on the wall, who desperately were trying to hold them back.

By the time Yakheed reached the ladders up the inner wall, people in the streets were fleeing to their homes, as if anywhere would be safe once the Nephilim breached the walls. Yakheed and Bur'el bounded up the ladder to behold a terrifying sight: enormous warriors cutting through defenders like stampeding mammoths.

He quickly looked around to those guarding the inner wall. "Soldiers," he bellowed, "all of you! Come with me!" He ran to the four men guarding the gang plank. "The moment one of those brutes breaks through our men and heads toward the plank, pull it!"

Yakheed quickly turned to Bur'el. "Quick! Command the captains below to send me reinforcements now! Get bowmen up here. Instruct them to shoot every Nephilim who comes within fifteen cubits of the ramps, and tell the guards of the gangways to pull them as soon as the reinforcements cross the gap. Go!"

Yakheed didn't wait for an answer, but dashed across the gangplank. On the other side, a deadly battle raged. At least thirty Nephilim had scaled the outer walls and were fighting viciously. Yakheed's defenders were falling before them, too terrified to strike hard.

Yakheed instantly saw their peril, for the Nephilim would win the battle unless his soldiers took the offensive. Roaring with anger, Yakheed began swinging his two axes almost haphazardly, wading his way into a battle between two Nephilim and a half-dozen defenders.

Before the invaders realized he was there, he had swung his right ax into the side of a vicious barbarian, who angrily screamed in pain. When he wielded his left ax, however, it only glanced off the armor of the second man, who instantly spun around, his spiked club narrowly missing Yakheed's bare head. Suddenly, they stood face to face.

This was the first moment Yakheed had ever encountered an opponent greater than himself and for a split second, he wavered, as if he were standing on the edge of a giant chasm, struggling to keep his balance. Above him towered an enormous soldier, invincible: a savage monster who knew no fear, insatiable in his hunger for destruction. Nothing could stop this creature, certainly not the weakling trembling before him. But Yakheed could not surrender to fear; surrender was against his nature. He recognized if he hesitated even a heartbeat longer, this Nephilim would vanquish him just as he had vanquished a hundred other faltering opponents.

He willed his right hand to pull free his ax and swing it with all his might into the side of the savage before him. Even as his right ax connected, he drove his left ax into the soldier's unprotected neck. The man gasped. At that instant, the battle stopped for Yakheed and his opponent; he heard no sounds, smelled no smoking brands, felt no tremors beneath his feet. All he saw was shock and fear frozen on the Nephilim's face; bulging eyes, blood spurting through his lips.

Suddenly the monster became a human. Yakheed saw how his beard swarmed with a thousand tiny jet black curls, how his eyebrows met together above his nose, how his nostrils were dilating and contracting. He smelled his breath, coarse and reeking of garlic. This was not an invincible behemoth. He was just a man, and at that instant, Yakheed realized they could defeat this host of mortal humans. He looked into his opponent's eyes and smiled, suddenly recognizing that they were now vacant of expression. The soldier began to waver and then slowly crumbled to the ground like a rag doll.

As the man fell against him, Yakheed jumped back. The noise of battle returned to him. He looked around himself and saw the other enemy, the one he had injured, attempting to hold his side, which bled profusely. Before Yakheed could react, three of his own soldiers attacked with knives. Within moments, the assailant was dead.

"You can beat them, soldiers!" shouted Yakheed. "They're not invincible at all. Follow me!" He began running toward a group of twelve Nephilim, who were plowing a path for their climbing kin to join them. As he ran, he roared in exultation, and many soldiers on the wall suddenly turned to see an amazing sight.

Eight or nine defenders were racing after Yakheed the Weaver, axes and knives brandished, eager to assail their foes. Within moments, the Nephilim discovered themselves inundated by furious fighters who wielded their weapons as if possessed by fire. Yakheed's men crushed into the invaders, pushing them back into the weapons of soldiers who only moments before were falling beneath them, but who now attacked with vigor. It was here the battle that day was won, for at this moment these men discovered that they too were fearsome adversaries.

Before long, the entire force of city soldiers was on the offensive, and no longer could two Nephilim hold back a squad of ten. The invaders fell before the defenders, and the guardians retook ladders, thrusting them off the city walls, flinging those scrambling up them to their deaths. They squelched the remaining pockets of opposition. After this, no Nephilim was able to make it over the wall to fight. It was not long before the Nephilim gave up the attack.

Fifteen times the Nephilim attempted to scale the walls, and fifteen times the city repulsed them. As hard as they tried to dismantle the gates, the aggressors could not. Yakheed had constructed these gates according to the plans of the man named Noah, making them virtually invincible.

The assailants' siege towers were ineffective as well. The only way for an invader to reach the fighting area was to squeeze through the openings in the wall, only to be slain by waiting soldiers. Even when the Nephilim had thrown an all out attack, with wave after wave of ladders, the now organized and confident defenders tripled their efforts to stop them. It was clear that these assailants would not win the city through might.

A few days after the fifteenth attack, Yakheed and Bur'el stood on the wall, watching a surprising sight; half of the Nephilim were breaking camp, readying to march. The eyes of the two friends followed a long line of carts already moving along the plain, and before long, thousands of soldiers, bearing bright standards, filed down the road toward the distant river and beyond that, to their own lands. Even in retreat, the forces summoned awe from those who had faced them in battle. All around the two friends, soldiers were speaking of victory, that their enemy had abandoned the city.

Bur'el, however, knew better. "They're readying for a siege, Yakheed. They'll keep enough soldiers to pen us in and send away anyone they don't need. That way they won't have to feed extra mouths. They're in this for the long haul now."

Yakheed nodded, a chill settling into his thoughts. "I knew we'd come to it, but I hoped they would have razed the city and slaughtered us all, before this happened."

Bur'el turned to his friend in surprise. "But you, more than any other man, have kept us alive. Without your courage and command, the Nephilim would have won the first day."

Frowning, Yakheed answered, "We are now at the same point as Mehujael when it failed. It wasn't the sword that beat them; it was the hunger and illness. They failed to prepare for the waiting."

"And will we succeed where they failed?" Bur'el asked quietly.

Looking out over the field of soldiers beneath them, Yakheed sighed. "No," he answered. "We have hardly improved Noah's plans. Perhaps we can survive a year, if our food doesn't rot. But I doubt it."

"Then let's hope the Nephilim lose patience with the wait," Bur'el said.

"No, we will lose this war, my friend."

Chapter Five

Year 1097

Six months passed, and Yakheed's prophecy remained unfulfilled. The wells supplied plenteous water, and the food remained fresh with the people carefully rationing supplies. The mood of the city was serious, but not despairing. They had no contact with the outside world, and no outside news of any kind passed the watchful guard of the Nephilim. Yet the war practically was at a standstill. The invaders never renewed their attack, trusting in starvation to defeat the city of Prathar. The city's preparations were complete enough, however, that they might be able to outlast the patience of their enemies.

The first disruption in their defense came from an unexpected source–rodents. Watchmen discovered grain was being consumed by a kind of black rodent never before seen in the city of Prathar. These rodents were much like mice, except larger and significantly more aggressive. Since no one had seen this creature before the siege, they guessed the vermin had come with the Nephilim, perhaps in the wagons which brought their supplies. Whatever their source, the animals, now named rats, wreaked havoc in the city. They had no natural enemies and bred rapidly.

For several months, no one had realized their presence, and during this period these rats began breeding with terrifying rapidity. By the siege's seventh month, the infestation forced the city to triple their guard of storage houses. Carpenters attempted to seal the houses, but the rats ate through the wood. Finally, craftsmen covered the wood with thin sheets of metal, which effectively stopped the rodents from invading the city's grain bins.

This solution, however, forced the starving rats into the general populous. Almost immediately, vermin invaded homes throughout Prathar. They established themselves in every imaginable hiding place and bred prodigiously. Their litters often consisted of ten or even fifteen offspring, and the young matured so quickly that within weeks they themselves were ready to bear their own pups. Since they had no natural enemies and–at first–possessed a plenteous food supply, they multiplied from just a few to thousands upon thousands in seven months.

The rats had a major part to play in what almost proved to be the defeat of Prathar. It all began quietly, in the smithies' quarter of the city. Yakheed had been summoned to mediate the dispersal of precious iron for weapons and tools. Carpenters correctly argued they needed iron tools for fashioning their wood products used by soldier and civilian alike, while the soldiers demanded more iron for knives and axes.

Yakheed patiently asked questions of both groups, knowing that no matter what anyone said, there was only a limited supply of iron, and all must compromise. In the midst of the debate, a carpenter was again explaining how each tool produced benefit for a larger number of people, when a little girl appeared in the doorway of the smiths' meeting hall.

The weathered soldiers and the muscular smiths dwarfed the child, who was perhaps no more than six years old. Light brown hair swept across her mahogany skin, her round dark eyes peering out in awe at the men seated before her. She stood still, desperately clutching a tiny doll, hoping someone would stop the noise long enough to listen. Yakheed raised his hand. "Gentlemen," he said with a smile. "We have a young lady here wishing to address this solemn assembly."

He rose, came to the girl and knelt down before her, gently taking her hand. "And what is your name, child?"

"Loree," she whispered.

Yakheed smiled. "Now, Loree, where are your parents?"

A frightened look came over her face. She pointed out the door. "They're at our house, but they haven't talked to me for two days and the rats are biting them."

Yakheed quickly picked Loree up and walked out the door. "Show me where to go, child."

She directed him to a house not far down the street. It was a smithy's shop, the name Sivit engraved on a wooden sign above the door. Yakheed put the little girl down. "You stay right here, child. I'll call you when it's safe to enter."

He swung open the door, peering into the dark room. A foul odor assaulted him, and he involuntarily gagged. Steadying himself for a moment, he called out, "Hello, Sivit? Are you here?" The room was silent, except for the sound of rats scurrying across the wooden floor. He found a candle on the fireplace mantel and lit it. Its light lent enough illumination to reveal a table, three chairs, various tools and weapons, but no people. Yakheed took the candle and moved through the room to a doorway. What he saw as he opened the door appalled him more than anything he had encountered in the battles he had faced thus far.

Before him, lying on a bed of straw, the bodies of a man and woman were covered with rats, rodents so voracious they did not even stir at the unwelcome candle light. The creatures had clearly been feeding for a long time, the result of which was so gruesome Yakheed could hardly bear the sight. He shouted at them, but they ignored him, either emboldened by their months of mastery over the city of Prathar, or made desperate enough they simply didn't care.

After surveying the scene, Yakheed returned to the street. Several people had gathered outside, waiting. Yakheed glanced down at the child, held now by a neighborhood woman. He caught the woman's eye and shook his head.

A look of fear passed over her face. "Come child," she said quietly and led Loree across the road.

Yakheed watched the woman and girl, waiting until they both disappeared into a nearby house. He then grabbed three bystanders. "We'll grab some weapons and tools inside, men. Come on."

If they expected to clear the room quickly of vermin, they encountered instead a difficult battle with a vicious enemy. Some of the rodents defended their meal, attacking the human intruders. In the course of the struggle, all four men received numerous bites. The room's darkness complicated their fight, since the only window was over the bed, and it was shut tight. They slashed and hammered for several minutes, cursing and shouting as they fought. Finally the animals recognized their defeat and fled, allowing one of the men to throw open the shutters.

Rays of the sun lit up the room, and Yak-heed gasped in shock. As horrible as was the sight on the bed, something equally grotesque lay before them on the floor. Beyond the creatures they had just killed, fourteen or fifteen additional rats lay dead on the ground, bloated and with blood trailing from their mouths. This was something he had never seen in an animal, and Yakheed wondered what on earth could have killed them.

Grabbing blankets from a shelf, with revulsion the men wrapped the two mutilated corpses and then carefully bore them to the street. As Yakheed led the men down the road, others began quietly to fall in behind them, swelling into a silent crowd. Finally the procession reached a humble cemetery near the eastern inner wall. The people looked at one another uneasily.

In a world where most people lived for seven and sometimes eight centuries, untimely death was foreign, almost incomprehensible. In another existence of the future, cultures would enshroud death in rituals. Here in Prathar, however, death was still too unfamiliar to bear masks, and so in muted voices they deliberated over how best to dispose of the bodies. A few women selected a spot and began digging holes for the couple. While they were working, Yakheed saw Bur'el across the road watching curiously, and he moved over to talk with him.

"Have you been to the house, Bur'el?" he asked softly.

The man shook his head. "Someone sent for me. He thought you might need some help. What happened?"

Yakheed frowned. "Have you heard of rats killing a human?"

Surprise passed over Bur'el's face. "Rats killing a human?"

Nodding, Yakheed answered, "Two humans, both lying in bed."

"Impossible."

Yakheed looked over to the corpses. "Then what killed them?"

He and Bur'el crossed the street and knelt down by the bodies. Gingerly unwrapping the man, Yakheed examined his head and neck, searching for clues, while Bur'el looked at the woman.

"Yakheed," Bur'el said almost in a whisper. "Look here."

He pointed to a couple of black bumps on her throat. "They're not from insects, and they're certainly not from the rats." He touched a bump. "It's hard as a rock. What is it?"

Yakheed looked down at the man's body, lying before him. "I don't know. He's got the same bumps." He looked up and seeing several people staring at him with a look of fear, he quickly re-wrapped the body.

The two stood, turned to a woman who had just finished digging the hole and nodded. "We must go back to the house and try to understand what has happened. Please bury these bodies and then care for the girl, Loree." The woman bowed and then returned to the bodies.

Walking along the street, Yakheed and Bur'el passed small groups quietly talking among themselves, looking nervous. "They're no fools, these people," Bur'el muttered, as they reached the Sivit house. "It won't take long for them to figure out that something very serious is happening."

Yakheed grunted. "But we don't have a clue what's going on! That's what I'd like to know. What are we dealing with?"

Entering the house, they surveyed the strange scene in the bed-room, with disdain poking at the rats lying on the floor, attempting to gain some insight into the situation. "My guess," Bur'el finally said, "is that the rats have something to do with it."

Yakheed nodded. "Whatever killed the rats, must have killed Sivit and his wife. There's some connection, but I don't know what it is. Whatever happened here, we need to get rid of the rats. Probably all rats in the city."

"All of them? That's impossible!"

"Every single house, every single shop," answered Yakheed. "I'm not going to feel safe until they're all gone." He looked again at the gruesome sight on the floor. "Hopefully, whatever killed the rats and Sivit will stay right here."

That afternoon, Yakheed summoned the city elders and urged them to begin a program designed to wipe out the now ubiquitous rat population. The elders appointed district committees to supervise sealing every house, protecting all food sources and hunting down and destroying rat nests. In addition, they appealed to the tinkers and craftsmen of the city to design devices for trapping and killing the rodents.

No one took this as seriously as Yakheed. In fact, he never went to bed that night, setting up a watch in the street outside the house of the unfortunate Sivit. The horrors he had just seen unsettled him and made him want to understand these rodents which were overrunning their city. By staying up all night, he might be able to learn the life of a rat, in order to defeat them. As he sat there, he sighted rats running through the streets, climbing up walls, scurrying across roofs, jumping through windows, slipping beneath doorways. *They're almost unstoppable*, he thought to himself.

Hours later, exhausted and deeply worried, Yakheed walked the streets in early morning sunlight. What he found on that walk daunted him as much as the sight he had seen the first day the Nephilim army assembled for battle so long ago: every thirty cubits or so lay a dead rat, in a courtyard, beside a well, on the cobblestone street. They were everywhere, often with a discharge of blood coming from their mouths, much like the rats on the floor in Sivit's bedroom.

That sight forced him to come to grips with what he already knew in his heart; some sort of illness was killing rats in the city. This new malady had been transmitted from the rats to Sivit and his wife, and it killed them as well. Yakheed, however, had no idea how it passed from the rats to the humans. It might have been communicated through anything–their droppings, their breath, their hair, their bites, literally anything. However it came, what if other rats had the disease? What if the entire population of rats had it? In no time, the whole city would be infected. They had to stop the illness now!

Yakheed remembered what the couple from Mehujael had said: some kind of mysterious illness had almost defeated that city in their war against the Nephilim. Dread gnawed Yakheed's thoughts; perhaps running through their streets was a more fearsome enemy than the Nephilim. The people of Prathar had to find a way to destroy the rats.

Once he came to this conclusion, he knew they must discover a way to kill rats easily and quickly. That led him to the craftsmen's district. His previous night's observations told him much about their new adversary, and he gathered together as many artificers as he could find, describing what he had learned from watching the rats.

"These creatures are lightning fast. They climb walls without ladders. They jump from roof to roof. They slide under doors, through narrow crevices, along walls, through the eves. Make us traps that move quicker than the blink of an eye. Make traps we can put into small places, on roofs, in corners, everywhere, and make them strong enough to hold the rats well."

An older artisan spoke up. "Do we want to trap them alive or kill them?"

Yakheed thought for a moment. "Anything you can do that works. We can drown any we catch alive. We only have one goal: get rid of them."

After leaving the craftsmen, he worked tirelessly throughout the rest of the day, moving from district to district, urging the committees to enforce rat obliteration. Few of them, however, appreciated the danger. Men and women who had already seen centuries of life had not yet experienced an illness that could end life. Some men in the city had never seen death, hardly believing it could happen. Even when Yakheed dragged them into a courtyard to discover still another rat corpse huddled in the shadows, his urging seemed unrealistic and therefore a waste of valuable time.

Several times Yakheed left a district and wondered if he was accomplishing anything. His time, however, was not entirely wasted, for a few took his warnings seriously enough to close down their shops for the day in order to search for rat nests, to seal doors and windows and to secure their food.

His last visit, not long before the sun set, turned out unexpectedly to be the most important. He was making his way along the outskirts of the city when a putrid aroma assailed his senses–the fetidness of the tanning district. *The last thing I want*, he thought to himself, *is to breathe that stench after a day like today.*

He turned up a street to escape it, eager to reach his home and rest. As he walked, a rat feeding on food in a courtyard caught his eye. In one fell motion, Yakheed grabbed a smooth stone from the roadside, aimed and threw. His shot missed his target, but at least it scared off the rodent. He walked over to the food, which turned out to be bread covered in mold. He shook his head. So rats can eat mold without getting sick. *Or. . .* He stood up straight. *Perhaps they can't.*

Perhaps they might not always know what is bad for them.

He stared at the bread on the ground, pondering what he saw. Surely it was possible to fool rats into eating something that would kill them, something poisonous. Who in the city might know something about poison? His mind raced to the obvious conclusion: the tanners. They worked with all sorts of unhealthy ingredients. He turned back and began walking rapidly toward the tanners' quarter. By the time he reached their street, most of the workers had ceased their work, and twilight bathed the district, but Yakheed didn't care. He banged on doors, called out in the street and even rang their warning bell. Before long a crowd had gathered around him, some looking irritated, but most looking either curious or worried.

"I am Yakheed, in charge of the city's defenses. Tell me, tanners," he asked with excitement in his voice, "you use all sorts of ingredients to dye your leather, don't you? Are any poisonous?"

For a few moments, no one answered. Then the crowd parted, allowing a city father to come forward. The man was clearly ancient. Centuries of sun, hard work and exposure had lined his face and hardened his deep brown skin. *I wonder*, thought Yakheed, *how old is he? Did this man know Father Cain?* Regardless of his age, the man was still obviously vibrant, and his massive arms made him appear stronger than most people Yakheed had met in his life.

With a sober face, the elder answered. "I am Phranko, son of Nod, and I can answer your question. We use oak for tanning and egg, saffron, indigo and berry for dying. We don't dye with poisons."

Yakheed's heart fell. Even though he was an expert in his own trade of weaving, leather working was entirely foreign to him. He searched through his brain to find the right question to ask.

"What about preparing the skin? Do you use any special ingredients for toughening it?"

A few faces in the crowd smiled, and a man at the back actually laughed out loud. Yakheed realized he had exposed his ignorance.

Phranko, however, did not laugh. "No, son. I'm afraid not."

Yakheed tried one more time. "Do you use anything special to lighten color? To make it more waterproof? To clean off the flesh?"

Phranko shook his head. "What are you seeking?"

"I need a poison to kill rats. I want to mix the poison with grain, so that the rats will eat it and die. The poison can't be obnoxious to the rats, otherwise they'll never eat it. I came here in hopes that your people might know of a substance poisonous enough to kill rats without making the bait repellant to them." Yakheed looked out over the crowd of perhaps twenty or thirty tanners. "Is anyone here familiar with such a substance?"

In the back, a woman looked up excitedly. After a moment, she began moving through the crowd to Phranko. Upon reaching him, she spoke quietly to the elder, and immediately his face lit up.

"Aidyl reminds me. We sometimes use a substance to remove hair. We barter for it from the ironmongers and tinsmiths."

The woman whispered to Phranko again. He nodded, saying to her, "Speak your mind, woman."

She turned to Yakheed. "My husband uses it instead of lime, and it works just as well." She smiled shyly. "But I think it could kill a rat. We use it in our garden to kill bugs, and it works well against them."

Yakheed spoke to the crowd before him. "Could you leather workers find enough of this substance to cleanse our city of rats?"

Few returned his gaze, telling him that no, they indeed would not do this for him.

Yakheed turned to Phranko. "Father, unless we stop these rats, we will not survive this war."

He looked out over the crowd, wrestling with what to say. On the one hand, telling them the truth about the illness could cause them to panic. They might try to leave the city, or attempt to convince the elders to surrender before the illness spread. On the other hand, if he chose not to warn them, they obviously wouldn't expend the effort needed to find the substance and distribute it throughout the city.

He decided to speak frankly. "The rats carry an illness," he said to the crowd. "Since yesterday night, I have found hundreds of rats lying dead in streets, courtyards, everywhere."

Phranko asked, "Isn't that a good thing?"

Yakheed nodded. "Normally, yes, but our real problem is this: yesterday morning an illness killed two people, an illness we have never before seen. I am convinced they caught the illness from rats."

A murmur ran through the people. "Think of how many rats infest our community. If these creatures are carrying a disease that can kill us, all of us are at risk. We simply have to destroy every rat we can before they start infecting all of us. That, obviously, is pretty much impossible. No matter how many traps we set, we'll never get them all. If your poison kills rats, you may have the only key capable of saving us."

No one spoke, but Yakheed saw how deeply his words had impacted them. Then he remembered. The couple who had survived the siege of Mehujael lived in this district before they fled the city. If no one else in Prathar knew about what a plague can do, surely the people in this section had heard about the terrible sickness that almost destroyed Mehujael. Glancing at Phranko, Yakheed knew at once he had found a comrade.

Phranko cleared his throat. "What do you ask us to do?"

Yakheed said with an urgency in his voice. "You must find this substance, as much of it as possible. Capture as many rats as you can, mix the substance with grain and feed it to them. If this kills the rats, send word to me immediately. This may be our last hope of survival."

Phranko thought for a moment. "We used to scrape it from the chimneys of the iron forges and smithies. I think among all of us here, we'll be able to round up plenty enough to kill rats. We'll set this experiment before we go to sleep tonight. Elder Yakheed," he said respectfully, "could you ask the smiths to help us produce more of the substance? They know far more about it than we."

"Normally, they'd complain," he said. "But not this time."

Phranko looked quizzical. "Why is that?"

"The first victims were smiths," he answered grimly. "The whole district is probably in a panic at this point. I'll talk to them tomorrow." He turned to leave, but then stopped for a moment. "Woman," he said to Aidyl, "what is the name of this ingredient I am seeking?"

She smiled. "Arsenic. It is called arsenic."

The next morning, Yakheed returned to the smithy's quarter. At first, the bustle on the street surprised him, since food was severely rationed, and any wares were reserved for the soldiers on the wall. Business on this street, however, seemed brisker than ever.

When Yakheed looked around at those who were purchasing, however, he immediately understood. He saw soldiers, craftsmen from other districts, leather workers and seamstresses. All of them sought the brass and iron tools and weapons necessary to arm and clothe the soldiers on the walls. The smiths were the tool makers of warfare, and they worked harder than soldiers to keep the city free.

Yakheed had assumed his quest for arsenic would be futile, since the tanners rarely called for it these days. Truk, the eldest of the smiths, however, immediately perked up when Yakheed explained his

mission. After leading him down several narrow streets, past bicker-
ing tradesmen and peddlers hawking their wares, they entered a dim
room, filled with shelves of covered pots.

"Arsenic lasts forever," he commented, "and it seems a shame to
waste it, so we store it here."

Yakheed mentally counted the pots in amazement, his smile growing broader and broader. "My friend, you have been storing arsenic
for just such a time as this. Now, catch yourself some rats and feed
them grain mixed with your arsenic. Let's see if the rats are hungry
enough to eat it, and let's see if arsenic is poisonous enough to kill
them. If it works, send messengers to the tanners and then to every
quarter in the city. Tell them to put it everywhere rats might stop to
eat. Make sure they don't waste it, but make sure as well they realize
their very existence depends on what rats eat for dinner over the next
four weeks."

After leaving Truk, Yakheed decided to return to his home, since
he was unusually tired and his muscles ached. As he plodded up the
street, he noticed fewer merchants here and wondered why. Up ahead,
the sign "Sivit" sent chills through his heart. The door was boarded
shut. No one was conducting business near that place. In fact, the
street remained empty here for perhaps fifteen or twenty houses before
he began to see men and women peddling their wares on the street.
The emptiness gave him a strange sense, almost a premonition of a
future he could not quite yet imagine.

He finally reached his small house by the east gate. The past few
days had exhausted his physical stamina and even though it was still
day, he collapsed onto his bed of straw arranged on the floor. He
desperately wanted to sleep, but found it difficult to do so, possibly
because of his excitement about the arsenic, possibly because it was
still day, but possibly as well because the horrors of his encounter with
Sivit kept replaying in his mind's eye.

As he drifted into sleep, rats dominated his uneasy dreams: rats
running, rats jumping, climbing, crawling, swimming, and, especially,
lying bloated in courtyards and streets. As the day and then night went
on, Yakheed found the border between dreaming and waking beginning to blur–sometimes he was surely awake, yet saw impossible
visions of thousands of rats climbing up walls and into windows and

doorways. The rats grew unimaginably immense, and he found himself helplessly fighting them with sticks and pebbles.

The night air, normally comfortable, became chillingly cold, and Yakheed desperately wanted to cover himself with warm blankets. He discovered, however, that rats had consumed his covers, along with all of his bedding and fabrics. Half awake, he began to see a thousand rats chewing through his walls until his house was entirely open. Now he could see into the streets, where millions upon millions of ravenous rats flooded through the city, devouring everything in their pathways. The flood swelled, and rats piled one layer atop the next until they filled the house to the ceiling and filled the city above the highest tower. In his own bedroom, squirming rats piled into the room until they entirely covered Yakheed. Their bodies were frigid cold, and he began shivering uncontrollably. Worse yet, their weight was unbearable, making breathing almost impossible.

Hour after hour Yakheed thrashed about in agony, sometimes bitterly cold, sometimes burning with heat. Occasionally voices filtered into his mind, but he couldn't comprehend who they were or what they were saying. Finally he drifted into a long, dreamless sleep.

At some point, he awoke. A voice, a woman's voice, was chanting a mournful song. He listened for a while and then rasped, "Who's here?" The harshness of his voice shocked him.

The singing stopped. He heard someone walking across the room to his bed. "My name is Achire," she said quietly. "You've been very sick these past four days."

"Four days?" he asked incredulously, turning his head toward her. Beside him stood a woman wearing a simple yellow shawl.

She nodded. "Bur'el found you lying all alone, burning with fever. He brought us here to watch you."

He felt confused. "Us?"

A shadow covered her features. "My two sisters and myself."

Yakheed smiled feebly at the woman. "And you have been here for days caring for me? Thank you for your mercy, and please thank your sisters for me."

She looked down, her voice catching. "I wish I could, but the illness took them as well."

His heart stopped. "You mean, I'm not the only one?"

The woman walked to the open window and looked out onto the street. She leaned against the wall, standing silent for a long time. The sunlight was softer, and the long shadows told Yakheed the sun would soon be setting. This was normally the time for the children of his weavers and carders to race through the streets, calling to one another, laughing and shouting, but the street this evening was entirely silent. Yakheed was desperate to know what was happening, but waited until Achire was ready to answer him.

Finally she spoke. "Elder, since you were taken, the illness has spread like the rats have spread, into every house in the city."

"And those who have been infected by it? Have they suffered as badly as I have?"

She looked at him from her station at the window, a curious expression on her face, obviously deep in thought. After a few minutes, she returned to his bed on the floor and knelt down beside him. Touching his forehead, she gauged his temperature.

Her face showed bewilderment mixed with something harsh, like bitterness. "Your fever's gone, and you're actually talking to me. So, Elder, I can definitely answer that everyone else has been affected much more severely than you."

The implications of her reply slowly sank into his brain. How could the illness be more severe? He had been delirious for four full days and was so weak he could hardly sit up straight. The only way it could be worse would be if others suffered the same fate little Loree's parents had experienced.

At this realization, Yakheed understood why Achire was crying. "What about your sisters?"

"Dead." The woman numbly sat down on the floor beside the bed. "My oldest sister, Eelanna, began to feel weak, and her muscles burned. I hurried her home, but when we came into the bedroom, my other sister was already there, feverish and in delirium. I tried to do whatever I could, but none of it did any good. By the end of the night, they both were dead."

"How horrible!"

Tears ran down her cheeks. "I couldn't move their bodies from the bed, because I had no place to put them. My neighbors couldn't help me; by then the illness had hit their houses as well."

Yakheed felt incapable of comforting or encouraging her. In reality, he could not imagine any comfort that could be offered. Her sisters were dead, and it looked as if the entire city was about to die as well.

Yakheed struggled to sit up and finally propped himself against the wall behind his bed of straw. He felt weak, and his muscles ached as if every inch of his being was bruised. He looked over to Achire who sat quietly beside him. "Is the disease this deadly with everyone?"

She nodded, eying him curiously. "Everyone, but you."

He closed his eyes, trying to grasp the magnitude of what she was saying. An illness was ravaging their city, an illness they could not comprehend. It was a consuming foeman, whose appetite would not be satisfied with anything short of complete annihilation.

With the Nephilim, at least the defenders could fight harder or call for reinforcements, or even attempt to negotiate a truce, but against this faceless, bodyless adversary they simply had no defenses, no battle plan. If the illness kept spreading like this, the entire city would soon be wiped out. They were altogether hopeless. Yakheed looked into Achire's eyes and sighed. "What of Bur'el?"

"Dead," she answered woodenly. "He took ill soon after finding you here. They carried him out three days ago."

With those words, Yakheed felt his last threads of hope completely crushed. Bur'el had been his closest associate and friend. The two of them had built their trade from nothing. They had worked long days and nights, planning, arguing at times, dreaming at times, but always working together. Yakheed had trusted no man until he met Bur'el, and now he was dead, leaving Yakheed without friend or counselor. Death rarely visited his world, but when it did, it came savagely.

He looked over to Achire, who was now crying openly. How appalling to think that this poor woman could not go home, knowing the corpses of her two sisters still lay rotting in her house. He surveyed the room, spying Bur'el's hauberk laying in a corner, and his ax standing up against the far wall. These were bitter reminders that Yakheed was now abandoned, able to depend on no one.

"What can we do?" the woman asked quietly. "We're all going to die. Either we catch the illness or the Nephilim simply kill us."

Yakheed nodded. "There was never much chance, anyway, woman. The Nephilim would have killed us sooner or later. Either we would starve to death or die of disease. What's the difference?"

She looked up, with an angry expression on her face which took Yakheed by surprise. Getting up, she began picking up the clothing which was strewn over the floor. For a long time, she said nothing, but her motions betrayed her fury at his statement.

"Is that all?" she finally asked. "'Not much chance?' Is that all this city is worth to you?"

"All I meant was—"

"All you meant was that you are giving up. Isn't that it?" she asked. "You don't want to fight any more, so just let everyone die."

She stuffed the clothing into a bag, which she then cast into a corner beside the bed. "What's the difference?"

He couldn't believe his ears. Yakheed had done more than anyone else to save the city of Prathar. Without him, they'd have been dead months ago. "Woman, I'm not giving up. But there's nothing left to do. We've lost."

"No!" she shouted. "It can't be that simple. You can't let this city go just like that."

Sobbing, she crossed the room to her shawl and put it on. Yakheed numbly watched her as she went to the doorway.

"Woman," he said weakly.

She stopped.

"What can I do?"

Her back to him, she answered, "Please, Yakheed. Try at least! You are our last hope."

"Then stay and help me think." He motioned to the spot beside the bed. She returned and knelt there, waiting.

For a long time, neither spoke, as Yakheed struggled to clear his mind enough to think intelligently. Finally, he began asking her questions. Were there soldiers on the walls or were they all dead? Were the city fathers organizing ways to dispose of corpses? Or were the city fathers all dead? In every household, how many died and how many never became sick? Her startling answer to this was "Half die and half have not yet become sick." Did she think the Nephilim knew of the city's calamity? Would they invade the city to take advantage of the defenders' weakness?

"No," she answered to the last question. "The Nephilim wouldn't dare attack. They don't want to get sick."

At this answer, Yakheed looked as if someone had slapped him on the face. He leaned forward and grabbed her arm. "Of course! This is the most terrifying experience I've ever had. They'd be scared to death if the illness came to them."

She looked down at his hand with surprise on her face and then nodded. "They may be able to fight us, but they would never be able to fight an enemy they can't see."

He nodded, excitedly. "Exactly! So we need to make this disease become our ally in war."

He went silent, wrestling with ideas of how they could use the illness to undermine the Nephilim. After a long time, Yakheed looked up, smiling broadly. "Achire, I need your help."

"What can I do?" she asked.

He looked out the window to an empty street. "Do you know if the tanners' poison actually worked against the rats?"

The woman nodded, got up and went into the other room. Moments later she returned carrying a small sack. "I received this bag of powder after sunrise today." She knelt down beside him, handing him the bag. "They have been circulating pouches to every household in the city. They told me to mix it in grain and put the grain where rats might go."

He opened the sack. Inside he found a finely ground powder. "Amazing!" he said excitedly. He looked back up. "I would never ask any more of you, after all you've suffered, but we have no choice. I have three different messages for you to deliver: to the craftsmen first, then one to the soldiers and one to the elders of the city. Would you do this for me?" He smiled gently at her. "Would you do this for our city?"

A pained expression came over her face, but nevertheless, she nodded. Yakheed gave her the messages, which she repeated back to him word for word. After she left, he crawled to the water bucket across the room, out of which he drank desperately. Satisfying his thirst, he then leaned against the wall in exhaustion and fell into a deep sleep.

It was dark, four days later, and Yakheed stood on the outer wall. All night long, he had been supervising soldiers as they carried out a gruesome task: hauling up corpses from the area between the inner and outer walls and then casting those corpses over the outer wall on to the ground below. The stench at times so overwhelmed the soldiers that many fainted or wretched over the wall. The need was so urgent, however, that the work continued regardless of the miserableness of the task.

Hundreds of soldiers and citizens labored either up on the wall or down below between the inner and outer defenses. Yakheed tried to see out into the dark where the Nephilim camp lay, but could make out nothing. So far, the Nephilim had not reacted, and Yakheed assumed this simply meant their guards were sleeping. Of course, it mattered little if the enemy discovered the city's activity. The corpses would continue to fall outside the city walls regardless.

Four days before, the elders sent word throughout the city that all victims of the rat illness would be carried away. Wagons would be sent to every quarter to cart these bodies to be piled between the walls. The procedure was difficult to carry out, because illness still raged in every quarter, with little relief. Many who survived the first wave of sickness succumbed to the second or third waves. The city elders, many of whom had already died, could find few workers either healthy enough to man the wagons or courageous enough to haul the bodies, knowing they might be next to fall prey.

The elders had also set in motion a second undertaking: trapping as many rats as they possibly could. Craftsmen worked feverishly on fabricating mechanisms for capturing the rodents. Within two days, hundreds of these simple live traps were being used throughout the city. When a rodent was caught, it was dumped into a crate (about two cubits by two cubits) with dozens of other rats. Those boxes were then brought to the walls.

By the end of four days, they had collected almost fifty such crates of rats. Of course, many of the creatures in the containers had died, either from the illness or suffocation, but many were still attempting to gnaw their way through their thick wooden prisons.

Now the city had almost completed its project. During the past hour, citizens had carefully lowered the crates by rope down to the ground outside the outer wall. Now Yakheed watched as men let down by rope a dozen soldiers. Below, he could barely make out the soldiers dragging the crates out in front of the thousands of bodies piled on the ground before the gates, while others unraveled and prepared bundles of hay behind the boxes.

Once all of the crates were between the bodies and the camp of the Nephilim, the soldiers removed the containers' outer panels, revealing a thin wood covering, something that would take the rodents a short while to penetrate. The soldiers raced back to the wall. As light began growing on the horizon, citizens hauled the men back up, and the defenders took their appropriate positions to do battle, in case it came to that.

Yakheed called for the archers and commanded them to light their arrows, wrapped in oil soaked rags. The flaming arrows flew into hay that had been soaked in oil, which now burst into flames. The only purpose of the flames was to drive the rats away from the gates and into the ranks of the Nephilim.

"Stand ready, men!" Yakheed cried, as he heard sounds of Nephilim soldiers in the camp shouting for ladders and bowmen. He added grimly, "They'll be attacking within a few minutes."

That attack, however, never came. At first, Nephilim soldiers raced toward the gate expecting to do battle, but the early morning light showed them a grisly new defense–a wall built of thousands of rotting corpses. The sight bewildered them. They could not understand the purpose of either the bodies or the flames in front of the bodies. Neither did they comprehend why the defenders on the wall shot no arrows. Nor did any Nephilim soldier guess why hordes of ravenous rats suddenly invaded their camp. Most importantly, no one ever connected the rats with the events that soon followed.

For within a few days, Nephilim soldiers began dying, a couple dozen at first and then hundreds and then several thousands. After three weeks, huge cremation fires began lighting the night sky, a desperate attempt to stop the illness from spreading. Then Nephilim went right to the gates of the city, unopposed and cremated the rotting bodies from Prathar which lay before the gates.

Still the disease ravaged their ranks. They tried burning tents, clothing, even food, but nothing seemed to stop the horror of the plague. The disease didn't stop, because the Nephilim never connected it to the thousands of black rats which ran freely through their ranks.

Because they did nothing to impede the rats, the illness continued to run unabated.

In the city, on the other hand, the poisoned food, rat traps, possibly even the rat's own sickness, and the people's vigilance in sealing off possible food sources caused the rats in the city to die off. Any rat corpses were thrown over the wall, in hopes of increasing the Nephilim's misery. People continued to trap live rats as well, stuffing them into bags and then throwing them over the city walls. As the weeks progressed, fewer and fewer citizens fell ill, and people began to wonder if perhaps they might survive this war after all. The price of survival, however, was beyond comprehension.

During those last days of the siege, Yakheed decided to revisit the smithy's quarter, to see where it all began. His journey was a silent one, except for wind sweeping through forsaken streets and shops. He passed buildings boarded up, houses abandoned, courtyards overgrown with weeds and thorns. The sadness that seemed to linger in every corner of the narrow roadway came not from the quietness, but from the memories of noise: children laughing, mothers calling, tradesmen bargaining. All now silent, except for those who could recall their sounds.

Yakheed remembered many other sounds as he walked along the way. The sounds of wooden wheels stumbling over cobblestones and criers summoning the living to bring out their dead. Sounds of weeping: a mother as she laid her lifeless babe on top of other lifeless babies, only to be covered by still others; a husband bidding his wife farewell as the wagon carried her away; a wife begging her dead husband not to leave her all alone, and the worst sound: two little children, forsaken, standing on the street, crying, but having no one to whisper to them any comfort or hope. All of these sounds etched themselves deeply into Yakheed's consciousness, and he doubted if they would ever be erased.

He came to the house of Sivit, abandoned now for months. The chill of the wind whipped past the corner and bit into his sinews, making him pull his cloak tight around him. As he looked at the boarded doorway, the memory of that first horror rushed back. He found he could not bear his recollection of what happened here and quickly passed along.

A short way beyond this, he came to the house that Sivit's daughter, Loree, had entered that day. To his disappointment, planks of wood barred entrance to this house as well. He shook his head, wondering. Did the woman here have a family or had she been all alone the day she took in Loree? How many died in this home? *How many?* he wondered. His eye caught a cloth object dancing about in the breeze. It was a small doll. Apparently someone had fastened it on the door, perhaps in hope that at least one man or woman might remember the doll's doting owner. He thought for a moment. *Didn't the little girl have a doll that day she interrupted their meeting?* Yakheed reached out and pulled the doll off the door.

How could such a horrible world exist? he thought as he gazed at the doll. How could so much suffering be possible? What did little Loree do to deserve such a fate, or the two children on the street, or the mother carrying her babe, or the husband or the wife? What justice could there be, what righteousness, what goodness? What possible purpose could all of this suffering accomplish?

Some fools prayed to an invisible god, begging him to save them, trusting him to carry out his mysterious purpose in the midst of all of their suffering. If such a god existed and had some purpose in what they had experienced here in this city, then that god must be twisted indeed. Yet so much beauty existed in the world. Could an evil god create so much good in the midst of such evil? That was simply impossible. Either this invisible god was good and did only good, or this invisible god was evil and did only evil. Or most likely, there was no god at all, and both beauty and suffering simply were parts of an empty reality. They simply happened in a world set loose from purpose or meaning.

He looked across the empty square, where the two children had stood that horrible morning. He was like them, standing forsaken on the street corner, surrounded by incomprehensible suffering. No one could whisper any comfort or hope to him, for there was none. He turned from the house, back toward his own quarter, clutching the doll in his hand.

In a month, the Nephilim departed from the city of Prathar. Yakheed watched the last wagon train make its way down the road toward the forest and beyond that, to the river. They left behind their tents, armament, clothing and food. Once the wagon train disappeared over the horizon, Yakheed sent his soldiers to their enormous abandoned camp. The first day, they set out piles of poisoned food, hoping to destroy at least most of the rats. After several weeks, they made enormous piles of clothing, tents, food and abandoned bodies, which they destroyed with fire. They saved only the weapons and tools.

And slowly, the city began to rebuild its world and work.

A year later, Yakheed found himself sitting across from Sister, in a cave almost a twenty day's journey from the city. She was stirring a stew of vegetables cooking in goat's milk, hanging in an iron pot over a fire. She looked up at Yakheed, smiling. "You know, boy, the word I've heard is that nothing can conquer you."

He laughed. "I promise you, Sister, the illness just about killed me."

She nodded. "But you still won, Yakheed! You learned your lesson well from your Sister. We take care of ourselves, by ourselves, don't we, boy?"

Yakheed said nothing, but nodded.

"And I hear that they've made you the chief elder of the city." She beamed at him. "And, they are calling the city 'Yakheed' now. Imagine, my Yakheed, the founder of the greatest city beyond the river!"

"Well, Sister, are you ready to come back to the city? We've started weaving again."

She smiled at this orphan child she rescued so long ago. "I think I'm ready to enter the city of Yakheed in style, with its chief elder carrying my bags for me."

Yakheed rose and smiled at his Sister. "Then let's pack those bags and get on our way. We have work to do."

Chapter Six

Year 1080

ere I come!" Noah looked up to see Han, his sixteen-year old field-hand, swinging toward him on the rope. He dropped down under the water and felt his feet skimming the surface just above his head before splashing into the lake. The waves rolled over him. From underneath the water he heard Nat's shout reverberating. This meant war.

He swung around, planted his feet on the floor of the shallow water, hardly more than three cubits deep and propelled himself on top of his friend, who, unfortunately was ready to wrestle him down, grasp him by the hair and begin dunking him beneath the surface. It took more than a minute for Noah to wrestle free, kick off and swim vigorously away from his assailant.

At Noah's escape, Nat's younger brother Tyal, who had been lounging along the water's grassy bank, splashed into the water to join in the onslaught. Behind him, Noah heard their older brother Sredael shouting warnings of doom as he sloshed through the shallows.

Noah quickly looked around him. Three hooligans descended upon him, and he didn't stand a chance. He wasn't entirely a victim, of course. It had been his idea to go swimming after they finished weeding the crops, and whenever they swam, they always ended up in battle, sometimes two against two, sometimes three against one, sometimes all against all. This evening, Noah was the victim, the three brothers his persecutors. The next time, perhaps the roles would reverse. Regardless, fate rapidly approached him, and he needed to respond. For a moment, Noah debated whether to flee or fight. Then he looked up to the sky and roared in exultation. Laughing, he turned, ready to take all comers.

An hour later, Noah and the boys sat on the bank, watching swans glide on the pond. The hush of evening had descended, and the gentle chiffon of twilight laid itself lightly upon the tree tops, softening everything that rested beneath its covers. He gazed at the pond, so placid that only the ripples of the swans interrupted its stillness. The noises of the world were subdued. The birdsongs soothed his mind and calmed his thoughts. Only here in nature could Noah ever find peace. He leaned back into the soft grass, began pulling apart a blade of grass and sighed.

"This is where I belong," he said quietly. A swan suddenly spread its wings and lifted off the pond, silently floating over the water. He watched it soar above the trees and disappear.

Nat looked at him curiously. "What do you mean, this is where you belong?"

Noah didn't answer immediately. The question forced him to probe his thoughts. He didn't hate farming; he actually enjoyed it. He loved working the dairy and had plenty of fun cultivating fields, especially when he labored beside the boys, a group of about six or seven youth, ages fourteen to nineteen. Since Noah was only twenty-four, they were close enough to his age to be lots of fun, even though Yenah regularly had to remind Noah about doing his job as a supervisor rather than as a friend of the field workers. Regardless, Noah thought to himself, farming was about the most enjoyable life he could imagine.

Nat interrupted his thoughts. "What do you mean, 'this is where I belong'?"

"This world," Noah answered. "With the bird songs, the sky, nature."

Sredael laughed. "You mean you don't like working."

Noah threw the grass at him. "No, I enjoy working, but I'd still rather be here."

"You, work?" Sredael asked, in a mock serious voice. "We run circles around you in everything you do."

Noah nodded his head. "That's what I mean. When you work, you're always in a hurry to get it done. I would much rather enjoy what I'm doing. Why push myself?" He looked past the pond to the fields. In the twilight, unending rows of grain shone a rich golden glow, and far beyond he could discern smoke from the farmhouse meandering up into rosy-cheeked clouds.

Tyal laughed, "I push myself to get it done, so I can do something I really want to do."

Noah looked over to his friend. "So, you make twelve hours of work miserable so you can make two hours of non-work enjoyable. Why not make your work pleasant?"

"Noah," Sredael said, "work is a curse. We do it because we have to, not because we want to."

"A curse?" Noah thought for a moment. "Not necessarily. The thorns are a curse. Weeds are a curse. The fact we have to work so hard to get our food is a curse, but we were created to work the garden. As the Promise Story says, 'The Yahweh God placed the man in the Garden of Eden to tend and care for it.'"

"Promise story?" Nat asked, laughing. "Another one of your creations?"

His question puzzled Noah. "I'm talking about the story of the Promise. You know, 'In the beginning, God created the heavens and earth. . .'"

"Beginning of what?" Tyal asked.

"The beginning," Noah answered slowly, "of everything. Sun, star, moon, earth, life animals. Before the beginning, only God existed."

Tyal sat up and looked at Noah. "Before the beginning, what existed?"

"Yahweh," he said, completely amazed. "You know, the Creator, the Lord, the Master of all things."

"Never heard of it."

"He's not an 'it', Tyal. He's someone." Noah looked at the three in astonishment. "Do you mean to say, none of you have heard about Yahweh before?"

Sredael laughed. "Noah, I don't know what you're talking about."

Tyal added, "At least it's more interesting than all that stuff about building bridges. Now, where did you hear of this Yahweh thing?"

Noah became solemn. "From Adam. I mean, not that I myself heard it from Adam, but my father did."

"And who is this Adam fellow? One of your imaginary friends?" teased Tyal.

His question stunned Noah. "You haven't heard of Adam? I mean, didn't your grandfathers tell you about Adam? He was the first man, and Eve was the first woman. Yahweh created them in the Garden of Eden out of the dust of the earth."

Nat laughed uncontrollably. "The first man created out of dust? That's rich!"

"No!" Noah said firmly. "It's the truth. Adam was a real man, and he told my father this story. My father knew him and used to bring sacrifices with him to the gates of Eden. But then," he added, "if you haven't heard of Adam, then you haven't heard of Eden either, have you?"

All three shook their heads, smiling at each other.

"So when," Sredael asked, "was this fellow Adam supposedly created?"

Noah thought for a moment, adding together the genealogies of his fathers. "A little over a thousand years ago."

"That's ridiculous," said Tyal. "Do you really believe that all of these cities and villages could have grown in just a thousand years?"

The question took Noah aback. "Of course. Just figure it out. My great-great-grandfather Jared is six hundred years old and has already fathered over four hundred children. If his offspring all have even just twenty children each, that's thousands of descendants, and if those children have offspring, it's tens of thousands. It doesn't take long to build cities and towns with that many people."

The three sat silent for a long time. Finally Sredael broke the silence. "Well, I've never heard anything about any Adam or Yahweh or creation before. I suppose it's possible."

Noah bowed his head. "Thank you."

"But," Sredael said, "You won't be able to convince me that work isn't a curse."

Tyal agreed. "It's a curse for me, anyway."

Noah lay back into the grass, staring into the sky. He wondered how these boys could look at a world without a creator. Why didn't their fathers tell them about Adam? Why didn't they explain the Promise to them?

"So. . ." he asked cautiously, "do you think all of the trees and stars and everything else just happened?"

Sredael laughed. "It's just always been here."

"But what's the purpose for it all?" Noah asked.

No one answered for several moments. Tyal picked up a stone and threw it into the pond. They watched as the ripples rolled out from where the stone landed finally reaching the shoreline.

Sredael finally broke the silence. "Noah, nothing has a purpose. It just is. We farm the earth, we craft our wood, we mine for iron and metal, we fashion scythes and plows and swords. Men and women marry and have children and their children have children. Who cares about purpose?"

Noah said nothing. How could they care about purpose, if they didn't know the story?

The next morning Noah and his co-workers were weeding the first field of grain. They had started early, at the first light. The cold season was finally coming to an end, so that the sun was rising earlier and setting later, much to Noah's relief. He liked waking up early, but only when the sun was already shining. The warm season gave them more time to work and, occasionally, more time to relax. Of course, the fields were also more productive during the warm season, and that did require a fair amount more labor, but he didn't mind.

Noah glanced down the row he was weeding. The grass, khitaw, had grown well this season, almost three cubits tall. The stalks were sturdy, and the heads overflowed with kernels. This would make Yenah happy, his milk cows and goats happy and therefore everyone else happy.

The boys were working hard and, as usual, were already ahead of Noah in weeding. They always beat him and usually did a better job of it as well. That, however, didn't bother Noah, since his real job normally was the creamery, not the fields. He worked the fields only at harvest and planting, or when Yenah sent him to supervise the boys, which had been often in the past few months.

Noah's real love, however, was working with Yenah's milk animals. He loved every part of it; cleaning the stalls, feeding and watering the goats and cows, midwiving calf and kid births and manufacturing different cheeses. Over the past three years, Noah had mastered the art of creating and preserving many different versions of cheese. He continually experimented, as was his nature, with new combinations and curing methods.

At first, Noah wanted only to establish the best and most efficient way to produce cheese, but before long, he began uncovering new flavors and textures of cheeses, and he also learned how to churn out far more cheese than any other farm in the area. After about a year of production, Yenah found himself with more cheese than he and his household could ever use and therefore began using it as barter for other goods. Because his cheeses were tastier and longer lasting than anyone else's, they commanded a high exchange, and people regularly began visiting his farm to procure cheese.

The demand led Yenah to change his focus to milk and cheese production. At first, to keep up with the workload, Noah labored from the sun's rising to its setting, but even that wasn't enough to stay on top of everything. That caused him to push beyond his limits, rushing himself often throughout most of the day, straining to keep up with the workload. To help out, Yenah hired two boys, twelve and fourteen, who did most of the milking, cleaning, watering and feeding. Noah still labored from morning to night in order to supervise the boys and process cheese, but at least now the work didn't stretch him.

Noah looked up and saw the brothers Nat and Tyal—one on the left, the other on the right— racing down his row to reach Noah first. "You're leaving a bunch of weeds behind you!" Noah shouted.

Nat scowled and forced his younger brother around to go back over what they had quickly covered. They turned in a few moments and began making their way to Noah.

Reaching him, Tyal smiled. "It's time for a break."

Noah made his way to a small shack on the outskirts of the field, where a horn hung on a nail. He blew the horn twice, signaling break time. Soon four other boys joined them.

The group sat beside the shack, under a giant tree, whose branches brooded over them, filtering out the sun's rays, giving them a comfortable lodge in which to rest. From the shack, Noah brought skins of water and cakes wrapped in oily leaves. They all eagerly unwrapped their food and began to eat. For a while no one spoke. Finally Noah looked up at them. "You know, in two weeks we harvest the first field."

Nat smiled. "Does that mean we get to work with your harvest invention?"

A serious look came over Noah's face. "I haven't decided yet. That machine is pretty dangerous, but I think you can help. You'll just need to be really careful."

Tyal spoke up. "Yenah told my father about the second planting. He said we'd need to start plowing the ground even before we finished the first harvest."

Noah nodded. "We're a little worried about that second planting. I wish we could just go ahead and plant it now, but we just don't have time with all we're doing here."

Tyal asked, "What difference does it make if you plant in three weeks or five?"

"Actually," Noah answered, smiling, "it makes a whole lot of difference. Plants need water and plants need sunlight. Take away either of them and the plant will die. Some plants, like khitaw, don't get their water from the rain."

Sredael said. "Grandfather told me that khitaw gets its water from the river beneath the ground."

"Right," Noah said. "There's a river underneath all three of our fields."

Nat looked confused. "A river? That's impossible!"

Noah picked up a rock and used it to draw a picture in the dirt. "This line here is the grass where we are. This line here is about twenty cubits below the surface, and it's an actual cave filled with sand and water. But, I believe that below those rivers is an ocean of water. I think that's where the rivers of water come from."

"So where do we get our water?" asked Sredael.

"Sometimes," Noah answered, "we dig wells down to the river beneath the ground, but not always. Sometimes our well water seeps through the ground. When you dig a hole next to the pond, it's always muddy, because the ground is soaked with water from the pond."

"All of the ground is filled with water," Nat said. "Every time we dig a hole anywhere, if it's deep enough, water comes up."

Tyal looked thoughtful for a moment. "So how did you hear about this river?"

Noah answered, "You mean, these rivers. They're everywhere. My grandfather told me about them and showed me how to find them."

Nat stood up and pushed aside the tree branches. "So," he said curiously, "there's a river underneath that field?"

"Right. Yenah knew the river was there when he claimed this land two hundred years ago, because khitaw was already growing in the field. Usually, that's how you find the river, when plants like khitaw or khorgul or khamis are there."

Nat looked back at Noah. "So what does that have to do with when we plant the field?"

"Since khitaw gets its water from the river rather than the rain, it needs to grow roots as long as thirty cubits. Once those roots reach the river, beneath the ground, the kernels start forming on the heads of the stalks. If we plant the khitaw too late, the sun will dry up the plant before its roots reach the river and the plant will die."

"So the point is," Sredael said, "we've got to get that second planting done as soon as possible."

Noah nodded. "Once we get the main part of the first harvest in, some of us will go over to the second field and start planting."

When Noah and his crew returned to the field, Yenah was waiting for him, and Noah knew why. Yenah wanted to give him more information about caring for the farm. About two months before, Yenah had made an important decision–as soon as he could he would journey to his ancestral home.

Sixty years had passed since Yenah last visited his ancestor Jabal. Jabal, originator of the clan, had been born six centuries before, and was the founder of the city named after him. Unless something had happened to him, he was probably still ruling the city. Yenah revered his great-grandfather and spoke often of him to Noah. Until Noah came, however, he had not felt safe in leaving his farm for the month-long journey. Now that Noah had worked with him for these three years, Yenah saw his opportunity to leave the farm in capable hands.

When two months ago Yenah announced his intentions to be gone for three or four months, Noah vigorously protested. "I'm not a farm manager, Yenah!"

The farmer smiled at him. "But you, Noah, know just about everything about this farm and the way I do things! You personally have improved our work in a dozen different ways. I can trust you."

"I'm a worker and a thinker," Noah said quietly, "you are a leader. I've had enough leading in my life and don't want any more."

Yenah, however, would not change his mind and now, with three days to go, he was training his unwilling apprentice in everything a farmer might need to understand. The young man was learning about nurturing crops, harvesting grain, storing produce and preparing for the next planting. Noah had no trouble grasping the routines, as well as the principles behind the routines, but each time Yenah deposited another task onto him, Noah's sense of panic grew. He had never wanted to be accountable for anything–ever since he was a small boy, whenever anyone pressured him, he had always slowed down, with- drawn or simply stopped trying.   Yenah, for all of his admirable qualities, could not understand Noah's terror of obligation.

Yenah called again. "Noah, please come here."

The young man came to Yenah, who took his hand and dropped several grains onto his palm. "Do you see this kernel?" He held up a grain, grasped between his thumb and finger. "When I roll it, the shell stays on. Look at the color—it's barely green, and I can feel just a little moisture on the tip of my fingers. That means you've got two weeks until harvest."

"Right," the young man said. "I've already hired five additional boys to help us."

Nodding, the owner took a grain from Noah's open palm and held it out for him. "Take it and roll it. I want to make sure you can read the grain."

"But. . ." Noah answered warily, "I would only need to read the grain if you weren't going to be here for the second harvest." He looked intently into Yenah's eyes.   "Five times already you have promised you'll be back here long before the second crop will be ready."

He smiled at Noah.   "Five times, because you've forced me to promise you five times."

"None of this information, Yenah," Noah said, ignoring the com- ment, "applies to me, because you're coming back as soon as you can. For that matter, most of the jobs you've been explaining to me today are irrelevant."

Irrelevant, at least, Noah thought to himself, *if you keep your promise.* No more than three months. He looked intently into Yenah's eyes.

Yenah did not look Noah in the eye. "Don't worry Noah, I'll be back in plenty of time. But. . ."

"But what?"

Yenah shrugged his shoulders. "But just in case. . ."

"Just in case. . . what?"

Clearing his throat, Yenah said, "Just in case something happens, you know."

"No," Noah said. "I don't know. Nothing must happen, Yenah. Please, don't put this onto me. I can't handle it."

The owner shook his head. "Noah, it's one thing to forget to fix a fence or miss weeding a plot of corn. That's just absentmindedness. Everyone has his little quirks."

"It's not a quirk, Yenah. It's who I am. I hate the pressure."

The owner put his hands on Noah's shoulders. "Son, a hundred different people depend on us for cheese. You'll be supervising a dozen boys who depend on you for their livelihood. I am depending on you to keep my possessions safe and my crops in order, not to mention our milk cows, sheep and goats. With all of us at your mercy, you simply can't fail."

Noah felt his chest constricting. He wanted to refuse, to walk away now, but Yenah had trapped him. *It's so unfair*, he thought to himself. *Why can't I live my life without pressure like this?* He gazed down the rows of grain.

In two weeks, a large crew would be working from the first ray of sunlight to the last drop of twilight cutting this grain. Even before they finished that job, Noah was to supervise plowing and planting the second field. Then he would need to process the grain from the first harvest, most of it for their cattle. Some of it they ground and compressed into pellets. Noah had discovered his cows produced more milk when they ate feed pellets in addition to their normal hay. After a long period of trial and error, he created a machine that stripped the grain, ground it and then pressed it into pellets. While all of this was going on, he would be supervising the care of the cattle and sheep, as well as producing cheeses.

"I can't do it, Yenah."

The owner laughed and began walking toward the farmhouse. "You'll do fine, young man. Stop worrying."

Standing alone, Noah watched his master walk down the row of grain toward the house in the distance.

Three days later, even before the sun had risen, Yenah was checking the ropes on his wagon. Three sturdy men were securing the horses to the harness. Noah stood at the gate, glumly watching his master's preparations. Yenah sensed the young man's mood, but his excitement for the trip simply would not allow him to take Noah's pleas seriously. Soon the men were ready to leave.

Yenah turned to Noah. "Noah, you've done everything I've asked for the past three years. I want you to know how much this trip means to me. You are like a son to me." He embraced him, signaled to his companions and led the horses and wagon down the path to the main road. He was sure that everything would go smoothly while he was gone. After all, Noah knew how to run the farm.

Noah watched in silence until Yenah disappeared into the shadows of the forest. He knew in his heart that something bad was coming.

In the beginning, Noah's fear seemed entirely unfounded. He hired four women to run the creamery, giving them detailed instructions for the production of various cheeses. After giving them a quick overview of what to do, he left for the fields. There his full crew awaited him, ready to go. The first day of harvest was so successful that Noah completely forgot his original fear. After finishing that first day, they were all congratulating him.

This was the first harvest using his invention, which was a scythe wagon. Its width covered three rows of grain, was pulled by two oxen and rolled through the rows on tall wheels, almost the size of a man. Noah had traded many barrels of cheese for the smith to forge five long, sharp scythe blades. These he fastened carefully to the wheels. When the oxen pulled the contraption, the scythe blades cut the grain and left it on the ground, to be picked up and put into the wagon by two workers who followed behind.

For the first hour or two, it actually took longer to reap with the machine than it would have taken by hand. Noah's helpers begged him to give it up and go back to the normal method of harvesting grain. Noah, however, did not want to abandon all of his hard work just because they ran into some starting difficulties. By noon, the machine was moving remarkably well and by evening, all agreed it was the best idea they had ever encountered.

The invention was so fast, however, that those following couldn't keep up with gathering the grain and putting it into the wagons to be processed. They lacked enough laborers to glean the wheat, and only had two wagons to carry it back to the yard. This is where Noah made his first critical error, an error he would rue in the weeks to come. When the machine left so much grain on the ground, foolishly Noah decided to wait until the end of the harvest, when they could haul the rest of the stalks back to the granary area.

Early in the second day, the boys and Noah were cutting the grain in the second quarter of the field.

"Noah!" Nat called.

Noah looked up. Nat was walking alongside the wagon, leaning with all his weight on the yoke.

Nat pointed to the scythe. "The ground here is uneven and your scythe is missing grain."

Of the three boys, Nat was the smallest, but still wiry and strong. To Noah's eye, however, the way he leaned on the coupling was precarious. "Nat," he yelled, "I don't think you should be pushing like that. It's. . ."

The cart hit a bump and Nat lost his balance.

"Tyal!" Noah screamed, "stop the oxen!"

In less than a heartbeat, Tyal began slowing the animals, Noah swung himself under the yoke and landed beside Nat, but it was too late. The boy was already on the ground, writhing in agony, grasping at his right leg. Noah knelt down to look at it.

The leg was clearly broken, badly enough, in fact, that the bone was sticking through the skin and bleeding profusely. Normally, a broken leg, unbearably painful, nevertheless healed overnight. Because this was an open fracture, somehow they would have to push the bone into place before it grew back incorrectly. Otherwise Nat would never walk normally again.

Tyal unharnessed the oxen and led them to shade, while Sredael ran to the farmhouse to find a horse and fetch his father. Noah knelt beside Nat, speaking quietly to him, trying to calm him. He anxiously kept glancing at the jagged bone. The bleeding had stopped, but they would need to work quickly to keep the bone from regrowing into a wrong position.

The town, where the boys lived, was a good distance away. It might take an hour before Nod, their father, would reach them, and an hour was clearly too long. Once the bone started the healing process, it would be impossible to bring the bone back together properly. Noah knew this from his work with horses and other animals.

Last year, when a horse had broken its leg, Yenah had taught Noah to guide the broken bone back into position. The animal, of course, had needed to be restrained, and the procedure was tricky at best. Noah had already done it three or four times and had not failed yet. He looked for Tyal, who was running back down the rows. They would need to do it right away.

"Find me two, long branches, as straight as possible!" Noah shouted.

The boy ran off. Noah looked at the wound. The bleeding had stopped, but that was not entirely a comfort. Probably the bone had already begun the work of regeneration. He had to fix it now, before things got worse. He jumped up and began dismantling the yoke on the cart, pulling off leather straps.

When Tyal returned, Noah gently slid four leather straps beneath Nat's leg. Carefully laying the two branches on the inside and outside of the leg, he prepared himself for the next step.

"Nat," he said mustering as much calmness as he could. "I am going to push the bone back into its proper position, but it's going to hurt like nothing you've ever experienced. You've got to hold on to Tyal while I do it. Okay?"

Nat nodded, and Tyal held down his brother's hands with all his strength. Noah took a deep breath and then pulled the first strap tightly. Nat screamed. He carefully pulled the next three straps as firmly as he could. Holding his brother with all his might, Tyal watched Noah gingerly guide the bone into position.

Noah prayed quietly, "Yahweh of Methuselah, put it where it needs to be. Don't let this leg be crooked." A few minutes later, he gingerly ran his hand along the leg. To Noah's eye, the leg was probably just about right. He sat down on the ground, overwhelmed.

It was almost two hours later before Nod arrived on horseback. The man was horrified at the extent of the injury and blamed Noah for the damage. He angrily supervised his sons as they placed their brother onto a wagon and took him home.

Before they left, Nod grimly informed Noah, "I want you to know: thank goodness you knew how to set that bone and thank goodness it looks alright, but my boys will not be working in your fields at all, Noah. Your scythe wagon is too dangerous, and I won't allow it!"

Noah's heart sank. Without those three boys, he would never be able to finish the harvest on time. "Could they start planting the new crop? There won't be any danger at all."

The second the words left his mouth, Noah knew he was in trouble. Nod's decision was made in the heat of his anger. Noah's request pushed him over the edge.

"No, they can work in the dairy, but nowhere else. Let them care for the animals."

"But the crops, I won't be able to harvest or plant. . ." Noah answered in panic. "It's too late to find anyone else to work."

"That," Nod said angrily, "is your problem, not mine." He yanked on the harness and the oxen began pulling the wagon. "I won't talk about this again, Noah. You're on your own."

Months later, when he allowed himself to think about what went wrong with the harvest, that moment stood out as the critical point in the disaster that followed. Everything bad that happened in the next two weeks began at that juncture.

After the accident, the other harvesters refused to work with the scythe wagon, which meant they had to return to reaping by hand. Normally, this would not have been a disaster, but Noah had lost three of his best workers, and the harvest slowed to a crawl.

Every night, Noah would return to his bed exhausted, pondering without success how to get the harvesting on track. During the days, the harvesting process ran into problem after problem, forcing Noah to increase the hours they worked. After five days, a worker complained about the intensity of the work and quit, cutting the number of harvesters down to three. Now the entire season was in jeopardy.

Noah worried about it so intensely that he couldn't sleep at night, and he found himself spending every waking moment in exhaustion. His fears, moreover, were well-founded; in the end, they spent an extra seven days working to finish that job. Even worse, they were so short-handed that Noah was unable to leave the harvesting in order to supervise the second planting.

That, however, was just the beginning of the trouble. At this point, much of the first day's work still lay in the field, never retrieved. Almost as bad, the grain from the first four days needed to be processed before it began to rot. The workers who still remained were too young to use Noah's grain compressing machine without careful supervision. He tried to show them at sunrise one day during the harvest, but they simply did not grasp the routine. Noah, however, had to manage the work of preparing the second field for its planting, already a week late. He was pretty sure they had enough time to beat the heat for that crop, as long as they started immediately. It turned out, however, that they never began at all.

The morning for commencing work on the second crop, Noah rose early, filling the wagon with seed and farm implements. He decided to check the creamery before leading the oxen into the fields, having been unable to visit it since the first harvest began. As he entered the barn, a powerful odor of spoiled milk assaulted his nostrils. This was not a cheese aroma, which admittedly at times could be pungent, but the smell of rottenness. He ran to the milk barrels, which were filled with ruined milk. Quickly he pulled up the first great cheese cask from the holding well and opened it. Empty.

That's when he remembered the messages his first week of harvest. The temporary creamery helpers could not figure out how to prepare his cheese recipes and to be honest, Noah had not done a good job in preparing them. The women twice had sent messengers out to the first field asking for his help, but the work out there was overwhelming him, and he didn't leave. He couldn't remember if they sent him any more messages. Now he went from place to place in the creamery, assessing the damage.

An hour later, Nat arrived. "I'm sorry, Noah," the boy muttered. "Father wouldn't let us warn you about the dairy." Noah looked up, utterly discouraged. "We told him how bad things were, but Father said it was your own fault, and you should pay the consequences for it."

"When did the women stop coming?" Noah asked glumly.

Nat looked at the milk in the vats. "About two days after they sent the first message."

Shaking his head, Noah walked over to the milk. "It's all spoiled. Go home and get your brothers, Nat. I'll teach you how to make cheese, and we'll get things going."

Once the boys arrived, Noah patiently trained them in his various techniques for preparing cheeses, which took until after noon. Then for another four hours, he carefully supervised them as they cautiously attempted to imitate what he had taught them. Once he was satisfied they understood everything, he explained to them how to store the cheeses in the great caskets, which they then would lower by pulleys into the frigid underground lake. By the time Noah finished his work with the boys, the sun had already set. Another critical day was lost.

That night, Noah dropped into his bed, exhausted beyond anything he had ever experienced. His muscles ached, and he desperately yearned to sleep all that night and the whole next day, but he knew this must not happen. Tomorrow would be the decisive day in their effort to save the second crop.

Of all times, Noah desperately needed a full night's sleep, but crops and cheeses crowded his thoughts like bees swarming on a honey-comb. The first harvest still needed to be processed. The grain might rot if they didn't care for it at once. His undermanned crew in the first field would have a heavy task on their hands for the next two weeks, and Noah doubted if they could work effectively without his oversight. The second planting, moreover, might already be too late. Those roots needed to get down to the river beneath the ground. Otherwise, the plants would simply wither on the stalk.

There was, however, hope; if Noah toiled from sunrise to sunset and if his workers labored without rest, they might still be able to plant the seeds in time, but even this was less than sure. Without a desperate effort, the entire crop would fail, and then what would Yenah do?

Noah lay staring at the ceiling above him. There was just barely a chance that he could make it happen. The creamery was running again, so at least something good had happened. The boys might be able to learn the grain compression machine. With some luck, moreo-ver, they might perchance fill the storage bins with grain. There could possibly be just enough time for the second planting, if everything worked just right. Potentially the roots might even reach the under-ground rivers, and the crop could be saved. At least these things were possibilities.

The very possibility of success, however, made the prospect heavi-er. Unless he worked harder than ever before in his life, everything would collapse in failure. Even if he did work hard, the chances against success were especially strong. It was all so unfair. He had begged Yenah not to burden him. All Noah wanted was a place to sleep, food to eat and a simple job to fulfill.

Other people always forced on him obligations, even though he begged them to leave him be. His father pressured him to work the farm, the people of Mehujael demanded he build their walls. Even the little girl Elizabeth impelled him to talk to her, to listen, to care. The more they pressured him, the more they stifled him, until finally he simply couldn't breathe. If only he could weave around himself an unassailable cocoon, safe from pain. *No one should have to bear the weight of what I bear*, he thought to himself. It simply wasn't fair.

Tossing and turning, Noah moaned out loud. "Yahweh, why do you hate me so much? Why do you lay this burden upon me? I never asked to be son of the Promise. I never wanted to be better at building than others. I never wanted to be smart. Why are you doing this to me? What have I done to you that all this grief should come to me?"

Yahweh, however, said nothing in the night, and Noah thrashed about in his bed until the early hours of morning. Sometimes, when he tried to close his eyes, all he could see was rows and rows of rotted grain, the thought of which choked his chest. Hundreds of possible solutions churned through his mind, all of which he immediately dismissed as useless fantasies. Several times he broke down in tears, begging the God of his father and grandfather to save him, help him.

Finally, right before the break of day, his bitterness and dread exhausted themselves, and sleep overtook him. All that day, until late afternoon, Noah slumbered. Twice laborers came to his hut, begging him to join them in the field, but Noah ignored their pleas and went back to sleep. The past four weeks had so consumed his strength that he simply could not summon the energy to worry about fields or grain. Not until sunset, did he finally arouse himself.

Beyond the typical sounds of animals, the farm seemed ominously silent, as if all of his laborers were gone. He knew in his heart they would not have planted the second field without his direction, and it was even less likely that the boys would have begun processing the first harvest. In other words, the farm had probably passed the point of no return.

At this juncture, Noah faced a decision: would he force himself to round up his laborers, even though it was probably too late? He sat on the floor beside his bed of straw, thinking. It was all so unfair. He never wanted any of this. From the moment Yenah asked him to do this, Noah had refused again and again. Yenah, not Noah, had done all of this.

The pain in his chest began to throb. It was impossible to save the farm, simply impossible. The more he thought about it, the worse it became to him. He simply couldn't face the farm. Yenah, the farm-hands, Yahweh Himself were all asking something of him that he was unable to do.

Getting up, he crossed his room to a chest in the far corner. He opened it and found four vessels full of wine. About a month ago, before this catastrophe began, a woman had insisted he take these containers as barter for cheese.

"It'll make you forget your worries, young man," she had said to him.

When he took them, he had no worries to forget. At this moment, here in his hut, Noah wanted to forget everything: his father, his gifts, his duties, his failures. He reached for a wineskin.

For the next three days, Noah the son of Lamech staggered through a drunken stupor. None of his workers could reason with him, for he raged incoherently, screaming obscenities at Yenah, at his father, his grandfather, Mehujael and at his Creator. For hours at a time, he lay in the dirt unconscious, only to awaken again and to rage more, curse more and drink more.

Eventually his wine ran out, and when it did Noah collapsed in a heap on the grain barn floor. Throughout an entire day and night, Noah lay not conscious of the precious time which was wasting away. When he at long last awoke, on the fourth morning, the opportunity to save the crops was gone.

Surprisingly, his head was relatively sober. He couldn't remember much of what had happened; he knew only that he had overslept when he should have been planting the second field, and then he had started drinking wine.

The thought of the field made him jump up. He raced to the bins where grain from the first harvest should have gone, but found them empty. No one had processed the grain. He grabbed a horse and rushed to the second field, which lay unattended. No one had planted the seed. When he returned to the sheep and cattle barns, he discovered at least that his milk animals were watered and fed. Beyond that, however, the farm lay in neglect.

A short time after noon, he rode his horse into the village. Coming to the home of Nod, the father of the three boys, Noah knocked loudly until the door opened. Noah looked up to see Nod viewing him suspiciously.

"Noah? What on earth is going on with you?"

"It doesn't matter. I need you to take over the farm. Your boys know the dairy part pretty well. They can run it without too much trouble."

The man frowned. "They tell me you've been drunk for the past four days. They tell me that they begged you to help them save the grain, but you just cursed and screamed and kept on drinking until you collapsed on the ground. They couldn't handle it anymore, so they came home."

Noah dropped his eyes in shame. His shoulders went slack and if any light was left in his face, it extinguished in that moment. Without looking up, he mumbled, "I need you to take the farm. It's too late for the second planting, but some of the first harvest can be saved."

Noah heard the man gasp. "You let the second planting go?"

He nodded.

"And now you're leaving everything?" Nod asked. "Just like that? After all Yenah has done for you?"

Noah had no answer. He stood before the man utterly defeated, wholly ashamed. He dreaded what Nod might say next. Nod might attempt to persuade him to stay, to make the best of a terrible disaster, to make things right, to save Yenah's harvest, fulfill his obligations, do what was right. All of that, however, was impossible. It was too late.

"Send your older boys to the farm this afternoon," he muttered, still staring at the ground. "I'll teach them to use my machine. Maybe they can save the first harvest."

Nod answered angrily, "How do I know you won't be drunk by the time they get there?"

Noah frowned and mounted his horse. He turned the animal toward the farm.

"How do I know?" the father shouted after him. "How do I know you won't get drunk again?"

Noah stopped and looked back into his face. "The wine is gone," he answered quietly. He bowed his head and guided the horse down the pathway.

Five months later found Noah cutting his way through grasses and stubborn vines on a steep mountain slope. Above him stood the mountain's peak, taller than any he had ever seen, perhaps six or seven times higher than the hills he knew at home. He stopped for a moment, wiping his brow. Most mountains were simply larger hills, with gentle woods and grassy slopes leading up to the crown. This mountain was nothing like that.

Giant boulders dotted its apron and covered the mountain's highest reaches. Its peak was visible for a great distance, which was what attracted Noah here to begin with. Early in the morning, when he had been trekking across the plain below, that mountain apex had beckoned him to investigate. In particular, one enormous boulder, almost at the pinnacle, had caught his eye, and he decided to ascend to it.

Noah had a plan; he wanted a home as far from human civilization as possible. If the past five months had revealed anything, they had exposed the hopeless corruption of his world. He passed through the charred remains of villages. He came upon husbands beating wives, children running through village streets half-naked and starving, beggars crowding him at city gates. Robbery and murder seemed to be occupations as common as carpentry and farming. People sold themselves as slaves or worse. Neighbor betrayed neighbor. He could no longer stomach the violence of the world around him.

The five month journey, moreover, also had exposed his own corruption. On the fifth week, he stayed a night in a small village on the edge of the wilderness. The next morning, he went outside the walls to fill his water sacks for the journey ahead. The sounds of the village–a blacksmith's hammer, a carpenter's saw, stray dogs barking–floated over the ivy covered walls. Yet oddly, even though it was the normal hour for women to fetch water, no one was at the well. It was curious, but he continued to pull water up from below. He finished his second waterskin when he heard a baby's whimper, not from the village, but nearby, perhaps in a small copse of bushes some twenty cubits away.

Putting down his pack, Noah investigated the sound. Before too long, he found her, a tiny baby, no longer strong enough to cry out loud, but still alive enough at least to make a pitiable sound. He knelt down beside her. It was clear that the tiny girl, who had been exposed to the elements without protection of clothing or blanket, would not live much longer, perhaps three or four hours at the most.

Who had put her here and why? The mother, or perhaps the father or grandparents had decided the baby wasn't good enough. Was it because she was a girl? Did they not approve of the lightness of her skin? Did they decide they didn't want another mouth to feed?

He looked toward the well, where women should have been drawing water that morning. That's why no one was there. They didn't want to hear the baby. So they busied themselves with weeding, sowing, building, working, blocking out the helpless sounds of a dying child. *Hypocrites*, he thought to himself. *If they weren't going to help her, at least they might as well listen to her die.*

But Noah made the mistake of looking again at the child. She could be saved, he was sure. Her skin was ashen, as if she had been out all night. Yet she was still pretty, and she had a surprising amount of hair on her head. Her feet were perfectly formed, but hardly moving now. He examined the long, fragile fingers on her tiny hands. Too weak to grasp anything, but with goat's milk and gentle care, she could grow strong in a few weeks. All she needed was—

He stopped and let the baby's hand drop. Looking around to see if anyone was watching, he rose slowly. Sounds from the village came over the wall; a mother called a child, a donkey brayed. Noah stood frozen, staring. Then, backing away from the copse, he furtively glanced toward the empty village gate. Turning, Noah walked slowly toward the road. He never looked back.

That moment had happened four long months ago. Now he found himself completely free of human habitation, a three month's journey away from the nearest village or town. Sooner or later civilization could come his way, but it might take centuries to happen. Until then, he could make this his haven of safety. He continued to climb the mountainside. It was so forbidding here, strewn with jagged rocks, an unfriendly world.

After three hours of hard climbing, he reached the boulder. From the plain below, he had tried to guess its size, but standing here, the rock surpassed his imagination, possibly four times the size of the largest behemoth he had ever seen. The boulder was jagged and dangerous, making it difficult to ascend and survey, but Noah was determined.

For the rest of the afternoon, he combed over the landscape surrounding the rock, looking for some kind of permanent shelter within its confines. Finally, he spotted a small hole beneath the boulder's far side. Kneeling down and peering within, Noah thought he saw in the midst of the blackness a shaft of light. He guessed this boulder might be blocking the entrance to some kind of cave.

Within an hour, he found a way into what turned out to be a remarkable cavern. As he explored over the next few days, he discovered a natural pathway leading down to an underground river. Although the cave was dark, several spots on its ceiling admitted light to illumine his way. Noah found that he might be able to allow even more light to brighten the various "halls" and "rooms" within his new mansion. One shaft of light revealed an exit to a hidden glen, surrounded by walls of jagged rocks. The glen would be big enough to support a large garden, and, much to his delight, wild khitaw grew there in abundance.

Four evenings later, Noah sat atop the great boulder, surveying the landscape below him. He saw no smoke from stove fires, no cultivated fields, no roads. Human life was at least a three month's journey away. He wondered if he were the first human to set foot in this place. Perhaps, he hoped, he might be the last. The thought encouraged him.

Eventually, he'd need to catch some goats and possibly even somehow find a bull and a couple of cows, but for now he wouldn't worry. He had khitaw and plenty of time to search for wild vegetables and fruits. He'd have to figure out a way to farm some land without making it obvious to others. Hopefully, this would be his last home. He stood and gazed toward the west, towards the last signs of human civilization far beyond the horizon. *Let them stay there*, he thought to himself.

He climbed over rocks, which earlier that day he had set to hide the cave's opening. He would miss friendships and human warmth, but not the shame and especially not the obligation. He'd much rather be alone and not have to face failing those he cared about. The sun was just about setting as Noah lowered himself into his cave. Here was his home now, and here he would stay.

Chapter Seven

Year 1441

F ather!"

Imas looked up. He saw Rehtak in the distance, coming hurriedly toward him. He laid his saw on the felled tree trunk and moved toward his ax, which was leaning against the stump. Something must be wrong for Rehtak to venture out alone. Quickly, he grabbed the ax and began racing toward his thirteen year old daughter.

Here, in the great valley, almost anything could go wrong. No other humans lived closer to them than a twelve day's journey. All by themselves in the wilderness, when anything went wrong, they were on their own. They harvested their own seed, cleared their own fields, spun their own thread and raised their own livestock--sheep for wool, goats and cattle for milk. Every single job pushed their abilities beyond anything they had previously known.

This new world, which they had been battling for over four years, forgave little. During the dark months of their first year, hunger had forced all fifteen of them into the forest, foraging for food while they waited for their crops to grow. Their next three crops barely answered their hunger, since they hadn't yet cleared enough land for large crops. The work of felling trees demanded much more labor than Imas had anticipated. Predators had already taken from them four of their animals. Three months ago, his oldest daughter Eisse had lost two fingers in their harvest machine's gears. The regenerative process was still not complete. Without a doubt, the wilderness provided a harsh home for Imas, Etena and their thirteen children.

He reached Rehtak, who was breathing heavily. She looked up. "Father!" she said. "A man is at the house. Mother sent me to fetch you."

Imas dropped down and put his hands on her shoulders. "Now, daughter, you must promise me you'll run home as quickly as you can run. I cannot wait for you."

Rehtak shook her head. "You shouldn't wait, Father. This man is. . . strange."

At this statement, Imas kissed his daughter on the forehead and bounded down the pathway toward his house, which stood at the end of the field. When he arrived, he found his door wide open and a tall, dark skinned, muscular man standing just on the inside of the threshold.

The first thing he noticed about the man was his coarse black hair. It flowed over his shoulders, falling almost to his waist. His black beard was probably even longer, although the end of it was stuffed into an especially large pocket. Imas wondered how the man could function without his hair getting in the way.

The stranger's clothing next caught Imas's eye. His tunic stretched almost to his knees and was covered with various deep pockets, most of which were obviously filled. His loose skirt, also populated with various deep pockets, which were also obviously stuffed, flowed almost to his ankles. He bore a leather rucksack, again covered with bulging pockets. What caught Imas's attention was not just the strange cut of this apparel, but the fabric. Even from a quick glance, the cloth seemed remarkably soft and flowing.

As Imas reached the doorway, the stranger glanced at him, then quickly averted his eyes and stepped back. Imas nodded to him and entered the room. As his eyes adjusted to the darkness, he made out his wife and several children standing behind the table. Her eyes met his and conveyed confusion and fear. He tightened his grip on his ax.

"What do you want, stranger?" he asked him firmly.

The man frowned. "I suppose I should answer, but I don't know if I should ask right away."

His answer surprised Imas, not exactly in what he said, but in the fact that he didn't say it to Imas, but rather to himself. "Ask what right away?" he asked.

The stranger looked startled. "Must not talk to myself out loud. How do I ask?"

"Stranger," Imas said resolutely, "we don't know who you are or why you are here. Unless you tell us what you want, you must leave."

"Are you hungry?" asked his wife, Etena. Imas looked over to her. Her expression showed compassion, typical of her character.

"Plenty of food," he answered, seemingly still to himself. The stranger deftly slipped off the pack and strode to the table. Etena backed up, but he scarcely acknowledged her presence. He began rummaging through the pack, pulling out various small bags.

Imas had never seen bags like these. They were cunningly made, with straps sewn into a seam, straps which apparently sealed the bag when they were pulled tight. The bags were all made out of another kind of fabric, different from the cloth he wore, with a harder, shiny surface. It wasn't animal skin, yet it couldn't have come from animal hair either. The ropes he used to string these bags together differed from any ropes Imas had encountered in his fifty years of life. They were so finely braided that one could barely see the weave. He could not guess how a man could manufacture rope to be so perfect.

The stranger deftly arranged twenty or so bags before him and began untying the straps. "Maybe they would be willing to trade for it. That's what I hope anyway." He busily opened each bag, discussing with himself the contents of every sack.

"I doubt if anyone has ever tasted cheese like this."

"These are the best apples we have dried in a hundred years."

"The honey on this cake doesn't mold like on others."

"This grain has a nuttier flavor than khitaw."

Imas watched the man in amazement. Even without tasting them, he recognized the foodstuff's sophistication. "What do you want, man?"

Not looking up, the stranger answered loudly, "Maybe they will trade for the food. I don't know when to ask." He frowned. "I must stop thinking out loud."

The conversation, if conversation it could be called, was almost humorous. Imas shook his head in sadness. If the world were not so violent and if men were not so cruel, he would almost be able to enjoy this one-sided encounter. It was because civilization had turned savage, however, that Imas had moved Etena and the children to this wilderness, to escape robberies, murders, and rapes. He looked at the man, carefully arranging his wares. They had traveled so far to avoid people just like this stranger before them.

The man sighed. "I would trade almost all of this for iron, brass, copper, tin or zinc. I hope they have some."

So this was it. He needed metal. Imas answered the question, saying, "I have no metal to trade."

The stranger looked up, his eyes for the first time meeting Imas's eyes. "None?" he asked, also for the first time not to himself.

Imas nodded. "We're far away from the nearest town. Maybe a twenty days' journey away, and they don't even have a blacksmith there."

The man frowned. "Will you ever be able to get metal? I need tools."

He certainly seemed sincere enough, Imas thought. *I want to trust him, but. . .* He looked over at his children. What if the stranger were simply looking for a way to take advantage of them? What if he were waiting until Imas journeyed to the village for supplies?

Finally Imas spoke. "Someday, I'll return there. Not soon, but someday."

The stranger stood silent, pondering what to do now. Imas watched him with curiosity, waiting for some response, but nothing came.

Finally, Imas broke the silence. "Food isn't good enough barter for metal, you know. No one would ever take it."

The man thought for a moment, then nodded. "Then what would be good?"

"Your cloth and ropes."

Surprise flitted into the stranger's eyes. Imas almost thought he detected a smile. For a long time, the man stood there, obviously processing what he should do at this point. Finally, he began placing his bags back into his rucksack. He grunted, slung the pack onto his back and turned.

"Time to go," he said quietly.

Imas saw four bags still lying on the table. "You forgot some."

Nodding, the man answered, "Gifts. Cheese." He strode to the door.

Etena called out to him. "Wait! Won't you stay the night? We would like to share a meal at least and talk."

The stranger mumbled something as he continued out the door.

"At least," she added, "you could tell us your name and your father's name."

This stopped him. He turned, looking at the woman, then at her husband, but said nothing. A look of fear lingered in his eyes. Perhaps it was regret. Imas could not tell.

"When will you bring the cloth?" he asked the stranger.

"A year. Maybe two." He thought for a moment, considering. "One year."

They watched him hiking quickly across the fields into the woods. He soon disappeared from sight. Etena took hold of her husband's arm. He looked down at her and smiled. "What kind of man would dress that way and talk that way?"

"Someone," she answered thoughtfully, "who has been alone for a long time."

He came again that next year, this time with a beast loaded with various kinds of cloth. Imas traded as much metal as he could, with a promise of more the next time. As soon as the exchange was completed, the man handed Etena four bags.

"Cheese," he said, smiling. He turned then and left.

As he led his beast down the path, Imas commented to his wife, "He barely said eight words. He must be incredibly lonely."

She nodded. "Lonelier than last year, anyway."

He looked at his wife in surprise. "Why lonelier?"

"Last year," she answered, "at least he was talking to himself. This year, not a word."

Imas smiled. "I noticed that. He was probably practicing all the way here."

"That," she asked, "must have been an unbelievably lonely journey, don't you think?"

Year after year, he arrived at Imas's farm, during the same moon, usually at the same exact phase, the last quarter. Every year he brought his cloth, rope and cheese, but starting the third year, he began staying overnight at the house, then leaving the next morning. The first time, Imas suspected the man simply was tired from his journey, but when the man departed in the morning, he lingered over an hour at the door, saying almost nothing, yet hesitant to leave.

On his fifth visit, the stranger began asking questions. He sat down at the table, folded his hands and quietly spoke. It was an odd, almost comical picture: A man with black hair to his shoulders and a beard stuffed into a pocket on his tunic, gently attending to his host's discussions about water, farming, animals, children and the life of a farmer.

Imas suspected the man understood these things profoundly. Continually throughout the discussion he would acknowledge various points with a slight nod or a shy smile. *Yes*, his eyes seemed to say, *I know all about birthing calves and building barns. Of course*, his nod suggested, *it is hard to clear a field assisted only by your children and wife.* Yet Imas never suspected the man to be anything less than entirely absorbed with what he said.

He was building a bridge, Etena suggested the following day. It was a bridge from his world to the world of humanity, cautiously constructing it one timber at a time, carefully placed, gingerly connected to the next. When his bridge was complete, he could cross back to human company.

On the tenth year, the stranger arrived to find Imas fifteen feet down a hole, struggling to dig a well for watering his cattle and sheep. Once he understood the project, he left Imas and the children digging and hauling dirt, while he himself began searching through the woods and fields, climbing through bushes and thistles and clambering over fallen trees. After almost an hour, Imas heard a gleeful "Ah!"

"Father," Eisse called down into the hole, "the stranger has found something."

Imas motioned to the children. "Send down the rope ladder."

When he reached the surface, he found the stranger standing there with an enormous smile on his face. "Khorgul," he said gleefully. "You've got three patches of it." Pointing toward the end of his field, he added, "Over there. . ." he said, pointing to the small hillock about five hundred cubits beyond the house. "And beneath your barn. . ." he added almost laughing.

Having never seen the man so animated, Imas paused before answering. To him, khorgul was an annoying weed, but obviously his visitor knew something Imas himself needed to know. "And why does that give you so much joy, stranger?"

"An underground river, Imas, passes directly under your field and your barn."

Hearing the stranger pronounce his name startled him. He looked at the man, who was so ecstatic that he did not recognize he had addressed the farmer as a person, almost as a friend.

"Don't you see?" he said beaming. "We can dig down to the river anywhere along that line," he drew an imaginary line between the end of the field and the hillock, "and access unlimited water."

"How deep?" the farmer asked with skepticism on his face.

"Don't worry about that," the stranger said. "Nobody knows more about digging wells than I do. I've been digging them by myself for three hundred years. We'll set up a well there," he pointed to a spot between the barn and the house, "and we'll use that for cold storage." He looked to the far end of the field. "See those gopher trees there? You can use them for storage barrels. I've got gopher wood casks that are two hundred years old and they still haven't rotted!"

Imas shook his head. "Gopher trees are impossible to cut down. They're like rock."

The man laughed. "I know. I spent thirty years finding a way to cut them and split them. We can do it. You'll be astonished."

Imas was already astonished. This quiet, taciturn hermit had suddenly found his voice and could barely contain himself. The farmer had no way to evaluate his ideas, but his instincts told him the man was probably right in anything he suggested. After all, the stranger had already demonstrated his ability to manufacture items far beyond what Imas had seen before. No one was able to produce cheeses as pleasurable as this man's. The quality of his rope put to shame anything developed even in the great cities. He glanced at his visitor's clothing. Granted, it was an outrageous design, with a knee-long tunic and an ankle-length skirt, not to mention the odd-shaped pockets, but regardless, the fabric itself was superb. Every year, the stranger's cloth brought the highest value in barter. No, this man probably would be a remarkable source of wisdom about farming, weaving and building.

Not until nightfall did the talking, planning and gathering end. Once they could no longer see, they began making their way across the field. In the distance a lantern set on the farmhouse door gave them their goal. The world was pitch black, for the moon was not out, yet the stranger easily led him along the rows of corn. When they reached the middle of the field, he stopped.

"Look at the sky," he whispered. Imas looked up. The man sighed. "Think of how many stars there must be--millions upon millions."

He was right. The sky blazed with stars. Even though Imas had seen the sight innumerable times, the majesty of the heavens that night drowned his words, and he gazed at the sight in silent awe. The breeze was still, but the sounds of the night washed around him like a mountain stream rushing over its stony bed. Crickets, frogs, doves and locusts all sang praises to the stars. An owl called out, its utterance answered by another somewhere across the field. In the far distance, a hyena cackled, a coyote wailed, a wolf yawled. Imas disappeared under the night flood, drowned beneath the weight of stars and songs.

For a long time, the two stood silent. Finally the stranger broke the spell. "You know, Imas, these stars haven't always been there. Ten generations ago, no stars existed, no earth, no moon, no sky. Only ten generations ago. Before that, solely the Creator existed."

He paused, apparently waiting for the farmer to reply, but Imas said nothing. Finally he spoke again.

"Our Father, Adam, was the first human. Do you know this name?"

Imas, still gazing at the sky, shook his head. "No, I do not."

The stranger became quiet. Imas could not see him in the blackness, yet sensed a struggle going on within him. For a long time, his neighbor wrestled with some unseen adversary. In the end, apparently the adversary prevailed. Imas heard the stranger stir and begin walking. The farmer followed him back to the house.

For the next two weeks, the two men worked side by side. The stranger's abilities astonished Imas, who had never seen as many clever tricks for digging, hauling, building and crafting. He taught the farmer to construct pulleys, which completely changed the process of digging a well. Once he improved the farmer's furnace, he took his own metal and turned it into useful tools for the farmer, carefully demonstrating how to work metal. During daytime hours, he guided the children to the best plants for making rope and after nightfall, he trained half of the children in simple rope braiding skills. Most of the daytime, Imas and his family were digging the first well by the barn, while the stranger spent his time improving various tools and implements around the farm.

The second week of work, he began constructing a rectangular cask out of gopher wood, held together by long gopher wood dowels. Once he had built five of the sides, he fashioned a lid and fastened it to the top by means of three lengths of rope, equally spaced from one another. He then attached three loops onto the ropes, which would enable the family to raise and lower the cask into the well. The project took him most of the week, with regular interruptions to advise, help and offer further instruction to the family as they worked the well and their crops.

The morning the stranger completed his project, he crossed the field to where Imas and his children were building a framework for hauling water up from the well. The stranger stood watching them for a quarter of an hour and then finally spoke.

"I have to get back. Can't leave my animals alone too long. Have to go."

Imas looked at him, curious. "How long will it take you?"

The man started to answer, then stopped. "A long ways," he said at last, as if the truth would somehow endanger his privacy.

Imas wiped the sweat from his forehead. "I can't tell you how much you've helped me, friend. I'll never be able to repay your kindness."

The man shook his head. "Don't need to." He stood there uncomfortably, as if waiting for permission to leave.

Imas picked up the shovel. "We used up all your metal on the tools you fashioned."

"I didn't come for metal anyway. I've had enough for a couple of years now."

The answer surprised Imas. He had assumed the metal was bringing his guest back every year. Now he wondered if it was human contact that drew him. "Why did you come, then?"

Shaking his head, the stranger frowned. "I don't know. I guess I said I'd come, so I figured I should. I don't know."

"Will you return?" Imas asked, wondering.

"Maybe, I don't. . ." He hesitated, letting his sentence trail off, as if he couldn't bear to commit himself. He turned to leave.

"At least let us give you food for the trip back," Imas called after him. "Rehtak, go back to the house. Tell your mother to make our guest some food."

The girl darted down the pathway toward the house. Imas watched the man begin walking. When he reached the house, he disappeared into the doorway. Not long afterwards, he emerged with the rucksack on his back. Looking toward the field, he waved. Then he turned toward the great woods and with long strides, disappeared into the trees.

Eisse carried a skin of water to her father, as he wiped sweat from his brow. "Will he come back next year, Father?"

He stared into the distance, a quizzical look on his face. "I don't know, really. But I don't think so."

This prediction, however, was proven wrong, for he did return and much sooner than in a year. He brought with him seven pack animals, loaded with cloth, ropes and tools. His arrival created a stir among Imas' offspring, since he bestowed cloth upon family members, some fabric crafted with unusual colors or patterns. The oldest boy, Bor, helped him cool the cheeses in the cask, which they lowered back into the well by the barn. Rehtak and Eisse led the animals to a cattle pen and brought them water and hay.

That night, they talked in the cabin by lantern light, like they had in years past. Now, however, the topics no longer centered on farming and building. He wanted to know about the world of men and women. He asked about the great cities and how the elders ruled their people. What was happening these days in commerce and trade? Did most people still live in poverty? He knew already that human habitation was creeping ever closer. Common sense made it clear that people would always push into the wilderness to escape the tyranny of civilization. What he wanted to know was whether mankind's lot had improved over the past three centuries.

As Imas described the state of human society, he kept using words like pillaging, despotism, suffering, robbery and violence. Children were regularly abandoned on hillsides to die. Daughters were sold for next to nothing as slaves to wicked men. Husbands beat their wives mercilessly, often sending them away when a younger woman appeared available. The visitor kept shaking his head in horror, muttering repeatedly, "It's much worse now than when I left."

After Imas finished, the stranger thought for a long time. Finally he looked at Imas with a probing gaze, asking, "It's the Nephilim, isn't it? They're the ones who make it happen. They still roam the countryside, and no one opposes them."

"They're not the problem," answered Imas, "but they certainly make things worse." He picked up a piece of cloth from the table and began running his hand over it. It was as smooth as a baby's skin, something he could not imagine in a fabric.

Imas shook his head. "Humans are the problem. I don't understand why, but I am convinced that somehow the human race is getting worse. The Nephilim disrupt things, things like commerce, farming and communities. I think they want to create chaos everywhere they can. Even so, I don't believe what the Nephilim do causes the human race to spiral down. Somehow something more fundamental than social anarchy is pushing us deeper and deeper into depravity."

The stranger thought about his words. "That makes no sense. How could an entire culture degenerate unless something is tearing it down?"

The farmer shook his head and sighed. "Maybe it's because we don't know what's good anymore. It's every man for himself in this world. The stronger you are, the more you can have. I used to think it was wrong to put children on the hillsides to let them die. But if I already have too many children to feed, is it wrong? I don't know. If my family is hungry and I see food in my neighbor's storehouse, why shouldn't I take it for myself if I'm stronger than my neighbor? The whole world is like that. These people who are burning farmhouses, raping women, stealing daughters--they're just taking whatever they want. If they're stronger than I am, who can say if it's wrong?"

"But it is wrong."

Imas put the cloth down. "And how. . ." he said glumly, "how would you know that?"

"Remember when I told you about the stars?" the man began slowly.

Imas nodded.

"In the beginning," he said, "someone spoke, and those stars simply began to exist."

"That. . ." Imas said, "is ridiculous. Who spoke?"

The stranger answered quietly. "In the beginning, God created the heavens and the earth."

"And who is God?"

Sighing, the man told the story of creation. Imas sat fascinated. It was all entirely new to him. He could not imagine a world where every tree, every star had a purpose, where human beings had a real purpose in life. When the stranger reached the part about the serpent and the fruit, Imas already knew the end of the story. Of course, they had disobeyed. Of course, they had wanted to change into petty gods who chose for themselves what was good and what wasn't. He found the description of Adam's expulsion from Eden heartbreaking and interrupted his friend.

"Does this place still exist?"

The stranger nodded. "I have been there. I have seen the cherubim. I have brought sacrifices to the altar there. It is very real."

"Tell me more about this story."

The stranger described Cain and Abel. He then recited the genealogies of Cain and Seth. This especially fascinated Imas. He knew vaguely of Cain's descendants and especially Tubal Cain. A few cities still carried their names, such as Mehujael and Nod. Imas had never, however, heard of Seth's line. Obviously Cain's offspring had made a significant impact on the world of humanity, but Seth's progeny had done nothing to distinguish their line.

He leaned forward. "Explain again about the promise to Eve. I don't understand it."

Carefully, the stranger recited the story. "'Then the Lord God asked the woman, 'How could you do such a thing?' 'The serpent tricked me,' she said. 'That's why I ate it.' So the Lord God said to the serpent, 'Because you have done this, you will be punished. You are singled out from all the domestic and wild animals of the whole earth to be cursed. You will grovel in the dust as long as you live, crawling along on your belly. From now on, you and the woman will be enemies, and your offspring and her offspring will be enemies. He will crush your head, and you will strike his heel.'"

"So the woman's offspring will someday crush the serpent's head. Who is her offspring?" Imas asked eagerly. "Was it Cain?"

The man shook his head. "No. The offspring comes through Seth's line."

"Seth. . ." The farmer considered this carefully. "Is this Seth still alive?"

"As far as I know, he is. . ." answered the stranger. "But he has passed the promise on to his son, and his son has passed the promise on to his son."

Imas was surprised at this succession of sons. "Do you mean that the promise passes from generation to generation? It wasn't Eve's son who will crush the serpent. Was it Seth's son?"

"Enosh passed the promise on to his son, who passed on to his own son."

Imas began counting through descendants. "Last time you said ten generations had passed since the creation. First Adam, then Seth, then Enosh."

"That's right," the stranger answered reluctantly. "Then Kenan, Mahalalel, Jared, Enoch, Methuselah and Lamech."

The farmer listened carefully. "And this is the line of promise. But that makes only nine. Who is the tenth?"

"The last son is Noah." He sighed. "He is the next son of the Promise."

"And the name of Noah's son?"

The stranger did not answer. For a long time, he simply stared into the lantern, wrestling with something that only he could understand. Even in the flickering light, Imas could see that a weight lay upon the stranger's heart, something so ponderous that he silently moaned under its bulk, far too heavy to bear on his own. Imas suspected the stranger wished to share this burden with him, but the man's courage failed and he looked hopeless, entirely abandoned. At last, he pushed the bench back from the table and rose. Walking wearily to the door, he grabbed his rucksack, opened the door, preparing to sleep in the barn with the animals.

Imas stared at the door in shock. It was obvious that the stranger was Noah. Imas carefully considered the story of creation and the story of Adam's sin. He had always wondered how a world could be so beautiful, yet deadly. What was it about existence that offered sweet fruits for the taking, and then extorted a slave's wages to gain their flavor? This Adam who ate the first wrong fruit had condemned his progeny to a life of weary labor. *Yes*, Imas thought to himself. *It all made sense.*

Now as well he understood the stranger who only once a year escaped from his wilderness exile to visit the sons of men. This was the descendant God had promised to Eve in the very beginning of the world. Imas wondered what it was that drove Noah into the wilderness.

This time, however, Imas would not let him run away. He rose from the table and followed the stranger into the yard outside the house. The full moon shone brightly on the man's face, who looked surprised to see the farmer approach him.

Imas grabbed the man's shoulders and whirled him around. "You are Noah, son of Lamech, descendant of Eve. You are the son of the Promise. The word 'Noah' means 'rest,' doesn't it? You are supposed to give us rest." He looked into this man's eyes, which were filling with tears. "That's why you hid yourself these three hundred years. That's why you ran away from civilization. It wasn't because you were afraid of humankind. You were afraid of the promise! For the past three centuries the whole world has been crumbling into a chaotic ruin, while you have closed yourself into your little lair. You play with your lifeless inventions, weaving soft fabrics and spinning rope. You sit in your forest den talking out loud to nobody but yourself, so that you need not speak to anyone who might actually listen and profit from what you have to say."

Imas' emotions overflowed, and he began shaking him furiously. "Don't you understand? This promise isn't for you, Noah, son of Eve. The promise is for my daughters and sons and wife. You have no right to hide this promise in your secret wilderness. You are our only hope."

Imas let go of him, and the man turned away. The farmer stared in the night gloom at the figure retreating into the barn. Soon Noah had disappeared in the dark opening. Imas sighed. Looking up at the sky, he stared in amazement. The millions of stars were somehow different now than they had been only hours before. They suddenly had a purpose. Someone had made them to mark off seasons and days and years. All of the animals, all of the trees and plants--they all had a purpose. He himself had a purpose. Life had a purpose. From the moment Imas had heard the story, he knew it was true. It explained so much of what was wrong–the depravity, the violence, the chaos. It explained why every action always carried consequences. There was a Creator who determined right from wrong, good from bad and judged that which was evil.

The story told him about his heritage, and it told him there was hope for his progeny. The children of Eve would not be forever lost, for God had given her a Promise. He knew instinctively that Noah indeed was the son of that Promise given to Eve. It was strange, he thought to himself as he returned to his house. Until the visitor first mentioned the Creator, he had always assumed that chance ruled the universe, cruel heartless chance. Now he understood creation's story-- everything came together into a coherent whole.

He entered the room, bolting the door behind him. As he lay down on the straw beside his wife, he discovered to his surprise he was crying. Perhaps it was his fear that Noah would abandon them again, returning to his wilderness, but he did not think so. It was, more likely, the shock of discovering that he, Imas, was not a meaningless wisp of smoke blown away by the morning breeze. He was formed in the Creator's image, a son of Adam, a son of Eve. He had meaning, as much as any king or ruler of a great army.

Imas closed his eyes, ready to sleep. "Creator," he said quietly. "If you hear me, do not allow this Noah to abandon us. Bring us rest through what he will do. Bring us rest, I ask." He fell into an untroubled sleep.

The next morning, Noah opened his eyes. Instantly, a sense of dread rose within him. The farmer knew both the story and that this stranger who had been visiting him was Noah himself.

For three long centuries, he had hidden from his own name. Now, having been discovered, he knew he could go back and hide again. A hundred times he had done it, those occasions when human needs had made demands upon him. Those times, however, when he had turned away, others suffered. If, so long ago, he had stayed in Mehujael, the city's food would not have rotted, their sewage would not have backed up, they could have found more water. He could have saved countless people from suffering and death, but by the time the Nephilim were throwing siege works against the city walls, Noah was already running away.

Dozens of times during his stay with Yenah, he could have improved life in the village--a bridge over the river, better roofs on their huts, a sewage system--but Noah had guarded his little world of security and kept silent. He felt so guilty about not helping the village people that he stopped going there altogether. Yenah assumed Noah was simply shy, but shyness had nothing to do with it. Noah didn't like feeling guilty. So the people had to work harder, live less pleasantly, and Noah was able to keep himself from obligations he didn't want to fulfill. Finally, he ran so far away that no duty could reach him, and he had managed to live without facing guilt for three hundred and fifty years.

Here on Imas' farm, however, he had discovered again what he had lost during these three centuries of solitude. He had lost humanity, with their different perspectives, human voices, children's laughter, ignorance, wisdom, fear, hope and surprisingly, need. The safety of his isolation prevented him from sharing the immensity of the starlit sky with another mortal. He had abandoned his soul to protect his spirit, and his spirit in the process had withered.

In the past eleven years, it had begun to come back to life, and he felt almost real again. Human contact, however, came with a deadly price--reality. That's why he had left so quickly after visiting the farm some eleven years ago. Etena that day had shown kindness, offering him food, and her act of mercy penetrated lies about humankind he had been creating and believing for three hundred years. That was what human contact could do to a hermit; it could invade his fantasy world. It forced him to make a choice; either he would fortify his private illusions and return to isolation, or allow truth to tear down his gingerly fabricated walls of peace.

He sat up and looked around himself. The stable was dirty, poorly constructed. The animals' stalls could be made much more efficient for milking cows. The roof was already rotting, because Imas used the wrong kinds of straw for his thatching. The smell of manure and urine permeated the air, because Imas did not understand how to set up a stable floor with slats, allowing manure to be pushed by animal hooves into an underground trough, to be washed away by water and urine.

Even though Imas had been farming here for over a decade, he only recently had come to understand that his farm rested over an underground river. Had he realized this from the start and grasped what it would mean for cultivation, he would have been able to yield twice the crops with half the work. The way he planted his seed, the way he weeded his rows of grain, the way he plowed his field, the way he harvested his crops; all of this was flawed. All of it could be improved. That was the problem with humans; they always came to you the way they really were, beset with defects and imperfections.

He stood up, and, bending over, grabbed his rucksack. Looking inside, he made sure that everything was there for him to return to the mountain, to disappear into his cave. It would take a while, but in time Noah was sure he could erase memories of the delight he had felt in working side by side with Imas and his wife and children. He would someday forget the wonder of asking questions and receiving an answer he could not at first comprehend, forcing him to ask the question in different ways until he finally understood the heart of another soul. At some point, he'd start conversing with himself again, talking to his animals and would actually convince himself such sound was as meaningful as looking into another person's eyes and understanding something of his heart within. In time, he'd become happy tinkering with inventions and animal husbandry.

He strode to the doorway, pulling the pack onto his back. Outside the children were already kneeling along rows of grain, pulling weeds. There were much better ways to deal with weeds than this, but of course, he had to leave that morning. Noah's world no longer was safe; Imas knew his secret.

He stood watching the children, knowing it was time for him to go. If he helped them here, then to Etena, who had shown him so much kindness, he owed a better flue for her chimney, a stronger latch for her door, windows that allowed light to enter. He owed all of them so much help, and this he did not want—to owe anyone anything ever.

Unless owing others was what made him a human being, and their need for him made them human as well. Maybe this was what it meant to be created in God's image; to choose to depend upon imperfect, flawed people when it would be easier to exist alone in peace. Perhaps being in God's image meant giving up one's insulated existence to merge with a dozen other fallible human souls, who sometimes lived in hurt and pain and other times wounded you deeply with your own hurt and pain. To reflect the Creator's image, perhaps, was to be able to choose to be hurt by others, and to choose not to inflict pain on them even when such a decision brought one great loss. If this were true, then to flee into the wilderness would be to deny his humanness, the precious image of God and ultimately, to deny the Creator Himself.

As bad as denying his own humanness, he thought to himself, *he would be denying Rehtak and Etena, Imas and Bor.* He stood staring at the children, chattering as they worked in the fields. He owed them the Promise as well; could he dare deny his obligation? He gazed for a long time, hardly thinking. Then, almost unconsciously, the pack came off his back, a knife slipped out of its sheath, and a sharpening stone began whetting the blade.

An hour later, a new stranger emerged from the barn. He was clean shaven, and his hair was cut close to his head. Imas was carrying hay to the sheep pen when he saw the man walking toward the farmhouse. The stranger was wearing Noah's tunic and skirt, but he no more looked like Noah than a tiger looked like a horse. The man looked up to see Imas staring at him and smiled awkwardly. Calling across the yard to the farmer, he said simply, "I would like to help you. What can I do?"

Chapter Eight

Year 1457

Noah worked with Imas for five years. For Imas, it was the greatest gift a farmer could receive, for Noah's understanding of everything, from cultivation to animal husbandry, was unexcelled. Etena, however, saw the most important work to be transforming Noah from an awkward hermit to a reasonably civilized man.

"Well," she would say when he protested another new rule for conduct, "we can't properly expect you to find a wife looking like that!"

They all knew from the start that when Noah felt Imas was ready, and Etena and the girls thought Noah was ready, he would leave. The wilderness was not the right home for the son of the Promise.

When the time came, he laid packs and bags on his horse and bid goodbye to Imas and his family. As he crossed the stream before the woods, he looked back to the house. The children were already in the fields, Imas was working the water wheel, and he imagined Etena back in the farmhouse managing the baby. He looked ahead and saw nothing but forest.

Imas had given him clear instructions. "First, you will come to the river. Turn north until you come to the ford. If you miss the ford, you will not be able to cross this river for seven days at least. Once you cross the ford, you will find a pathway. It is the last pathway of civilization, the first pathway you will encounter. It will bring you to the nearest village."

Imas' directions, however, were outdated. A fairly large village, perhaps forty or fifty wooden houses, sat on the near banks of the river ford. The forest had already been cleared for at least two thousand cubits from the waters edge, and crops were growing. As he passed by cultivated land, he saw two farmers working in the fields, and he hailed them. When they looked up, Noah decided to cross the fields to speak with them. They watched him with interest.

The farmers wore knee-length skirts with no tunic and wide brimmed headpieces not unlike a large disc or a shallow cone. Their skin color was especially light, something he had rarely seen in his travels. They looked as if they had been working all day. Their faces were not unfriendly, but were not entirely welcoming either.

"Where are you from?" the taller worker asked.

Noah pointed into the wilderness. "About a seven days journey east."

"Seven days!" he answered. "There's nothing out there but trees and wild animals." He looked at Noah as if perhaps the man might be exaggerating.

Noah smiled. "I can promise you, sir, nothing is out there but trees and wild animals. I've been living in a cave for over three hundred years and with a few exceptions, it's all wilderness." He had decided to tell the truth, but chose not to mention Imas and his family. It was hard to imagine bandits traveling seven days to pillage a solitary farm, but he didn't want to push his luck.

The second worker looked him over carefully and then asked, "What's your name and your father's name?"

"Noah, son of Lamech, son of Methuselah. We come from the line of Seth."

The farmer shook his head. "Never heard of him, but that's not surprising. I come from Cabel's line, and you probably haven't heard of him either. My name is Tam, and this is my brother Cram."

They greeted one another. Noah silently thanked God for Etena's lessons on greetings, which was not the last time he expressed that sentiment. Noah was deeply curious about the village below. "Your village, how long has it been here?"

Cram thought for a moment. "I'd say it's been here about four or five years. We wanted to get enough forest between us and other settlements to discourage any bands of brigands from showing up."

"Is the world out there really that bad?" Noah asked.

Tam shook his head. "If you think that's bad, you might as well turn around and go back to the wild. It's far worse than anything you could ever imagine, friend."

Noah looked from their vantage point to the village below, surrounded by fields. To the left of village, he saw long tall rows of some sort of plants held up by wooden latticework. This was new to him, and he wondered what they were.

When he asked the brothers, Tam said, "Oh, that's our treasure crop. We care for that more tenderly than our own lives. Grapes, my friend."

"Grapes? All of those rows for fruit?"

"Fruit?" Cram laughed. "Not on your life! That's for wine, the drink of forgetfulness."

Noah frowned. "The one time I drank wine, I was a madman."

"That's why we love it so. You'd better get used to it, because you'll be seeing a lot of men in this village drinking a lot of wine."

Changing the subject, Noah looked over the village. "Tell me, brothers Cram and Tam, do you think I might find someone in this village whom I could serve in exchange for food and a place to sleep? I'd be happy in a stable."

Cram laughed. "That all depends on what you can do, friend Noah."

"I am four hundred years old," he answered smiling. "I can do many, many things."

The brothers looked at each other for a moment, as if thinking the same thought. "Can you dig a well?" Cram asked, hopefully.

Once he had dug two wells for the brothers, he began digging wells for other villagers. In addition to helping them find good sources of water, he also constructed unusual systems for bringing it to the surface, and that made him a popular worker in the community. At first, he traded his skill and knowledge for lodging, but after a month he was permitted to live in an abandoned barn. From that point on, he bartered for tools, metals and food. When the demand for wells diminished, Noah assisted the two brothers in cultivating their land more productively. Word got out, and others began calling on him. Before long Noah became an indispensable member of the village.

It was, however, a harsh life. The vulgarity of speech often shocked Noah, not just in the words they used, but also in their coarseness. It was a small village, and everyone knew everyone else. They should have been able to respect each other, but these people were refugees from a brutal culture, and they bore the marks of the world they had fled. Even stranger were the relationships between men and women and sometimes between men and men. Only half of the men had brought wives. For a long time, Noah could not understand the others. There were perhaps a dozen single women in the town who seemed desperate to be taken as wives, but for some reason, inexplicable to Noah, these women were completely ignored. When the two brothers explained to Noah the relationships the men carried on, he was appalled. Yet to the brothers, this was simply a part of life.

Perhaps the most annoying part of village life was the drinking of wine. After a long day of hard labor, Noah would come back to his barn, which opened right onto the village street, preparing to sleep. For a while things would be quiet enough, but then the carousing would begin. Men, never women, would begin laughing boisterously, singing raucous songs and talking loudly. Sooner or later, someone would get into a brawl, which would often go on for an hour as Noah tried desperately to ignore the commotion and fall back to sleep.

Occasionally the disturbances would be right beside his barn, so that he took to securing his door with two heavy planks, to make sure he did not end up with unwanted nighttime visitors. The drunkenness was almost universal among men, except for Noah, who never wanted to put himself in such a state again.

The drinking was annoying, but most disturbing was the way men treated children and women. When a child would displease his or her parents, they would violently strike the child, scream at the child, or punish the child cruelly. The families had many offspring, sometimes fifteen or more. Boys were more highly valued than girls, something Noah had seen when he was a young man in his journey east. They received the best food and clothing, which was none too good and were allowed to sleep in the best places. The girls were handled as if they were farm animals, sometimes left in the wild to die, sometimes sold off as wives or servants or immeasurably worse. Some boys, especially in families with too many mouths to feed, ended up being sold to single men.

The lot of women was no better, as Noah observed regularly and experienced first-hand. About four months after Noah had arrived, he found himself teaching a farmer how to set his rows of grain to make better use of his new well. As they talked, in the corner of his eye Noah spied the man's wife carrying two large buckets of water into their shack. Suddenly movement caught his attention, and he turned his head to see the woman trip over a root and tumble onto the ground with a crash. The water spilled all over the ground and the buckets crumbled. Noah jumped up, as did the farmer. He angrily strode across the yard and, to Noah's horror, began screaming at the woman and kicking her mercilessly. Noah shouted, and the farmer, looking at him furiously, turned from his piteous wife, who was writhing on the ground.

Raging across the yard, with both hands the farmer grabbed Noah's tunic at his neck, pulling him right up to his face and screamed, "Don't ever tell me how to treat my own, stranger. I will do what I want. Do you understand?"

Noah, overcome with amazement and fear, at first didn't answer, but pushed himself away. Then he saw the woman again, lying on the ground. He would not let this go by. "This is wrong. How can you treat your own wife that way?"

Before he had finished his sentence, the farmer pulled back his right fist and smashed him in the face, then whirled around with his other fist and smashed again. Noah was so overwhelmed that he didn't know what to do. That, unfortunately didn't matter, for the farmer quickly hit him again and again, until Noah collapsed. As he hit the ground, everything went black.

At some point, he woke up, his face in the dirt. It was morning, and the sounds of village life suggested late morning. Noah sat up and discovered he was back in his own barn. Somehow, the farmer had transported him here and dumped him unceremoniously onto the floor. He got to his knees carefully and then stood, slowly walking to the door and opening it to bring light into the room and onto himself. He examined his clothing. The tunic and skirt were both covered in blood, his blood, he guessed, and he imagined his face and hair probably were covered as well. Running his hand over his head, he was relieved to find everything still there, until he came to the nose, that is. It was somehow wrong. The farmer had hit him hard enough to break the nose, but unfortunately, it had already healed in the wrong position.

He stepped out into the street. Village life was in full force, as it was every day. Looking down the road, he saw three children pulling a rope, dragging a rock toward a house on the left. All three were barely clothed, their bodies filthy and gaunt. Not far from him, a woman trudged up the way, toting a pole which balanced two buckets of water, one on each side. As she passed, he yearned to relieve her, somehow to help her, but knew it would do no good. She probably had a husband or master, and he knew his interference would only earn her a beating. That was the way of this village. At that moment, Noah realized he did not belong here, but back with Imas and Etena and the children, or better yet, back in his cave. This world, with its violence, drunkenness and unnatural cruelty, was not his.

Yet it indeed was his world, for all of these people—drunken men, laden women, gaunt children—all were created in God's image. It was hard to believe that the moral filth he had witnessed already did not deny their uniqueness among all creatures; nevertheless, these were God's highest creation. God had placed all things under their feet and had appointed them as rulers of His works. Noah shook his head. He could not connect the two realities, but knew without question both were true. Why did they live like animals when they bore such a weighty calling?

Part of the answer was desire. When humans serve desire, it becomes a cruel taskmaster, and they end up enslaved to lust. Another part of the answer, he suspected, was rebellion. They purposely chose to live this way, because they did not want God's lordship over their alleged freedom. How odd it was that people would rather be enslaved by sin, which drove them to beat children and wives, be lost in drunkenness and in the end, wallow in misery! Yet rebellion was always more attractive than submission to their true Lord.

There was another reason, however, that humankind lived this way. They did not know the story of the Creator, the truth about the first man and woman, the first sin and the Promise. Their lives were unconnected to truth. Because there was no story, they did not realize they were a part of a greater history. Thinking they simply existed in a mindless universe, they spent their days in meaningless pursuits, hopelessly searching for a reason to keep living, desperate to stave off death from hurling them into an empty void, clawing to discover for themselves a purpose when, apart from their Purposer, there could be none.

All of them should have known the chronicle of creation. For some reason, only Seth's descendants had preserved the true account.

Noah pondered what this might mean. The son of the Promise came through Seth's line. Only Seth's line entrusted the message to their descendants. Therefore, he wondered, had God appointed this task to the son of the Promise? He remembered how carefully Lamech, a son of the Promise had taught him the words, the same words Methuselah, a son of the Promise, had reinforced when Noah was a boy of ten. Adam had taught those words to Seth, who had taught Enosh, who then committed the story to Kenan, then from generation to generation until finally it had reached Noah.

He began walking through the center of town, making his way to the fields. He needed someone to remind him of why he should stay there in the village. He hoped the two brothers would at least take the time to give him a purpose for remaining. When he reached their field, he spotted them working on their water wheel, and he trudged across the land to the well.

"Good morning!" he called out, smiling. The brothers looked up, with a dark expression on both their faces. They continued bringing up water.

Noah decided to wait until they were finished, but had the distinct impression he was not particularly welcome there.

After a few minutes, he asked hopefully, "Can I help?" but neither brother responded. The task was mostly finished by the time he arrived, but they seemed to dawdle, as if they were trying to avoiding finishing and therefore being forced to talk to him.

Finally Noah decided to meet it head on. "Did you hear about what happened yesterday? Are you men angry with me?"

Tam looked up, his white face flushed. "You are treading in dangerous territory, friend, when you interfere between a man and his woman. That's no way for a newcomer to make himself wanted."

"But he was killing her," Noah answered resolutely. "If I didn't say anything, she would be dead."

Cram looked at Noah with anger in his eyes. "And if she died, what business would that be of yours, anyway? She isn't your woman; she's his!"

Noah foolishly tried to defend his action. "When a man kills someone, don't you punish him for it? Otherwise, he'll just do it again."

Cram approached Noah threateningly, his face red with fury. "If you don't like the way we do things, you're free to find a village you

do like. If you choose to   stay, friend, you'd better learn right now
there's a time for speaking and a time for staying quiet. When a man is
beating his woman or his children, that's no time for speaking."

"But. . ."

Cram grabbed him. "Can't you hear?" he shouted. "You have no
business telling us what kind of living we're supposed to be doing." He
roughly pushed him away.

"Cram, listen!"

Cram spat on Noah's feet. "I've said my piece. It's time for you to
go."

Noah stared at his two friends, who were gathering materials and
loading them into a cart. As far as they were concerned, Noah was no
longer there. He suspected that for them he no longer existed.

He returned to the village. When he reached the barn, his heart
fell. There, lying on the side of the road, sat all of his belongings.
Someone had boarded up the door to his shack, so that now he had no
home. Apparently, with all of their brawling and violent speech, the
people of the town still joined together when they faced a common
enemy. Noah now was that enemy.

He gathered together his possessions and stuffed them into his
rucksack. Standing up, he stared at the boarded building, trying to
formulate a plan. A thick dark sense of abandonment rose up within
his chest.   Things began to seem hopeless in his mind. As he slung
the pack over his shoulder, half the contents came streaming out. He
had forgotten to fasten it. *Idiot!* he thought to himself. *Failure!*

It now hurt for him to think, to act, even to bend down and gather
his scattered possessions. Collecting each item became a struggle,
because pain now stifled his willpower and his courage. Once everything was replaced in the pack, he drew the lashings tight and slowly
slipped his arms through the shoulder straps. Having no idea of where
to go, he turned to the easiest direction, downhill, toward the river. He
walked slowly.

The sense of isolation now choked every other sense. He became
aware that passers-by were keeping to the other side of the road; they
were shunning him. *Why?* he thought to himself. *I did what was
right! Why would God allow this to happen?* After a drawn-out walk,
he reached the water.

The river was shallow where Noah sat. He picked up a small stick and tossed it into the current, watching it float idly downstream. Tall trees– terebinth, oak and gopher–lined the river bank on the other side. Noah saw a pathway at the opposite shore. *The road to civilization. . .* he thought bitterly. There was nothing civilized in beating your women, starving your children, or spending your nights in drunkenness. That, however, was the current state of the human race, and he hated it.

Noah realized he had to go back to Imas' farm or the cave. He had failed here; he would fail in any society he encountered. It wasn't his fault, for they were simply too depraved to hear his message. He had tried to speak the truth and do what was right, but the entire village rose up against him. *I don't understand it, God*, he complained. *Here are all these people living entirely rebellious lives, but they do fine. I'm trying to obey, and you let me fail miserably.*

It was hopeless. He had to go home. The fog of despair now entirely blanketed his thinking and feeling. There was no point in staying; he was a failure, as always.

The only obstacle to returning to the farm was the village in front of him, which he would have to pass through in order to be on his way. He couldn't be sure if anyone there would actually physically attack him, but he expected with every step to feel their hateful stares. There was no way around it, however, and Noah forced himself to begin walking. He had a definite sense he was doing the right thing for once. A man could do only what he was able to do. Noah had never been able to carry out a difficult task for others. By nature, he was a loner. Furthermore, he had tried, even had stood up to the farmer when he was kicking his wife. Whatever sense of guilt echoed in the hidden chambers of his mind, the sense of loss, rejection, abandonment and failure gave him all the evidence he needed to persuade himself to return to where he belonged.

In many ways, walking through town reinforced his resolve. Even the women and children plainly avoided him, taking the other side of the road. Coming upon a group of several men whom in the past he had helped immeasurably by digging wells or advising on cultivation, he found himself afraid they might turn on him. Two of them actually spat upon him as he passed. The entire journey through the small village showed him it was impossible ever to bring positive good to the people here. They were too closed and now too bitter toward him.

At the upper edge of town, where the buildings ended, he came upon an emaciated boy, perhaps five years old, sitting beside the road and playing with a bucket of water. The child was filthy, and his clothes consisted of two or three rags barely sewn together. As Noah approached the child, the boy's song, seemingly nonsense words, filtered through Noah's cloud of self-pity.

> Boy for sale
> Just for you
> He will do
> What you want him to.

Noah knelt down next to the child. "That's a strange song. . ."

"I know. . ." the child said. "My father taught it to me and makes me sing it."

Looking around, Noah asked, "And where are your parents?"

The child pointed to a shack sitting in a distant field. "Do you want to buy me?"

"I'm sure," Noah answered, not sure at all, "that your parents would never let anyone buy you."

He shook his head. "Yes they would. Father set me here this morning and warned me that I can't move until one of the village men is willing to pay for me."

Noah gazed toward the shack in the distance. He couldn't see anyone working the field right now, but suspected no one there particularly cared what happened to the boy. "Why would your father sell you?"

"Father says I'm useless," the boy answered. "And he can't be feeding a useless mouth, so I have to leave. I am useless," the boy said quickly, forestalling Noah's protest. "My leg is twisted, and I don't walk well enough to help in the field."

Sure enough, the boy's right leg was terribly contorted. It had reset at an impossible angle, and he doubted if the boy would ever be able to walk quickly, let alone run. "When did this happen?" Noah asked.

"Two weeks ago. I broke Father's wineskin. He was really mad."

Two weeks ago, Noah thought. Two weeks ago, he might have been able to purchase the child, but he doubted it now. After last night, the chances that Noah could even approach the father without getting his own leg broken were slender. Even if the father were willing to trade, Noah had nothing to offer, beyond some tools. Furthermore, he would not be able to feed the boy, and he certainly could not bring the child back to the cave or even Imas' farm. The journey was too hazardous for a crippled child. Besides, if he were to ransom every neglected child here, he would end up with the whole village. This was not his mission.

He looked down at the child. "Boy, what's your name?"

"Darbe," the child answered, looking hopeful.

Noah looked to the point ahead where the road emptied into the great forest. Everything in his mind and heart urged him to return to the wilderness. He desperately wanted to escape from the debauchery of human civilization. He then looked at Darbe. This boy's immediate future was almost certainly going to destroy his spirit forever, and his distant future would end in despair. Noah doubted if hereafter he himself would encounter anything as harsh as what this child would face as soon as somebody bought him for. . . He could not finish the thought. He was not going to leave this boy the way he had left the dying baby so long ago. At least he would try to help him.

He smiled at Darbe. "I may meet you again, and I may not. We'll see. May God protect you!"

Noah cut across the fields away from the boy and his parents, heading toward the farm of the man who had broken his nose. He admitted to himself it was an insane idea and probably would result in further pain, but he was going there in any case. He couldn't quell the growing fear churning in his chest, but thinking of that poor boy being bought by an unmarried man inspired him not to turn back. Once he caught sight of the farmer, he forced the issue by calling out to him. The farmer looked up, and Noah almost smiled, imagining his shock. The man picked up a shovel and strode confidently to meet him. Noah braced himself.

"What are you doing here, outcast?" the farmer asked, moving closer as if to strike him.

Noah answered as positively as he could, in light of his quaking heart, "I didn't finish my work for you, sir."

The man laughed harshly. "What? You want me to break the rest of your face?"

"Sir, I haven't built your wheel for the well," Noah answered. "Once we get that finished, I'll take my leave." The farmer's expression was dangerous. He was obviously expecting a fight and could not grasp why Noah would come back with anything less than revenge on his mind. He watched Noah with incredulous suspicion.

Noah casually tried to disarm his misgivings. "I just don't like the thought of you having to work so hard to water your crops and your flocks and herds, when the water wheel would make it go so quickly. I wouldn't want to do it without the wheel, and so I figured the best thing would be to help you finish it."

"Are you crazy?" the farmer asked.

"Sir, what's bigger? Your well, or my nose?"

The question caught the farmer off guard, and he began to laugh uproariously. Slapping Noah on the back, he reached out his hand and grabbed Noah's shoulder. It took all of Noah's willpower not to flinch back in self protection, but he found himself being escorted to the well and put to work. All that week, the two men labored to set up irrigation and watering troughs. Noah received back his home and amazingly, earned a new respect among the villagers.

As far as the boy went, Noah was allowed to purchase him, by digging a well for his father. The boy became Noah's constant companion and helper.

After another two months, Noah every evening picked a spot in the center square of the village, which was nothing more than a place where the only two roads intersected. He sat down on a basket and began telling stories. At first, only children listened, but after several weeks, the whole village ended up giving ear.

In the days, Noah and Darbe would labor long in the field, but at night Noah related the stories his father had spoken when he was just a child. He described the garden of Eden in great detail, explaining about the perfect world which sin destroyed. Noah took his time with the story, added what his grandfather Methuselah had recited to him, building up suspense. When he came to the story of the fruit of the knowledge of good and evil, he tried to end the story at Eve's point of decision, but the crowd demanded he continue. The story was so enthralling, that he recounted it for another hour before he left to go to bed. That sleep was the first Noah could recall to be free from the sounds of drunken brawling.

On another night, his description of Cain's murder of Abel was especially poignant, for several men there had killed someone out of anger, perhaps a child, a woman, or even another man. That night, as every night, Noah brought his story back to the Promise God had given Eve. God had warned the foe of all humans, the serpent: "From now on, you and the woman will be enemies, and your off-spring and her offspring will be enemies. He will crush your head, and you will strike his heel." Someday a descendant of Eve would crush the serpent's head. Someday, they would be rescued from their sin and rebellion against God. The Son of the Promise would deliver them.

Telling the entire story took months, partially because every night, the men began asking questions. Who was this God? How did He create all things? Why did he punish Adam and Eve? How can it be fair that we suffer for sins committed by our ancestors? The questions Noah could answer, he did as clearly as possible. Some questions, he simply recited the story that spoke to it and admitted that he did not know any more than that.

Even though not everyone in the village believed the story, they all came every night, because life there on the wilderness's edge was harsh, and anything that might soften the severity of their lives was more than welcome. Certainly a part of their response was simply the pleasurable experience of hearing a captivating story.

Just a few, however, listened and believed the story. Noah could tell by the questions they asked in the evenings. These people began recognizing their own rebellion against the Creator. Noah found occasionally, he would spend half of his day working in the fields for a farmer, and the other half explaining to the farmer the meaning of the story.

After several months, when he had nearly reached the end of the story, Noah built an altar between the village and the great forest and began offering sacrifices for sin. Since he himself owned no cattle or sheep, he presented only grain sacrifices. Three others, however, took the costly step of bringing whole burnt offerings to the altar. A few women also brought grain to present, but Noah suspected many more women did not come for fear their husbands would beat them.

After the months of storytelling were completed, Noah began teaching every evening. At this point, almost all of his listeners stopped coming. To the few who continued, he showed what it meant to be created in God's image and what it meant to love God and others. In three families, both husband and wife embraced Noah's message and changed how they walked before God. Parents were kinder to their children, and husbands stopped beating their wives. The majority of villagers, however, continued in their old ways. The farmer who broke Noah's nose himself did not believe the story, although he enjoyed it immensely. Amazingly, however, he allowed his wife to come in the evenings with two of her older daughters. If Noah had not presented the story first, he knew this never would have happened.

One evening, Darbe's parents, who had attended every story since the first week, waited after Noah's teaching time to speak with him. The father looked nervous. He had been shy about asking questions, and Noah had wondered at times if perhaps his guilt kept him silent. Nevertheless, his was one of only three families that had continued to come, which encouraged Noah that the man was serious.

After hemming and hawing through an awkward conversion, he suddenly blurted out. "My wife and I have been talking. I sinned against the Creator in beating the boy. I can't undo what I've done to him, but I want to make the best of it for him now. Will you sell him back to me?"

Left to himself, Noah would have simply given the boy back for free, but the man would not allow it. The man argued that Noah had worked hard for him in exchange for the boy, and the man owed him for his labor. As Noah considered the man's insistence, he decided to accept his help as the first step toward leaving the village for the larger world. It was time to move on. He could not even guess where he should go, but he knew without a doubt that God had given him a mission. He was the son of the Promise, and it was his duty to hand the story on to the next generation.

This village's response had amazed him; some people had actually turned from rebellious lifestyles and were living according to God's ways. Others must also have the opportunity to change. In order for this to happen, however, Noah needed food and clothing for his journey. Thus, in exchange for the boy, the farmer supplied Noah with everything he required to travel to the next village.

Not long after, early in the morning, a group of seven people stood on the bank of the river. Noah, the son of the Promise, was wading across the ford as he set out on his mission. Before him waited a century of villages, farmhouses and cities, where Noah would preach God's righteousness as revealed in the Story of the Promise. He was going to face threats, beatings, slanders and expulsions during the days ahead. A tiny number would hear the story and walk in fear before God, but most would ridicule it as insulting or ridiculous. Over the decades, he would come to be known as the preacher of righteousness among those who feared the Creator. The rest would see him as a fool.

As he waded through the water, of course, Noah could guess none of this. He understood only that a village awaited him some seven days journey away. He reached the far shore and waved to his friends on the bank. Noah then turned toward the pathway into the forest and disappeared into the shadows. A century of preaching had begun.

Chapter Nine

Year 1555

When he reached the top of the hill and saw the river far beyond, he smiled. This spot had written itself into his memory, though almost five hundred years had passed since he stood here last. In this place Noah and Lamech had first sighted the river, threading its path across the fabric of the land. The excitement that surged in his heart as a boy continued to echo, as he still imagined the great waterfall, the icy waters rushing through the Garden of Eden, passing through the hedge into the wilderness. Along its shores, Adam and Eve had lived most of their lives. The river flowed from Eden into his country, the country of Adam and Eve.

From the overlook all the way to the river, green grasses rolled over the gentle rise and fall of the landscape. Occasional clumps of shrubs dotted the wide open grasslands, with islands of boulders scattered randomly amidst the sea of grass. Massive forests lined either side of the pasture lands all the way down to the river. To the left, along the hills leading up to the trees, grazed several large flocks of sheep. The sky sat over the scene with blues as deep and rich as the greens below, and flocks of clouds grazed peacefully in the pastures of the heavens.

Below, Noah could barely make out a tiny village of ten or twelve dwellings huddling at the river's shore, but he knew the buildings well. He smiled again. As much as he loved the hill and its view, he decided it was time to see his family, and he began moving. As he walked, he kept his eyes on the hills, seeing perhaps as many as ten figures busy at work among the flocks. He wondered if they were shearing the sheep and decided to head for the pastures first. A long time passed before Noah was close enough to figure out for sure that the people were indeed fleecing the sheep, but he still could not see anyone distinctly. Someone there, however, pointed to him, and the others all stopped their work to gaze.

One man put down a sheep and began weaving through the animals as if he were coming toward Noah. Noah increased his pace. Once the man broke free of the flock, he began walking rapidly, but suddenly he shouted something to the others and broke into a run. At this, several figures left their work to follow, but the first man stayed far ahead. With a rush of excitement, Noah recognized the man as Lamech, and he began racing toward his father.

Finally they burst into each other's arms, the father kissing his son and openly weeping. It wasn't until this moment that Noah was sure he was home. Their reunion was soon interrupted by a half dozen more—Methuselah and five strangers, who turned out to be Noah's siblings. The family poured out a stream of questions and comments, but they were too excited to give Noah any chance of saying more than a few words in reply to each.

After the evening meal, they sat beneath the sky and talked, late into the night. Noah recounted a broad outline of his life thus far. His story was remarkable in its breadth and meaning. Although everyone had questions and many times tried to interrupt the narrative, Methuselah quelled all inquiries, commanding them to wait until later to have their curiosity satisfied. This story belonged to Noah, and Methuselah ordained that Noah should tell the story as he saw fit.

When Noah's story finally reached the borders of the present time, he stopped speaking. The circle was quiet. By telling the chronicle as a single whole, the weight of its message bore especially heavily upon the entire group, affecting different people in varying ways. For Noah, the story became for him an enormous portrait of God's mercy at work in his life. His father Lamech, found himself amazed his son was even alive to tell the tale. In others, however, a suspicion was growing that God was preparing Noah for something even greater than the work he had already done. For a long time, no one spoke, staring into the dying embers of the fire before them. Finally Methuselah cleared his throat.

He glanced around the circle. "I will allow only one question, since we all need our rest to finish fleecing our flocks." He turned to Noah. "As you have told us about your preaching over the past one hundred years, it sounds as if in the course of time fewer and fewer have responded to the Story of the Promise. Is this true?"

"That's the strangest part of all," Noah answered, shaking his head. "In the past fifty years, almost no one has turned to follow the Creator God, and I'm positive the world is much worse now than when I first started preaching righteousness. It doesn't make any sense to me, because the message hasn't changed at all, and I understand it so much more clearly now. Even so, I see violence and immorality becoming more visible and less condemned. If when I first set out, I had seen the kind of decay that's going on now even in isolated villages, I probably would have run as fast as I could back to the safety of Imas' farm. The decay hasn't happened because of the Nephilim either, because some places I've visited have never even seen a Nephilim warrior." He turned to Methuselah. "Grandfather, I don't know what it means."

Methuselah nodded. "Nineteen years ago, Yahweh God spoke to me in a dream. 'My Spirit shall not wrestle with humanity forever, because he also is flesh; therefore his days shall be one hundred and twenty years.' At the time, I assumed that each man's lifespan was about to shorten to one hundred and twenty, which saddened me greatly. After hearing your story, Noah, I wonder if Yahweh has been using your message to prepare the earth for something much more terrible than a shortened life."

"What could be more terrible than that?" Lamech asked, amazed. "I can't imagine a life lasting only one hundred and twenty years! At two hundred years I still had dozens of skills just waiting to be developed."

Methuselah rose from the ground. "I cannot answer your question, my son. Perhaps we may not live long enough to know what God has planned. I do know this. Shortly before Noah was born, Seth and Enoch departed this life. Since Noah left, Enosh, Kenan, Mahalaleel and Jared are gone. The sons of the promise diminish down to the three men standing here. Yahweh said this: 'My Spirit shall not wrestle with humanity forever, because he also is flesh; therefore his days shall be one hundred and twenty years.' Could it be that something remarkable is about to happen, the end of all flesh? Could it be that God will judge humankind for our horrendous sins against him?"

He shook his head. "Of course, I may be wrong. In the meantime," he added, turning to Noah, who had stood along with the rest of the families, "I believe that Lamech has a task to perform for his son, Noah."

Noah looked surprised. "What would that be, Grandfather?"

"Lamech," he answered playfully, "must find my grandson a wife."

Noah stayed with his family for three months. During that time, his understanding of God's ways deepened, and he began formulating answers to difficult questions he had encountered in preaching. As in his youth, he also helped his father and grandfather create better ways to carry out a multitude of tasks. Most of the time, when they would ask where he gained this skill or learned that invention, he would respond, "In the cave." After several weeks of hearing the same reply, Methuselah exclaimed; "Grandson, what did you do for three hundred years in that cave?"

"All I did," he said, "was study plants, animals and inventions. Any time I encountered an inconvenience, I decided to create a better way of doing things. I wandered days on end studying every creature I could observe: what they ate, when they slept, how they lived. Many of them I brought back with me, but that didn't always work well, because a lot of animals have a difficult time surviving in a pen or cave, and with plants, I learned how to improve them, make them stronger and help them grow larger fruits or more seeds."

Methuselah looked thoughtful. "That suggests to me," he said quietly, "that your time in the cave may not have been entirely lost."

"Over the past one hundred years," Noah said, "I have often used my knowledge to support myself in the villages or cities where I preached."

One afternoon, Lamech came to his son, who was finishing a machine for processing grain. "Son, could you stop your work for a while and come with me down to the river?"

The two followed the pathway to the banks of the great river. Noah sat down, leaning against a tree root that arched over the bank into the water below. For a long time he simply watched the current pass by on its way from Eden to the outer world. Lamech sat across from him, watching his son, deep in thought.

"Noah, I have a wife for you."

A bemused look came over his son's face. "Oh really, Father? and where are you hiding her, because she surely isn't anywhere near here!"

Lamech looked out over the river. "Have you heard of the city called Yakheed?"

"Who hasn't?" Noah said. "It's the only city to beat the Nephilim. That was a long time ago, I know, but the Nephilim have never tried to attack them again. I would guess it's probably the most prosperous city outside of Tubal Cain."

Lamech nodded. "My brother has lived in Yakheed for centuries. He has a great-granddaughter for you to marry."

Noah looked into his father's eyes. "I don't understand, Father. How could he have a granddaughter for me to marry? I've been separated from the family for almost five hundred years!"

"All I know is this," Lamech said. "When she was born, her father pledged her to wed the son of the Promise, and she has kept herself faithful to this pledge for thirty years. My brother's great grandson told me of this last year when he visited."

Noah thought about this for a long time. "And she is living in the city of Yakheed?" He looked up toward the gathering of houses on the hill. A couple of figures, his siblings, he imagined, were carrying a load into a barn. Noah sighed. "I was hoping I could stay here for the rest of my life."

"That's what I want for you, Noah," Lamech said quietly. "Your arrival has been the most wonderful gift I've gotten since your Aunt Qanath was alive and well." He picked up a twig and flicked into the water, watching it float down river. "Your grandfather, however, has been urging me to send you away. He believes you must marry soon and bear sons. According to Grandfather, only when you have begotten the next son of the Promise will your final mission become clear."

Noah carefully considered his grandfather's convictions for some time before answering. Finally he spoke. "This woman, do you know her name?"

Lamech thought for a moment. "Her cousin called her Emah, daughter of Wehtam."

"Emah means 'mother," Noah said thoughtfully. "Her parents named her 'mother' from the day she was born. You named me 'rest' at my birth. I still don't understand my name. I haven't given anyone rest, and her name is even more mysterious. Mother of what?"

Lamech answered, a bemused look on his face. "Mother of the son of the Promise?"

"I suppose so," Noah said, but his expression suggested the answer didn't quite fit. There had been nine mothers of the sons of promise, but not one of them was set apart from birth. He stood up and held out his hand to his father to pull him up. "Let's go back to the village. It sounds as if I am supposed to find a bride. It's time to prepare for a long journey."

The first time one travels to the city of Yakheed, the visitor experiences a sense of awe usually reserved for natural wonders. The walls loom above the plain and when the sun reflects upon the brilliant white ramparts, the observer finds himself almost blinded in its brightness. Since for close to a day's journey, the countryside is flat, one can first descry the blaze of the city walls from a great distance, looking like a star shining in a noonday sky. It's difficult to lose one's bearings when the city of Yakheed is the goal; it dominates the landscape. The closer one comes to the alabaster bulwarks, the more their massiveness overwhelms the senses, so that those who enter through the monolithic northern gate sometimes comment that they feel as if they have been swallowed up by the sun.

All of these sensations simply heightened Noah's awareness that his life was about to change in drastic ways. He was to marry, forever committing himself to one woman, to raising children and to carrying out family responsibilities. He had no inkling of what that one woman was like: was she harsh and demanding, or was she compassionate and patient? For him, the dread he sensed at the sight of the city was as much related to his uncertainties as to the city's greatness. Not only was he to marry, but apparently a great mission awaited him in the city.

Methuselah could not say what that mission might entail, but Noah could guess; he probably would preach the story of the Promise to the citizens of Yakheed, which almost certainly would mean persecution. As difficult as it had been in the past to undergo ill-treatment, the situation was about to change dramatically. He must worry not only about himself, but especially about his wife and future children.

He passed through the gate into a wide plaza. This was not the first city Noah had known, having lived in several others over his lifetime. The city of Yakheed, however, was unlike anything Noah had experienced. Immediately he recognized a flavor of simplicity and strength in the square before him. There was nothing fancy: neither gold, nor ornate grillwork, nor statues gracing the plaza.

Noah tried to guess why the buildings were so simple. *Probably,* he thought, *the elders want to keep the Nephilim happy. The city is safe from attack, but knows its humble place.* Even with this thought, however, he thought he could detect a deeper theme running through the buildings. This was a city not of the mighty and rich, but of the humble and simple.

Noah immediately began inquiring after Wehtam, who turned out to be a respected citizen of the city, having fought in the Nephilim's siege several centuries earlier. Wehtam currently was a smith and if Noah were to find him, he must travel through the streets to the eastern wall, the sector for smithies. He found it interesting that he, his grandfather and his cousin Wehtam all enjoyed working metal. *It must be,* he theorized, *in their blood.*

The journey to the smiths' quarter was fascinating. As he walked, he noted the variety of stones that seemed to characterize this city. Stone paved the streets and supported every building. Some were dark, others light, some even with pink or gray running like evening clouds set in a white sky. Like the northern gate plaza, the houses and shops refrained from intricate patterns so typical of other cities. Noah did not find the architecture gloomy by any means, and vendors and hawkers filled the streets with colorful carts and booths to keep things lively. Nevertheless, Noah, the builder, sensed a purposeful attempt to set the jewel of the city in straightforward stone, as if to reinforce to anyone who passed this way that people here were simple, solemn and purposeful.

Of course, unlike wilderness towns, a city tended to change very little. Generally, the same elders ruled for centuries, and they liked things to run as things always had been run. This city in particular had a reputation for firm rulership, beginning with elder Yakheed, not exactly the founder, but without a doubt the most important man in the city.

Noah had heard good things about the moral fabric of the town. No infants were left on hillsides to die. Men who beat their wives suffered severe punishment. Cheating was punished by permanent exile, and the fabric trade in particular was carefully regulated. Furthermore, when Noah entered the city gates, a polite but watchful guard interrogated him as to his destination, his plans, and informed him that no one could move to Yakheed without permission from the elders.

Noah stopped a merchant, asking politely for Wehtam's shop. The man pointed down the street to a shop with a silver painted sign. Noah thanked the man and began walking slowly. He felt his heart beating. What would she be like? What would her father say? He could hardly imagine what might happen in the next hour.

There it was, the name Wehtam on a silver sign. Taking a deep breath, Noah, son of Lamech entered the smithy. A woman, busy sewing a garment, looked up and smiled. She was light skinned, with light brown hair cut somewhat close to her head, as was often the custom for married women. Her nose, unlike his, jutted out mildly from her face, but was not large. Her strong jaw suggested to Noah a confident character. Emah? Perhaps, but she seemed too old and was probably married.

"I am seeking... Wehtam...," he stammered. "The smith. . . "

Noah noticed her curiously looking at him. "Wehtam is out back in the courtyard." Noah glanced behind her to see a gray curtain, presumably leading to the courtyard. "May I tell him who wishes to speak with him?"

"Noah. Tell Wehtam that Methuselah has sent Noah, son of Lamech to meet his daughter Emah."

Shock set her face. Her eyes widened, but she did not reply. Nodding, she nervously folded her apparel and carried it with her through a doorway in the back.

The moment she left, Noah inwardly moaned. *Why did I tell her everything in one sentence?* he thought to himself. These words should have been for the father, not the wife. He was sure now it was all a mistake and would have run out the door if it weren't for the promise he had made to his father and grandfather. He stood, fidgeting with his tool belt, brushing back his hair. His ears strained to make out the muffled voices, but he could not be sure of the words. There was a commotion, presumably in the courtyard. He heard a woman's excited squeal and footsteps. The curtains flew open and a younger woman, also light skinned, burst into the room, much like the other, except with long hair ending in a riot of curls spilling over her shoulders. Her face was bright, with eyes that couldn't decide between brown and green and gray, full of light. She was not tall, probably to Noah's shoulders, but seemed fit and strong. She was wearing a leather apron, pocked with burn marks. *So*, he thought, *she also is a smith*.

Suddenly, she blushed bright red, fled the room, swishing the curtains shut. More mumbling went on. Again, Noah strained his ears to figure out what people were saying, all talking at once, but heard crying, a sharp command from a man– presumably the father, Wehtam–and almost frantic pleading. *If only I had waited to speak to the father*, he reminded himself, *none of this would be happening now*. The tension in the house was so palatable, Noah felt in greater danger than even when he had been dragged before the city council as a trouble maker. Time seemed to stop as he waited for the calamity in the courtyard to calm down and for someone to summon him to meet Wehtam.

Finally, the curtain parted again, and a man entered the shop. Noah gasped, for the man looked almost exactly like his grandfather Methuselah. He was muscular and tall, with light brown hair and deep chestnut skin. His own leather apron, also marked with burns, half covered a brawny bare chest and ran down over his skirt to the knees. Noah was amazed at this man's sinewy arms, more powerful even than Methuselah's.

He threw his arms around Noah, engulfing him in a doughty embrace. "Cousin! You look just like my uncle Lamech! Amazing!"

"And you, cousin," Noah said, catching his breath, "look more like our grandfather Methuselah than Methuselah does!"

Wehtam grabbed Noah's arm and dragged him through the curtain into a courtyard, designed for a smith's trade, with bellows, anvil, tools and water. He immediately saw the woman from the shop, her arm around the one who had burst through the curtain. The mother was now wiping tears from the girl's eyes. The girl looked up at Noah and began crying again, the mother saying only "Shhhh. . ." over and over. The father, his arm around Noah's shoulder was beaming with excitement.

Noah stood dumbfounded. He had stood before city elders, mobs and wild animals and always ended up knowing what to say and do. Now he stood before a woman who cried every time she beheld him, and he helplessly stared as if frozen. The father, Wehtam, actually laughed.

"Well, Noah, son of the Promise, meet your lovely bride."

The girl looked up at her father, and her weeping overflowed into loud sobs. The mother herself began crying, and Noah heard a sniffle even from Wehtam, who said tearfully, "Well now, don't worry about her crying. That's what she does when she is exceedingly happy, which is exactly how she feels right now. Isn't that right, Emah?"

The girl looked up and nodded and then burst into heightened wailing.

Wehtam smiled. "There's one thing you need to do, cousin, and that's to appear before the city elders. You can't live in this city without their approval. Otherwise, we'd have a million people stacked on top of each other. And, he said confidently, "you can't marry one of the city's daughters without them saying it's alright. Tomorrow is the fourth day of the week, so, we'll just wander over there in the morning and say hello to them, don't you think?"

Since this information set the tears to new levels, Wehtam tugged on Noah's arm. "Come on, cousin. Let's take a walk, so you can tell me about yourself in the peace and quiet of the market place away from all of this wailing. Then I'll bring you back here to sleep in serenity on the covered porch in the courtyard."

The next morning, Wehtam led Noah and Emah, who was still silent, through the busy streets to the meeting hall for the council of elders. The building was indeed impressive, with at least thirty tall vertical beams framing a marble white portico. Although still not embellished with ornate artwork, the council hall surpassed any structure Noah had encountered yet in the city. This was also the only building that one entered by climbing a series of perhaps seventy steps.

Once they entered, Noah gasped at the way light illuminated the enormous room. He looked up to see a stunning dome, obviously ancient, with windows cleverly built into its structure, allowing light without admitting the sun's most burning rays. Before him was a half-circular meeting hall, with the council members seated far below, accessible by walking down about eighty levels of steps which seated citizens for large gatherings. Noah was impressed not only by the grandeur of the building, but also by the way sound carried. As they entered, a small delegation was receiving a lecture from a city elder far below, yet as Noah, Wehtam and Emah descended, they could clearly hear every word uttered. They reached the main level and a steward motioned for them to sit, which they did.

Although five men sat on the council that morning, Noah immediately picked out the real leader, whom Wehtam identified as Yakheed. Even seated the man impressed him with his physical strength and confident appearance. His skin was light, and his hair was thick and curly. Noah was surprised to see him wearing a leather tunic, which, although free from burns and scratches, was nonetheless much more practical than the usual flowing robes of leaders. His ankle length skirt was a simple gray, with no design or emblem.

What surprised Noah most was the fact that the man obviously still worked hard at some craft or trade. Yakheed's hands–strong like the roots of an oak tree–were calloused and stained from some kind of dye, as if he either worked with leather or cloth. His face revealed lively passion. Noah guessed that here was a man who loved life and poured himself into whatever task he met.

It was now their turn, and Wehtam motioned for Noah and Emah to approach the council table. They bowed, and the council members returned a nod of the heads.

The man to Yakheed's left, apparently a secretary, asked, "What is the nature of your business?"

Wehtam cleared his throat. "I, Wehtam, announce a joyous event for our family. This cousin of mine comes from a distant land to take my daughter's hand in marriage. He has requested to live in our fair city and to work here. This has been promised in our family since my daughter's birth thirty years ago."

The secretary shook his head. "We simply have no room for another family, Wehtam. We honor your service to our city and your courage, but we have turned away at least thirty requests this year."

Wehtam nodded. "It would break my heart, but I am willing for my daughter to accompany my cousin to make a home in another place. May they have permission for this?"

The secretary spoke again. "Your daughter is a lovely young woman. We have many men who would delight in marrying such a fine person. Why can't you marry her to one of our own?"

"It is a long story—" Wehtam began.

Yakheed cut him short. "She seems to be awfully young to marry a man who is obviously well on in life. Sir, how old are you?"

Noah, surprised, thought for a moment. "Four hundred and ninety nine years, elder."

The elder stopped in surprise. "What month were you born?"

"The fourth moon, sir, on the fifteenth day."

Yakheed shook his head. "Amazing. . . The very day I myself was born." He thought for a moment. "And why should you marry this particular woman?"

"Well," Noah began cautiously, "I have been gone from my family for most of my life until eight months ago. My cousin here devoted his daughter to marrying me when she was born, and my grandfather requested that I come here to make her my bride."

From Yakheed's face, Noah could tell he found this story dubious. The elder leaned over, "And who, sir, is your father?"

"Lamech, son of Methuselah, son of Seth," Noah answered slowly.

"And your mother?"

Noah said, "Katina, but she died at my birth. A band of Nephilim attacked my father's farm."

A grim smile came over Yakheed's face. "Sir, I have lived a long time, but never once have I met a man whose story mirrors my own so much." He turned to the other members of the council. "I am almost tempted to invite this. . ." He looked up to Wehtam. "Did you mention his name, citizen? I don't seem to remember it."

Wehtam bowed. "Noah, sir."

A look of curiosity came over the great elder's face. "Noah? The defender of Mehujael?"

Wehtam looked completely at a loss. Yakheed turned to his cousin. "Well, are you the same Noah?"

"I am," he answered quietly.

Shaking his head, Yakheed turned again to his fellow council members. "Gentlemen, standing before us is the man who saved the city of Prathar from the great siege of the Nephilim."

He stood and bowed. "It is the greatest honor to welcome you, Noah, son of Lamech, to our city. It was your design for the inner and outer walls that stopped the ladders of the enemy. We used your plans for building grain storage, improving water supply, even for the means of dismantling stone buildings to build the outer wall. Without a doubt, unless we had discovered your technique for building the outer wall, we would never have survived the Nephilim."

Noah stood transfixed. He had heard, of course, of the city's victory over the Nephilim and had yesterday passed through the city's massive walls. He would never have imagined, however, that his great tragedy in Mehujael might have somehow enabled the city of Prathar to repel the Nephilim. Yet perhaps this might be God's way of opening an opportunity for preaching righteousness to the people of this city.

As Noah, Wehtam and Emah stood silently, the city elders conferred in whispers. Several times, Yakheed looked at Noah, shook his head and exclaimed, "I can't believe it." In a few minutes, they had clearly come to a unanimous decision.

"Because of your illustrious contribution, Sir," the council secretary began, "we would like to confer upon you the status of favored citizen of the city of Yakheed." He smiled. "This entitles you to live in the borders of our city free from taxation and exempt from ordinary civic obligations. It so happens that one of our oldest families has only recently moved from our city to the country, leaving a fine house available to occupy. We had awarded this house to elder Camut here, but he now refuses it, desiring instead to give it to Noah and his bride."

At this point, an ancient man rose and bowed. "I will never forget the sight of watching the Nephilim armies march away from our city so long ago. At the time, I thanked Yakheed many times for his brilliance in designing and constructing our impregnable walls. Every time, however, our elder would remind me; 'Thank the man Noah for the design; thank me for the dead rats.'"

Noah returned his bow. He then bowed to the council. "I am overwhelmed by your remarkable generosity, elders. I pray I will serve you in this city until my final days."

Yakheed chuckled. "And to think, that we were born on the very same day and that both of our mothers died in childbirth. Who could have imagined it? Citizen Noah, you and I must become friends, I think."

That night, Wehtam and his wife brought Emah, clothed in a sky blue wedding dress which flowed almost to the floor. Her mother had woven tiny white flowers into her hair, flowers which she also braided as a necklace. Wehtam led his daughter to Noah, who knelt as she knelt beside him. The father laid his hands on their heads and committed their marriage to Yahweh, the Creator of all things. His wife, tears streaming down her face, kissed her daughter, tears also streaming down her face.

Wehtam bent over to whisper in his wife's ear, who then embraced her daughter. Wehtam waited a moment, extricated his wife from Emah, then tenderly led her–actually dragged her–out of the room. As Wehtam closed the door, the last thing Noah saw was the mother peering though the opening with tears running down her face.

They sat on two small benches, facing each other, Emah drying her eyes, Noah absentmindedly running his hands over a fold in his skirt. Almost immediately after the door closed, he spoke.

"Are you alright?"

She looked at him, surprised. "Alright? What do you mean?"

He immediately regretted his choice of words. "I mean. . . the weeping."

"Weeping?" she asked, puzzled.

He nodded. "You've been weeping. . ."

She looked at him as if he were feebleminded. "When?"

"Since you looked through the curtain yesterday and saw me, until a moment ago."

Smiling, she straightened her hair and smoothed her dress. "Oh, that wasn't weeping. . . Those were tears."

"Tears."

She folded her hands on her lap and leaned forward. "Tears." She stared at him as if lecturing a small child. "When people are exceedingly happy, tears sometimes form in their eyes. We call this experience 'tears of joy.'"

"So. . ." Noah said cautiously, "when you first saw me you weren't weeping because I am unbearably ugly."

She examined him, starting with his hair and ending with his nervous hands, still playing with the fold in his clothing. "No," she said solemnly "you are not unbearable at all."

"Old?"

A faint smile formed at the corner of her mouth. "You seem to have a couple of hundred good years left in you."

He considered this, relief thawing the tenseness of his features. "Why then did you have so many 'tears' when you first saw me?"

"I have always believed," she answered slowly, "that I could marry only the son of the Promise. I am thirty years old, Noah, son of Lamech and have watched all of my sisters and dearest friends wed and give birth to babes. I never coveted their husbands, only their completeness. Last year my cousin traveled to the gates of Eden to discover from Methuselah who this son of the Promise might be, for he wished my hand in marriage. When he returned to tell me you had been lost for four centuries, I gave up almost all hope."

Stirred by her story, he asked, "Why didn't you give up and marry your cousin?"

"Because of my name," she answered. "Because of my name."

He nodded. "I understand what you mean. My name means 'rest.' When I was born, after my mother died, God spoke to my father that I would bring rest to those who struggled from the curse."

"When I was born, God told my father that I will be mother to all humankind."

Noah reached over and gently took her hand. "Do you understand the meaning of your name?"

"No, but I believe I soon will. . . do you?"

He shook his head. "I believe, as you do, that we will understand the meaning very soon." He squeeze Emah's hand. "We are somehow meant for each other, my bride. Together God has something mysterious for us to do."

"Then together we shall be," she said, taking his other hand.

Noah sat silent for a long time, pondering. "Emah," he said finally, in a quiet voice. "You speak of the son of the Promise. Do you know the story of the Promise?"

"In the beginning, God created the heavens and the earth. . ." she recited. For a short while, she told the story until Noah raised his hand to quiet her.

He smiled. "You know the story well and that's a good thing, because you and I will be telling this story together, you to the women and I to the men."

Chapter Ten

Year 1556

N oah glanced over to Emah, wiping sweat off her brow. She was seated on her upside-down basket, surrounded by at least a dozen fascinated women, who deftly sewed garments as they listened to her story. He looked around himself. The square in the seamstress's quarter was modest compared to some. The shops were well kept, but did not impress the visitor with imposing pillars or massive vertical beams. Colorful carts peddling bright fabrics and articles of clothing adorned the square's perimeter, and Noah could peer down any street and see an almost endless forest of traders, peddlers, hawkers, cobblers and buyers. Walking along, one could hear little comedies playing out between customers and hagglers. Either all of those buying were as poor as they claimed to be and the material was as cheap as they claimed it to be, or else they were as rich as the peddlers made them out to be and the material was as perfect as the peddlers made it out to be. Noah loved watching them dicker, knowing they would reach a price acceptable to both, a price they had mentally determined before a single offer was made.

He looked back over at his wife. She looked terribly uncomfortable sitting there, with an extended belly holding their coming child. The baby would be born soon, perhaps in weeks she said, and yet here she was reciting the stories. Noah suddenly remembered; he himself needed to get out into the square and start inviting men to listen to his own telling of the promise story.

He walked back and forth past the various stalls and booths. As customers were handing gold or barter to the peddler, Noah would smile and say, "Excuse me, sirs. In about fifteen minutes, I will be

telling a fascinating story for free in the center of the square. I welcome you to join with me and hear the story."

Generally, regardless of the response, he would smile, bow and
then move on to the next. Although some shopkeepers warned him to
stay away from their customers, most knew him as the one who
showed them little tricks to improve their sewing techniques or color
dying. Even the many craftsmen who were older than Noah had not
learned the kinds of methods Noah employed. The needlemen could
not join him during the day, and Noah did not expect them. His goal
was to invite customers to listen.

He always gathered a good group, sometimes even twenty or twen-
ty-five, and today was an unusually good day, for twenty-nine men
joined him in the center of the square. He motioned for the men to sit
down and cleared his throat, announcing the tale was about to com-
mence. The people of Yakheed loved a good story, and Noah never
disappointed their expectations. He began each gathering with the
same explanation.

"Before the heavens were there," he said, pointing to the sky, "and
the earth was here," he continued, sweeping his hands to indicate
everyone and everything before him, "God was. God is not land or
sea, animal or creature. He is not breath or flesh or human. He is
Yahweh, Creator of the heavens and the earth, but Yahweh is not on
the earth or a part of the heavens. In the beginning, God created the
heavens and the earth."

As he spoke, his audience hushed. In the corner of his eye, he felt
rather than saw a few bodies making room for another, but he did not
desire to lose the rhythm of the story, so he chose to ignore the disruption. Today he decided to tell Adam's creation and God's warning
about the fruit. His hope was that perhaps one of his listeners would
wait behind to hear more. Sometimes this happened, much to his
encouragement. Often, not one man responded. Today, even though
his listeners hung on every word he spoke, his intuition warned him
that no one would take his message seriously. He brought the story to
God's warning about the fruit of the knowledge of good and evil.

"Then the Lord God placed the man in the Garden of Eden to cultivate it and guard it. He said to him, 'You may eat the fruit of any tree
in the garden, except the tree that gives knowledge of what is good and

what is bad. You must not eat the fruit of that tree; if you do, you will die the same day.'"

Noah then smiled broadly at the gathering. Suddenly, his eye caught sight of an imposing figure seated to the far left of the crowd. It was Yakheed. The sight unsettled Noah's concentration for a moment, but, he regrouped his thoughts and forged ahead to his conclusion. "I have much more of this story to tell you, but I cannot keep you any longer. Next week at this same time, I will tell about the woman and how she was created and what the woman and man did with the fruit of the knowledge of good and evil."

He bowed. "You have honored me by your careful attention. May Yahweh, the Creator God, grant you his protection this week."

The crowd quickly dispersed. No one thanked him or commented. After years of telling the story, he had learned to expect his audiences to dismiss his message. Nonetheless, their lack of response still saddened him. He had come to realize that no matter how polished this city seemed on the outside, it was just as hardened to his message as any backwoods village.

Noah had preached in multitudes of villages, towns and cities and few carried on their activities as courteously and cleanly as the people of Yakheed. Their restraint, however, covered a facade of violence. Once the sun set, wise citizens barred their doors, for nights here raged with drunken abandon. The noise of brawling and besotted laughter made sleep hard to endure. Thieves would roam through alleyways searching for semi-conscious revelers and would steal from them or worse. Often in the morning one would find two or three bodies lying in the street, some warm and some very cold. The sins of relationships--especially between men and women and grotesquely between the same genders--nauseated Noah's sense of decency. For all their social decorum, the men and women of this city lived in open rebellion against the will of the One who created them. Noah suspected that his listeners had deadened their hearts, because they did not wish to face the Creator God who owned all things, including humans themselves.

He watched the men filtering back into the crowds. Suddenly he remembered Yakheed and turned to see if he had left as well. There he stood, however, with a bemused smile on his face. "I have seldom heard a better story teller, and I have seldom heard a stranger story."

Bowing, Noah answered, "You honor me, Elder."

"Bah!" Yakheed said. "I wasn't trying to honor you, Noah, son of Lamech, and don't call me 'Elder.' 'Yakheed' will do fine. Where did you learn this story?"

"My grandfather," he answered.

Yakheed began walking and motioned Noah to join him. "And who taught it to him?"

Noah answered, "Adam."

Yakheed stopped in his tracks. "What? Are you saying this Adam was a real man?"

"My grandfather," Noah said, "lived with Adam for two hundred and fifty years. He knew him well and taught me everything Adam said about the beginning of all things."

Noah's reply visibly unsettled Yakheed, who answered sharply, "That's impossible. The heavens and the earth have been here forever. You'd have to be a fool to believe someone or something created this world out of nothing!" He started walking again.

Noah smiled. "I know my grandfather. I trust him. Therefore I also trust what Adam said. He's not going to lie about it, and neither am I."

They walked together for a long time, without comment. Noah wondered if his companion could ever trust him enough to believe his story about Adam. Sometimes, not often, listeners would begin considering the story of the Promise because they counted Noah himself as worthy of trust.

After a while, Yakheed spoke again. "The real reason I stayed behind, Noah, son of Lamech, is your skirt."

The comment flustered Noah. "My what?"

Yakheed looked down at Noah's skirt. "Our city is the most famous center for weaving in the world. We weave almost all of the fabric worn by kings and rulers throughout the lands. But never have I seen cloth like your skirt. It is so smooth and supple, it makes my own materials feel like tree bark. Where did you buy it?"

Laughing, Noah answered, "I didn't buy it. I made it."

"That's impossible!"

Noah smiled. "I found the plant, and I learned how to cultivate it. While I was improving the strain of plant, I also created ways to clean, spin and weave the fiber. It took me a century to perfect the whole process, but it was worth it, I can assure you!"

For a long time, Yakheed walked along in silence. He was obviously deep in thought. Finally he spoke. "Where is this plant?"

"Further east than any city or village," Noah said. "On the side of the greatest mountain I have ever seen. It's at least a four month journey from here, unless one could reach it by the river. Then the journey might only take a month."

"Could you travel to this place and bring me seeds?"

Noah considered this. "My wife is about to give me my first child, and I do not want to leave her alone." He thought for a moment. "Of course, I could draw you an excellent map. You certainly have my permission to send a few adventurous souls to my cave past the edge of civilization. Let them bring back whatever they find there. I only request the right to examine what they have, in case they might bring something precious to me now that I am a husband."

"Will they find this plant there?" Yakheed asked tentatively.

Noah shrugged. "I can't imagine that it has died out. Your men would probably find enough to grow a seed crop. And, of course, I could help a lot there, because I worked on cultivating the plants for such a long time."

They came to a house, large, but not pretentious. Yakheed smiled. "I would invite you to join me for dinner, Noah. We could negotiate an agreement favorable for both of us in regards to this plant and your help."

This took Noah completely by surprise, and he began to laugh. It took him a few moments to calm down enough to reply. "I don't want anything at all. I've been wondering how I could get some of my plants back here, so I could weave clothing for Emah and the baby. You're just working it out for me."

Yakheed smiled. "You are not a businessman, Noah. I offer you this: free fabric for the rest of your life, as well as for the lives of your wife and children."

Noah nodded. "Only if the plants actually produce your fiber. Otherwise, I get nothing from this."

"This is a backwards way to bargain," Yakheed said. "I agree to your terms. Now, will you dine with me?"

Noah shook his head. "My pregnant wife is probably walking alone all the way back to our lovely home. I think I need to be with her."

"Then meet me in the elder's council room in four days after sunrise, with maps and instructions," Yakheed answered. "Have mercy on my men. Give them as much help as possible in finding this plant."

Noah smiled. "I will see you in four days with everything you need."

As he walked down the street toward his own home, Noah was amazed at how different facets of his life--the city of Mehujael, his farmwork for Yenah, his self-imposed exile in the cave, his years of wandering as a preacher--were now working together to grant him great favor in the city. *God must be preparing me for something*, he thought to himself. *When will He reveal His plan?* he wondered. The answer to this was about to come.

For the next four days, Noah prepared maps, drawings and instructions for the expedition. On the first night, a thought continually grew in his mind. During his years in the cave, he had especially worked with one particular grain, which had produced far more cereal than the grain grown anywhere else. During his third year in the cave, he had discovered the plant and began cultivating it soon after. Over the period of several hundred years, Noah's experiments with cross breeding plants produced remarkable results. Now in the city of Yakheed, he had an overwhelming sense to secure as many seeds as the expedition could find at the mountain. Of course, the seed would bring enormous benefit to the people here, but it was obvious this was not the source of his convictions. The seed was a part of God's plan for his future as the son of the Promise who brought rest.

Four days later, he presented to Yakheed maps, drawings, and instructions for finding the mountain, cave, gardens and fields. For hours he explained to Yakheed and his men the journey to the mountain, especially if they came by river. "The Great River flows from the Garden of Eden."

Noah's statement visibly startled Yakheed. "How do you know this?"

Noah pointed to his largest map. "I have been there. In fact, I came to this city from Eden only a year ago. I could not enter its gates, but sat beside the Great River many times."

Yakheed said nothing, but the look on his face suggested that he doubted Noah's statement.

Noah looked around to the travelers. "The Great River branches into four rivers; the Tigris, Euphrates, Pishon and Gihon. Those rivers flow from Eden east, northeast and south." He marked out the direction on his map. "Of these rivers, the Tigris flows straight east. The journey there will bring you past many distributaries, rivers and streams branching off of the Tigris. You men must stay on the Tigris itself, which will eventually bring you to the village of Slaf. The last I heard, this is the furthermost east civilization has ventured. A century ago, I lived in this city, and some people there may remember me."

After carefully plotting out their journey to the mountain and explaining how they would find the fields, gardens and cave, Noah paused. Smiling at the men, he said in an embarrassed way, "I also have a request. I have planted many crops over the years, but my favorite is this grain." He showed them several drawings of the plant. "I am hoping you will be able to find as many plants as possible. Here are the locations I cultivated it over the years. Surely some should still be thriving there; it was a hardy breed."

He glanced over to Yakheed, who was listening to this with great interest. The elder nodded and smiled, as if he suspected Noah of trying to profit from the journey, something of which Yakheed approved heartily. For several more hours, Noah and the men went through questions and details about the trip. By the time they finished their consultation, evening was descending. Noah wished the men Yahweh's favor, a statement which communicated very little to them and took his leave. He hurried to his dwelling.

When he arrived home, he found three women in his house, all with serious looks on their faces. Emah was sitting, leaning against the wall, her face flushed, eyes closed. She was breathing heavily, as if trying to control her pain. One of the women was holding her hand, wiping sweat from her forehead. Noah knelt down beside her. She opened her eyes and looked at him.

"The child is coming, husband."

The labor was long, lasting the entire night. When morning finally broke the horizon, a boy's lusty cry broke the hush in the house. Once the women had cleaned the child, they handed him to his mother and left the room. Emah was obviously exhausted, but smiled joyously. "It's a boy, Noah. He's beautiful, isn't he? And big! A miracle! What is his name, husband?"

"Shem," Noah answered. "He is Shem."

Emah looked at her husband intently. "And is he. . .?"

Nodding, Noah answered, "He is the son of the Promise."

After a while, Noah took the child to allow his mother to rest. One of the women, still waiting in the outer room, laid the sleeping babe in its cradle and stood guard over it. Noah retired into his workroom, closed the shutters and lay down to sleep. The enormity of what had just happened was beginning to form itself in his mind. He had a son now, one who would carry on the message of the promise to the next generation. The boy, tiny as he was, carried in him the seed of Eve. Perhaps this son would crush the serpent's head. Could this be the boy who would re-open the way to the tree of life and redeem humanity from sin?

"Yahweh," he prayed quietly, "reveal your purpose for me. Show me your plan."

He fell into an exhausted sleep. As he slept, images began flashing in his mind. He saw many great cities: Mehujael, Tubal Cain, Nod and Yakheed. His vantage point was as an eagle's, soaring over the walls and then flying rapidly just above the streets. Sometimes he passed through windows into inner rooms, sometimes above rooftops, sometimes in places of work. Everywhere he flew, men and women were sinning. He saw human greed in businesses and in homes; men murdering men; he came upon fighting, deceit and hatred. He heard a hundred voices whisper gossip and slander, shouting blasphemy, arrogance and boasting. He saw multitudes of people, all of whom had no comprehension of the God who created them. Because they did not know God, they loved only pleasure and feeding their own desires.

Then his dream left the great cities and searched the villages and the countryside. He traveled over shops where traders cheated, homes where husbands beat their wives, hillsides cluttered with the bones of babies left to die. He heard the wailing of children forever defiled by depraved men who took what they wanted and threw away the remains without shame. Everywhere humanity betrayed humanity, betrayed its children, betrayed itself, betrayed its Creator, and still he swept over the land, seeing further corruption and destruction.

Noah recognized the villages and cities he himself had visited. He saw faces of men to whom he had told the story of the Promise. There were children, now suddenly men and women, who had understood long ago the message of God, but now were entirely rebellious. He watched villages burning, armies battling and fields cluttered with the casualties of war. As he journeyed over these fruits of human degradation, Noah understood: it could not continue like this. It must stop.

With a shock, he awoke and sat up, covered in perspiration. The room around him was dark, although he knew it was still day outside. He could hear sounds in the next room–a baby was crying and women were hushing it. He could not understand why, but a feeling of terror beyond anything he had ever encountered was descending upon him. His heart was beating wildly, and his chest seemed as if it were about to explode. An invisible weight crushed his entire body, engulfing his senses and overwhelming his being. His heart pounded audibly in his ears, pulsating like the hammer striking the anvil, his head throbbing with every painful clang.   Falling down to the floor beneath the heaviness, he lay prostrate, unable to move, barely able to breathe.

A Voice spoke. "Noah."

Now he understood his terror; Yahweh had come to him.   He closed his eyes. "Yes, Yahweh?"

The Voice said to him, "The end of all flesh has come before Me; for the earth is filled with violence because of them; and behold, I am about to destroy them along with the earth."

Noah's heart sank. Methuselah's prophecy; the end of all flesh.

The Voice spoke again.   "Make for yourself a barge of gopher wood; you shall make the barge with rooms and shall cover it inside and out with pitch. This is how you shall make it: the length of the barge three hundred cubits, its breadth fifty cubits and its height thirty cubits. You shall make a window for the barge and finish it to a cubit from the top; and set the door of the barge in the side of it; you shall make it with lower, second and third decks."

Noah gasped. *Three hundred cubits long and fifty cubits wide? It couldn't even fit on most rivers! How could I build it?* All of these thoughts rushed through his head in the blink of an eye.

God spoke again. "Behold, I, even I am bringing the flood of water upon the earth, to destroy all flesh in which is the breath of life, from under heaven; everything that is on the earth shall perish. But I will establish My covenant with you; and you shall enter the barge–you and your sons and your wife and your sons' wives with you."

Every living creature! Every human! Every tree and meadow!

"And of every living thing of all flesh, you shall bring two of every kind into the barge, to keep them alive with you; they shall be male and female. Of the birds after their kind and of the animals after their kind, of every creeping thing of the ground after its kind, two of every kind will come to you to keep them alive."

The improbability of the task struck him. He was to fill this enormous barge with two of every kind of animal. No one could do this.

God spoke one last time. "As for you, take for yourself some of all food which is edible and gather it to yourself; and it shall be food for you and for them."

Noah lay there prostrate in the silence, barely able to breathe. Slowly, the heaviness lifted and the terror dissipated. He pulled himself up into a sitting position and held his head in his hands. *How could this be happening? How could this be happening?*

After a few minutes, he rose. The baby was crying, and he followed the sound into Emah's room. She was sitting up in her bed on the floor, cuddling the child, rocking him in a gentle motion. Noah quietly crossed the room and knelt beside her. As the baby grasped a fold of bed clothing, Noah examined each tiny finger, captivated by the intricacy of design. The child's face seemed a mixture of mother and father, a mixture of grandfathers and grandmothers. The nose seemed little more than a bump on his face--this he received from his mother. The babe opened his eyes, and the father suddenly saw Emah's mother, with wide eyes that sparkled with life. His hair arranged itself in tight little black curls, close set to his head, a gift from Methuselah. All that Noah saw in the baby overwhelmed his senses. The child was perfect and incomprehensibly, this was his child, his son.

These powerful emotions which welled up as he gazed upon his newborn child could not, however, blot out the experience he had just undergone in the other room. God was bringing judgment upon the human race, a horrible judgment. Noah began to see other babies, as innocent, fragile and helpless as Shem. He saw that the little boy on his mother's bosom was only one of a vast world. Those babies grew into wide-eyed children, who saw the world as a place of wonder, whose voices brought life to lifeless places, returned energy and excitement to a world of hardship. Hardship, Noah realized, was the stuff out of which this world was made. All of those babies would grow up into adversity, the world of manhood and womanhood, the world of sin and suffering. He thought of the hungry and lost who roamed this city, begging on the streets for food. He thought of the drunks who spent their days in hopeless pursuit of enough wine to drink themselves insensible at night. He thought of men and women who labored hard under a brutal sun to provide their children's dinner and a roof over their head. All of them came into the world as innocent as this little perfect human who now snuggled in his mother's arms.

Noah poked his finger toward the tiny one, and the babe instinctively grasped it. He could not imagine any emotion more overwhelming than the love he was experiencing toward this son of his. The child began to cry, and his mother prepared to nurse him. She whispered to the baby, cuddling him and positioned him to feed. Noah watched in amazement as the child greedily drank from his mother. Even the sound of the baby's sucking elated him and gave him more joy than he had ever known.

Yet deep within his heart, he also heard other sounds, the sounds of his vision, the rolling waves of God's pronouncement, and, especially, the cries of a million voices about to encounter God's righteous anger. How could these two contradictory oceans of feeling both exist in a human heart without entirely breaking it? Tears formed in his eyes, rolling down his cheeks.

Emah looked up at him; "Tears of joy?" she asked with a smile.

Noah, son of Lamech, son of the Promise, could not answer.

Noah's preparations for his mammoth task began quietly. He assumed his first priority would be to find a place to build the barge. The location, however, turned out to be a bit tricky. It needed to be near a large supply of gopherwood trees. He did not want to build too close to the city, for fear that skeptics might attempt to damage it. Yet he also wanted to be close enough to the city that he and Emah could continue to tell the story of the promise. God was bringing the flood because humankind refused to submit to His will. If Noah and Emah could persuade the people of this city to turn from their sins, perhaps God would spare them. Perhaps He would spare the world. Thus Noah wanted the best of all worlds: to be close enough to preach righteousness to the city, but not close enough to invite violence. In addition, of course, he needed an enormous supply of gopherwood.

Until he could find the right location, Noah set his mind on fashioning barge models. Even though God had provided the vessel's dimensions, Noah had to construct his boat with a clear understanding of how flood waters would impact it. His first model floated perfectly on a canal, but when he put it out on the real river, within a few moments it had smashed into rocks and disintegrated. As time went on, he tried model after model, and a pattern emerged; Noah could protect his barge from water, but not from rocks. In a flood, a towering wave might catch the barge and fling it into a mountainside, where Noah was sure it would splinter and all aboard would be lost. In a flood, fast moving water would turn innocent looking rooftops or wagons into battering rams. If Noah and his family were to survive the flood, they needed to avoid fast moving water and debris.

This discovery complicated his quest for the right location. The only protection against such dangers would be to build the barge somewhere high. At first, the waters would sweep away low lying towns and cities. Those first stages of flooding would be a whirlpool of swirling houses and trees; nothing could survive in that environment. As the water continued to rise, enormous waves would crash across the countryside, tossing floating objects such as the barge as if they were splinters. Not until the water was truly deep would the uncontrollable surges calm to the point that a boat might survive.

After a month of planning and careful consideration, Noah had narrowed his possibilities. He must build in the middle of a plenteous supply of gopherwood trees; this God had clearly commanded. The place must be close enough to an enormous source of fresh food, especially grains, so that he could process the food within a year of the cataclysm. In all of the years he had worked to develop storing food long term, he had never succeeded for longer than two years. The location also had to be far enough from the city to discourage violence, but close enough to reach easily. Finally, the location had to be as high as possible. The only likely location to match this would be Halftop Mountain, but he did not know if any gopherwood trees even grew there.

Two months after the vision, Noah and Emah and little Shem left the South Gate early in the morning to survey Halftop. They transported themselves across the fast moving river by means of a raft. A pulley system with ropes connected the raft to each shore, and travelers could draw themselves to the far side easily enough, although without the rope, it would be challenging indeed. Beyond the river, lay a wide plain leading to the foot of the mountain. They crossed the plain and reached the woods and noted how the ground began to rise. It was a clean wood, with little undergrowth and as far as the eye could see stood tall trees, mostly perhaps a bit more than half a cubit in diameter.

"Emah," Noah exclaimed. "These are gopherwood trees."

"It looks like the entire forest is gopherwood," she said. "Perhaps all the way to the top."

He nodded. "And hard as rocks, they are." They stopped, and Noah ran his hand down a trunk. "When I was in the cave, I had gopherwood trees all around me. It literally took me thirty years to work out a saw that wouldn't break when it cut gopherwood."

"What's that?" she asked, cocking her head.

They both listened intently. A distant rushing sound filtered through the trees. They headed toward it and after several minutes came upon a stream tumbling down the side of the mountain. Noah took Emah's hand and the three of them, Shem fast asleep on her back, followed the stream perhaps thirty cubits to a waterfall. The sight delighted Emah, who had never seen a fall before.

She sat down on a large rock, just to watch clouds of floating water, seemingly suspended in the space halfway between the top and the bottom, a height of perhaps fifteen cubits. The sight also intrigued Noah, but for different reasons. He knew waterfalls well, having used them extensively over the years of his cave life. This cascade might provide them with help for their projects.

"Streams are always moving," he thought out loud, "and that means we can use them to move wheels."

"How do you get the water to move a wheel?"

He smiled, thinking back to the works in his cave. "I tried everything. It got pretty frustrating for a while, but in the end I put something like buckets on the wheel. The water caught the first bucket and moved it along and since the bucket was attached to the wheel, the wheel moved along too. By that time, the water caught the second bucket and then the third and so on. The wheel started turning pretty quickly, and I figured out pretty quickly how to use that motion to grind my grain, to pull loads up and all kinds of things."

She looked surprised. "I've never seen anyone do that before."

"Oh, I'm not the inventor," he answered grinning. "I saw somebody doing it when I was a boy, so I had the idea already. I just couldn't figure out the buckets."

"Amazing!"

Noah looked over at the waterfall pouring in front of him. "My best waterwheel," he said thoughtfully, "worked on a waterfall just like this one, only mine was a bit smaller. That one whirled like a potter's wheel. It's a shame this falls is all the way down here."

She looked uphill. "That's a long way to haul wooden beams."

"Too long," he said, feeling disappointed.

"Of course," she added, "if you had another waterwheel, and somehow you could line a rope from here to there and then back to here, like the rope for the raft across the river, you could pull a wagon—"

"Especially if the wagon were on some kind of road made out of . . . maybe planks of wood or something."

"You'd need a couple of people here on the bottom to load and attach it."

"A couple of people at the top to receive it."

"Of course, it would be awfully slow. . ."

"Yes but everyone could be working while it was coming and going."

Noah bent over and kissed his wife. "Well now, that's an idea that may save us a lot of labor." He considered the falls, the hill, the stream above, the trees surrounding him.

He looked upward. "Let's get to the top and see what it's like up there."

They started climbing again. Noah began feeling as if he were back at his old cave, for the kinds of rocks they climbed past here were jagged and full of holes. "I'll bet we're going to find caves in this mountain sooner or later, just like my mountain."

When they reached the top, the ground began gently descending into the crater. The trees were somewhat thinner here, but still about the same size. After about twenty minutes of hiking, they reached the lake. Emah gasped. It was crystal blue, as still and deep as the sky. "It's almost perfect!" she said.

Her husband nodded. "We can make it work very well, I think."

A confused look came over her. "But Noah, this isn't your mountain?"

He smiled at his wife. "Well. . . I think God has a way for us to use the mountain and the wood."

For the next three months, Noah worked on drawings and then on painstaking models. He and Emah continued to preach in the different districts of the city, but the vision changed the heart of his message. No longer did he simply describe the story; he now forcefully urged people to turn from sin. At first, the change surprised his audiences, then it antagonized them. Before long, almost no one came to listen. The same happened to a lesser extent with Emah's women. For some, they stopped coming at their husband's command, but most avoided her because of the harshness of the message.

Sooner or later, Noah knew Yakheed would confront him about it, so he was not surprised when he received a summons to the meeting hall. He arrived, worried about what to say and how this might turn out. His discomfort increased even more when the servants at the hall gave him the strangest looks as they led him into the chambers. Would he be exiled? Might they take Emah and the baby away from him?

All of his worries, however, were completely confused when he arrived in the chamber and saw, to his shock, the men Yakheed had sent to his cave and the table before Yakheed piled high with Noah's fabric. Noah did a quick figuring in his head. It must have been at least five months since they left. Looking them over, he could see the five months had been anything but comfortable.

They bowed strangely to Noah. Curiosity dominated Yakheed's face. He respectfully nodded to his friend and then turned to the travelers. "Well, men, I understand you have brought back quite a store of goods from your journeys. My servants say you have wagons of commodities. Did you go on a trading spree?"

The leader shook his head. "We didn't organize for any of it, except the plants you requested and the plants the visitor requested." He turned to Noah. "By the way, the people of the town by the river send their greetings. Civilization has gone far past the river now, friend. It is within a two day's journey of your mountain. I doubt after what has happened that your cave will remain intact."

Yakheed put his hand to his chin, stroking his beard. "What on earth happened?"

"Well, after a long search, we came on the cave, but we didn't go in," the man answered. "Instead, we searched the mountain using our excellent maps and were able to cull several bags of the two plants and their seeds. Some of the men wanted to leave at that point, but the place itself had enticed my curiosity, and we chose to explore."

The man looked at Yakheed with excitement. "You see, in the gardens and fields we found the strangest machinery I have ever encountered. An irrigation wheel was supplying exactly the right amount of water for the fruit trees, even though the trees themselves had clearly not been pruned for ages. After all this time! A gateway guarded an entryway into the cave from a hidden glen. One simply had to tug on the rope, which was, by the way, still intact, and the gate lifted by itself."

The man paused for a moment, glancing at Noah. "You will forgive us, I hope, but we not only intruded on your home; we pillaged it. It was piled high with fabrics, strange instruments, tools such as I have never seen, a platform connected to pulleys that one could use to lower oneself down to the depths of the cave, or raise oneself up to its attic. The artifacts in the cave amazed us so much that we returned to the town, purchased animals and wagons in order to haul as much as we could."

He turned to Yakheed. "Elder, excuse me for being forward, but the man standing before you is this city's greatest treasure. If you had seen the wonders we observed in this cave, you would probably appoint him chief architect and designer of the city of Yakheed. I suspect once you have examined our booty from his cave, you will agree."

For a long time, Yakheed simply stared at Noah, deeply impressed by what the men described. The look on his face was not one of jealousy, but respect, surprising in a man who governed his city through his reputation rather than by force. He finally spoke. "And the fabric plant–do you have plenty of specimens?"

The traveler nodded.

Yakheed smiled. Turning to Noah, he asked, "Well, what do you say to all of this?"

Noah shrugged. "What else could I do for three hundred and fifty years? Knitting gets boring after a while."

"All I wanted from this expedition was my fabric plant," Yakheed said carefully. "The rest of the 'booty,' as our captain called it, shall be brought to Noah's home. It is, after all, his possession."

The captain bowed, but Noah spoke quickly. "Oh no, elder. I don't want any of it. We bequeath all of these artifacts to you, to distribute as you will."

Noah caught a glint of something, perhaps triumph, in Yakheed's eyes. He wondered if Yakheed had already inventoried the cargo and was simply orchestrating this meeting with the expectation that Noah would never accept the gift. It was always better to amass new wealth by diplomacy rather than through force. Noah of course, already realized how the fabric plant would end up making this city even richer than it already was. Yet he didn't begrudge Yakheed's plan; the city needed these things more than he did.

Yakheed turned to him and bowed. "You have again put our city in debt to you, Noah, son of Lamech, son of this so-called promise. How could we repay you for your gift?"

Noah sensed that something was happening here. All of a sudden, God was opening to him a plan, and it was his responsibility to take the next step. He prayed silently. Then, his heart beating furiously, Noah answered.

"I would ask the city to sell to me the hill called Halftop Mountain."

Yakheed laughed. "Halftop! That place is worthless. It's full of gopherwood. You can't be serious. What are you possibly going to do with it?"

Noah held his breath and carefully said his next assertion. "Yahweh, the Creator of the universe, has commanded me to build a barge on the top of it."

The room stilled. Noah glanced at Yakheed's face and saw deep disappointment. His own heart sank. Five minutes ago, everyone in the room had thought he was a genius. Yakheed's expression said that had changed in an instant.

"Your so-called creator has talked to you?" he said icily.

Noah nodded, feeling utterly ridiculous. He desperately wanted to run out of the room, or explain away what he had just said, but knew he couldn't.

Yakheed asked him, shaking his head; "A barge? Why on earth would your Yahweh want a barge on top of Halftop Mountain?"

Noah swallowed nervously and then took the biggest step in his life. "He is going to destroy all flesh with an ocean of water."

"Destroy. . ." Looking at him as if he were insane, Yakheed stroked his beard, thinking. For a long time, he said nothing. Then he turned back to his seat and sat down. He stared into Noah's eyes, obviously thinking and wrestling with what to do. Noah stood still, half praying, half complaining to God for being boxed into this situation. He looked back up to see Yakheed still gazing at him.

Finally the elder spoke. "And do you have anything valuable enough to entice us to sell an entire mountain?"

"A mill," Noah answered. "Well, actually, several mills."

Curiosity lit up in Yakheed's doubting eyes. "We have plenty of mills, Noah."

"But our mills all run by draft animals," he said cautiously. "My mills would run by water power." His natural excitement began to overtake his humiliation and fear. "I could build for you a mill for sawing wood, a mill for grinding grain and a mill for running looms."

Yakheed shook his head. "Why do we want water mills when we have draft animals? I guess I don't understand the point."

At this, the captain, who had been listening quietly this entire time, interrupted. "Excuse me, elder, but I have been in this man's cave and have seen these water wheels for myself. I think all of my men would agree, they work far more effectively than draft animals ever could work."

Noah nodded, adding with excitement, "You see, water doesn't get tired, it moves much faster and you don't have to feed it. It works from sunrise to sunrise. If you know how to build your gears and your axles and pulleys, water is amazingly powerful as well. You can use it to carry on a hundred tasks."

Noah studied Yakheed's expression, but could not read what the elder was thinking. He remembered Yahweh and silently asked Him to bring the best solution. Yakheed looked at the men and the cloth lying on table before him. He ran his hand over the fabric. A hard business look braced his face. Noah could tell that business was overruling Yakheed's personal distaste of Noah's claim about an ocean of water. Finally, he looked up.

"Your first mill will obviously be a sawmill to cut wood for the other mills. Your second mill, however. . . could it be a loom?"

"Of course—"

"And," Yakheed continued, "could you build a loom to weave as you have woven this fabric?"

Noah nodded. "The very fabric you hold was woven on a water powered loom." He paused, thinking. Then he added, "Although it would help me greatly if you could teach me what you know about constructing looms. I ran into more problems developing that loom than almost any task I ever tackled."

This brought a smile to Yakheed's face, and Noah silently sighed relief. "Good idea, Noah, son of Lamech. Looms have been my life for the past five hundred years. You'd do well enough without me, but together, there is nothing we couldn't accomplish. Now," his smile tightened, as if artificial: "When is this ocean of water supposed to come on us?"

Noah spoke nervously, "In ninety-nine years."

"And you feel sure about this?" Yakheed asked, back to being the businessman.

Noah answered, nodding, "More sure than about anything else I know."

Yakheed lifted up the material and smiled a trader's smile. "Then let's rewrite our agreement for the plants you've given us. I will give fabric to you and your descendants for the next one hundred years. We will grant you the mountain to do with as you please, for the next one hundred years. You may live in your present house in the city for one hundred years. At end of that time, all of this will revert to the city. In exchange for this, you will design for us a water powered loom, a water powered gristmill and a water powered sawmill."

"But that hardly seems fair, Yakheed. It feels like stealing."

The elder smiled. "You say it will all be under water anyway, so what difference does it make to you?"

"That's what I mean," Noah answered with concern. "I feel like I'm taking advantage of you. The mills, the river, the city will all be gone in a hundred years."

Yakheed's face turned dark. He looked Noah in the eye with a steely gaze. "I'll take my chances," he finally answered. He dismissed Noah with a bow of his head.

As Noah climbed the steps of the council chamber, he heard the captain whisper to the elder, "Sir, in all my life, I have never seen so many wonders as I encountered in that cave! This man is a genius."

As Noah reached the top step, he heard Yakheed answer in a whisper, amplified through the entire chamber. "He may be a genius, but he is also a fool." With a broken heart, Noah returned to his home.

Over the next five months, Noah worked on plans and models for the three water powered mills. At first, he expected to do all of the work and pay for all materials, but the opposite happened. Within a week, Yakheed had sent him a foreman, who began gathering workers to fell trees and prepare the land beside the river. They surveyed different sites and agreed on three. In order to make the plan more effective, Noah requested permission to build a bridge over the river, which the city gladly permitted. All of these projects took most of the year, during which time Emah presented Noah with his second son, named Ham.

One unexpected benefit of all this activity was Noah's working relationship with Yakheed. Their friendship had almost vanished when Noah announced the coming flood that day, but Yakheed had to overcome his anger in order to design the weaving mill. This brought them together almost every day for an entire month.

So many factors complicated the task of weaving fabric: fulling, spinning and the looms themselves. Noah wanted all of them to be powered by water, which would make the work much easier and produce higher quality material. Yakheed was a genius about tricks in constructing looms, fullers and spinners. Once Noah taught him the principles of water power, gears and rope pulleys, Yakheed began applying his experience with weaving to this new source of power. Sometimes when he went too far, Noah would explain how Yakheed's ideas undercut the basic principles of water power. A couple of times

Yakheed insisted on trying his idea, but when the models were built, Noah was right. This cemented his respect again.

Beyond this planning and building, Noah also rented a field from Werd, the richest farmer in the city. Werd owned two thirds of the farmland beyond the city walls. His farming system was effective; he leased the land for free the first year, and then required tenants to pay for the next year with one half of the first harvest. This way new farmers could start with no capital outlay and would feel tied to Werd's land, because they always had to pay for the coming year.

When Noah and Emah, of course, cultivated their land, they planted the grain he had developed when he was in his cave. The crop grew wonderfully and bore the best harvest he had ever seen. Since the yield came three weeks early, Noah sent notice to Werd that the landowner might receive his share of the harvest. Werd's foreman arrived the next day, saying nothing, but carried away the crops in his wagons.

The following morning, Emah answered the door to discover Werd himself, requesting an audience with Noah. After customary greetings, Werd reached into a pouch and pulled out a handful of grain.

He came right to the point. "My foreman tells me your crop had at least twice as much yield as any crop he has ever seen, and the grain itself is delicious! The flour is stickier and my baker thinks it will make better breads. Where is this grain from?"

Again, Noah sensed that this discussion was enormously important for their future task. He prayed silently and then answered in a light manner, "Oh, I developed that in my cave. It took me at least one hundred years to bring it to the point that was just right. Why do you ask?"

Werd stared at the grain in his hand. Noah suspected he was struggling with how to negotiate this. He could use the seeds they had collected from Noah without brokering an agreement, but they both knew the city elders would consider this to be a kind of theft. He said in a mildly anxious voice, "I would like to begin using your seed for planting crops."

It was Noah's turn to bargain. "I haven't figured out yet what to do with my grain. I suppose I could sell it to you. Then you'd have a pretty good harvest next year." He paused, thinking. "Of course, all of the seed is really mine in a way. I developed it."

Werd's eyes narrowed. "What do you want in exchange for me using your seeds?"

Suddenly a thought dropped into Noah's mind and he smiled. "You may use these seeds in any way you see fit, however the elders permit you, of course. All I would ask is that you provide me, my family and workers with food for free."

"That's all? Noah, don't be ridiculous. This grain will make me the richest man in the city!"

Noah considered this before speaking. "The second stipulation is a little more unusual. Are you familiar with what the Creator God has said about the ocean of water?"

"I'm familiar about what you have said this so-called god told you. Everyone in the city knows about it!"

Noah nodded. "Then here's my request. In ninety-eight years, you will have a great harvest. I want half of it. Not just the grains, mind you. I want the fruits, vegetables and grains. I want the grain transported to the grist mill and the fruits and vegetables delivered to the foot of Halftop Mountain. Once you have brought those items to me, you are free of me forever."

Werd looked surprised. "One half? That will be my entire share! What do you expect me to do without my profit for a whole year?"

Noah thought for a moment. "You can spend that whole year just counting all of the money you will have been making from my seeds for the first ninety-seven years."

"And I will be free from feeding you after that year?" he asked quietly.

Shaking his head, Noah said. "Werd, you will be free, but the waters will destroy everything you own. Don't you understand? It's all going to end."

"Noah, let me tell you what I understand," Werd answered. "I understand farming. I understand business. I understand people. You may want to believe this foolishness, but the only thing I want to believe is farming and doing business. I will bring this agreement to the elders. If they approve, they will bind us to it, and we can do business together."

Werd left them. Emah came to Noah, who stood beside the door. "They're all going to die, aren't they? They'll never believe until it's too late."

Noah watched Werd making his way down the street. "They'll never believe until it's too late."

Far away, a man walked slowly to the Great River that flows from Eden. He was tired and wondered when God would bring his final rest. Since Noah had left several years before, every day the man had come to this river to pray to Yahweh, the Creator of the heavens and earth. He had asked Him for Noah's safety and wisdom. He had faithfully implored Yahweh to direct Noah's steps. He was now confident that God was going to bring a terrible calamity upon the human race and upon nature itself, a calamity that would destroy all flesh. Yet he also knew Lamech's word, that through Noah, human-kind would find rest from its painful labor.

Methuselah sat down beside the river, watching the flow. Lately the water had not given him serenity, but a sense of foreboding. What this meant he could not fathom. He felt certain that God had set in motion something only God could direct. With this, Methuselah looked to heaven. "O God, I trust in your unfailing wisdom. Keep my grandson safe, Lord. Direct him step by step according to your plan for all flesh. Protect him from persecutors, Lord and teach him to love those who mock him. Amen."

He sighed, watching enormous behemoth along the far shore. Just to see them drink from the water amazed him. For a while, he simply lost sight of anything but the miracle across the river. Then he remembered one last request of Yahweh.

"If it is possible, Yahweh, I ask to be taken before the calamity begins. Amen"

Chapter Eleven

Year 1639

B e careful with that pole!" he shouted angrily. Yakheed shook his head. "Don't you see those pots of dye stacked over there?"

The worker looked up to his left and spied a shelf two feet above his head. He glanced back at his chief. Yakheed could see fear in the man's eyes.

The owner grunted. "Don't worry. I won't fire you." Waving his hand to send the worker on, he added, "Just be more careful when you carry those things."

He watched the man hurrying down the aisle and smiled to himself. Since they had built these mills, he had seen hundreds of workers come and leave his employment. They arrived from farms, shops and even orphanages in distant cities. One characteristic typified everyone who labored there–they all treated Yakheed almost as if he were a Nephilim warrior or bloodthirsty tyrant. Scanning his workers, Yakheed could tell they were all putting in extra efforts because he was standing there, and he wondered what it was about him that frightened them so.

It wasn't because he avoided being around his laborers. On the contrary, he worked right beside them. They could always count on him adjusting a beater or separating threads and often repairing broken machines. Without a doubt, nobody in the mill worked harder than Yakheed. Nor could anyone accuse him of not taking care of them. He paid them well, far more than any other employer in the city. He watched out for all his mill workers almost like a father, knowing not only everyone's name and the names of their spouses and children, but even visiting them at their homes when the need arose.

Generally, he didn't mind people being afraid of him. Yet at times he wondered if he was perhaps too harsh on them, a bit too demanding. Not that he could do anything about it, since all of his life he had been rough around the edges. He paused, watching the gears and shafts turning, the beaters swinging and craftsmen deftly moving the warp and woof into place. His people feared him, yet many in the city vied to work in his mills. It wasn't just the money. He had heard from his fellow city elders that for all of his gruff manner, his workers loved the mills. Perhaps it was because he loved working with them almost as much as he enjoyed the business of weaving fabric. But not quite.

Weaving was his life. Yakheed had built a room on the lowest floor of the mill, right above the river. Even though he had a handsome house located beside the southern wall of the city, he seldom slept there. He preferred his workplace, which was more a home for him than any mansion he could imagine. All throughout the night he slept to the sounds of the river below him and the mostly empty factory–the groaning of the waterwheels and a solitary loom that continued to run all night. This was his passion, and he never felt himself lonely or empty. Occasionally a city elder might urge him to find a wife and settle down, enjoy life rather than work it away. Suggestions like that always made him laugh.

"The only thing a wife is good for is having babies," he would answer, "and I've never seen much use in babies, unless your idea of usefulness is staying up all night listening to them whine and cry."

He smiled at the thought of having a family. How could that compare to building a city? What could be more gratifying than being the most prosperous tradesman for a twenty days journey in any direction? No, he decided. This is where I belong. As he mulled this over, his foreman interrupted his thoughts. "Master, a woman has come here asking for a job."

"We don't have any openings right now," Yakheed answered. "I have a waiting list two pages long. Take her name and tell her if anything comes up we will let her know."

The foreman looked uncomfortable. "Master Yakheed," he said cautiously, "I think you should at least talk to this woman."

"Unless she is stronger than a Nephilim warrior," Yakheed answered, "I don't see much point in talking to her."

The foreman cleared his throat. "Master," he said, "I wouldn't feel right about turning her away without at least you meeting her."

His curiosity aroused, Yakheed nodded his head and motioned for the man to lead him. They passed through the main weaving station and began making their way toward the stairs to the outer entrance. As he passed through each section, he could actually see his workers intensify their labors, which again caused him to smile.

When he finally reached the entryway, Yakheed saw standing in the doorway the outline of the woman. She was not terribly young, nor was she slender as so many maidens seemed to be these days. Her hair was covered by a brown handkerchief and a tattered shawl draped over her shoulders. Her skirt reached the floor and had been patched in several places. Yakheed could tell this woman had seen difficult times.

When they reached her, the foreman said, "I brought him to you, Miss. The Elder will be able to help you with whatever you need." He turned, bowed to Yakheed and left.

"How can I help you?" Yakheed asked.

The woman glanced up. She appeared tired and her clothing was worn, but her eyes surprised him with their warmth. Mixed with the warmth was resignation, not the kind of resignation that comes from those who constantly whine and complain. Instead, he could tell she understood how little chance there was for finding work in this mill, but she had to try anyway. Her eyes seemed to join wisdom and compassion, a rare combination in Yakheed's experience. For the first time in his life he found himself taken back by a woman's glance, and he did not know what to do.

"I was hoping you might have work for me," she said gravely. "I can do many things well."

Yakheed shook his head. "I'm afraid we simply don't have any work available at the moment. I have a waiting list with about fifty names on it."

Normally at this point Yakheed would dismiss the job seeker and walk away, letting the person find his or her own way out. For some reason, however, Yakheed decided at least to escort the woman out of the building. He motioned toward the door and she looked at him earnestly.

"Do you mean you are not giving me a chance?" she said with disappointment. "I'll do any menial job if it will buy me a place to live and some bread to eat."

Yakheed placed his hand on the woman's back to move her gently toward the exit. She said nothing more. When they reached the outside, he helped her down the steps even though it was clear she needed no help. He heard her sigh quietly.

Yakheed felt awkward. He could do nothing for the woman, yet he did not want simply to bid her good luck and send her on her way. Whatever was urging him to linger there made him wish she would say something, even though Yakheed had no clue what he wanted to hear. Clearly she possessed wisdom. For a moment, he entertained the absurd notion to ask advice about his employees and their fears. Yet was it wisdom he wanted from her or something else? Maybe it was just because she was so unlike him. Until that moment he had never considered the possibility that knowing someone gentle and stable might actually smooth out some of those rough edges.

Still she did not speak, leaving the next word up to him, which of course was only fair. He unfortunately could find nothing worth uttering. In this impossible dilemma, Yakheed offered to escort the woman back into the city. She accepted his offer.

They walked along the streets of the city, chatting as they went. The woman, whose name was Tirina, loved to talk. She told Yakheed about her life, which had been hard for many years. He found himself telling her about his own experiences. Surprisingly he did not try to impress her by his high position or even his heroic rescue of the city so long ago. Instead he shared with her his most precious memories– growing up with Sister, rescuing babies left to die, and about how he loved life as a weaver.

Tirina seemed most fascinated by his passion for life and continually asked exactly the right questions to coax out his next story. Many years had passed since Yakheed had found someone interested in him as a person rather than as an employer or elder of the city, and he enjoyed the experience greatly. Their journey led them through several city districts until finally they reached the eastern wall, lined with warehouses and granaries.

Tirina stopped and smiled. "Well Elder," she said lightly, "I have entirely enjoyed our time together, but now I must say goodbye."

He stood staring blankly, thinking furiously. If they parted company now, they likely would never meet again. *Why should I worry about a woman I don't even know?* he thought to himself. *Maybe I could offer her a job at the mill. That was ridiculous, since she knew they had no openings. My life is going just fine the way it already is. I should just turn and leave!*

He glanced again at Tirina. "No," he said out loud.

When she looked at him, he wasn't sure whether he saw surprise in her eyes or a guarded hope. Tirina, however, did not reply but simply smiled.

"I mean," he said apologetically, "I think I would like to talk more if you are willing to spend some time with me."

"Elder," Tirina answered in a measured voice, "I am willing to spend time with you, but I must admit I have not eaten all day."

Yakheed pointed down the road to a market place not far away. "I think we can soothe your hunger easily enough." He took her arm and began leading her toward the booths there.

Once he had purchased food, they found a bench and sat. As they were eating, Yakheed looked up suddenly in shock. "You're not married are you?"

She shook her head and smiled. "You're not married, are you?"

He laughed. "Not yet anyway." He thought for a moment. "If I asked you to marry me, what would you say?"

Tirina became very serious. "What do you think, Elder?"

His face broke into a broad smile. "Then I will begin making arrangements. I must speak to your father."

"My father?" she asked. "That would be impossible. I never knew my father and my mother has been dead for years." She paused and her eyes pleaded with him. Speaking slowly, she continued, "If you need to speak to anyone for permission, it should be me."

Yakheed stood. He offered her his hand and helped her stand. "Somebody has to give you away and you will need some kind of mother to prepare you in your bridal dress. You must have a proper wedding if you are to be a bride."

Tirina stood absolutely still for a long time. He watched her face, wondering why she wasn't answering. Finally she turned and began walking toward the eastern wall district. He looked at her in surprise.

"Where are you going?" he called out after her.

She stopped and looked back at him. "There will be no wedding," she said soberly.

He stared at her in a stupor. "No wedding? But I thought you said—"

"I said," she interrupted, "if you need to speak to anyone for permission, it had better be me. But you haven't done that yet." She turned and walked briskly away.

Yakheed did not know what to do. He was not used to women speaking back to him. For that matter he was hardly used to having anyone speak back to him. His anger surged. She hardly knew him and yet had the audacity to turn her back to him and walk away. *Nobody can talk that way to me*, he thought to himself.

He angrily pursued her. It did not take long to catch up and as he did, he marched alongside her, protesting vigorously. "How can you just leave like . . ." He stopped. Tears were streaming down Tirina's face. "What on earth?" he muttered in shock.

She looked up at him and said through her tears, "All of my life I have been dreaming of the day when someone would ask me to marry him. Then you come along and without even as much as a please or thank you, you simply take for granted this is what I want."

"Well?" Yakheed sputtered, "isn't it?"

She nodded, "Maybe, but I just need a chance to tell you myself. Couldn't you at least give me the opportunity to say no?"

Yakheed looked at her for a long time, wrestling in his emotions. Even as his anger urged him to walk away, something was making him hold back his natural rashness. He looked around himself. She was crying, and Yakheed worried people on the street might notice, but apparently Tirina did not care whether she attracted a whole crowd. He stared at her, knowing he should do something to soften her discomfort, but felt ill at ease. So he stood there, his arms hanging loosely at his side, unable to speak.

Finally he put his hand on her back and awkwardly pulled her toward him. Immediately the woman collapsed onto his chest sobbing more loudly than she had even onto this point. He softened his embrace and she molded into his arms. For the first time since he had been a boy Yakheed found comfort in human touch, and he wondered how he could have survived all of these years without it.

For a long time they simply stood there on the street, ignoring the strangers who passed by. It was ridiculous, he knew. The woman was a complete stranger, and he hardly knew her. He would make a difficult husband. For many years he had protected himself from the many women who tried to make him their own. Now someone had finally gotten past his defenses and he was crazy enough to consider marrying her. Even worse, he was worried she might not accept him and was ready to do all he could to convince her he was right for her.

His common sense told him to let her go and to run back to the safety of his mill. Yet in his heart, Yakheed did not want to turn away from the wisdom and gentleness he had seen in this woman's eyes. All he had to do now was swallow his pride and ask her to be his wife. When she finally stopped crying, he proposed and she quietly accepted. Two months later, Yakheed and Tirina were married.

Before the first year was out Tirina gave birth. Ever since she had first informed him, Yakheed had assumed the child would be a boy or even two boys. When the midwife informed him the child was a girl, he stared without comprehension. He almost left the room.

The woman looked into his shocked eyes and smiled. "Here," she said quietly, holding out the baby. He shook his head, but she simply pushed the child into his arms and let go.

The baby moved, and he looked down. It was exquisitely beautiful, with tiny hands and perfectly formed fingers. Her face was pink, and soft eyelashes lined her jet black eyes. *She has a strong nose like her father*, he thought to himself. The baby's legs were moving as if she were uncomfortable, and he wrapped the blanket around them to keep them warm. He poked her hand with his finger, and the child instinctively grabbed it.

All of a sudden, Yakheed realized he had never wanted anything but a daughter. Holding that baby in his arms, delicate and fragile, he realized that all of his life thus far had been only a shadow–this was the reality. He forgot about battles, city planning, positions of honor and weaving. Only this baby and her mother meant anything; the rest was just a distraction.

"I name you Tinith," he whispered.

The baby's eyes closed, and he kissed her forehead. Gingerly he carried her into the room where her mother was lying on the bed. Tirina looked up and smiled. "She's beautiful, isn't she?"

Yakheed leaned over and placed the child into her arms. He smiled. "What shall we call her?"

Tirina stroked the soft hair on her head, cuddling the baby gently. "I would like her father to name her, as long as it is a beautiful name, a name she will be pleased to bear."

"Tinith," Yakheed said immediately. "I want to call her Tinith."

She kissed the baby. "You like that name, little Tinith? I like it, and your father likes it too."

A midwife entered the room and bowed to Yakheed. "It is time for your wife to gain some sleep, elder. She has had a hard labor."

Yakheed nodded and began to leave. When he reached the door, he turned and spoke quietly to his wife. "I will be right here if you need me for anything."

He crossed the room to the outside door and stepped onto the busy street. It was late afternoon and people hurriedly passed by him. Nobody seemed to notice him even though his entire existence had been forever changed by the child inside the house sleeping on her mother. He was a father.

As long as I live, Yakheed promised himself, *I will take care of that little girl. Whatever she needs she will have.* The people continued to pass by, but Yakheed hardly noticed. All he could think about was Tinith. *As long as I live I will take care of that child.*

When the child was five he began bringing her to the mill. "I want her to learn how to work hard," he explained to her mother. "My daughter is not going to be like all of the elders' daughters who are pampered and spoiled. She's going to learn to be a weaver like her father and a seamstress like her mother."

From her very first day at the mill Tinith learned how to wash and sweep the floors. She was carrying small loads back and forth from the weavers, who willingly played along with the game, even though it did slow them down at times. Before long, Tinith had become popular among the workers, who treated her as their mascot. They asked her to eat with them and sometimes even brought her toys.

Unexpectedly, laborers began treating Yakheed differently, something he had not expected. Although they never became intimate with him, nevertheless now when they saw him on the street they would smile and greet him warmly. In their eyes, little Tinith transformed Yakheed the Elder and mill owner into Yakheed the father of Tinith.

After lunch time Yakheed would bring her back to her mother, who could not live without her daughter for an entire day. The three of them would take midday walks through the city streets, sometimes leaving the gates to stroll along the river. Then Yakheed would kiss his wife goodbye, hug his daughter and begin to go back to the mill.

Always as he walked away, Tinith would race through the crowd to her father and grab hold of his leg. "Daddy," she then would say, "You forgot to give me a kiss."

Once he fulfilled that duty, she'd return to her mother and head for home. For the rest of the day, Yakheed would find himself continually checking the position of the sun, and wondering how soon it would set and let him leave his workplace to return to his wife and daughter.

It was late spring when the fire struck. Tinith and her father were eating their lunch at the mill when a messenger burst into the eating hall shouting the name

"Elder Yakheed!"   Immediately the entire room went silent. "There is a fire—".

Yakheed jumped up from his seat. "Where? Where is it?"

"At the southern wall," the messenger answered breathlessly.

Before the man could say anything more Yakheed had leaped from the table and was running for the door. Passing a laborer, he shouted out "Care for my girl!"

She did not even have a chance to answer, for he was already out the door and making for the bridge. As he entered the city gate, he heard people talking about a fire, but he did not dare pause long enough to gather news. Frantically he pushed through the crowds, shouting at them to move out of his way.

In the goldsmith's district people were staring at the sky, where thick clouds of smoke were pouring above the rooftops. The sight spurred him on, terror coursing through his veins more devastating than anything he had encountered through the many dangers he had faced over the centuries. Turning a corner and reaching the wide lane of his own street, he burst upon a panicked scene. Crowds were shouting confused orders, and men were racing toward the end of the block where a house blazed with fire–his own house where Tirina had been making candles all morning.

In an instant he pushed his way into the open space where buckets passed from the well to men desperately trying to douse the fire. Flames shot out of the windowsills on both the first and second stories and spiraled through the roof into the sky. Yakheed looked frantically around for help and saw his neighbors pouring water on nearby buildings.

Racing to one of them, he cried out, "Tirina! Is she safe? Have you seen her?" The man shook his head. Yakheed groaned in exasperation. He ran to another man and then another, but no one had seen her.

All of this happened in a matter of moments. It did not take much for Yakheed to determine what he must do. He grabbed a bucket from the line and poured water over his head. Then he ran toward the door of his house. He had to find Tirina before it was too late.

When he was about ten cubits from his home, a crashing sound from above broke through the commotion and caused Yakheed to look up. The roof was collapsing and an entire segment was shifting, breaking off the main section. He jumped back as the burning timbers careened to the ground. Men shouted and several began throwing water on the pile of blazing beams. As Yakheed searched for a path around the flames, more crashing sounds erupted from within, as if the floors of the house were giving way. Suddenly strong arms grabbed him from behind, and he turned.

"You can't go in there," a burly man shouted above the commotion.

"My wife—she's in the house. I've got to get her out!"

The man pointed to the roof. "Look at the trusses! They've already fallen through to the second floor. The second floor has already collapsed onto the first floor. Nobody could be alive in there."

"Let go of me," Yakheed screamed. "I don't care. She's in there, and I've got to get her out!" He struggled to pull free.

The man shouted and several fire fighters left their line to block Yakheed's way. One of them, the shoemaker, was covered with dirt and soot. He grabbed Yakheed's shoulders and stared into his face.

"What about your little one, Tinith?" he shouted above the commotion. "Is she in there?"

"No," Yakheed answered, shaking his head. "I left her at the mill. She's safe."

The shoemaker strengthened his grip. "If the girl is alive, you cannot go into the fire," he shouted. "That girl needs you, Yakheed. You cannot make her an orphan, even if your wife is in that house."

Yakheed moaned. "I can't just let Tirina die, shoemaker!"

The man shook his head. "She's dead already, man." He pointed toward the flames. "Look!"

More sounds of crashing burst from within the burning building. Sparks flew through the air. Another flaming section of roofing broke free and lurched toward the ground. Heat drove the group back across the street.

Yakheed tried to peer through the smoke, screaming with all of his powers, "Tirina! Tirina! Please don't leave me, I beg you!"

But only the sounds of disaster–crackling, roaring flames and collapsing floors and ceilings–emanated from the house. He slumped, falling to his knees. The group of men left him, racing back to the bucket brigade, while Yakheed wept, calling out her name, but knowing she would never answer again.

Sometime after the sun had set, loud knocking broke the silence of Noah's home in a far-away city district. When he and Emah opened the door, there stood Yakheed, covered in soot, holding his Tinith. The girl was clutching a large rag doll.

The elder said quietly, "I'm in trouble, Noah. You see, there was a fire and my Tirina. . ." He began to weep and could not finish his words.

Emah rushed to him, taking little Tinith from his arms. Noah embraced his friend and then led him to his workroom. Emah watched them close the door and then whispered to the little girl, "Child, let us talk to Yahweh. He will listen, and He will help us."

Five years passed. Tinith and her father were working at the mill. "Daddy," Tinith said sweetly, "can we go to see Aunt Emah today?"

Her father did not look up at her, but continued working on the gearbox. He talked to himself for a few minutes while he tried one tool after another, none of which seemed quite right. He looked up. "Tinith, fetch me that bag, please."

"Yes sir," she said and ran to grab her father's tool bag. Reaching inside she pulled out a small wrench.

Her father shook his head. "No, no, that's not what I want. Just give me the bag, and I'll find it for myself."

After a few minutes of working, he smiled and looked over to his daughter sitting patiently on a bench nearby. "Collect all of the tools and gather up all the spare parts and put them in this bag, please. When you get the whole place cleaned up, I think we should go on a picnic. Hmm. . . where should we go?"

Tinith scrambled to pick up her father's tools and then carefully assembled the parts. Within a few minutes she was sweeping the floor to make sure she had missed nothing. She put the boxes into a pile, replaced the tools to their proper position and neatened up the workshop so that it looked better than it had before they had begun their work. The girl raced down the hallway to their apartment below, where she quickly changed her clothes into something more appropriate for a journey up the mountain.

When she was ready, she called up the stairs to her father. "Daddy, what kind of cakes should we bring with us on our picnic?"

Within an hour, father and daughter were making their way up the mountainside to visit Tinith's favorite aunt, Emah. These days Uncle Noah and Aunt Emah spent most of their time at the top of Halftop Mountain, where they were building an enormous boat. Tinith could not understand why they were building the ship, and her father had up to now refused to explain it.

Tinith didn't come to see the barge anyway, but to spend time with her aunt and uncle. Always, as soon as she and her father arrived, Uncle Noah and Aunt Emah would stop whatever they were doing to come and spend the rest of the day with the two of them. Father's friendship with them differed from his relationships with people at home. Tinith was only ten years old but she could tell that the people in the city were careful with her father. They bowed before him, spoke respectfully to him and always seemed to want something from him.

Not so with Uncle Noah and Aunt Emah. They seemed to enjoy seeing her father just to be with him, and she suspected Aunt Emah viewed her more like a daughter rather than as a niece. Whenever they visited, Aunt Emah would create for the two of them a new adventure right on the spot. Sometimes they would go looking for waterfalls. Sometimes they would make up fantasies and play games of intrigue and suspense. And whatever the adventure, while they would walk or sit or climb, Aunt Emah would tell Tinith tales about Yahweh or the descendants of Adam and Eve. Even though in her younger years Tinith enjoyed the adventures more than the conversations, as she matured she found herself increasingly encouraged by Aunt Emah's words about Yahweh and His ways.

Father would never let her go into the boat. Whenever she asked him about it, he would always say, "That's just some crazy idea your Uncle Noah has. Don't worry–it doesn't mean anything at all."

Of course, Tinith secretly wanted to see the inside, imagining some strange and mysterious creatures must be hidden within it, if Father would not let her enter. She knew better, however, than to disobey.

This day they made their way up the mountainside, gazing at fascinating waterwheels Uncle Noah had constructed alongside the stream. Some of them powered a saw mill, but some also powered a unique transportation system. Tinith had often watched the cart puller in action. Shipments would arrive from the town. The carriers would load their goods onto a wagon which was then dragged by a set of pulleys and ropes all the way up the mountainside. Shem, Uncle Noah's oldest son, sometimes walked beside it on its journey and sometimes rode it.

Of course, Tinith continually begged her father to let her ride in the wagon, but he always forbade it. Just watching it go, however, delighted her as it did her father. Today, however, the wheel turned but no wagons were attached.

Below this waterfall stood a much larger fall with an enormous wheel. This ran the lumber mill. She could not enter that building, but her father allowed her to watch through the window as the blade ripped logs into boards of various lengths and sizes. Even though the lumber mill here was similar to the one that her father owned by the river, this mill was simpler and more interesting to watch.

Soon she and her father resumed their journey up the hill. Usually when they traveled, they discussed a wide range of subjects. Father had always believed people could only have worthwhile lives if they learned to think for themselves instead of believing what everyone else simply took for granted. He never let a chance go by to stir his daughter to conversation about anything worth thinking. It had paid off richly; his ten-year-old daughter was in many ways far more mature than most adults he knew.

This is why they would never stop talking until they would reach their friends at the top. Tinith enjoyed every step of it and considered herself to be one of the luckier girls in the city. Even though her mother had died five years ago, and Tinith still sorely missed her, she had a closer relationship with her father than most other daughters had with either parent. Father had taught her to work hard in the mills. He even included her when visitors from other lands came seeking trade for fabrics. They might be uncomfortable having a young witness to their negotiations, but her father did not care. Always in the back of his mind he was planning for his daughter someday to join him in weaving and trading.

The child did miss her mother in many ways. Her father could advise her on how to think well and work hard, but he had little to say about growing up to be a young woman. Not that Tinith envied other girls, for often their mothers would beat them for little or no reason. Even worse, many of the wealthier girls were pampered and spoiled. Tinith rarely talked to such girls and did not enjoy being around them. Yet she sorely missed her mother's wisdom about etiquette and manners. There were times she found herself making social blunders that might have embarrassed any other father in public. Even more she missed her mother's gentleness, and that Father could not supply.

It was for this reason she so often urged her father to visit Uncle Noah and suspected this explained his willingness to leave the mills and his work to go there. Perhaps, however, Father did not do it only for her. A worker had suggested the visits were also good medicine for her father. The fire had taken away his exuberance for life. Several had mentioned how much friendlier her father was when he came back from Halftop Mountain. It was as if Uncle Noah gave Father more hope to keep on living.

In the midst of a spirited conversation about the city elders, they crested the top and began descending into the cone. Decades ago, a forest of trees had filled the mountain top, but ever since Tinith had been coming here, one could see from the rim all the way to the ship. Even though she had visited so many times before, the barge still amazed her. The hull had been finished for several years. These days Uncle Noah and his sons were building floors, rooms, stairwells and storage areas for the barge. Down at the base of the barge stood several wagons filled with wood. A tall crane was lifting the wood to the large opening two stories up.

The machine operated by the power of animals. The animals were harnessed to long poles coming out like spokes on a wheel. As the beasts walked, a series of gears pulled a thick rope running through a pulley at the top of the crane. Uncle Noah's sons attached the rope to heavy items and then started the animals walking in the circle. Using this ingenious method, they were able to raise enormously heavy loads to the top of the barge or into one of the interior compartments.

Today they were raising a thick beam almost twenty cubits long, and Tinith wondered how the animals would be strong enough to pull it. When she asked her father about it, he smiled, pointing to the top of the machine. "See those large pulley wheels up there? That makes the work much easier. Also, look at the place where the animals are attached to the poles. They are all the way out, not in the middle or close to the center. The further away the animals get from the center the easier it is for them to turn that poll. Even though only five animals are walking around that circle, they can do a lot more work than they could simply dragging the beam by themselves."

Soon Uncle Noah and his wife came out to greet them and Tinith and Aunt Emah went for their walk. It was a thoroughly delightful day, and Tinith had lots of questions for her Aunt. The two were so lost in conversation they had no time for games or adventures. They were both sitting on rocks on the far side of the lake when they heard the bell clanging, causing Aunt Emah to look up in surprise.

"It must be time for you to go home," she said with a smile. "Now that we've had our little talk, are you feeling better about some of those older boys in town?"

Tinith nodded. "It helps to discuss things with a woman. Father and I can talk about almost everything, but there are some things he does not seem to understand at all."

They began making their way along the lakeshore toward the barge. Aunt Emah took Tinith's hand. "That's the way God made us, child. Men are not bad and women are not bad. We just don't always understand each other, that's all."

Ahead of them Uncle Noah's sons were drawing the last load of wood into the ship's opening. Tinith often held her breath apprehensively, but no one had yet been injured seriously.

"Why would God make us so different? It makes things so much harder than it would have been if we were all the same."

Aunt Emah laughed. "And since when are easy things necessarily better? I thought you told me that the girls in town who have comfortable lives are usually more selfish. Just because something takes less effort, does not guarantee it will be better. When you have to work hard to understand another person, you learn how to love that person."

"Oh, that explains it."

Emah looked over to Tinith. The little girl was smiling, almost shining. "What are you thinking young lady?"

"It's just that Father is always asking questions about everything I think and feel," she answered. "I assumed it was because he did not trust me or because he was angry at me." She stopped walking and looked up into her aunt's face. "Could it be because he does not understand things about me since I'm different from him?"

Emah reached over and brushed hair out of her niece's eyes. The girl had so much wisdom, not just beyond other girls her age but even beyond many adults that she knew. She had been raised well. "I have never known a father," she answered gently, "who worked harder than yours to love and care for his daughter. I'm sure that's why he's asking so many questions."

Tinith embraced her. The bell rang, and they began walking again. "Even so," she said, "I'm glad Father lets me visit you. It's nice to have someone who does understand without asking questions."

"Do not forget," Emah reminded her, "that Yahweh God also understands. When you talk to Him, He listens, and He answers according to what is best for you."

An hour later Yakheed and his daughter were climbing over rocks at the base of the mountain. Behind them up the hill they could hear the sound of a waterfall, but right now they were more interested in watching and listening to the cascading water in the stream beside them. Tinith leaned over and embraced her father warmly. He hugged her back.

"What's that for?" he asked, surprised.

She squeezed harder. "Oh, it's just something that Aunt Emah said to me. She told me you are the best father a daughter could ever have, and I believe it."

"Did she now?" He grunted. "That's funny. I have always thought that you are the best daughter a father could ever have, and I believe it too." He looked up to the sky. Dark red clouds were slashed across the horizon and wisps of orange clouds feathered the distant mountains. "Child, we had better make our way back home before it's too dark."

The two of them rose and began walking back towards the city gates. Within the walls, vendors were hawking their wares or haggling with customers. Workmen were transporting their tools and materials back to their shops, and children ran through the streets laughing. The sounds of evening swirled around Yakheed and his daughter, but they didn't notice. Instead they walked along the busy street hand in hand as father and daughter.

As they approached their home Yakheed noticed the shoemaker's shop, the man who had begged him not to abandon his daughter in order to save Tirina. How much Yakheed would have lost had he disregarded the man's warning that day. How much Tinith would have lost. Even though he had suffered much, he still had his daughter, and that was a treasure more precious than any one man could ever wish to possess.

Chapter Twelve

Year 1655

Tinith stuffed the fruit and cakes into the rucksack and pulled the straps tightly. She looked over to her father, who was finishing instructions to his servants. She sighed. Ever since Mother died, when Tinith was only five, her father had carried out both a mother's and father's job. He managed the household, oversaw the servants, raised his daughter and governed the greatest city in the world. Whatever greatness the city of Yakheed might have, it all came from Father, Yakheed the elder. His courage and cunning had defeated the Nephilim, and the city's trade and prosperity owed everything to him. Without Father, this city would have been little more than a hovel under the thumbs of the Nephilim. She watched him place his hand on his head servant's shoulder, a sign of great respect in their city. Few men treated their servants and workers better than her father. He cared about them and watched out for their best interests.

He stood in the doorway and watched the servant make his way down the street. Tinith smiled. She thought her father handsome, with his light colored skin, brown hair and strong features. Everyone said that Tinith had received many traits from her father. She had her father's jutting nose, his deep eyes, his rich brown hair and his quick smile. Yet she also had her mother's chestnut skin and beauty. When she walked down the street, some people immediately recognized her as the daughter of Tirana, a woman whose beauty was still legendary, even though fifteen years had passed since she died. Others, however, could tell she was the daughter of Yakheed. Tinith was proud of that, just as she was proud of her father.

He looked back at her, "Well Tinith, are we ready for a little journey?"

"I've been waiting for you, Father," she answered playfully.

He smiled. "Have you now!" he said. "Then this would be the first time in my life that you actually were ready before I walked out the door. Let's go." He turned to leave.

"Wait just a second," she said. "I'll be right there," and ran into the back room to fetch her shawl.

He stepped out the door and called back, "I'll be waiting for you, as always."

They made their way through the busy streets toward the South Gate. It was impossible to carry on a conversation when they walked through the city; every pedestrian, every shopkeeper, even the guards continually interrupted their chats with greetings, requests and expressions of thanks. Tinith loved the adulation, not because it made her feel special, but because she always wanted others to see how great a man she knew her father to be. She had heard stories of his courage and had observed firsthand how selfless he was as a leader. He had started off as an abandoned baby and now ruled a mighty city. All of this position did not turn him arrogant either, for her father was a servant in the true sense, committed to others, fascinated by their stories, hardworking and good. If his temper got him in trouble at times, she could overlook it. He always asked for forgiveness, and he always went out of his way to make things right. Regardless of his idiosyncrasies, Father was a great man.

Once they passed the mills and crossed the bridge, the crowds disappeared and then the fun began. She and her father could discuss any subject without limitation. He loved to bring up difficult questions about trade or governing or the raising of children, and then they would be at it. She would theorize, he would critique, he would then theorize, and she would critique.

"It's the thinking that you need," Yakheed would always say. "You need to examine questions as if the other person may be right and only make your decision when you have seen the strengths of the other person's position."

Sometimes, actually often, she changed her father's mind about different issues. He was open to listening and learning. Sometimes she changed her own mind about an issue. The rest of the time, they agreed to see things just a little bit differently.

Today, however, she could see that her father wanted to talk, and she could tell it was serious. Once they passed the mills and the river, he cleared his throat. "Tinith," he said. "What do you think about your Uncle Noah's crazy idea?"

Tinith inwardly sighed. She and Father had discussed this question many times, starting before her Mother had died. When they came to their final conclusion, he had always explained why Uncle Noah could not be right, and until last year, she always accepted it without thinking. Lately though, she had begun questioning his convictions. Unlike their other debates, this was one where Father did not bend. If any topic might cause trouble on their walk today, this would be it.

"Why do you ask, Father?" she asked.

"I ask," he answered, "because in less than a year, Noah, Aunt Emah, Shem, Japheth and Ham will be locking themselves in the barge, waiting for the waters to come. They'll have enough food to gorge themselves for about five years, but once they admit it was all a farce, they'll never be able to look our people in the eye again. That crazy man has spent almost one hundred years on this barge of his. I just want to make sure you understand how idiotic the whole thing is."

She was quiet for a moment, trying to figure out how to answer. "Well," she finally said, "we certainly don't have any proof that he's right."

"That's for sure," Yakheed said quickly.

She continued. "The only kind of claim that can't be proven or disproved, is when someone hears or sees something no one has heard or seen. We'll never know if Uncle Noah's vision really happened the way he said it did, because none of us were there."

Yakheed turned to her enthusiastically. "My point exactly!"

"On the other hand," she added, "Uncle Noah is the most trustworthy man I have ever met. You know as well as I do that he believes he heard the voice, so we should at least accept the probability that he is not lying."

It was obvious her father didn't like this line of reasoning at all. He started to argue with her about it, but she interrupted him.

"He's also the smartest man in the city. If he believes his story about creation, then I suspect it's true. His own grandfather Methuselah actually knew the first man and woman. That's pretty convincing to me anyway."

Yakheed scowled. "His grandfather must have been a fool, that's what I think."

"Father," she said, "If Uncle Noah's grandfather was a fool, Uncle Noah would have figured that out."

He laughed. "And where is the precious proof that some God named Yahweh created everything? Is there any proof at all?"

She thought for a moment. "Aunt Emah is always saying that everything had to come from something. And, if you think about it, the way things happen in the world is too complicated to be just by chance or something. I'm always amazed when I look at babies, at how intricate they are. How on earth can a baby be formed in a woman's womb unless Someone had planned out the whole process?"

"Hah!" Yakheed blurted out. "There's no plan. They just happen that way."

She shook her head. "Some things may just happen, but not everything. I can understand about rocks and clouds just happening that way, but not babies or trees or animals. No, Someone designed those things. The rocks and clouds are great, but it's humans and animals and plants that amaze me the most. These things don't just happen; Somebody planned them."

"And who created this god, this Yahweh?"

She thought for a moment. "Good question, Father. I don't have an answer."

Her father smiled. "So I stumped you for once."

"It had to happen sooner or later," she answered playfully.

They walked uphill in silence for a while. Over the past year or so, they'd been taking this back pathway to avoid all of the clamor from gawkers and mockers. She found Father's relationship with Uncle Noah difficult to understand. Father wouldn't believe a word about creation, Yahweh, Adam and Eve, God's standards for righteousness and especially the coming oceans of water. Yet every other week, Uncle Noah came to the city to visit Father and the next week, Father would always climb up the hill to visit Uncle Noah. Even if Uncle Noah's wild ideas annoyed Father, at least Tinith could tell how deeply Father respected his friend in every other way. She had heard from others that when her mother died, Father had immediately sought out Uncle Noah for comfort and encouragement. Father had scores of friends, but none as kindly and compassionate as Uncle Noah. There was something about him that kept bringing Father back up this mountain to visit. That was why Father forced the city elders to protect

Uncle Noah from troublemakers. The man might be crazy, but he was too good a man to ignore.

Tinith finally broke the silence. "I will say this, Father. I know Uncle Noah wouldn't give up everything to build the barge unless he was sure these waters are coming. But it's just too fantastic to be real. I don't understand how, but in some way he must have imagined that voice. Until I see real honest proof, I just won't believe."

"That's a girl," Yakheed said, smiling. "Just keep on using your head."

They continued to talk about other subjects: harvests, children and cutting back on drunkenness. This was a frequent discussion between father and daughter.

"Let them have their fun!" Yakheed would say.

Tinith would always answer, "They're destroying their families!"

Finally, the two came over the top. Although they had been here every other week since Tinith was just a little girl, the sight still overwhelmed her senses.

Before them lay a huge crater, formerly covered in trees (not, however, in Tinith's life-time), but now bare. The ground all sloped down to a relatively small point at its center, where laid a stunningly blue lake. A massive barge stood on the lake's shore, three hundred cubits long, fifty cubits wide and thirty cubits high. Standing on almost one hundred stone pillars, the vessel brought visitors a sense of awe, sitting here by itself on the top of a bare mountain.

It was not quite accurate, however, to describe the boat as sitting by itself, for all kinds of paraphernalia surrounded it. Draft animals, such as horses, oxen and buffalo were corralled or caged beyond the bow end of the barge. Several enormous levers, some as tall as the ship, were standing idly by.

Tinith had watched Uncle Noah's sons use those levers to raise the massive gopherwood beams onto their positions on the ship's sides. Uncle Noah or his sons would lash ropes to the beam, then through a series of ropes and pulleys would raise them by the strength of their draft animals. She usually held her breath watching the beam swinging in the air, but every time the lumber dropped into place without incident.

Tinith gazed over the sight. Beyond animals, carts, levers, buildings and tools for construction, she noticed something new–a maze of
some kind of stalls, as if for animals.

"I can't believe it," Yakheed muttered. "He actually thinks animals are coming!"

The comment stirred something in Tinith's mind, and she didn't
immediately answer. Yakheed looked over to his daughter, curiosity
written on his face. "What are you thinking, Tinith?"

"Well, since Uncle Noah's story is too crazy to believe without
facts, if no animals show up, we'll know it was all a dream. If they do
come, Father, we'll have to admit the waters are on their way too.
Once I see those animals, I'll believe everything else he preaches."

Yakheed laughed. "I wouldn't believe it even if the animals did
come, which they won't! How could a good god create everything and
then kill all his handiwork? That would be like me having a child and
then putting her to death for no reason at all."

"It's not like that," Tinith said. "This Yahweh God created humans to rule over the earth. The Father of humanity, Adam, rebelled
against Yahweh, and the world was changed from good to evil. Aunt
Emah says that every time we do not trust the Creator or refuse to love
other people, we are in rebellion, just like Adam and Eve."

Scowling, Yakheed said, "How could I be in rebellion when I
don't even believe in this Yahweh god? I'm a good man, and nobody
can say differently. Look at how I have kept this city alive for hundreds of years."

Tinith frowned. "I don't know, Father. If Yahweh is real, and I
think He is, then it would be pretty bad to ignore him."

By now, they were approaching the great ship. Tinith spotted
Shem, Uncle Noah's oldest son, leading a wagon up to the great ramp.
His face lit up when he saw them.

"Greetings Elder!" he called. "My father is inside the barge.
Climb up the ramp if you want to speak to him."

They ascended the ramp, a long incline parallel to the boat. It rose
to a point perhaps fifteen cubits up the barge's hull. The ramp was
broad enough to allow wagons to pass each other. Tinith noticed four
grooves running from the ground all the way into the barge.

When she pointed them out to Father, he thought for a moment,
and then said, "Very impressive." He pointed to where the ramp met

the ground. "They run the wagon wheels down there into the ruts and then pull the wagon up the incline by that rope attached to the draft animal circle over there."

Tinith saw draft animals attached to a contraption that looked much like a giant wheel, its five spokes running out from the center. When Uncle Noah needed power, he would start the animals walking in a circle. A simple set of gears and pulleys transferred the energy of their work to pulling the wagons, lifting loads on the crane, or pulling beams across the yard.

The entry hatch before them was perhaps twelve cubits wide and ten cubits high. As they neared the top, Tinith said, excitement in her voice, "I've never been inside before."

"Well," Yakheed answered wryly, "be ready for a surprise."

They entered to the smell of smoke from oil lamps. Tinith gasped. An enormous cargo hold stretched out before them. To their immediate left, a ramp led upwards to the third deck, while a ramp to their right led downward to the first level. Before them, a wide aisle cut straight across the barge to the far side, where she could see intersecting aisles to the right and the left. Along the hull, she observed massive trusses connecting to ribs at regular intervals.

When she actually looked at the edge of the entryway opening, she discovered to her surprise four layers of planks. She could tell that the outside layers were horizontal to the floor, but the two inner layers seemed to be at an angle. That made her curious, so she walked around the upward ramp and examined the wall. The planks were entirely covered with a shiny substance, slightly sticky to the touch. She ran her hand over it.

A voice spoke behind her. "That's pitch."

She turned to see her Uncle Noah, carrying a torch and smiling. "We built the hull walls in four layers, section by section. As we built each section, we laid the first layer straight. We lined it with pitch, which we've been gathering from the trees in our gopherwood forest every year. Pitch acts like a glue and also repels water. Then we built the second layer for that section and covered it with pitch, but that layer we set at a forty-five degree angle. The third layer we placed at the opposite angle, covering it with pitch. The fourth layer, as you can see, is straight again."

Running her hand over the surface, Tinith exclaimed, "Amazing!"

Noah looked over to Yakheed, his enthusiasm growing. "I got the idea, in a way, from building the walls of Mehujael. You remember it, don't you?" Yakheed smiled. "Well, then you recall how the outside layer was hard rock to repel anyone who tried to tear the wall down. The only purpose of the middle layer was to provide weight to absorb heavy blows, like battering rams. The backside was only there to keep the inside from pouring out."

He knocked on the hull. "Our problem with waves isn't battering rams, but bending. The ship goes up and down, or the bow goes up and the stern goes down, or the bow goes down and the stern goes down, but the midsection stays up. All of this twisting puts an incredible amount of stress at the middle of the boat. So I'm using my outside wall to repel the water and any floating objects, my inner two layers to deal with the stress (that's why they're at an angle) and the inside wall to hold it together. Different layers accomplish different tasks. Does that make sense?"

Laughing, Yakheed slapped him on the back. "Does it make sense? It made enough sense to stop those Nephilim! That's good enough for me." He looked around. "Why don't you give Tinith a tour?"

They returned to the center aisle at the ramps and walked toward the far side. As Tinith gazed down each row, she saw heavy trusses cutting across the entire midsection at cross angles and a long line of booths, pens and resting places for the animals. When they reached the far side, they turned left. The first pens they passed were perhaps for animals the size of sheep. Above the pens, they found two bins, one atop the other. Pellets the size of the tip of a thumb filled the lower storage compartment. A crib above this contained mounds of hay. Tinith looked curiously at the pellets, having never seen anything like it.

"They're grain pellets," Noah said, answering her unspoken question. "This is what we're doing with most of the grain harvest the farmers bring us. We built a mill on the river just for processing grain into these pellets. We compress them as tightly as possible. They've got lots of fiber in them, but also the grain itself. So, they take far less room and keep the animals alive." He looked above that bin. "Of course, the hay is important too, and we've been working night and day bringing it in and stuffing it there."

They resumed walking, passing dozens and dozens of similar sized bins. "How do you know what all of the animals eat?" Tinith asked. "You can't feed them all the same things."

Noah nodded. "I know that. We're going to try to feed grain pellets to as many as possible. For meat eaters, we have dried as much meat as we can over the past year. For the rest, we'll find out when the animals arrive."

"What do you mean?" she asked, curious.

Noah answered, "Animals that need special foods will go foraging. We'll try to follow them, to see if we can bring enough to sustain them."

Yakheed cleared his throat. "You can feed them your dreams, Noah. 'Cause that's all that'll be coming here."

Noah smiled. "My friend, I hope you're right. With all my heart, I hope you're right."

Tinith glanced over at her father and saw a flash of anger flit into his eyes. She grabbed his hand and squeezed it. He kept looking ahead, clearly trying to restrain a nasty reply. Miraculously, he said nothing. Tinith marveled at how deeply he must have loved Noah to check his temper.

They continued walking down the row, looking at the various cages, and Uncle Noah seemed unaware that he had sparked irritation in her father. After a few minutes, however, the elder relaxed and began joking again.

As they toured the lower level, Tinith noted the floors of many stalls were slatted and asked her uncle about it.

"Well, we know we'll have plenty of larger animals, and we simply can't handle all of their waste. I tried this first in a limited way in Mehujael, then a bit more in my cave, but perfected it on a farm I worked for several years before I went out preaching. The animal's solid waste drops onto the slats. As the animals move back and forth, their hooves or feet push the waste through the slats into large bins underneath. The liquid drains off and the solid stays. As long as the liquid is gone, the solid won't be a problem."

Yakheed grimaced. "The smell would be enough to kill you."

"I know," Noah said. "I used a system like this in a dairy barn I ran for two years. The smell wasn't too bad, because the liquid drained off. The liquid is what makes it really unbearable. Regardless, after a while you get used to it."

"You have a lot of your pens lined with straw," Tinith said.

Noah pointed to such a place. "I worked on a farm once for about eight months, where the owner raised dozens of wild animals. He kept all of them in pens with thick beds of straw. Their waste material filtered through the straw, and he never changed it the whole time I was there. I didn't like the idea, but it seemed to work at least for those eight months."

Tinith looked horrified. "How cruel!"

"It's all a matter of perspective," Noah said. "I've spent much of my life in the wilderness. You do whatever you can to survive. That's all we need to do–survive."

When they reached the human quarters of the boat, they all reclined on pillows. Tinith examined the various aspects of the room. The furnishings were austere, just enough to get by, but little more. She noted doorways into four bedrooms, which surprised her. "Aren't you all sleeping in the same room?" she asked with curiosity. "Wouldn't that be a little more comforting in a world surrounded by animals day and night?"

"Actually, I have a feeling we'll want to be by ourselves," Noah answered with a chuckle. "Besides, my sons will be bringing wives with them."

"Wives?" Yakheed exclaimed. "Do you really think any woman would be crazy enough to marry one of your sons and climb up that ramp into this madhouse? They'd better do it the Nephilim way; raid the village, kidnap the tallest woman on the street and hope for the best."

Noah sighed. Tinith guessed that her father's comments had hit a sensitive spot.

"My sons have been terribly busy, and I suspect you are right, Yakheed. Emah has been telling the story of creation for a hundred years, and few women have responded."

"And I suppose," said Yakheed, "that none of those women happen to be available for marriage."

Noah acceded the point. "All I know is this; if God is powerful enough to bring the oceans of water, then God is powerful enough to bring the animals. If God is powerful enough to bring the animals, then most certainly He will bring wives for my three sons."

"A lot of ifs," Yakheed said. "And not a whole lot of facts."

Nodding, Noah said. "I promise you, friend; not a day goes by that I don't wonder whether I'm as crazy as you think I am. But almost one hundred and twenty years ago, my grandfather Methuselah had a dream warning him about the end of humankind. Then my vision came to me, and it was as clear as your voice right now. I won't give up this work; I can't give it up. As far as we can figure, in about seven months, the end will come."

Not long after, Yakheed and his daughter Tinith left their good friend and returned across the bridge to town. Noah's unshakeable convictions unsettled both father and daughter, even though neither admitted it. For Tinith, the only real issue was Uncle Noah himself. This man was far from a fool, and both she and her father recognized that. His theory seemed too fantastic to accept, yet how could she deny what he was doing? He never apologized for devoting his life to a vision he had received a hundred years before. The foundation of his faith was the story his father and grandfather had passed on to him since his childhood. He had never actually professed this, but Tinith suspected him to be the son of the Promise described by Aunt Emah in her many stories.

Furthermore and even more importantly, for a good while Tinith had believed in the Creator Yahweh, and she understood why Yahweh would judge the world for its sin. She had seen her own selfishness and rebellion, and at times she was appalled by her twisted heart. If the Promise story was true, and Uncle Noah turned out to be the son of the Promise, she could almost imagine that this Yahweh God might have spoken to him. An enormous barge, however, filled with grain and hay, divided into thousands of animal pens–this was ludicrous. It wasn't Noah's story that made her doubt; it was this Yahweh's command to build a ship. Why not simply miraculously save them all? Why appoint a man to gather, build, feed and deliver?

Yakheed, after this visit, began doubting himself. He couldn't put his finger on why he was convinced Noah's boat just didn't make sense. The problem was, if the story turned out to be true, then Adam and Eve were true, and sin was true, and Yahweh was true, and judgment was right. If a man lived his life the best he could, but ignored Yahweh, then the man would be a sinner, no matter how good a man he was otherwise. That concept was so insulting to Yakheed, who had spent his life working hard with his hands, thinking clearly, serving his people, succeeding in trade and saving an entire city from destruction. If Yahweh demanded humans to obey him and love him, then even though Yakheed was one of the most celebrated heroes in the entire region, that would count for nothing, because he did not love God or obey him. *Outrageous!* he thought to himself. *No god could overlook all the good I've done, just because I didn't care to believe and serve him.*

Methuselah toted the firewood into the house and threw it beside the fireplace. According to his calculations, the end of all flesh would be within seven months. Lamech and Qanath had died five years ago. All of Methuselah's other offspring had migrated away from the shadow of Eden, leaving the ancient man entirely alone. It was not pleasant, being the last man to dwell within Eden's shadow. His routine was always the same. He would rise early, work in the garden, care for the animals, clean and sharpen his tools and then rest. In the afternoons, he walked. Most of the sheep were set free now, since their wool no longer met a need. The projects were completed, since he hardly needed to build anything new, and whatever was broken might as well stay that way. At times, Methuselah felt like the only man on earth, and often he wished it were so. For the judgment was sure to come and humankind would be no more, except that is, for Noah.

How ironic, Methuselah thought to himself, *that Noah's name meant 'rest.'* Humankind would surely rest from their labors, but it would be the sleep of death which would overflow the world in waves of wrath and judgment. Seven months and it would all be over.

Chapter Thirteen

Year 1656: The Last Days

Five Months Before the End

The first report was almost impossible to believe. Tinith was working in their garden plot when her father appeared at the courtyard gate. "Daughter," he said wryly, "there's a sight on the south side you probably would like to take a look at."

He held out his hand and led her to the stairs on the south gate, which they ascended to the catwalk along the outer wall. She looked out over the land beyond the city walls and gasped. At least thirty different behemoth, all absolutely enormous, were congregated beside the river, to the west of the mills. Some of these animals, who had never come near the entire region, were foraging in the brush and woods, dragging sticks and brush across the grassy area.

Tinith had never before beheld a large behemoth, and she was struck by their lumbering gait. Some of the animals seemed vicious, with tooth filled mouths and threatening looks. The entire group, however, seemed at peace with one another.

Yakheed sighed. "I have seen a few behemoth during my days, but never so close! That one over there," he pointed to a slightly smaller animal on two feet, "looks like it's ready to kill the whole lot of them! Imagine, right here at our city walls."

Tinith looked at her father. "You mean, right here at Noah's boat, don't you?"

He snorted. "I thought you might say that. But I've been on that barge, and it does not have one space big enough for an animal a quarter that size."

She thought about his comment and smiled. "I didn't see any spaces that big either. But it is awfully strange that those animals would show up with five months to go."

The arrival of the first behemoth stirred each of the five workers on Halftop Mountain differently. Ham, the middle son, laughed when news reached them. "Finally," he muttered. "Finally these people will stop mocking us as fools. Now let's see who does the mocking."

Japheth looked at the mountains of pellets and hay still needing to be loaded into the various storage bins. "Unless we work without rest for the next five months, a lot of animals are going to go hungry on this boat of ours."

Shem came to Noah in despair. "Father, we have no wives, and it's time to launch our barge. You've got to go to the town and find three women willing to join us." But Noah was not yet ready to leave their work.

Emah sought out her husband, putting her arm around him. "I always knew, my Noah, that God had given you this vision. Now everyone will know you are God's promised son."

Noah did not answer. The appearance of the beasts had further unsettled the turbulence in his thoughts.

Four Months, Three Weeks Before the End

A week or so later, mastodons, mammoths, elephants and other enormous animals arrived. Strangely, these also were too large to fit the boat, yet Tinith could hardly attribute their appearances alongside the behemoth as coincidence. By the end of the month, an entire population of enormous creatures filled the plain beyond the city walls on both sides of the river. They stayed away from the mills and bridge, but few men or women dared to venture onto the road leading up Halftop Mountain.

It was about this time, that Yakheed finally understood what the animals were doing. The hairy animals were preparing to give birth, and the behemoth were creating nesting areas to lay their eggs. This was all happening without any human interaction at all. No one dared interrupt the habitation of the animals; the calamity it might engender would be far too dangerous to take the chance.

Four Months Before the End

The first to bear twins were the mastodons, and crowds watched from the wall with fascination. Afterwards, others also bore offspring, all twins as well. In the face of every other miracle, Tinith assumed they were male and female twins. Before long, more animals had appeared, all large and all preparing nests or birthing areas. Tinith could no longer could deny the obvious; these animals had come to Noah. Although none had ascended the mountain, they nevertheless were coexisting with one another in peace, something which normally could never happen in the wild and especially where newborns were involved. The enormous area beyond the south gate became a land of impossibilities. For Tinith, the greatest impossibility became a reality; Noah's vision was true.

Even with the sudden appearance of animals, Yakheed steadfastly denied what Tinith had finally conceded. One day, as they monitored the events beyond the south gate, he suddenly exclaimed, "How could a good god destroy so many wonderful things? It's impossible. How could a good god allow so much suffering in the world? How could he let fathers defile their daughters, or mothers leave their babies to die on barren hillsides? How could he be good and let so much evil rule the earth? But he can't be bad either, because a bad god wouldn't be able to make good things, and there's a lot of good in the world too."

Tinith answered him quietly. "How could a man know that in one hundred years animals would come to gather at the foot of a mountain? How could animals normally at enmity with one another live side by side while giving birth? How could there be a hundred different creatures, all of which birth twins?"

He shook his head in disgust. "Your questions don't answer my questions. I see the animals. Yes, they are amazing, but they don't explain how a good god, would allow the kinds of pain I have seen in my life. I don't care about animals suddenly giving birth to twins. The god of Noah is not a good god, and I cannot believe he is creator of all things."

Tinith glanced at her father in surprise. It was not the facts he denied; the facts were nursing their young on the plain before him. He did not like the kind of Creator Noah preached. Even though the story of Adam and Eve explained the suffering surrounding them, that story did not satisfy Yakheed, because he could not, or was it that he would not, accept a god who allowed suffering in the world. As long as suffering ruled the planet, Yakheed would always see the Creator as false. Was this not a form of hatred, to refuse to accept someone as he was rather than as one would wish him to be?

Tinith suddenly understood human rebellion. They had plenty enough information to believe in the Creator. Humans, however, didn't like the Creator the way He really was and therefore they rejected the information as well. She opened her mouth to speak, but stopped. If the promise was true–and she no longer questioned this–then many more animals would begin appearing. As that came about, Father would have no choice but to believe.

Three Months and Two Weeks Before the End

When Methuselah came down from the flocks, he saw from the distance a figure standing by the river. As he walked, he tried to guess who it might be, since in the past few years visits had almost entirely ceased. It wasn't until he actually reached the shoreline that he recognized his grandson Wehtam, the father of the girl pledged to Noah. His grandson was staring at the waters, obviously deep in thought and had not yet noticed his grandfather's approach.

Methuselah broke his solitude, saying, "Wehtam, you have made a great journey to visit your grandfather."

Wehtam looked up and a smile broke out on his face. "Grandfather!" he exclaimed. "It's so good to see you!" He rose and embraced Methuselah. "Four months ago, my beloved wife died, and I thought that I would rather be with you at the end than be lost in a panic-stricken city."

Over the next hours, Wehtam told him of Noah and the impact he had made on the city of Yakheed. He described the marriage of his daughter, the birth of the son of the Promise Shem, the vision, the building of the barge, the opposition of the people and the closeness of the end. Methuselah soberly absorbed the information in silence.

At the end of the discussion, the grandfather looked out over the river, thinking of what was shortly coming to all living things. He sadly shook his head. "And your Emah, is she contented with her husband and the fate that awaits her?"

"She believes she was born for this work, Grandfather. She is contented."

Methuselah turned back to his grandson and smiled. "Then you and I must be contented with our part in the story. I am glad you have come to be with me at the end."

Three Months Before the End

One sunny morning, Tinith stood watching the growing multitudes of animals camping beyond the city walls. In the distance she saw Uncle Noah himself walking among the beasts, apparently fearless. *He's probably observing their eating habits*, she thought to herself, *and is making his final adjustments to what he will provide for them.*

Tinith watched most of the morning, fascinated by the impossible assortment of creatures. Several times, Noah approached some of the largest beasts, but she could not guess his purpose. Toward noon, he crossed the bridge and made his way to the south gate. She immediately ran to find her father, who reluctantly agreed to escort Uncle Noah to his destination.

They were standing at the gate when he arrived. Even before he reached them, some of the bystanders there were murmuring threats. "What is this troublemaker doing here? He's the one who brought all these animals, disrupting everything we're doing!"

Yakheed and Tinith quickly pushed through the crowd to their friend, and upon seeing the city elder, the voices quieted for the moment.

As they left the gate and made their way to the house, Yakheed anxiously looked behind them. "Nobody's following. At least that's a good sign."

The three continued along the streets, uncomfortably aware of glaring passers-by, who occasionally made unsettling comments. They finally made it to the house and slipped inside in relief.

As Yakheed shut and bolted the door behind them, he said quietly, "I think it might be better if you didn't return to our city, Noah, at least until all of this is past."

Noah walked slowly over to a bench and sat down. "I didn't expect antagonism, just indifference."

Yakheed pulled up a bench and sat across from him. For a long time, he didn't reply, but was obviously wrestling with how to answer. Tinith watched her father, curious. Finally, he spoke. "It's the animals, Noah. They all blame you for those animals being here. It makes no sense to me; the beasts are just a freak of nature. The people are frightened and want to know when those cursed animals are going away."

Leaning forward, Noah answered in a quiet voice, "Yakheed, they all know when the animals will leave. I've been telling them for a hundred years. In three months, the beasts will be gone, but at that point, nobody will be worrying about the creatures."

"I don't believe it," Yakheed said tensely. "I can't accept this fantasy that some creator god would destroy the world simply because a few human beings don't obey him." He leaned forward. "I've never seen him, and you're supposedly the only one who's ever heard him speak. How could he judge me for not believing in what I cannot see?"

With quiet conviction, Noah said, "You do see, Yakheed. You see what He's done. The whole creation, especially living creation, could only continue on if it was planned by Someone."

"That's ridiculous!" Yakheed said with contempt. "It just happens. Nothing more."

Noah considered for a moment. "Suppose you came upon a city in the middle of the wilderness. Suppose that city had a thousand empty buildings. Wouldn't you say someone must have built them?"

"Not necessarily," Yakheed answered. "You lived in a cave for three hundred and fifty years, and nobody built that. Your cave had rooms, water and light. No, I think it could all just happen that way."

Noah smiled. "Alright, you decide to explore this strange city which seemed to happen just by chance. As you're walking down the street, you hear a whirring and a grinding sound, and you follow the noise to the river. There you see an enormous grist mill, with a water wheel, pulleys, ropes, gears, millstones, shafts and buckets. Now, would you say someone must have built it?"

Yakheed said nothing.

"You walk through the building, counting every gear, every sprocket, every shaft. One hundred and twenty three gears, fifty sprockets, twenty shafts. Every single piece fits perfectly. If one tiny sprocket was the wrong size, the whole giant gristmill would grind to a halt. Just one wrong size."

The elder watched him darkly, but Noah continued. "Once you've counted everything, you look at the whole machine with amazement. 'Somebody really intelligent must have planned this mill!' you say to yourself. 'I'll bet my good friend Noah was here! This looks just like the way he plans his mills. Every single gear fits just right.'"

Yakheed shook his head. "It just happened that way."

"Maybe some things do just happen," Noah said, "but I can promise you, things like animals or machines can't just happen. The looms in our mills couldn't just happen. You and I designed every single part for the machines we built, and each part had to be exactly right. If the smallest gear was too big or too small, the loom couldn't have turned at all. If we didn't make the shuttle at the perfect angle, the whole thing would catch and break into pieces. When you have working parts in something, parts that only function when other parts are working, then we know somebody had to plan how the parts were going to interact with each other."

He looked intently at his friend. "Yakheed, a fool would never be able to design that mill, and you and I both know it. It took all of your wisdom and experience, and it took all of mine. It took a lot more wisdom for Yahweh to design each tree, each animal."

Turning away his gaze, Yakheed said, "But that's different. Looms and mills don't just happen in nature. Animals do."

Noah shook his head. "What does that mean? That just because we see animals every day, therefore nobody had a plan to make them work? A male and a female sheep come together, and in months lambs are born. I've seen the inside of a female sheep, and no little lambs are hiding in her. So where do they come from? They form inside the mother, according to a plan! When the lamb is born, it has a heart, a liver, a kidney, a bladder, a brain, muscles, blood and literally a hundred other organs. Every single one of those organs has to fit just right for the lamb to live. Somebody had to figure out the plan, Yakheed, to make sure each one of those parts would work together properly. If a loom can't happen by chance without a plan, how can something far more complicated happen without a planner?"

"So explain to me," Yakheed spat out bitterly, "how this Yahweh of yours created his world in order to destroy it all on a whim."

Noah closed his eyes and frowned. "It's not a whim. We are Yahweh's reflection. He appointed Adam and Eve to rule over every plant, every animal in creation, just as Yahweh Himself rules. They were responsible for creation, to care for it, to serve it, to protect it, but Adam chose to throw it all away by submitting to his wife and sinning. When he sinned, the whole planet was thrown upside down. Adam no longer served Yahweh. Creation no longer served Adam, but fought against Him in every way. If the ruler rebels against his ruler, then all of his subjects will rebel against him. That's where suffering comes from and that's why creation will share in the horrors of God's judgment against Adam's race."

Tinith looked at her father fearfully. Fury lined his face, and she was beginning to suspect he would not listen, no matter how clearly Noah explained.

Suddenly Yakheed exploded in anger. "But what about the children? Is God judging them?"

"When I was a young man," Noah answered quietly, "I came upon a baby left to die outside the city gates. Who was responsible for that baby's suffering?"

"It's parents!" Yakheed said bitterly. "They chose to have the child, and they should have protected it."

Noah agreed. "And did the baby do anything to deserve such a horrible fate? No. The parents should have protected it because they were made in God's image. They were responsible for the baby. They didn't want to submit to God's ways and therefore they killed their baby. Who suffered? The baby. That is not right, but it's what happens when those in Yahweh's image refuse to obey their Creator."

Yakheed said nothing, listening in silence.

"That baby suffered," Noah said, "as a consequence, of the parents' choices. The baby did nothing wrong, but because the parents were responsible for the baby, the baby suffered. God gave the parents this responsibility. When the flood comes, babies will die because their parents refuse to believe in Yahweh and turn from their sin."

"And how," Yakheed asked in anger, "is that possibly fair?"

Noah leaned forward. "It doesn't seem fair now, but God will bring justice at the end. When the child suffers and the parents go free, God sees the sin. He promises that in the end the parents will bear the consequences for murdering the child."

Looking Noah in the eye, Yakheed said, "I have never murdered a child, Noah. I have never allowed anyone in this city to leave a child to die like that. So why does Yahweh judge me?"

"The day I saw that baby," his friend answered quietly, "I stood there wrestling with what to do. I was leaving civilization and had no way to raise it without changing all of my plans. The baby could be saved, I knew, but then I'd have to deny everything I wanted. So I left it there to die. Was that murder?"

Yakheed looked at Noah. At that moment, Tinith felt as if her father loathed him more than the lowest thief or murderer. "You killed that baby just as much as its parents did."

Noah paused for a moment before continuing. "So I can murder someone without ever touching her. I can be responsible for someone whose name I never knew. When I do not care for my fellow human, I am committing murder. My fellow human suffers the consequences and at first, I get away for free. Therefore, in the end, God must bring His judgment."

The room went silent. Tinith watched her father in anticipation. He opened his mouth to speak, but stopped, as if slapped in the face. She wasn't sure why, but wondered if perhaps Noah's argument hit home.

Finally, Yakheed answered ominously. "And what if I cannot see this murder I have committed? How then could your Yahweh judge me?"

Quietly, Noah considered his friend's response and then answered gently. "The parents of the baby, if they thought what they did was right, should they be judged? And I, when I abandoned that same baby, should I be judged? The baby paid the consequences for her parent's and my sin; therefore her parents and I in the end must pay the consequences."

"And how do you pay the consequences, Noah son of Lamech?" Yakheed said angrily. "When Yahweh's waters destroy all flesh, you'll be hiding away on your barge, safe from paying for all the sins you committed."

"Well. . . I. . ." Noah faltered, unable to reply.

Yakheed smiled bitterly. "So, are you better than the rest of us, Noah? Have you been more faithful to your Yahweh than the rest of us? Why you?"

Tinith stirred. "He is the descendant of Eve, Father."

"I thought we all are her descendants," Yakheed answered harshly.

She nodded, answering cautiously. "We are, but in the story of the Promise, God promised Eve that her descendant would crush the serpent's head. God promised that someday a man would bear the penalties for all men's sins, if they trust in the Promise. Noah is the next man in the line which will someday lead to the one who will save humankind from the serpent."

"That ridiculous!" Yakheed said, his face livid. "Are you saying he's somehow better than the rest of us?"

Tinith steadied herself, thinking through her answer. "No. In fact, Aunt Emah has always taught me that the only way she or Noah could be saved from God's wrath is through the sacrifices they offer to Yahweh. Noah and his family take animals and lay their hands on them, confessing their sins. Then they kill the animals as a picture of the Promise that will come when Eve's descendant saves us from our sins."

"And you believe this nonsense?"

She nodded meekly. "I have believed for a long time now in Yahweh and Adam and Eve. When I saw the animals arriving beyond the south gate, I believed the vision of Noah." She walked to the window and looked through the cutout into the street. "I believe the waters are coming, Father. You and I don't have long to live. You need to believe too."

Yakheed rose slowly, his face red with rage. "Get out of my house, Noah son of Lamech. You have deluded my daughter into believing your idiotic nonsense." Noah immediately rose. "And you, Tinith, must stop believing this tripe. I will not have my daughter calling me a murderer."

"But Father—" she began.

Yakheed interrupted her, furious. "We will not discuss this again. Not the animals, not the barge, not the creator! Do you understand, girl?"

Noah was now standing beside the door. "Yakheed, at least consider allowing Tinith to come with us on the boat."

"What?" he shouted. "Have you lost your mind? My daughter will never join you."

Tinith looked at her father in shock. "But the animals, Father. You know it has to be true. The waters are coming. Do you want me to die?"

Yakheed grabbed her arm. "I will not allow you to have anything to do with this lunatic, Tinith. I forbid you from ever speaking with him again."

She tried to pull away from her father's iron grip. "I don't understand this. You leave me in the city to die, simply because you don't want to believe in Noah's God? How are you better than the parents who leave their babies to die outside the city gates?"

Yakheed slapped his daughter in the face, the first time in her life her father had struck her. She pulled away from him in shock. Noah opened the door, leaving Yakheed standing in bewilderment. Tinith ran into her room, crying uncontrollably.

One Month Before the End

Over the passing of the next two months, more animals arrived across the river. The name Noah was no longer a joke, but a curse. Rumors had spread through the city that Noah was trying to kidnap young girls as wives for his three sons. Tinith heard from several women that the day Tinith and her father had escorted Noah, he had left the city alone, and she wondered what he would do without wives for his sons.

When she tried to find out information about the animals or Noah, she quickly found the subject impolitic, usually resulting in icy stares and cold attitudes. An ugly mood had settled on the city, and no one wanted to talk about anything to do with the animals, the barge or Noah. Drunkenness increased, as did immorality. The streets became unsafe, even during daylight hours.

Tinith began to realize that she was alone in her faith and decided not to speak about Yahweh to anyone, fearing they might inform her father, who would almost certainly confine her to the house. No matter what the people of the city believed, however, Tinith no longer doubted that disaster was about to befall the world. She did not want to die in an ocean of water pouring over city walls. Noah had offered her a place on the barge, presumably as wife of one of his sons, but her father had forbidden this without any qualification. Yet she was sure going with Noah was the right thing to do and also thought it her responsibility to find two other women ready to follow. Where, however, would she find even one believer in a city so dead set against Noah's message? For years, no one had responded to his appeals about the Promise. At least, no adult.

Tinith thought back to those days when as children, she and her friends would gather in the square to hear Emah's stories. Did any of those girls back then believe? She concentrated her thoughts on the children who sat on the hard stone, all eagerly listening to Noah's wife. One face surfaced in her mind, a child named Aleac. *I need to find Aleac*, Tinith thought to herself. *The girl always had questions for Aunt Emah. Perhaps she still believes.*

With little time left, Tinith began searching for her childhood acquaintance. Day after day, she questioned every woman in every market she could find. No one remembered the girl or the name, and she began to worry her quest might be hopeless.

Two Weeks Before the End

Two long weeks passed before she finally found someone in the city who had heard the name Aleac before. She was a rag peddler in the oldest sector and after selling Tinith several bundles of useless fabric, she suggested that perhaps Tinith should check the blacksmiths' quarter, for a young woman there went by that name.

The next morning Tinith made her way through the streets in the smiths' quarter, searching for her friend, wondering if she would even recognize her. After hours of wandering, she came upon a woman sweeping off a doorway in a smithy's back alley.

"Excuse me," Tinith ventured cautiously, "are you familiar with a woman named Aleac?"

The woman looked up, a curious expression on her face. She stared for almost a minute at this strange inquirer and then cautiously whispered, "Tinith? Is that you?"

Tinith threw her arms around the woman, and they fell into a stream of questions and answers. Finally, Aleac looked into her friend's eyes. "What on earth ever led you to find me here?"

Tinith took her hand. "Do you remember Emah's stories when we were children?" Aleac looked furtively around them, as if afraid someone might overhear. She nodded secretively and then led Tinith away from the doorstep through the alleyway to a small garden by the inner wall.

"Do you believe in the Promise?" Tinith asked.

Aleac checked to make sure no one could hear them. "Yes."

"How have you and your family reacted to the animals coming near our city?"

"It has terrified me to see such huge and ferocious looking animals, but my family won't even discuss it. They seem so angry at Noah. They blame him completely."

Tinith looked sadly at Aleac. "I know this will be hard for you, but are you willing to join me on the boat?"

Aleac glanced nervously to the street, appearing to check for family members or even suspicious neighbors. She quietly whispered, "Yes. But Tinith, can you arrange this for me?" Tinith nodded her head.

Aleac looked earnestly at Tinith. "I have a friend who also believes in the Promise. Do you think she can join us also?"

Tinith felt relieved to see how Yahweh was providing for all of them. For the next hour, they planned how they might escape their families to join Noah on his boat. They would have to wait, worried about leaving too soon and inciting perhaps a riot or attack upon Noah's family. As they discussed it, they decided to wait until the very last moment to come to the barge. Aleac agreed to recruit her friend, and Tinith agreed to inform her Uncle Noah.

That night, after Yakheed had fallen asleep, Tinith crept out of her room, opened the outside door and quietly made her way down the street. After what seemed to be an eternal journey, she reached the small door beside the south gate, which was barred for the night. A sentry stood watch beside the door, and Tinith approached him nervously. He fortunately did not recognize her and willingly accepted the small bag of gold to allow her to exit the city onto the outside plain.

She followed the road over the bridge and came to one of the wagons used to haul food up the mountainside. Carefully, Tinith placed a note and two large pieces of cloth on the seat of the wagon. In the note, she explained their request. If Noah wanted Tinith and her two friends as wives for his sons, they were to fly the black flag from the far side of the bridge. If they rejected the offer, they should plant a white flag there. She hurried back to the gate and then to her room and fell into a nervous sleep.

At noon, Tinith came to the wall. A black flag flew from the bridge. She sighed. In two weeks, the end would come. She would need to prepare Aleac and her friend, Hannah, who was also coming with them, for what would happen next.

She guessed they must ascend the mountain before the animals crossed the river, yet the threat of her father's anger worried her. If they left the city too soon, what would Father do? Would he organize an army to attack the group atop the mountain? Would he attempt to burn them out of the barge? She could not take that chance. On the other hand, once the animals began ascending, she doubted if anyone would dare attack, out of fear these passive beasts might turn on them.

The plan, then, was to leave the city right before the animals began making their way up the pathway. Looking out over the field, filled with the mighty animals, it would take all of her courage just to pass across the grasses, walking among behemoth and mammoths to ascend Halftop Mountain. Tinith sighed. It would take even more courage to leave her father.

Nine Days Before the End

Nine days before the end, Shem found Noah dismantling a shack along the path to the rim. "Father," he said urgently, "We still have no wives. I know that Tinith has promised she will bring two women to us, but the end is almost here."

His father nodded and stared at where the pathway descended to the city. "I have been praying about this all week, all day in fact. Tinith is a sharp young woman and knows how to think for herself."

"What if Yakheed forbids her to come?"

Noah thought for a moment. "He's already done that. He could, I suppose, imprison her, but normally, that's not his way of doing things. I'm a little worried if she comes to us, that he may try to stop us."

"I'm worried about that," Shem answered. "I guess if God can protect us from the waters, he can protect us from the city."

Eight Days Before the End

Eight days before the end, the three women secretly packed bags and smuggled them out of their homes, stowing them in an empty shop by the south gate. They were hoping to reach the barge before the animals began boarding, but could not work out a way to tell when that might happen. That afternoon, however, news came to them which made their decision easy–hundreds of animals were arriving on the battle plain north of the city walls. The animals, apparently, had begun arriving in the morning and seemed to be making their homes all along the vast plains which opened before the city. Citizens began worrying about trade, since no one would dare travel the road across the plain surrounded by hordes of wild beasts, many of which normally might be quite vicious.

The tidings changed their approach to escaping the city. Since the animals were obviously here as a stopping point on their way to the barge, the women would simply watch the northern fields all day over the next eight days. The journey around the city would take the beasts enough out of the way that once the women saw them move, the three women would be able to pass through the city, cross the bridge and ascend the mountain. Even if they didn't reach the bridge before the exodus began, Tinith knew about another way up which she doubted the animals would take.

At this point, then, the three women took their posts on the north wall. It was now only a matter of time.

Wehtam found his grandfather standing on the banks of the Great River. He was looking across the waters at two mighty behemoth drinking from the river. "They're amazing, aren't they? It breaks my heart to think they will not survive this flood."

"But Grandfather," Wehtam said. "Before I left the city, behemoth were already preparing to bear young for the barge. The earth's greatest beasts will be in the new world."

Methuselah smiled. "Of course! They bear young, and raise them enough to be ready to board the ship. Amazing! Everything is coming together according to Yahweh's plan."

Seven Days Before the End

From her vantage point on the northern wall, Aleac saw a movement among the animals on the plain beyond the gates. Some of the
first animals were approaching the city. Her heart pounding, she
scrambled down the steps to the streets below, where she found Tinith.
What Aleac had just seen so startled her, that she attracted the attention of bystanders who watched them somewhat suspiciously. Aleac
caught Tinith's eye and nodded silently. The two held hands as they
hurriedly began making their way down the street, passing shops,
homes and street venders. As they approached the city council building, Tinith grabbed Aleac's arm. "Get Hannah and bring her to the
south gate. I must say goodbye to Father! Wait only a few minutes.
If I'm not there soon, leave without me." She raced up the long marble
stairs leading to the public meeting chambers. Aleac called out,
"Hurry!" to her, but did not slow her pace. Time was running out.

That evening, Methuselah looked at Wehtam, who was tending a
fire. "Grandson, I think it's time for a journey, don't you?"
Wehtam smiled. "A journey? We have nowhere to go!"
Methuselah pointed northward. "About a two day's trek from here,
we'll come to an altar. I think it's time for us to bring sacrifices to
Yahweh. Are you disposed to join me for the last journey to Eden?"

Noah was loading hay on a wagon near the ramp, looking toward
where the pathway descended the mountain. It was time to gather the
family for the last preparations. He dropped the hay and strode to a
hollow metal pipe hanging from a scaffold. Taking the hammer, he
struck the pipe several times, summoning his sons and wife. As he
waited for the family, he looked at the work they had done. The ship
had been ready for a year. The supplies were almost all on board now.
Their only remaining task was to disconnect the ramp from the ship
once the last animals had arrived and close the door, although he was
not sure how from the inside of it, they could make it wholly secure.
In a few moments, Emah and her sons had gathered around Noah,
looking at one another, fear etched into their faces.

Noah sighed. "Now it begins."   He turned to his three sons. "Leave everything you've been doing; whatever it is, we'll have no more time for loading and fashioning. Help me clear the pathway from the road to the barge. Then, I need you men to tear down any building that stands higher than these supports for the barge."

Glancing over to the rim of the crater, where animals would soon begin appearing, he said, "I have a feeling we won't have time to direct them to where they need to be in the boat. God has brought them here and therefore we'll trust Him to lead them to their proper pens or cages." He looked to heaven. "Mighty God, give us wisdom now, and Lord, protect the women who will shortly join us and bring them to us at the right time."

Tinith entered the public chambers, where the stairway led below to the great table. Her father Yakheed sat at the table, alone. He looked up at her, smiling sadly. "I thought you might come here today, daughter," he said quietly. He watched her as she descended down the steps to face him, shaking in fear.

"Father, the animals are heading toward the mountain now," she said, her voice quavering. "If I am to go, I must leave immediately."

Yakheed shook his head. "I have forbidden it. I will not change my mind."

"You and I both know how right Uncle Noah was about the animals," she answered desperately. "You might as well admit it; he must be right about the flood as well. I don't want to die, Father. Why won't you give me your leave?"

He leaned over and said sternly; "You, child are my daughter. You must obey your father."

She said nothing at first, her dilemma overwhelming her. Seated before her was her father. This was the greatest man in the city and more important, the greatest man in her life, whom she respected and adored above all others. Here he sat at the center of his civic power in the public meeting room for the city council. Hundreds of years ago, the elders had built this chamber in a giant semi-circle, rising in tiers, each level providing seating for the public. She could feel the room towering behind her, reducing her to an insignificant little girl. Who was she to oppose the great Yakheed her father?

Tinith glanced back to the exit of the meeting area, standing at the apex of the stairs. Little time remained; the animals were already on the move. Even though she desperately wanted to save him, help him, please him, submit to him–nevertheless she knew in her heart what she must do.

Holding her breath, she turned to her father and spoke in a fragile voice, "No. I cannot stay here. I must follow Yahweh." She wanted to say more, but could not.

Yakheed stayed seated, watching her with mounting anger. He said to her, "Then you are not my daughter."

Tinith turned and ran up the stairs.

Yakheed called out to her, this time more loudly. "Then you are not my daughter!" When she came to the top of the steps, he screamed in fury, "Then you are not my daughter!"

At the doorway, Tinith turned to face Yakheed, elder of the city, her father and friend. "You will always be my father, and I will always love you." With tears streaming down her cheeks, she pulled her shawl over her face and turned. "Goodbye, Father," she whispered and was gone.

Noah watched his sons disappear over the mountain rim. He could not imagine what they would do if the women did not arrive, for his heart told him the animals finally were approaching the ship. His sons were journeying to the foot of the mountain, no further than the bridge, in hopes of escorting their new wives to the barge above. They could not, however, afford to wait very long. Time was quickly running out.

Tinith raced to her two friends, who frantically awaited her by the wall. When she reached them, they grabbed her hands and dragged her through the southern gate. No one saw the women exiting the city; the citizens' eyes were set on the field of animals beyond the river. Something was happening there; the many twins were leaving their parents, making their way across the field toward the pathway. The women below, racing to the bridge, saw this as well, and Hannah cried out in fear; "We won't make it before they begin!" This thought drove them on all the more. Amazingly, however, when the first animals reached the track, they stopped, as if waiting for some final sign to start them on their ascent to the summit.

Tinith found running difficult, her eyes being blinded by tears. Her heart, soul and strength all begged her to turn back, to comfort her abandoned father, but she knew her course lay ahead and not behind. It was not simply fear that drove her on; it was an unshakable conviction that God had called her to this new life. Behind her lay all she knew and loved. Before her lay a Promise. She reached the bridge and crossed. On the far side, Noah's sons awaited them.

Each son reached out a hand. Tinith grasped the hand of Shem, son of the Promise. Exhausted, the women and men hurried up the mountain to the awaiting ship.

Yakheed slammed his fist against the table in the chamber. "I won't allow my daughter to destroy her life on that boat!" He bounded up the stairs to the outside door. As he scrambled down the steps to the street, he found himself in the middle of a drunken wedding party. The revelers precariously bore the bride and groom on their shoulders and were dancing on the steps of the city chambers. He gruffly pushed past the crowd, and made his way toward the southern wall.

Soon he had arrived at the outer stairway and sprang up the steps. When he reached the top, he looked out to the land beyond the river.

No one was on the bridge or the road leading to the mountaintop. Tinith was gone.

The three sons of Noah and the three women reached the ramp. As they ascended, the women wept, and the journey became their longest and hardest. Tinith looked above them to the door, looming over her like a gaping, bottomless hole. Once she fell into it, her heart forewarned her, she would never escape. Behind them, far away, they heard the sound of a mighty behemoth, bellowing a mournful cry.

The sound caused Aleac to turn and then cry out, "Look, at the rim! The animals!"

They turned to see a column of various kinds of behemoth twins making their way toward the ship. The women and men continued upwards until they reached the platform at the end of the ramp. Tinith peered into the opening and saw nothing but blackness. She stopped and surveyed her own world behind her, about to be lost forever. Everything wonderful and good lay beyond that rim where animals now filed toward the ship. A hand gently touched her arm; she looked up.

Aunt Emah was there, standing just within the threshold, a sad look on her face. "Daughter, it's time to enter."

Tinith paused for a moment longer, then followed her, disappearing into the gloom.

Five Days Before the End

"Where in this house can I find a wrench for the gearbox?" Yakheed muttered to himself. Since his mills were temporarily closed, he had spent the last two days cleaning his home and fixing any items in need of repair. Now he was attempting to improve the mechanism which opened and shut his gate, but lacked the right tool.

After scouring the house, he realized Tinith might have kept her tool bag she used when she worked at the mill. He climbed the steps to her room on the second floor. As soon as he entered, it was obvious he should not have come here–the room was perfectly kept, carefully laid out with memories and treasures, and he did not think he could bear the hurt.

Against his will, Yakheed's eyes ran over the items fastened on the walls: a wildflower from an adventure in the past, a picture she had drawn with charcoal, a piece of driftwood. Then his eyes stopped. A brown kerchief hung from three well placed nails–the kerchief Tirina wore the day she came to the factory looking for a job. He crossed the room to the spot and gently ran his hand over the fabric. How much it reminded him of his beloved wife. She must have allowed their little daughter to bring it to the mill sometime before the fire. For all these years, he had never known it was here.

Yakheed removed the scarf and held it gently, thinking about its owner. Tirina had been so wise, so gentle, so vulnerable. He shook his head. Tinith was like her in many ways. She had grown into a beautiful woman who ministered to the needy, freely laughed, was always ready to talk and loved her father more than any daughter could. She seemed to carry on for her mother, who, had she survived the fire, would have set aside a special room just like this, a treasure house of the past, filled with memories. As Yakheed studied each item, he realized how many of Tinith's prizes in this room came from adventures he and his little girl had shared. A tear formed in his eye– his daughter saw her time with him as a great treasure. And in anger he had sent her away. What a fool!

He stopped himself from thinking about it. She was gone, but at this point he could do nothing about it. The tool bag was hidden somewhere in this room, and he needed to find it, probably stored in her chest on the far wall. Inside of the chest, Yakheed immediately spotted the bag and pulled it up. As he did, he spotted something familiar lying beneath. Uncovering it, he lifted it from the chest. It was the rag doll in a simple blue dress. The fabric was smooth and had obviously been repaired many times over the years. Until she was an adult, Tinith had never slept anywhere without that doll, not since the day Tirina had died.

It was a silly thing– just a doll–but Yakheed could not escape the memories it recalled; of that night he had carried Tinith through the streets, the two weeping uncontrollably, desperately hoping Noah and Emah might bring to them some comfort and possibly some hope. That doll became for Tinith her most poignant connection to the past, something her mother had sewn for her, something her mother had held with her, and now it represented to Yakheed his own past, linking together the wife and daughter who were both torn from him forever. He found himself falling to the floor, grasping the doll and weeping uncontrollably. He had sent her away, his beloved Tinith. Now, all he had to speak of her was a tattered little doll.

Four Days Before the End

Yakheed stood on the wall, looking over the field. Animals continued to proceed up the pathway toward the mountain, to the ship where his daughter had fled. He scowled, frustrated at his outburst of anger.

"Why did I tell her she was no longer my daughter?" he asked himself in disgust. "The last thing Tinith will remember about her father is that I cursed her!"

He stared at the steady line of animals. Somehow he had to reach her and explain that he didn't mean it, that she still was his only child, the reflection of his beloved Tirina, who had died so long ago.

He returned to the street and made his way through the crowds to the southern gate, but it was now barred as a defense against possible animal attacks. Yakheed approached the men guarding the smaller door. "Let me out there. I need to see Noah."

The soldiers looked at him in surprise. "Elder, you can't get across the river any longer. Haven't you seen the behemoth?"

He frowned. "I've been looking at the behemoth for the past five months!"

"Sir," the man answered, shaking his head. "The behemoth have moved. Now they are gathered just on the other side of the bridge. I don't think it would be physically possible for you to pass them."

He returned in dejection to his empty house.

Three Days Before the End

Methuselah pulled tight the strap of his pack and motioned to his grandson. "I have put just enough food in here to feed us on our way to the altar and to keep us alive while we bring offerings to the Lord. It's strange to think of packing my last meal on earth. Are you ready to go?"

Wehtam nodded and the two began walking, the sheep and bull following obediently. They steadily ascended the hill that rose from the little hamlet. When they reached the top, Methuselah halted and looked back. Below them, beyond the gathering of stone houses, the river cut its way across the land. The breeze passed over the grasses, and he watched them dance beneath the sky. It was a beautiful sight, this home of Adam and Eve, this earth which had been his home for nine centuries. He sorrowed to bid it farewell, but he turned and traveled beyond the peak of the hill, the river disappearing behind him. He had begun his final journey.

The Day Before the End

A messenger found Yakheed sitting alone in the council chamber. The man bowed.

"What do you want?" the elder mumbled.

The messenger spoke. "The guards on the northern wall send you word that no more animals cross the plain, elder. By late tonight, or perhaps early tomorrow, our troubles will be resolved."

"So?" Yakheed growled dangerously.

Confused, the messenger asked him, "I beg your pardon?"

"So?" Yakheed was almost shouting. "What do I care about the stupid animals?"

The messenger responded cautiously, "The captain of the guard—"

"I don't care," Yakheed screamed. "I don't care about the captain or anything else! Get out!"

The messenger fled.

The sound of mighty beating wings had dominated the air for hours, but this was Wehtam's first sight of the Cherubim which guarded Eden's gate. Their swords flamed with blinding light, and the noise they created unsettled him. It was not their sound, however, but their faces which brought terror into every sinew of his being. They spoke of a holiness Wehtam had never before encountered, and he realized here at Eden the depth of his depravity.

It was the day before the end, and their spirits were heavy as they approached the ancient resting place, with its stone shelters and fire hearths. To this shrine their ancestors had come for a millennia and a half, and now at last–at the end of all flesh–Methuselah and Wehtam drew near to bring sacrifice to Yahweh at the doorway to the Garden of Eden.

The Last Day

Sometime during the night, the animals had stopped boarding the ship, and now all lay asleep in their stalls, cages and pens. In the early sunlight, the family worked feverishly to dismantle the ramp. Noah had designed it so that they might bring it with them, and the ramp came apart in segments. He had prepared an area within the boat to store the various pieces, and as four of the family disassembled the sections down below, the others hauled them up and into the boat. Once they finished the ramp, which took several hours, they attached their ropes to the enormous wooden door, lying on the ground beneath the opening. After they had entered the ship, they would pull the door from the ground, and then hopefully the eight of them would be able to secure it firmly into its place on the ship.

As Emah had been working side by side with Tinith, she had noticed how often the young woman kept glancing nervously to the now empty pathway leading down to the city. It wasn't until they finished their task, which took several hours, that she came to Tinith, gently putting her arm around her and saying, "You are hoping your father will come?"

Looking at her new mother sadly, Tinith answered, "No, not really Aunt Emah. But if he does come, I just want to be sure I don't miss him."

Methuselah and Wehtam knelt before the altar. "Yahweh," Methuselah prayed hoarsely, "We have sinned. I should be dying. Wehtam should be dying, but we kill these two lambs in our place. We should be paying for our own sins, but these lambs pay instead. Please accept this symbol of the Promised One who comes to save us all." He laid his hand on the head of his lamb and motioned for Wehtam to copy him. He then picked up his knife.

Yakheed stood upon the city's southern wall, staring out across the now empty plain. No animals could be seen, and he assumed the barge had filled to its limit. It was a strange morning in the city of Yakheed. The entire population had declared a holiday, and its citizens filled the streets, drinking toasts to the departure of the animals, as if it were something to celebrate. But he knew better. He looked up the mountain, straining to make out its rim. *She was up there*, he said to himself hopelessly. Tinith had left him and now he would be alone forever.

What kind of god would be so selfish as to take a little girl away from her father? Ten thousand young women were drinking in the streets that morning, laughing, singing and dancing to the sounds of flutes and strings. Why couldn't Yahweh have chosen one of them and at least left Yakheed with the comfort of his daughter at the end? The question answered itself; Yahweh was a cruel and selfish god who cared only for his own twisted desires. Over the past six hundred years, Noah's god had stolen so much from Yakheed, and now robbed him of his only child. He looked out over the river and cursed the god of Noah.

Methuselah and Wehtam laid the final sacrifice on the altar and stepped back. A horn sounded, and they looked toward Eden. From the depths of the garden a light blazed dazzlingly bright. The swords of the cherubim paled, the sun paled and the two men fell to their knees.

They watched, amazed, as the Tree of Life rose from its place on the hill within the Garden and followed the path toward the gateway. As it moved through the Garden forest, the trees seemed to fall prostrate before it, bowing before their King. When it reached the entrance of the Garden of Eden, the tree paused. The cherubim rose from their posts, their swords almost extinguished by the brilliance of the tree. The tree then ascended toward the heavens, accompanied by the cherubim in glory.

Methuselah and Wehtam stood awestruck at glory so great that everything else would fade beneath it. The horn sounded again. Suddenly flames leaped from heaven and consumed the sacrifices lying upon the altar before Eden's gate. The cherubim and tree ascended into the heavens, but Methuselah and Wehtam did not observe their departure, for at the second sounding of the horn, they had fallen to the ground, no longer alive and they along with the offerings and the altar, had been received by the glory of God.

The family of Noah climbed the ladder back into the boat and stood before the entrance. Their preparations finished, they gazed out over the landscape, wondering what might happen next. Suddenly, the enormous door which Noah had constructed slowly began rising from the ground below them. They all stepped back, astonished and fearful. The great door of the ship continued to ascend to its position, unaided by man and his machines. If any had stood outside the barge to observe it, they would have seen eight figures standing forlornly at the entrance, desperately clinging to their last glimpse of a world they had loved since birth. The door crashed securely shut, their faces disappearing from the outside world, never to be seen again by any soul dwelling then upon the earth. Tinith backed into the darkness of the ship. "Goodbye, Father," she whispered.

Chapter Fourteen

Year 1656: The End of All Flesh

The catwalk on the outer wall trembled, and Yakheed looked down. Loose gravel around his feet was quivering, as if the ground were shaking. He grabbed hold of the wall and felt vibrations. To his right, chains attached to the gate began to rattle. A spear leaning against a sentry post slipped and fell clattering to the ground. Behind him, he heard a cracking sound. Whirling around, he observed the city inner wall undulating slightly in a wave running as far as his eye could see. A pottery jug tottered and fell from a ledge, shattering. The wooden guard shack creaked, and he almost detected it swaying, which would have explained the hanging lanterns, which rocked back and forth nervously.

Behind him, the distinctive sound of creaking, immediately followed by a snap grabbed his attention, and he whirled around in time to discover a giant oak tree crashing to the ground beyond the river. Almost immediately another fell, and within moments a dozen or so more came smashing down. The rest of the trees swayed, as if some invisible force had grasped ahold of their roots and was violently shaking them.

The river churned fiercely, rolling and slamming against its banks. Suddenly, a cacophony of snapping branches and trunks pierced the tumult, as eight or nine trees tottered then careened, smashing into each other as they dropped to the ground. To Yakheed's surprise, white water from the hill abruptly poured over the downed trees in wild surges, its flow doubling with every heave. Within moments, the new water, now a wall, joined with the swelling river. The combined forces peaked and then rushed toward the mills. Yakheed watched the whitened waters crashing along the high banks as the first wave slammed into the gristmill. An enormous groan sounded over the roaring watercourse, and a water wheel from the gristmill snapped off like a twig from a branch and then flipped into the waters.

Yakheed examined the plain across the river, the resting place for creatures over the past months. The ground was rolling, almost like ripples running across a pond, and within a heartbeat the land itself began ripping in half as easily as if it were an old worn cloth caught on a nail. The plain ruptured, trees on the edge of the field edge tottering and collapsing into the rapidly widening breach in the earth. As Yakheed watched in terror, water rose up from the gap in the land and overflowed onto the once level ground. Within moments, the entire plain had become a turbulent pond, then a lake. Before long, it would join with other lakes and merge into an ocean.

A new rush of water, much more substantial, careened toward the gristmill. When it reached its goal, it twisted the building from its roots and dragged it into the current. Within moments, the water-course angrily smashed the gristmill's rubble into the next mill, which exploded into a boiling stew of beams and boards. One by one, the growing waters transformed debris into deadly battering rams, which mercilessly decimated the rest of the mill buildings. Within minutes, the entire row of fifteen mills had completely disappeared.

Behind him, in the city, Yakheed could hear stonework caving in and buildings collapsing. He felt more than heard calamity on the streets. Men and women were shouting and screaming. No one could find shelter from the falling debris, which piled upon them as their homes, businesses and buildings collapsed under the strain of rolling earthquakes. The great fortress city of Yakheed came upon its inhabitants like an unexpected enemy, full of death and destruction. As its collapsing walls and buildings ravaged its citizens, it drew no quarter, slaying old and young, strong and weak, brave and terrified, and no one could save them.

The battle, moreover, had only begun. The combined forces of earth, stream and river had united and sent its troops against the city fortress, for the water now rose precipitously. Yakheed had hoped somehow that his mighty walls might repel the onslaught as those same walls had once defied the Nephilim, but before long the battering rams of trees, the broken bridge and rubble besieged the gates, crashing savagely against them. Finally the gates surrendered and burst asunder. The ocean outside the walls rushed in. Now swelling waters charged through the streets of the city, joining forces with other waters already rising out of city wells and springs, burying the dead and hungrily seeking the living.

Far away, in Eden, above the waterfall, the Great River convulsed. Enormous waves surged abruptly forward. The billow traveled rapidly, swelling like a colossal wall until it reached monstrous proportions. The onrush arrived at the falls, and it paused tremulously, shaking the mountainside, which tottered, broke into pieces, then slid with a roar down to the waiting forest below.

If Eve could have watched Eden for that hour, she would have seen the ground tearing apart and then collapsing into a void. She would have watched water bursting out of the breach, melting away earth, then overflowing the land. The constant, thunderous crashes of falling trees would almost have deafened her. If Eve could have found a solid foothold in this sea of transformation, she would have observed earth falling away, collapsing on itself, folding into its molten womb below until nothing was left but a watery mass of broken trees and rocks.

In the beginning of all things, God said, "Let the waters below the heavens be gathered into one place, and let the dry land appear"; and it was so. God called the dry land earth and the gathering of the waters He called seas. The seas were gathered into one place, and the earth was not divided into many landmasses, but was one in itself. Now, as earth and seas met, the cataclysm spreading across that one landmass brought calamity to every corner. Rivers exploded into masses of raging water, and springs transformed into tempestuous outpourings. Hills and valleys convulsed, often collapsing into the void beneath the surface. Everywhere the catastrophe overtook terrified animals entirely unaware of what was happening and why the earth was breaking loose beneath their feet.

What befell the city of Yakheed came upon every place, and humanity raised an anguished voice to the God of heaven whom they had, until then, denied.

Not far from that city, eight people patrolled long aisles within the ship; checking animal stalls, securing hatches and preparing feeding routines. As they worked, tremors unsettled the floor beneath their feet, and they paused often to steady themselves. The cacophony of creature noise enshrouded any sounds they might have heard from the outside world, but nothing of what was occurring in the city would have reached them anyway. The walls of the barge served as barriers to the world of humankind.

Noah had assigned to Tinith the task of maintaining the animals' foodstuff. She had been doing this work since she entered the barge. Emah had demonstrated to her where to find the feed, how to carry it to the animals and the best way to fill the cribs. The task of caring for several thousand animals required each crew member to work from the time he or she arose to bedtime at night.

On this afternoon, as she worked on her assignment, Tinith was making slow progress. It had taken her all morning to reach the middle row of the ship where the ramps led upstairs and down. This was where they originally entered the barge, the entrance which now, of course, was tightly sealed. She came to the last bin, standing above a column of four small cages and filled it with pellets of grain.

"How's the work going?" a man's voice asked. She looked over to see Shem, carrying containers of pellets, standing at the hatchway.

"Fine," she answered, ". . . I guess."

He laid the buckets down and came to where she was working. "You guess? In other words, you are not fine."

"It's my hands," she said weakly. "I can't seem to. . . I'm not able to. . . You see, they're trembling so." She dropped the scoop, and pellets scattered over the floor. Tears began running down her face and she found her body giving way. She slid down along the cages to the floor. Sobbing, she tried to continue, "I just can't seem to hold the. . ."

But she could not finish her words. Surges of grief overflowed her heart, wave after wave of remorse drowning her in sorrow. She could not seem to get her breath and found herself sinking into blackness. Shem dropped beside her, putting his arms around her and rocking her gently. She looked up at him.

"My father. . ." she tried to explain. "He's down there, all alone. . ." Again the heartbreak broke through her walls of self-protection and smothered her words. As Shem held Tinith, he felt her collapse in his arms, swept away by what was happening on the outside. Her weeping continued in heartbroken sobs, and even through the animal noises, the others heard her grief.

Down below, beside the city gates, the elder Yakheed held on to the trembling outer wall. The rushing waters continued to pour into the city, tearing at the great stones supporting the bulwark, raging flows undermining its foundation and rapidly eroding the mud bricks supporting it on the inside. The city itself was mostly under water.

Although from his vantage point Yakheed spotted various figures huddling on roofs or clinging to floating lumber, he suspected most were probably dead by now. Looking at the gate, he saw the flood's irresistible force tearing at every stone, every joint of mortar and every supporting timber. It would not be too much longer before the whole structure would be swept away in the current, carrying with it the last remnants of the city.

Yakheed tried to peer through the spray, screaming with all of his powers, "Tinith! Tinith! Please don't leave me, I beg you!" But only the sounds of disaster–crashing trees, roaring waves and buildings and bridges collapsing–emanated from the world beyond the city walls.

"It isn't fair!" he shouted out into the void around him. "How could you fashion such a world and then have the audacity to punish us because we aren't good enough? You made us!"

A stone at the gate finally broke loose, and the wall lurched. For the moment the bulwark held. Yakheed staggered to a wooden post and threw his arms around it.

Looking out toward the waters again, he cried, "What if we are sinners? You made us that way, didn't you? I never agreed to enter your world. I was made by you. I didn't create your perfect garden of Eden, and I wasn't stupid enough to put a tree with fruit that could plunge us all into depravity. If there's any blame, it belongs to you!"

He looked up into the darkening sky. "All of that," he screamed, "all of that was your decision! You made us, you equipped us, and you depraved us. HOW DARE YOU JUDGE US!"

The sky thundered ominously, and a bolt of lightning struck somewhere within the city. Desperately clinging to the post with one arm, Yakheed the elder shook his fist at the sky. "Go on! Send your thunderbolts! Send your floods! You have no right to judge us! You have no right!"

Then Yakheed, Elder of the city, began crying uncontrollably, saying the words "Tinith" again and again. He slumped, falling to his knees. An enormous crack rang through the tumult. The arch over the gate twisted and shattered while Yakheed wept, calling out his daughter's name, but knowing she would never answer again. The stonework fragmented, the ramparts lurched, and a gigantic wave crashed over the wall, sweeping Yakheed away. For an instant, his hand broke through the water's surface, desperate to grasp anything that might save him from the wrath of the flood, but nothing could deliver him now. The waters swirled, and he disappeared beneath the surface.

The rains began and joined the floods now pouring over the face of the earth. Sheets of water fell from the sky like bludgeoning hammers, crushing plants and trees, animals and humans alike. Those few not caught by the initial flooding clawed their way to higher ground and huddled miserably in hopes the devastation soon might end. This wrath, however, knew no mercy. Lightning storms of fearsome power ripped through the air, bolts screaming pitilessly one after another after another. The night sky flashed continually with gruesome shocks of light.

Beneath the ocean floor, the earth groaned and flexed. The fountains of the deep were breaking and spouting boiling waters high into the air. Tumults underneath the sea wrenched the ocean bed and rolled its floor much like a huge rock falling into a pond rolls the water's surface. Fiery mountains pushed their way through the sea bottom and spewed molten rock, boiling water and towers of steam. Each new roll and flex beneath the sea spawned a series of enormous waves which rushed in a deadly path toward the land.

The few men and women still alive on the tops of hills and mountains clung to the hope that the worst was past. But the sea floor was rising, and as it rose the waters spilled beyond the boundaries set by God to separate earth from sea. The fountains of the deep poured out their store of water onto the land. The rains poured out their store of water onto the land. In time, the displaced sea water would roll over the land and cover the entire earth and in the end all the mountain tops would be covered. As the floods rose, sea waters tossed about in chaos, and enormous waves originating from points all over earth crashed into one another, swirling in mammoth vortices.

The first night, Shem found his father in the bottom deck, feeding the two young mammoths. "Now you need to understand," Noah was explaining, "you are on your own now." He added, shaking his head.

"I can't teach you anything about how grown mammoths are supposed to act. But for now, you need to eat these pellets." He offered a handful of grain pellets to the male, which greedily consumed all. "But don't eat too much," he added. "We don't have room to deal with giant mammoths!"

Shem smiled. He supposed his father never entirely freed himself from his hermit ways, regularly talking to himself and animals. He differed so much from people like Yakheed, who met and overcame difficult circumstances with courage and determination. If that was the definition of greatness, Father did not qualify. Yet here Noah stood, father of the entire human race. Surely this was a new kind of greatness, the greatness Yahweh bestowed on the weak who trust him to the uttermost.

Shem hated to interrupt his father's one-sided conversation, but circumstances required some immediate, if embarrassing, action. He cleared his throat and said quietly, "Father, we have a little problem, and we need your help with it."

Noah looked up, surprised. "A little problem?"

Shem's face became hot. He shifted uncomfortably. "Well, it's just that. . ."

"Just that what?" Noah asked, entirely curious.

Shem grappled for words. "It's just that the women. . . I mean, our wives, well. . . they don't feel right about being wives until they've received their fathers' blessings."

"Their fathers' blessing? But. . ." confusion slipped over Noah's face, "their fathers are all out there. . ." he said, pointing beyond the walls of the ship.

Shem nodded. "Right. Of course. . . But they don't feel comfortable with. . . with. . . Oh!" he muttered in exasperation.

Noah thought for a moment. "Should Mother and I bless them? She crafted gifts for each girl, and I would be glad to pray with them."

"Tonight?" asked Shem, anxiously.

Noah smiled. "Let's find your mother and the girls."

Three hours later, in her own bedroom, Emah was weaving white flowers into Aleac's hair. The other two women were sitting silently on the bedding, holding each other's hands in quiet grief. All three wore the traditional blue wedding dresses, perfectly embroidered with designs of white and blue flowers running from the shoulders all the way to the floor. In any other place, at any other time, this evening would have been the most blessed moment of their lives. This night was, however, the worst. As Emah dressed her hair, Aleac's tears flowed freely down her cheeks. Her suffering broke Emah's heart.

Wiping away the tears from her new daughter's face, she said softly, "I know. Your mother should be doing this, child, and here I am, almost a stranger, preparing you for your wedding night."

"I'm sorry," Aleac answered in a quavering voice. "It's just that, I remember as a little girl watching Mother braid the flowers for my older sister and thinking, 'Someday, she'll be doing that for me.' and now. . ."

Emah took her hand and squeezed it. "You are being brave, daughter, and I'm proud of you." Biting her lip, she tried to fight back her own tears, hoping she could be brave enough to help these poor young women bear such loss. A few moments passed as she threaded the last flower into Aleac's hair, and then she sighed. "All done."

She reached into her basket, pulling out a necklace fashioned from tiny white flowers. As Emah placed the necklace around Aleac's throat, Tinith looked at the basket and then back at Emah. "Those are the baskets you carried this morning, aren't they?"

"I asked your Uncle Noah. . ."

"Father," Tinith said.

"Your father. . ." Emah repeated tentatively. "I asked if I could gather a few baskets of flowers. I doubt if he will ever understand why, but even so he let me do it." She stepped back from Aleac. "You look lovely."

Glancing at the other two women, she asked, "Well, brides, Aleac is ready. Are you?"

They nodded. Emah helped each woman up and then whispered to the three of them, "Wait here." She disappeared through the doorway, and the girls could hear her speaking to Noah and the men. They heard the sound of a few tables and benches moving, and then the curtains parted and Emah reentered.

Tinith watched Emah gently take Hannah's hand and lead her through the doorway. She returned and led Aleac past the curtain into the other room. Shortly thereafter, she came back through the curtain and walked across the room to the young woman. Taking both of Tinith's hands, she smiled, and Tinith saw tears running down her face.

"I had always prayed for a daughter, but God chose not to give us one," Emah said quietly. "He had other plans, plans I did not understand at the time." She sighed. "The day your mother died, your father appeared at our door, carrying you in his arms, just a little thing, five years old. The poor man hardly knew what he was doing at that point, so I took you out of Yakheed's arms, and Uncle Noah led him to the other room."

Emah adjusted a flower braid in her daughter's hair and pushed a strand into its proper place. "They stayed there for an entire night and day, talking, listening, weeping, and you cried on my shoulder all night until you finally fell asleep."

She smiled. "That evening, I vowed in my heart to be a mother to you until your wedding day." Pausing, Emah looked up into Tinith's eyes. "This is why I taught you of the Promise. This is why I came so often to visit. This is why I prayed for you every morning and every night since I first held you in my arms, and God has answered my deepest prayer, for here you are on your wedding day, as the bride of my eldest son."

Emah kissed her daughter on the forehead. "Come child, let us meet your husband."

A few moments later, Tinith was kneeling beside her husband Shem, offering him a timid smile. He had taken her hand and was holding it gently. Noah was already laying hands upon Ham and Aleac, praying for them, blessing them. He then did the same for Japheth and Hannah and then Shem and Tinith.

After this, Noah and Emah led the first couple to their own room, blessing them again. They then returned to the next couple and did the same. Finally they brought Shem and Tinith into their room. Laying his hand on their heads, Noah prayed a blessing upon them. He kissed Tinith on the forehead and smiled. Then, taking Emah's arm, he led her (dragged her) to the door. The last thing Tinith saw of the outside room was the face of Emah, covered with tears, gazing through the crack of the curtain as Noah pulled it shut.

Hours later, Tinith woke with a start. At first, she stared into the darkness, wondering what had aroused her. She felt the bedding beside her, hoping Shem might have awakened as well, but he was not there. The floor lurched and she gasped; something was wrong with the ship. Frantically, she searched the floor for clothing and found a work dress, which she hurriedly pulled over her head.

She made her way through the doorway into the dimly lit gathering room, hoping to find someone who might explain the movement, but no one was there. Looking toward the hold, she could see the faint glows of lanterns lining the aisle to the ramps and decided to investigate. The boat rocked again.

Walking past the pens in the dark proved to be an unpleasant experience. Most of the animals stayed quiet, although a few seemed to grunt or sigh as they slept in their stalls. Yet the darkness and the sudden ship movements made Tinith worry the whole barge might suddenly capsize and spill a hundred animals on top of her. At each lurch, scraping sounds reverberated throughout the hold, and she could not imagine what would make such a noise. Finally she saw a candle moving ahead of her, and she hastened to catch whoever it was.

It turned out to be Noah, and he looked worried. "The ship is launching itself," he said. "The boat rests on about a hundred rock pilings. I'm a little concerned that as the water begins lifting us up, the barge may keep smashing against those pilings and damage the hull."

Tinith was horrified. "Do you mean the waters have come this high already? They're covering the mountain?"

"No, no. . ." he answered, shaking his head. "Remember the lake next to the ship? We built the boat up here on the mountain crater to take advantage of the lake. The crater acts like a funnel, channeling all the rainwater into the center. The plan has always been that the lake would overflow to the ship and then raise us up. That's what we're experiencing tonight. We'll be floating for weeks, maybe months before the flood reaches the summit of Halftop Mountain. In the meantime, we'll be sitting on a cushion of water, safe from earth-quakes and any enormous waves."

The ship rocked again, and the scraping sound sent chills down Tinith's spine. The sound also clearly unsettled Noah. He ran his hand over a beam. "We built the hull out of gopherwood, which is as strong as rock, but I sure wish the rain would get us away from those stone pillars."

Tinith silently prayed. Even before she finished, she felt as if the ship were sliding forward, and she grabbed onto the slats of an animal pen. The boat now rocked back and forth, scraping along the pilings almost the total distance of the boat's bottom. Suddenly, the entire vessel lunged, throwing Tinith to the floor and rocked violently.

The motion seemed to relieve Noah's fear. "We're free," he said excitedly. "All we want now is to float away from the launch site until we're entirely above it." He listened to the creaking ship. "Oh Lord," he prayed, "keep us clear of those pilings until your rains raise our ship to a safer level."

Looking at Tinith on the floor, he offered his hand to help her up. Smiling, he said to her, "Now begins the first phase of our journey, here on the mountain. How long it will take for us to lift away from this spot, only God knows."

For forty days the barge floated on its mountaintop lake while the planet convulsed with storms and savage waves. The ocean floors continued to rise, and this movement forced even more sea waters over the land mass and thus covered the land at ever increasing depths. The flood level grew until it covered the summits of every hill and moun-tain on the earth, higher than the highest peak by a depth of fifteen cubits.

On the fortieth day, a long ocean wave came rolling across the mountaintop. It pushed the boat along and then lifted it over the rim of its safe harbor, bringing it out into the open sea. Tinith was cleaning stalls in the second aisle on the bottom floor when she felt the ship roll with the sea.

"We're free from the mountaintop," she said to the bull in the pen.

The thought was both exciting and frightening. They could no longer depend on the mountain's protection from massive waves, but as well they were finally free to float to their new home, wherever that might be. From this point on, from early morning to late night, those rolling waves became as much a part of life as breathing. The ship's journey had entered its second phase.

When Tinith looked back over those months, she remembered wind, rain and wondering. Wailing winds woke them in the morning and lulled them to sleep at night. One might expect such a constant barrage to sink into their mental background, but it never did. Perhaps it was because the wind had a baleful tone, foreboding and severe. Accompanying the wind, violent rain continued to pummel the ship every moment of every day. Everyone wondered, although no one expressed it, when the ordeal would be over.

One morning, over five months after they had first entered the barge, they awoke to silence. Tinith jumped up from her bed and ran to stand beneath the window, which stood ten cubits above the floor. She could see the sky. True, it was a foreboding dark gray, but at least she could see a sky. One by one, the others joined her, craning their necks to see the heavens. Through the morning, Japheth and Shem built a platform and ladder, in order to assist them in looking out the window. Everyone on the boat felt lighter, as if this nightmare might soon be ending. The day of work went more easily than it had since the beginning.

That night, they talked about what they dreamed for their lives at the end of this voyage.

"God is making a new Garden of Eden out there," Noah said with excitement. "That's what the flood was all about; cleaning away the filth of human civilization and starting everything over again."

"I don't know, Father," Japheth answered cautiously. "It may be brutal out there. No trees, no iron, no bronze. . . We may find ourselves in a wilderness all over again."

Ham laughed. "You are such a pessimist, brother. I've got a feeling about this new world."

Shem cleared his throat. "You've got a feeling? What's that supposed to mean?"

He smiled at Shem. "Sometimes I get feelings about things, and they're usually pretty reliable. I have a feeling about this new world, that we will be able to do anything we want. If we want to build a city next to a river, we'll just plant ourselves down and get to work. That's the kind of world we're facing when we get off this ship of ours."

Noah nodded, but added soberly, "We will need to stay together, especially at the beginning. It will probably take a couple of centuries before we have enough offspring to move apart from each other."

"That may be," Ham said, "but I promise you, Father, I want my sons to do whatever they desire. Nobody has ever faced such an incredible opportunity, not since Adam left Eden."

"Ham," Noah said carefully, "it may be a hard life in the new world."

Ham smiled eagerly at his father. "I don't care what kind of life it starts out being; my sons are going to make it theirs."

Japheth scowled at his brother. "Don't forget, Ham. We will all have sons and grandsons."

That night, lying on their bedding, Tinith whispered to her husband, "Did you feel uncomfortable with what your brother Ham said?"

"So you noticed?" answered Shem. "I thought maybe I was just being a faultfinding older brother. It sounds to me as if Ham wants his sons to become the new Nephilim."

Tinith lay silent for a while, thinking. "What did Japheth mean about all of you having sons and grandsons?"

Shem thought for a moment and then answered. "I think we may have trouble on our hands between my two brothers and their descendants."

"What does that mean for our descendants?" asked Tinith.

Shem found her hand and squeezed it. "It means we'll have to teach them to know and trust Yahweh when others are more interested in getting what they want."

The waters began to recede. The fountains of the deep sealed, ocean floors lowered, and the landmasses buckled up, resulting in new mountain ranges. The highest mountains before the flood had been perhaps two thousand cubits high, but some of these new mountains rose to heights of over seventeen thousand cubits. As they rose, they broke the water's surface and ascended into the skies.

One afternoon, Tinith was hauling baskets of pellets when a shudder ran under her feet. "We've hit something!" she shouted, running toward the ramp.

Ham met her, racing down as she rushed up. "Did you feel that?" he said excitedly.

"Have we hit something?" she asked urgently.

A broad smile flooded his face. "We've hit land, woman. That's what we've hit."

The days of floating on the water's face had ended. Now began the days of waiting to disembark. For the next two months, all of the passengers found themselves climbing up onto the platform several times a day, gazing out the window on the waters, hoping to see land. Yet day after day, they saw nothing but water. Finally, one morning, Tinith heard her mother shouting at the top of her lungs. By the time the young woman reached the sound, seven people were crowding each other on top of the platform, chattering in excited voices, pointing out the window.

"What do you see?" Tinith asked eagerly.

Emah smiled. "There's a world out there, my daughter, full of islands. Your husband thinks they are mountain tops. All I know is that they are some kind of land with real rocks and dirt, and a prettier sight I have never seen." They spent several hours gazing at the new sights.

Now began the great debate about when to disembark the ship. Even though the vessel was resting on land, they could not see the ground through their window. Nobody knew if the land was even dry enough to walk on. Furthermore, Noah was convinced they should not leave the barge without God's direct command to do so.

"God told us when to get on the boat, and He will tell us when to leave," he argued.

"Father," Ham said, "God told you how big the barge should be and what materials to use for it, but he didn't tell you anything about how to build it. He expected you to use the experience and wisdom you had gained over the years. Isn't that what God wants you to do now?"

Noah shook his head. "What kind of wisdom could possibly tell me when we're ready to leave the ship? I've never been in a flood before. Ham, I've never floated on a ship before, and I'm really without any wisdom."

Ham asked, "Why not send out a bird?"

"What will that tell us?" Noah asked dubiously.

He shrugged. "If it doesn't come back, maybe there's something out there."

So, nine months after they boarded the boat, Noah set free a raven. They watched the bird fly off, wondering what it might tell them.

Unfortunately, it never returned, and they couldn't be sure its absence had any real meaning for them. Ham, however, wasn't ready yet to give up.

"How about a dove? We've used doves to send messages back and forth. They're really good about finding their way."

The first dove, to everyone's disappointment, came back without finding a resting place. A week later, however, they decided to repeat the experiment, and this time it was successful, for the bird came back with an olive leaf in its beak. They now knew two things: first, land was lying somewhere near the ship; and second, trees had begun repopulating the earth. The group begged Noah to send the dove out once more. This time, however, it did not return and they all guessed it had found a resting place. This event began a series of debates among the eight survivors.

The real debate was between Ham and his father. Ham wanted to open the covering, so they could at least see where their ship had landed. The entire family basically agreed with him, but did not want to argue with their father, a scruple not shared by Ham. Tinith could not understand Noah's reasoning, but it did not matter. As long as he forbade opening the door, she was willing to obey him. After all, God had not revealed the flood to any of the sons, but solely to Noah. Therefore, she trusted God to tell Noah when it was time to leave.

Ham, however, did not give up begging his father, and after three weeks, Noah finally relented. Early that morning, the sounds of hammering filled the ark. When Tinith finally left her rows of cages to investigate, she felt a new breeze of fresh air. Rushing down the ramp, she came to four men gazing out a large opening to the land before them. For they could certainly see abundant land, stretching up to the mountain peak. This was the final assurance their ordeal was coming to an end.

For the next fifty-six days, they prepared for disembarking. During the day, they did their normal work of caring for animals and cleaning out stalls. In the afternoons, however, they began making tools ready, such as saws, hammers, axes, scythes and knives. Certain areas of the boat were no longer needed, and these they dismantled, readying the wood for their future homes and work houses. Once it became too dark to work, they gathered in the common room and talked about their futures together.

More than the others, Shem worried about keeping the new world free from human sin. "I just don't know how to protect my sons from what we saw in the city and countryside."

Japheth disagreed. "A lot of those problems came because of the Nephilim. Their armies constantly brought disorder to villages and cities. That was their whole plan: ravage the lands to keep the people from organizing a real government. Without the Nephilim, I think we can make the world a better place."

Shaking his head, Shem said, "At least for a while, we won't have that kind of chaos, but—"

"Shem, we're going to need strong rulers," said Ham. "We need to make a new kind of government. We're going to have to build armies if we want our people to stay in line."

Noah looked incredulous. "Armies? Strong rulers? What kind of world do you think we're creating here? We want a world of peace, not war!"

"I agree that armies are a problem, Father," answered Ham, "but the moment one city creates an army, everyone else will have to do it."

Shaking his head, Noah pointed to the ship's hull. "Outside those walls, we have an unspoiled world waiting to be filled with the best we can give. God gave me the name Noah, which means rest. I do not intend to fulfill it by creating a new world of war and hardship."

For a long time, nobody answered. Tinith could see how deeply Noah's words had impacted Shem. Glancing around the room, however, she detected quite a different response in the other two brothers, and it worried her.

Ham stirred and spoke. "Father, if one of our descendants decides he wants to steal, we're going to have to stop him. If he builds an army to pillage towns in the countryside, then we'll have to build an army too. That's just reality."

"We must build a world of peace, Ham," Noah said to him, smiling. "We must lay better foundations than Adam did after he left Eden."

Tinith watched Ham's face. He smiled and agreed with his father, but she saw in his eyes a different response, and it frightened her.

Four weeks later, three hundred and seventy days after the animals first began boarding the ship, Noah stood watching the land. Suddenly the wind stopped, and the sun itself muted.

A Voice spoke, the same Voice which had spoken over a hundred years before. "Go out of the ark, you and your wife and your sons and your sons' wives with you. Bring out with you every living thing of all flesh that is with you, birds and animals and every reptile, that they may breed abundantly on the earth, and be fruitful and multiply on the earth."

When the wind resumed, and the sun returned, Noah joyfully informed his family about the good news.

Within a few minutes, all eight humans had descended a ladder to the ground. When Tinith's feet first touched the earth, she dropped to her knees, running her hand over the grass. It was thick and as high as her knees, and its coarse blades felt delicious to her fingers, and the smell! She lifted up her head and breathed deep drafts of crisp air, odors free of animal waste and human sweat, free from the smell of gopherwood and seawater. Her lungs greedily drank in the freshness and purity. She stared above into a profoundly deep blue sky, the wind hurrying along enormous white clouds. Above her stood the mountain peak, but she wondered what lay beyond the ship and therefore walked to the end of the boat. As she walked, her dress whipped about her, and she pulled tight her shawl.

When she came around the ship, the sight before her stole away her breath. They were in a new kind of world, a world with soaring mountains, and they themselves stood below the peak of one of the mightiest. To her left rose crests of other mountains, some of which Emah had first observed through the boat's window months before. The summits of these mountains seemed to pierce the crisp sky, and wisps of clouds adorned their crowns like mantles. In the old world, mountains were simply large hills, but in this world, their majesty dizzied the senses.

To her right, she saw a panorama of land below, green, vibrant and dotted with a thousand lakes. Although no trees yet populated the mountainside where they stood, saplings grew everywhere, which surprised her. How their seeds could have survived the flood, she could not imagine. Perhaps God chose to restore the plant kingdom without help from Noah. Even though it would take years for those trees to provide them wood, what mattered now was that there would be trees in the world to come, and this made her glad.

The party stood transfixed for at least a half an hour. Beyond exclamations of wonder, no one felt equal to the glory they now experienced.

Finally Noah broke the spell, announcing, "We must send Shem and Japheth back onto the boat." He looked to his sons, pointing to the boat's opening. "You men will tie ropes on the pieces of the disassembled ramp and then lower them down to us one at a time. Ham, the women and I will begin rebuilding it."

The sons nodded and climbed the ladder back into the ship's hold. Before long, they were all at work, having been preparing for this procedure over the past month.

By evening they had completed the ramp. Tinith bounded up, and in a few minutes came down with an armful of bedding for herself.

She walked past Noah, smiling. "It's going to take a lot to get me to sleep inside that thing again." After two more trips, she had made a nice spot beneath the ramp for Shem and herself.

The animals began descending the next morning. The process took several days to complete. Once they reached the ground, some animals stayed close by, but most continued walking and eventually disappeared from sight. Even as the animals descended, Noah, Shem and Japheth worked to build an altar before the boat, gathering the largest stones they could carry. Noah designed the altar to mimic what Adam had built before the gates of Eden, a simple box-like table. Once the stones were laid in place, the entire party carried a large flat stone to serve as the work surface. They placed it upon the carefully piled rocks. The family then brought wood from the barge, laying it in great piles on the table.

Not until Noah assembled one of every clean animal was their journey truly complete. A year ago, God specifically instructed them to bring seven of each kind of ritually clean animals. In obedience, they set aside animals such as oxen, sheep, and goats, plus pigeons and doves. Now, Noah carefully brought one of each of these animals to a makeshift pen and sent Ham to bring fire to the wood.

He lifted his eyes to the heavens and prayed. "Yahweh God, You have cleansed the earth from the stain of humanity's arrogance against you. Yet we the survivors are still unworthy to stand before You in this new world. These sacrifices, Lord, remind us that we cannot cleanse ourselves from sins we have carried out against You, the Lord of heaven and earth. Yahweh, send Your Promised Savior to deliver us from our sin!"

Shem led a sheep to his father, who then motioned to the family. One by one, they laid their hands on the animal, confessing before Yahweh their sin. They stepped back, and Noah slit the animal's throat, Shem catching its blood in a bowl. Noah gutted the animal, skinned it and then quartered it. Noah and Shem carried the blood, organs, skin and quarters to the now blazing fire atop the altar. Noah sprinkled the blood on the altar and then poured the rest at its base. He placed the animal pieces and skin on the altar and stepped back.

Suddenly, he fell to his knees, bowing his head. The others watched amazed, for they had heard or seen nothing, yet they could see that Noah himself was hearing much, for tears were streaming down his face. For a long time, they watched him hoping against hope that Yahweh the Creator had spoken words of comfort, for themselves and for the new world they now encountered.

Finally, Noah looked up. "Yahweh has spoken to me, children. He said that the smell of our sacrifices rose up before Him as a rest-giving aroma. He told me that He received the aroma and said to Himself, 'I will never again curse the ground on account of man, for the intent of man's heart is evil from his youth; and I will never again destroy every living thing, as I have done. While the earth remains, seedtime and harvest and cold and heat and summer and winter and day and night shall not cease.'"

They continued to sacrifice, until each clean animal kind had been offered to Yahweh. At the end, suddenly a Voice spoke. This time, however, each person heard His Voice.

God blessed Noah and his sons and said to them, "Be fruitful and multiply, and fill the earth. The fear of you and the terror of you will be on every beast of the earth and on every bird of the sky; with everything that creeps on the ground and all the fish of the sea, into your hand they are given. Every moving thing that is alive shall be food for you; I give all to you, as I gave the green plant. Only you shall not eat flesh with its life, that is, its blood. Surely I will require your lifeblood; from every beast I will require it, and from every man, from every man's brother I will require the life of man. Whoever sheds man's blood, by man his blood shall be shed, for in the image of God He made man. As for you, be fruitful and multiply; populate the earth abundantly and multiply in it."

Then God spoke to Noah and to his sons with him, saying, "Now behold, I Myself do establish My covenant with you and with your descendants after you; and with every living creature that is with you, the birds, the cattle and every beast of the earth with you; of all that comes out of the ark, even every beast of the earth. I establish My covenant with you; and all flesh shall never again be cut off by the water of the flood, neither shall there again be a flood to destroy the earth."

God said, "This is the sign of the covenant which I am making between Me and you and every living creature that is with you, for all successive generations; I set My bow in the cloud, and it shall be for a sign of a covenant between Me and the earth. It shall come about, when I bring a cloud over the earth, that the bow will be seen in the cloud and I will remember My covenant, which is between Me and you and every living creature of all flesh; and never again shall the water become a flood to destroy all flesh. When the bow is in the cloud, then I will look upon it, to remember the everlasting covenant between God and every living creature of all flesh that is on the earth."

And God said to Noah, "This is the sign of the covenant which I have established between Me and all flesh that is on the earth."

Chapter Fifteen

Year 1657

Tinith pulled back on the tether, and the oxen slowed to a halt. Wiping her brow, she looked over the field, which stretched for hundreds of cubits from the stream to their small house. Beyond the house, a forest was already growing, with some trees almost taller than she. Even though only a year had passed since they had left the barge, the world was rapidly recovering, and the woods offered hope for better times to come. Turning to view the land running to the stream, she wondered if the watercourse might at some time overflow its boundaries and flood the crops. That, she assumed, would significantly hurt their chances for survival. *Of course*, she thought as she noted the tips of plants already breaking the surface, *we've planted far too many seeds to harvest anyway.* Noah had urged them to do this, realizing how different the weather, the soil and the sun were from their days in the city of Yakheed. Most plants would probably not survive the transformed growing season.

She reflected on their future. Shem would survive, because he was the son of the Promise. God assured the human race that a Savior would deliver them from the serpent. Shem was either the Savior or his progenitor, and she herself would therefore be the mother of the next in line. The Promise itself, however, confused her, for she did not understand why humans needed a Savior from a serpent. If serpents presented a danger to humankind, why didn't God simply choose to exclude them from the ship? Since God had brought snakes to the barge, the serpent who deceived Eve must have been more than just an animal.

She recalled the words Noah had taught her: "Now the serpent was crafty, more than any beast of the field which the Lord God had made."

That seemed sensible, since no animals could talk, and her year on the barge had proven all animals to be far different from the serpent in the story. Could this evil enemy of the human race have appeared to Adam and Eve in a serpent's body, but be more than a serpent? Perhaps this enemy might even return to humanity in another guise. The thought troubled her, especially since in the Garden, the serpent's obvious goal was to lead Eve into sin and death. If the serpent returned, she suspected he would again attempt to lead the new world into rebellion against Yahweh.

Noah still believed it possible to create a world of peace and righteousness. *Was it possible?* she wondered. Even if she and Shem were the only two humans left, it still seemed unlikely they would be able to forge a world without sin. Already Tinith had found herself sinning against her husband, her brothers-in-law and even Noah. She thought about how easily she became angry about anything that went against her wishes.

At the outset of their new life, she had fought Japheth's choice of land. Even though Shem was oldest and therefore should have had second choice after Noah, Japheth had insisted on planting away from the stream. Noah was so worried about keeping peace, he urged Shem to defer to his brother, even as Tinith begged him to assert his own rights. Shem's decision to accede gave rise to a week of tension within their marriage. Tinith fought to bring her heart into submission to her husband, but several times had angrily confronted him about his decision. She wanted morally to do the right thing, but her desires continually contradicted what she knew was good. She wasn't alone either–all of them were still entirely human and therefore likely to sin. Yet she had seen what happens to a world where humans no longer even care about doing the good; Noah could not allow things to return to such depravity.

Looking over the fields, she spotted two figures walking along the pathway toward their home. Ham and Aleac were visiting. She glanced over to Shem, who was already leading his oxen back to the building. Plowing would have to wait, and she began leading her team along the furrows toward the barn.

As she walked, Tinith wondered why Ham seemed so different from his brothers or father. Ham did not like submitting to Noah or even treating his father respectfully. In the short year since they had disembarked, at least three times Ham had actually refused to obey Noah's direct request. His defiance shocked and worried her. If he were this bad now, what would his sons and daughters be like in the future?

By the time she had set the oxen in the cattle pen, Shem was already visiting with his brother. *Shem is so steady,* she thought to herself, *and I am so hotheaded like my father. After what Ham said last month to Noah, I wouldn't even speak to him, but Shem forgives.* She made her way across the yard to their one room shack, where the three of them were sitting on benches beneath a porch roof. Shem looked up and smiled.

"Ham has finished plowing his fields already," he said.

This surprised Tinith. "We must have at least four days left," she said. Turning to Ham, she asked, "How did you get it done so quickly?"

A look of excitement came over her brother-in-law's face. "You won't believe it!" he said. "I'm like Father; I tried an experiment to speed things up and it worked."

Shem smiled. "Well, brother, share the wealth of your knowledge, and maybe we'll finish early too."

"I planted poles at the end of each row before we started plowing," he answered looking exhilarated.

"Poles?" asked Shem, mystified.

Ham nodded. "I pulled some poles from the boat, cut them so they were about ten feet tall and then pounded them into the dirt. Then I sacrificed one of my oxen."

Shem started in surprise. "You sacrificed an ox? Does Father know this?"

He shook his head, answering, "No, not yet." He paused for a moment, then continued with fervor. "Anyway, I painted the pole with the ox's blood and then fastened one of its organs to the top of each pole."

"An organ? Are you serious?" Shem stared at his brother in utter disbelief.

"Then," Ham leaned forward, "I put a little bit of the blood in the oxen's watering bucket. We stood back and watched the oxen as they drank their water. All four of them lifted back their heads and bellowed and snorted, like they were ready to fight. We hitched them up to the plow right then and there and got to work. I swear they never stopped pulling until the sun went down and the next morning were awake and raring to go at least an hour earlier than usual, and that," he smiled, spreading his hands out much as a storyteller might, "is how my oxen worked twice as fast as yours in breaking ground."

For a long time, Shem simply gazed at his brother, apparently having nothing to say in reply. Finally Tinith broke the silence. "What would doing those things have to do with making oxen work harder?"

Ham laughed. "Don't you see? Yahweh told us the animal's life is in its blood. So I used blood to give them more life, more power. The animal organs are soaked with blood and that pulls the oxen straight to the pole. I hardly have to guide them."

Tinith glanced at her husband, whose expression was wary. "You gave the oxen blood to drink," he said with concern. "Yahweh has forbidden us from eating or drinking blood."

"He didn't say anything against oxen drinking it," the brother said. "Besides, why do you even ask? We already know blood has life power, and my experiment proved blood makes oxen work harder."

Shem stood, walking over to the edge of the porch and looked out over the field. He finally said, "How did you ever come up with such a crazy idea, brother?"

Ham shook his head. "I don't know, Shem. It just came to me in the middle of the night. I was sleeping, and all of a sudden, I got the strangest feeling, as if something were happening outside. So I grabbed my ax, unbarred the door and took a look around the barn. It was a strange night; the wind was blowing and making the queerest sound you can imagine."

Aleac shivered. "I hate it when it does that."

"Anyway," Ham continued, "I went out to the fields and there it was: a red glow in the sky."

Shem turned to look at his brother. "In the middle of the night?"

"In the middle of the night," Ham answered. "And suddenly, almost as if someone were putting ideas into my head, I realized red is the color of blood. I thought to myself, why would I be thinking about blood here in the fields, unless I was supposed to do something with blood on my crops. That's when I decided to use the power of blood with the oxen."

Tinith glanced at Shem, who had turned again to gaze out into the fields. She tried to discern what he might be thinking. She herself was wondering if perhaps Ham had discovered a new way to advance farming, wondering also if perhaps Ham was going too far. Her guess was that Shem felt the same way. Indeed, after a long pause, he shook his head. "I don't know, Ham," he said cautiously. "It doesn't sound right to me. If Yahweh wanted us to use blood as a power, then wouldn't He tell us?"

"That's just stupid," Ham answered, obviously aggravated. "Yahweh didn't tell Father how to use water to run a mill, did He? The water was simply Father's source of power. Now we've discovered blood as a source of power. That's all I'm doing; finding a new way to make our crops grow better. If God didn't forbid it, then it must be fine."

Aleac added. "Ham is going to mix blood with dirt and then sprinkle it all over the fields where we plant. We think we'll get healthier grain and vegetables that way."

Shem sighed. He was obviously struggling with how to judge this new approach to farming. Several minutes passed as he stared out across the land. Tinith looked over to Ham, who was watching her husband carefully, almost eagerly. She could understand why he was so excited about this new-found power, but she was also confused about herself. Why did the idea unsettle her so, and why did it also unsettle her husband?

Finally Shem turned to his brother. "I can't explain it yet, Ham, but I see a difference between water power and this so-called power of life in the ox blood." He paused, thinking again. He caught his wife's eye, and she shook her head slightly. "Tinith and I are not going to use this new approach, unless Yahweh makes it clear that we should."

Anger flashed across Ham's face, but disappeared almost as quickly as it came. He got up, laughing. "Well, since Yahweh seems to speak to us about once every one hundred years or so, I guess you're going to be waiting for a long time. While you're doing a lot more work for far less productive crops, I'll be enjoying my newfound secret." He reached out his hand to Aleac, who rose, and the two stepped off the porch and across the grass to the path. As they walked, he called out over his shoulder, "You'll come around, brother, when you see the kinds of crops I'm producing. Don't worry; you'll be doing it in five years."

Tinith came to her husband and took his arm. Together they watched the two crossing the fields to the distant house. She stayed quiet, allowing her husband to mull through what his brother had just announced. The light was beginning to fail, and she squeezed his arm and pulled closer to him.

"We need to talk to Father," he said gravely.

An hour later, they were sitting with Noah and Emah. Noah was shaking his head and saying to his oldest son, "And he specifically described it as a sacrifice, not as slaying or slaughtering?"

Shem nodded. "That's the part worrying me the most, Father. How could he sacrifice an ox for anything but Yahweh?"

Noah answered slowly, "Maybe it was sacrificed to Yahweh. He could be rebelling against my authority, wanting to bring his own offerings."

"No," Shem said, shaking his head. "He didn't have an altar, and he didn't burn the beast with fire."

Tinith agreed, "I don't think the sacrifice was about the Promise."

Noah stared at Tinith, entirely baffled. "Not about the Promise? What else could it be?"

"The blood?" she asked quietly.

Shem thought about what she said. "The life is in the blood. He's looking for some kind of life power in the blood."

Shaking his head, Noah said, "What would the sacrifice have to do with that? The sacrifice is a sign of God's Promise."

Tinith felt confused. "That's what I don't understand about it, Father. How is killing an animal a sign of anything?"

"Think about each part of it," he answered. "You and I have sinned against Yahweh and should die. We select the best animal from the flock or herd, we lay our hands on it, confessing our sins. Then we kill the animal. God promises that someday a Savior will come—"

"Our seed," Shem added.

Noah continued, "and that Savior will crush the serpent's head. The sacrifice is a sign of our sin, our confession, the coming Savior, death and forgiveness."

Even though Tinith still did not understand how an animal's bloody death could symbolize Eve's descendant, she nevertheless grasped the heart of the issue: this symbol had nothing to do with the kind of power Ham wanted. The sacrifice symbolized how sin had broken each human's relationship with God and how that relationship could only be repaired through the death of an innocent substitute for the guilty sinner. The blood of the animal symbolized its poured out life on behalf of the sinner. It simply had nothing at all to do with power.

"So," she finally said, "Ham is taking a symbol about sin and our broken relationship with Yahweh, and he is turning it into some kind of tool to get power from animal blood."

Shem thought about her statement for a moment, adding, "The most impossible part of this story is the fact it actually works. Tinith and I have been laboring from sunrise to sunset plowing our fields. Our oxen are every bit as strong as Ham's, and our dirt has far fewer stones in it. Nevertheless, Ham did plow his field in half the time. Somehow what he has been doing with ox blood actually enables him to work faster."

Noah looked at his son. "We have never had a reason to suspect blood has special power. I don't think that's real. What you say, however, is true; the blood has been working."

Emah considered this for a moment, then suggested, "Does this mean Yahweh approves of this technique?"

"That can't be," answered Noah. "God Himself created the sacrifice, and God Himself told us what it means. That sacrifice is God's Word of Promise to us."

Shem added, "When Ham changes how the sacrifice is done, he completely changes what the Promise means. God would not approve of changing His Word to mean something different."

Confusion unsettled Emah's eyes. "Ham makes a sacrifice, puts blood in the water and on the poles. He then plows his field in half the time. If the blood is not doing this and Yahweh is not doing this, what made the oxen so much stronger?"

To this question, no one had an answer.

The following year, Tinith gave birth to a son, whom they named Arpachshad, and both Aleac and Hannah also bore sons. Over the next ten years, children were born every year, and the tiny families began farming their land together. Although his father forbade it, Ham continued offering blood sacrifices, and his crops were significantly more productive than Shem's. After five years, Japheth finally decided to try the sacrifices, and that year his crops produced abundantly for him as well. That year also, Noah confronted both brothers about this so passionately that Ham warned his father to stop speaking about it, or they would leave to find a new home. Ham's ultimatum forced the father to choose between longing for peace and enforcing righteousness. In the end, Noah's desire for peace led him to stay quiet, and after this the family continued to dwell together in uneasy harmony.

Neither Shem nor Noah could understand how these blood sacrifices produced such bounteous harvests and Ham consistently confessed his own ignorance on the issue. As the years progressed, however, Shem began to suspect Ham was holding back a secret about the blood. Whatever that mystery was, it took ten years before it finally came out. That was the year of the drought.

Even before they planted, all four families noted how dry the winter had been. The ground was harder than in the past and took more work to till. After they had plowed their furrows, Shem and his children decided to dig an irrigation ditch to the stream, bringing water to their crops just in case rains didn't come. One morning, as they worked on the main ditch, they heard voices from across the fields. Shem looked up to see his brother Ham, along with Cush, his oldest boy, approaching them.

Ham reached them and exclaimed, "You men are incredible!" His eyes followed the ditch all the way to the first field. "Cush, look at all of the work these fellows have done! I doubt if we could do even half as well."

Shem wiped sweat from his brow and stood. "Alright boys, why don't you play with Cush for a few minutes while I talk with your Uncle Ham?" The boys bounded out of the ditch and began talking in excited tones with their cousin. Shem, meanwhile, dropped to the ground in exhaustion, his brother coming to sit beside him.

Ham looked over to Shem and shook his head. "You guys work so hard to beat Nature, with your ditches, planting techniques and fertilizing."

Shem grunted. "I've seen you and the children in the fields; you work plenty hard."

"We work hard, but we have more help," Ham said, somewhat cryptically.

Shem stared at his brother in confusion at first, then suddenly laughed. "Oh, you mean your blood sacrifices."

Ham grinned, "Sort of."

"Sort of?" Shem asked, confused. "There's something else?"

Ham picked up a stone and threw it across the field. "Sure. . . There's something else. Or, I guess someone else."

Shem felt a stab of fear run through his thoughts. "Someone? I don't understand."

Looking to the stream, for a while Ham sat in silence as his brother watched him. He picked a blade of grass and began stripping it. "I wonder if you realize," he said carefully, "Yahweh isn't the only person in the world."

"Obviously," Shem said. "But. . ." at this he looked into Ham's wary eyes, "I suppose you are talking about persons other than humans, aren't you?"

Picking up another stone, his brother reached back and tossed it toward the stream. "No, not human, but very real." The sounds of the children running along the stream rode the breeze to their vantage point, but Shem hardly noticed. For a long time, he had suspected Ham's rituals had become more than just experiments with natural laws. He noticed his heart was beating rapidly and wondered why. What could possibly be frightening about his brother's answer?

"They talk to me sometimes," Ham said cautiously.

Shem stared at him. "Talk to you? They?"

He nodded. "I used to say always I had these feelings about things. They almost always were right. Remember?"

Shem nodded.

A furtive look stole into his eyes. "That feeling was them, I mean, the gods."

Appalled at what Ham just said, Shem simply sat there in silence.

"Do you remember the night I saw blood in the sky?" his brother asked. "It was the gods speaking to me. They gave me the idea to use the sacrifices. They explained the power of the blood, and it hasn't stopped since then either. They've been telling me a lot of things over the past ten years. They're very powerful, Shem, and they can make things happen."

For what seemed to be an eternity, the two brothers simply sat, staring out over the fields without speaking. Shem had a dozen questions for Ham, but didn't know how to begin asking. Why did his brother dare to call these things 'gods'? What about Yahweh? Were these things truly speaking to him, or was he just feeling something everyone else feels as a part of normal life? Even as these questions surfaced, Shem realized how futile it would be to uncover the falseness of Ham's rituals. His brother had already proven their effectiveness in producing rich harvests. Yet Shem needed to know something about these so-called gods. He asked a cautious question. "What kinds of things do they make happen?"

"Beyond the crops and the oxen and our harvests?"

Shem nodded. "Beyond those things."

"You know the twins?" he asked. Shem nodded. "I sacrificed two lambs the night they were conceived. I had this feeling if I doubled my normal offering, the gods would give me twice the power. You can ask Aleac about it. I told her it was going to happen months before they were born."

Shem looked at his brother urgently. "Maybe it was Yahweh telling you. It doesn't have to be other gods."

His brother laughed. "Yahweh? They hate Yahweh."

Fear was rising precariously within Shem, but he remained silent.

Scowling, Ham said, "They say that Yahweh created everything, but won't give them power. The only way they can get it is through us." He looked out over the stream. "You see, we have bodies and they don't. We can speak words of power out loud. We can touch oxen and spill their blood, but the gods are trapped in the spirit world. So they need us to give them more power. Blood has power in it. Some trees have power in them. Nighttime is brimming with power. The stars have power. Even some of us have power." At this, he looked at Shem, who saw perverse pleasure dominating his brother's countenance.

"If I can give them enough power, Shem," he said with excitement, "I can live forever."

That night, Shem sat with his wife, his father and mother. As he described his conversation with Ham, the family sat dumbfounded. Noah was the first to respond.

"How could there be other gods?" he asked incredulous. "Yahweh created the heavens and the earth. Yahweh spoke with Adam and Eve, and Yahweh even spoke to me. Doesn't Ham remember what happened in the flood? He saw Yahweh destroy every creature on earth! Why would he turn from Yahweh to these so-called gods when Yahweh rules over everything?"

Shem said. "Ham's gods don't care about sin. He can live anyway he pleases, as long as he gives them the power they need. They use him, and he uses them."

Emah looked at her son. "That's convenient."

Shem nodded. "Think about it. In the real world, death is the consequence of sin. In Ham's world, these gods promise they can overcome that consequence if humans bring them power. That, however, is obviously a fantasy. If God judges, who can stop Him? The flood was God's judgment against human sin. Could these gods have stopped the waters? When Ham gives power to his gods, even if it's real power, those gods still would not be able to stop Yahweh from bringing justice."

"But they offer him unending life," Emah said.

Noah scowled. "No one can make that offer. That's the whole point of the Promise and the sacrifice."

As the import of these words sunk in, Tinith suddenly understood. Ham's story, the crops, the oxen, the blood, even the strange feelings and impression–all of it made perfect sense. She looked at the others in fear. "You are wrong, Father. This offer has been made before. In the garden."

Shem stared at his wife, amazed. "By the serpent."

Emah quoted; "The serpent said to the woman, 'You surely will not die! For God knows that in the day you eat from it your eyes will be opened, and you will be like God, knowing good and evil.'"

Tinith saw the horror on the faces of her husband, mother and father, and she sighed. "Ham is dealing with the serpent."

"Our greatest enemy," Noah whispered.

Emah took her husband's hand. "We have to warn him, Noah, and Japheth."

Shem shook his head. "We'll warn them, but they won't listen. They'll always choose whatever works, and right now, the serpent is working out everything they want."

"But why," asked Emah, "is the serpent requiring blood sacrifices? Wouldn't that remind Ham and Japheth of the Promise?"

"No," Tinith answered. "It changes the symbol of the Promise into a source of illicit power. Unless our brothers and their wives repent, they will never be able to look at a sacrifice and feel shame for their sin, nor will they hope for God's Savior. They'll only see power— power for themselves and power for their evil gods."

Noah considered her words carefully. "So these sacrifices are like the fruit of the knowledge of good and evil. The serpent told Eve she would live forever, but she died. The serpent is promising Ham and Aleac they will live forever, but nonetheless, they will die." He looked up with the sudden shock of understanding. "The serpent doesn't need or want these sacrifices! He wants my children to die in their sin, separated from Yahweh eternally. The sacrifices are just a sham."

"The first time humankind obeyed the serpent," Emah said in a hushed voice, "they became the slaves of death. What will happen this time?"

Shem looked toward the mountains, blanketed with snow. Thirty-seven years ago, when they first left the ark, only trees covered these summits, but now even at the end of summer, the upper halves of the mountains were still white. It had been almost thirty years ago when the weather began cooling. *It's the sky*, he thought to himself uneasily. *We haven't had a clear day in ten years.* Without sunshine, their world was turning cold. Worse yet, the long winter ate into their growing season, and early frosts wiped out many of their crops.

Ham's pagan sacrifices didn't seem to work against the cold; he claimed he needed new kinds of offerings suited to weather gods rather than fertility and animal gods. When Shem pointed out the obvious fact that Yahweh was judging them for sacrificing to their gods, Ham asked why Noah and his only faithful son suffered along-side everyone else in the disaster.

To this Shem had no answer.

He looked out over dwellings which dotted the countryside and beyond. His family had grown enormously over the decades. He now had eighteen grandchildren, who were a great joy to him. Eight children enlivened the household of Arpachshad, Shem's oldest son, whose wife Neela was expecting their ninth child any day now. In fact, she was staying with his mother until she gave birth. Shem's other sons and daughters still brought their little ones to Grandfather, who carefully taught them the story of the Promise. Of Noah's three sons, Shem alone remained faithful to passing on the story, and this worried him. With the many offspring of Ham and Japheth, it would not take long for their tiny village to expand into a city. Perhaps within fifty more years, they would number in the tens of thousands. What would happen if none of them knew the story?

He heard a shout from beyond the irrigation ditch, and spotted Ham making his way across the field toward him. A young man followed closely behind, probably Canaan, Ham's youngest son. Ham seldom visited this farm and had never come before with the boy, the youngest of Noah's grandsons, about twenty years in age.

Shem stared at the two figures. He wondered what would bring them both, unless the boy was proposing marriage to one of Shem's daughters. This, however, would never happen as long as Shem still ruled his household. Two years before, Shem's oldest daughter had come to him privately about Canaan. What she told her father about the boy and his relationships with both women and men drove Shem to forbid his daughters or sons even to talk with Canaan. They lived far enough apart, however, that such interaction seldom had opportunity to develop.

Shem prayed and then strode to greet his brother and nephew. Ham beamed. "Well brother! How are your crops?" He looked over the fields. "Dying like mine, I see. Before long, we'll be eating pine cones." He laughed.

"Hello Ham, Canaan," he said soberly.

Canaan nodded, but a curious expression came over Ham's face. "I almost get the impression we are not welcome here, brother. What have we done to you?"

Shem paused, considering how to answer. He decided to ignore the comment and face the situation. "So, Canaan, I'm assuming you are here to request one of my daughters as a wife."

Canaan looked at him with an unfriendly expression. "That's correct Uncle. Yaneth has caught my eye. I am successful, with my own fields, flocks and herds. She'll have a real house and three completed farm buildings." He stopped and looked sulkily at Shem. "That's all I've got to say."

Shem looked the young man in the eye, and the boy flinched. "And what about your other three wives, Canaan?" he said solemnly. "How will they feel about a new member of the household?"

The young man's eyes snapped in anger. "I'm their husband. They'll accept it."

Still gazing into his eyes, Shem said, "I see." It was clear his scrutiny disconcerted Canaan, who squirmed under his stare and backed away. Shem did not like what he had seen of the boy over the years, and after what his daughter had said, he knew he could not give Yaneth to him as a bride. For that matter, he would never allow any of his girls to wed any son of Ham or Japheth, for these men all served the serpent and would therefore all come to the same end.

"So," Ham said with a good-natured smile, "when shall we come to pick up the bride and her belongings?"

Shem steeled himself for the dam about to burst. "Never," he answered as calmly as he could bring himself to speak. "I will not give my daughter to a man with other wives, and I will not give any daughter to a man who serves the serpent."

If Shem had slapped his brother on the face, the shock would not have been any less abrupt. Ham stepped toward him, and Shem prepared to defend himself. His brother's eyes blazed, and his face tightened with rage.

"You have no right to hold any daughter from my sons!" he hissed. Shem saw anger in his brother unlike anything he had experienced, even in the days before the flood. Ham spoke again. "We are brothers, and you owe me and my son as many daughters as we need!"

Shaking his head, Shem answered evenly, "Your son has too many wives already. I won't give him my daughter, and I cannot allow my girls to live in a household under the serpent's lordship."

"Fool! I am going to Father about this. Yahweh commanded us to be fruitful and multiply. Our Father will compel you to give up your daughter; be sure of that."

Shem kept his temper calm. "Father and I have discussed this many times, brother. Not only does he agree with me, but Father himself first suggested it." He glanced at Canaan, whose anger was even more dangerous than his father's. Beyond what his daughter had already told him, this young man's ill nature convinced Shem that he had no choice but to protect his Yaneth. Even if he could have foretold the pain his decision would soon bring, as a father, he would still have answered no. When Ham realized his older brother would not back down, he tramped away shouting warnings, threats and curses.

Emah watched her husband filling baskets with grapes. Last year was the first time his vines had produced, and this year his yield was abundant. Noah never spoke of the grapes, nor mentioned what he did with them, but she knew. He had begun drinking wine again. He was desperately trying to find a way to ease the grief that haunted his days and nights.

The past thirty-seven years had shown how hopeless human progress actually was. Already, his offspring rebelled against God just as defiantly as humankind had rebelled before the flood. Ham and Japheth had all but abandoned Yahweh. Even though Japheth still attended Noah's offerings to God, he inevitably went right back to serving the serpent. The middle son, Ham, not only rejected Noah's sacrifices, but also opposed his father constantly, at times actually mocking him. Shem and his children alone stayed faithful to the promise.

Noah could see the path his children took and knew it led to death. He and Emah had anguished over what to do, but finally realized they were helpless. Night after night they begged Yahweh to turn their children back. Their two sons and grandchildren nevertheless continued to go their own way. Watching two generations slipping into sin before their eyes was more painful than witnessing God's wrath poured out upon the human race at the flood. At least then, they could hope that future generations might serve Yahweh. Now, those future generations were failing their hope. Only Shem's offered promise of faithfulness and how long could that last? Noah's grief was driving him to seek forgetfulness in wine.

In the distance, Emah saw Ham making his way down the pathway toward the vineyard. Once he reached his father, although she could hear nothing, it was clear Ham was quite angry. He was waving his arms, pointing back toward Shem's fields and shaking his head. Furthermore, whatever Noah answered did not satisfy him, for he continued to argue and cajole. Noah seemed to slump under his son's barrage of anger. She wished she could be there, confronting her impious son and reminding him of his duty to honor and obey his father, but it would do no good.

After several minutes of this spectacle, Ham turned and strode away. She viewed Noah, standing alone on the path, watching his middle son retreat. Whatever had occasioned this outburst, Emah had little doubt what impact it would bring to her husband. She observed her husband stoop to gather up his baskets and begin walking toward a large tent they used for nurturing newborn lambs. Before he reached the opening, however, she saw him stop and turn again to view his son. Then Noah disappeared into the tent.

He did not return that evening for supper, nor did he return that night for sleep, and Emah's fears deepened. Her grandson Arpachshad and his wife Neela were staying in the house, awaiting the birth of their ninth child. Emah did not want them to see their grandfather drunk. For several hours, she tossed and turned, wondering what to do. Finally, unable to stand it any longer, she lit a lantern and made her way across the barnyard to the tent facing the house. Entering the darkness, she found her husband sitting in the hay, a wineskin in his hand. He looked up at her and smiled.

"Husband," she said quietly, "our bed is cold and needs you to warm it."

He laughed cynically. "The world is cold, woman. Haven't you noticed?"

She didn't answer.

He pointed to the mountains beyond the tent walls. "Haven't you seen the snow? Haven't you felt the cold winds blowing from the north? When did you last see sunlight or blue sky or stars sprinkling in the heavens? Don't you realize, wife, what is happening? Yahweh is withdrawing His warmth from the world. He shuts down the earth like a fire doused by morning rain. Soon ice will cover not just the mountain peaks but the slopes and feet and yes, even this valley will drown in its flood, until the whole world is cold and dead."

She stared at her husband, wondering what to say, what to do. Tears now streamed down his face. She spoke to him in a gentle voice. "Husband, what did Ham do to you?"

"Do to me?" Noah answered drunkenly. "He did nothing at all. He simply told me the truth. He hates me, Emah, because I will not serve his evil gods. He hates me because I will not give my permission to defile my only pure granddaughters with his vile and rebellious sons. Do you know what he dared say to me?"

She whispered, "What?"

"I told him he was destroying the human race, and he looked me in the eye and said, 'Father, the day you finished that barge and allowed even one human to board, the human race already was lost. You have done this, Father, not I.'" He put his head in his hands. "He's right, you know."

Standing there in the doorway, with only a lantern to light the room, she answered firmly, "No, husband."

He looked up to her, weeping.

"No," she repeated. "Yahweh warned you of the coming flood. Yahweh commanded you to build the ship. Yahweh brought the animals to the ramp. Yahweh led us to this valley beneath the mountains. You did only what Yahweh commanded, and Yahweh will fulfill His Promise."

He stared, clumsily trying to understand her words, to grasp what she meant, but he was too drunk, far too lost in his own self pity, and he shook his head. He smiled and lifted the wineskin to his mouth.

"Leave the lamp," he muttered.

She turned, and, weeping silently, left the light with her husband inside the tent. It was difficult to find her way to the house in the darkness, but she finally reached the doorway of her house. A few minutes later found her kneeling on the floor, praying. "Yahweh, please spare my husband any more pain. Please protect him from the hatred of his sons and grandsons." As she knelt there in the dark of her room, she did not know a figure was making his way from the path to the tent doorway.

Outside the house, in the tent, the crack of a twig broke the silence, and Noah looked up. Canaan his grandson, stood before him. The boy's quiet demeanor was more dangerous than he had been in his fury earlier that day, but Noah was too drunk to notice. He lifted the wineskin toward Canaan and said drunkenly, "So, have you come to drink with me?"

Canaan shook his head.

"Ah," Noah said with exaggerated wisdom, "You're here for my granddaughter, aren't you?"

Again, Canaan shook his head.

A ridiculing smirk came over Noah's face. "Perhaps you're looking for your gods. Well, boy, they're not welcome here. They don't like Yahweh very much, or didn't you know that?" He leaned toward him, whispering loudly, "He created them, and He doesn't like them very much either. They're afraid of Him, you know."

At this, Canaan started. "That's not true," he answered darkly. "They do not fear Yahweh. They despise him."

"No," his grandfather said in derision. "They despise you, boy. They despise you as much as they despise Yahweh, because you are fool enough to believe all their lies."

In a moment, the boy was across the room, grabbing his grandfather by the cloak, pulling him up and shaking him violently. "You are the fool, old man!" he hissed. "The gods are powerful, more powerful than anything you have ever seen." He looked into Noah's face with utter contempt, spat and then pushed him back onto the bed of hay.

For a moment, he stood in the center of the tent, surveying its contents. Then his eyes fell upon whatever it was he sought. Grabbing the lantern, he strode to a small animal pen, placed the lantern on the floor and reached over the gate. Noah watched him pick a lamb up by the scruff of its neck. Moving his hand to his sheath, Canaan slipped out a menacing knife and approached his grandfather, carrying the lamb in his other hand.

Noah, too drunk to defend himself, pulled back in exaggerated fear. Canaan laughed mockingly. "You don't think I'd kill you, do you? You're not good enough for what I want. I want power." Up he swung the lamb into the air and with one swift motion, slit its throat.

Noah cried out in shock, as blood burst from the animal and spilled onto his head and clothing. Canaan lifted the lamb above his face and let its lifeblood pour into his mouth, which he gleefully swallowed.

Then he dropped the animal onto Noah and shouted in ecstasy. "This is power!" his voice boomed. "I am the god, Noah son of

Lamech. Fear me, for you will never meet power as awesome as this! I am the god!" He turned and ran from the tent.

Noah, pushed the lifeless lamb off himself in revulsion. Clumsily grabbing at his clothing, he discovered himself soaked with blood, and he moaned. Suddenly, terror surged up inside of him, terror of this hideous blood. He was desperate to be free of it, desperate to get away from it. He tried ripping at the cloak to get it off of him, but his fingers kept slipping on the fluid, and he found himself unable to rend the material. Frantically working to free himself, he became obsessed with the smell of blood. Finally, in his drunken daze, he managed to pull the cloak off and to cast it down onto the floor. This, however, was not enough, for he still felt the defiling blood splattered over the rest of his body. In panic, he tore off every piece of blood-stained clothing, flinging it away from himself until he was entirely naked. Only after this did he fall back onto the hay, and from that point on, he knew nothing else.

Early in the next morning, Shem awoke to Ham's jubilant voice. "Wake up, brother. I want you to look upon our marvelous father this morning."

Before long, Shem, Ham and Japheth were approaching their father's tent. As they walked, Ham told his brothers the story he had learned from Canaan. "He's in there, Shem, your precious father, drunk with sweet wine, not a stitch of clothing, probably lying in his own vomit."

"Why are you doing this?" Shem asked angrily. "Don't you care enough about your father to treat him with respect?"

Ham laughed. "I respect him for what he is–a naked drunken fool. Isn't that just being honest?"

They reached the tent door, and Ham stopped. "Well, brothers, are you joining me?"

Neither Shem nor his youngest brother Japheth moved. The middle brother smirked at them, bowed, and they grimly watched him disappear into the tent entrance. Within moments, they heard laughter, loud rolling laughter, which continued for several minutes. Shem found the experience nauseating and wished he could be anywhere but there. Finally, Ham stumbled out, hysterically guffawing. He came to Shem and hung on him, still laughing. Shem pushed him away.

That helped Ham finally to get enough control of himself to speak. "It's quite a sight in there brothers. He's as naked as he was the day he was born, lying on his little bed of hay. Looks like his wine got all used up." He patted Shem on the shoulder. "You really should see him, brother. It would make you proud."

He walked past the two of them, reached the pathway and began making his way back to his own farm. In disgust, Shem watched him leave. When he turned back, he saw his mother standing at the door of the house, holding a long garment. Crossing the yard, he embraced her for a long time. She said nothing. Then he took the garment and brought it to Japheth. The two of them entered the tent walking backwards and covered their father's nakedness.

Many hours later, Tinith arrived from their farm to Noah's land to sit with Neela at the birth of her child. She saw Shem, and Japheth standing together in silence. Shem quietly described to her what had transpired the previous night and that morning. The three of them guarded the entrance to the tent throughout the morning. Not until the sun reached its zenith, did they hear stirring within. Before long, their father emerged, his face and arms covered with blood and dirt. Glancing at his sons with a shameful look, he examined himself, grimacing in disgust.

Without saying a word, Noah turned toward the stream and his two sons accompanied him, who both waited as he washed himself free of the stain. Once he was finished, they returned to Tinith, saying nothing. There Noah stood before the tent, wrestling with the urge to avoid facing what had happened here during the night. Finally, he entered the tent alone, staying within for several minutes, then emerged with a sober expression. One look at his face convinced Tinith her father knew what his youngest descendant had done to him.

For a long time, Noah gazed across the fields to the house of Ham. Finally, he turned to his sons and daughter-in-law. "This cannot go on," he said grimly. "I must speak what Yahweh has put into my heart."

Noah motioned to one of the children playing nearby them. "Run to your Uncle Ham's home. Ask him to bring Canaan here to the house."

Noah looked out across the land. "I used to believe we could create a new world of righteousness, without sin and without war. Now I understand how futile that would be. As long as we are human, we will always choose the fruit of the knowledge of good and evil and reject the tree of life. It is written into the very sinews of our being."

Tinith glanced at her father-in-law. He shook his head in sadness. "Ham was right; as soon as we allowed humans aboard the ship, we were again dooming humanity to absolute failure. We cannot overcome our sin by changing human government. Humanity itself is the problem. As long as humans rule this planet, it will never return to Eden's perfection."

Tinith placed her hand on Noah's arm to comfort him.

"This new world is worse than the old. In this world, the serpent entices my sons to serve him, and they choose to turn the sacrifice, a symbol of Yahweh's Promise, into a ritual designed to gain them power. They throw away the coming Savior and sell themselves instead to the serpent as slaves. Now that the serpent has returned to humankind, we will have no peace until the seed of Eve crushes his head."

Tinith could see in the distance her brother-in-law Ham and nephew Canaan making their way across the field to the house. Turning to his youngest son, Noah spoke quietly. "Japheth, everyone who serves the serpent will become his slave. You must not obey your brother's gods, for they will destroy you in the end. The serpent only cares about murder and deceit. You cannot trust him." His son did not reply.

Tinith looked up to see Canaan and Ham on the pathway at the end of the field. Noah turned and solemnly gazed at them until the two reached the tent. "Behold your nephew Canaan," Noah said loudly, as Canaan and Ham reached them. "He has chosen the serpent over Yahweh. He has defiled himself before me, and his father has disgraced me without shame. Therefore hear what I now declare to you: Cursed be Canaan; a servant of servants He shall be to his brothers."

Noah turned to Shem, and laid his hands upon him. "Blessed be the Lord, The God of Shem; and let Canaan be his servant." He then turned to Japheth, laying his hands on his youngest son. "May God enlarge Japheth and let him dwell in the tents of Shem; and let Canaan be his servant."

His words shocked Tinith, and she glanced at Ham, whose face surprisingly showed fear, although she could not imagine why. Canaan was insolently scowling, but said nothing.

The sound of an opening door broke the silence. "Noah," she heard Emah calling out, clearly unaware of the drama being played out before her. "Neela is giving birth. Could Tinith come and help?"

Noah looked to his daughter-in-law and nodded, and she hurried across the yard to the house. As she entered, she looked back to see the men moving from the tent.

The birth happened quickly. Once the child came out, they washed it and wrapped it in a cloth. Tinith gently rocked the baby, smiling at its perfect fingers, its perfect face and its perfect feet. In the midst of their grief, a new life entered the world. She began to hand it to Neela, but Emah stopped her and bent over her granddaughter lying on the bedding.

"Neela, let me present the child to Noah first, and then we'll bring it back." The mother, a curious expression on her face, nevertheless nodded, and Tinith and Emah carried the baby into the next room, where Arpachshad stood anxiously waiting. "We bring the child to Noah," Emah said quietly. "Come with us." The three of them found the men standing in the yard.

"Your great-grandchild, Noah," Emah said quietly. "I thought you should see him first."

Noah looked up at her in surprise. She placed the babe into his arms and stepped back. Tinith watched Noah quietly studying the newborn, obviously deep in thought. She wondered what led Emah to bring the child to Noah. At first, she supposed her mother wanted him to see again the beauty of human life, but surely he had met too much grief to find comfort in the birth of another child. Yet something in his face told her this child was comforting him, rather than driving him to despair.

Emah spoke. "So husband, is this the one?"

He said nothing at first, still staring at the baby. They waited quietly. Finally he looked up. "This is the one," he answered. "God's Promise to Eve continues. He has sent us another gift of hope."

He placed the child in Arpachshad's arms and smiled. "Grandson, you must name this son of the Promise."

Arpachshad gazed at the boy for a long time, saying nothing. "Shelah," he finally answered. "He is the sent one."

Emah touched Tinith's arm. "Your daughter-in-law needs us. Come." They walked toward the door of the house. There they both stopped, looking at the group in the yard.

Although Tinith did not know the future, she still could see the fate of all the nations standing before them. Noah, the father of the human race, was lifting his eyes to the heavens, hope again renewed. Shem, father of the sons of Promise, stood quietly beside his father, committing himself to pass the story on to the child. Ham and Canaan, fathers of idolatry, turned from the scene in disgust, and began making their way to their own places. Japheth, father of many peoples, in confusion watched them leave, struggling between the seed of Shem and the power of Ham and Canaan's gods.

For Tinith, however, hope lay in Arpachshad's arms. Yahweh continued to fulfill his Promise. No matter how far humanity turned its heart from serving Him, God still had sent Shelah. Perhaps this was the Son who would crush the serpent's head. Perhaps this child would open the way to the Tree of Life. In the midst of their grief, Yahweh brought them hope.

Applying *The End of All Flesh* to our Lives today

If you are a regular reader of the Bible, I trust this story has unsettled you. Hopefully whatever you disliked about the book (theology, storytelling, viewpoints, etc.) did not keep you from seeing Yakheed as a real person (in a fictional sort of way) and feeling sad when the flood waters dragged him away. People who love God need to see God's wrath as tragic, not heroic.

If you are not a regular reader of the Bible or if you are not enamored with biblical truth, this narrative may have offended you. Did you wonder why on earth a writer would glorify the "senseless" destruction of innocent children and frightened men and women, people who sought to do the best they could? Granted, some of them may have committed terrible crimes, but the grand majority were ordinary people, no worse than the millions of faithful churchgoers who call themselves "saved." It may seem wrong to you that the so-called God of love arbitrarily snuffed out the lives of those who displeased Him. On this point, many identify with John Stuart Mill, who wrote; "I will call no being good who is not what I mean when I apply that epithet to my fellow creatures; and if such a creature can sentence me to hell for not so calling him, to hell I will go" (An Examination of Sir William Hamilton's Philosophy—1865).

Of course, the God portrayed in the Bible most certainly does judge people. Countless stories in the Old Testament chronicle His wrath. Jesus continually warns of God's condemnation. "'And you, Capernaum, will not be exalted to heaven, will you? You will descend to Hades; for if the miracles had occurred in Sodom which occurred in you, it would have remained to this day. Nevertheless I say to you that it will be more tolerable for the land of Sodom in the day of judgment, than for you.'" (Matthew 11:23-24) We are told in Hebrews ". . . it is appointed for men to die once and after this comes judgment. . ." (Hebrews 9:27). We may find Yahweh's approach to justice frightening and repugnant. That, however, does not change the reality: God in the Bible punishes all sin with suffering, death and eternal separation from all that is good.

Anyone who denies this is simply ignoring what the Bible teaches. If you say, "The God I believe in is not a wrathful Being," that's fine, but I do wonder where you get your information. Unless you have some source of divine revelation, you must really be saying "I prefer a God who is not wrathful." We all would prefer a Creator who does not judge sin, but we really need some hard facts before we change what He is like to fit our personal tastes. Not only is it arrogant (supremely arrogant when it comes to the Creator) and dangerous, but it is also a terribly unloving attitude. Love demands that we accept people as they really are, not as we would like them to be. None of us respects a man who marries a woman and then tries to force her into his own mold, or a woman who marries a man and then manipulates him into what she wants him to become. We call that abusive or controlling, but would never call it love. When we try to force the Creator into our own personal mold, it isn't love either. We need to accept Him as He is in reality, don't we? After all, when Moses asked His name, God answered: 'I AM WHO I AM'; and He said, 'Thus you shall say to the sons of Israel, 'I AM has sent me to you.'" (Exodus 3:13-14) What kind of a name is that? It is a name which means, "No matter what kind of God you want Me to be, I am what I am." When we refuse to accept Him as He is, we are not loving Him at all. The sin of remolding God into a more acceptable form is idolatry, a sin committed by the Israelites when they created an idol and called it Yahweh (Exodus 32).

Sometimes people make the mistake of embracing one characteristic of Yahweh (His love, for example), while denying another characteristic (His righteous judgment). We argue, how can a loving God condemn people who do not understand His will for them? Therefore, we say, God does not send people to hell. Yet the authors of the Bible, including Jesus Himself, saw God's wrath and God's love as entirely compatible. Is the real problem the fact that God is somehow twisted, or instead are we humans simplistic and limited in what we can understand? After all, my inability to understand Einstein's theory of relativity does not disprove the theory, but simply points out the obvious fact that I am not as smart as Einstein. If a scientific theory can be too complex for me to grasp, I should realize how limited I will be in trying to comprehend the Creator of the universe, the One who created DNA, who composed a universe of laws and processes far beyond the most brilliant minds alive today.

On that basis, either we reject the Bible's picture of God altogether, or we acknowledge what the Bible makes unavoidably clear: God is the Lord who judges. He calls Himself "Yahweh, the Lord God, compassionate and gracious, slow to anger and abounding in lovingkindness and truth; who keeps lovingkindness for thousands, who forgives iniquity, transgression and sin; yet He will by no means leave the guilty unpunished, visiting the iniquity of fathers on the children and on the grandchildren to the third and fourth generations." (Exodus 34:6-7) When we ignore our Creator, we are not loving Him. We are not loving Him when we say, "Well, I don't like the way He says He is, so I'm going to ignore Him. I won't say anything bad about Him, but I won't listen to what He says either." This is rebellion. It is like the time you walked past an unpleasant person and acted as if he wasn't there. It may not have seemed like hatred when you did it, but it sure wasn't love and was a sort of passive hatred.

The story of Noah is first and foremost a story about how Yahweh poured out His wrath upon those humans who rebelled against him, either actively or passively. Most of those who died in the flood did not raise their fists in anger the way Yakheed did, but simply ignored God's claim upon them. That, however, is as serious a sin as cursing the Lord. We humans are entirely the possessions of the Creator God and must submit to whatever He chooses as our purpose in life. Yahweh created the heavens and the earth and therefore Yahweh owns everything. "The earth is the Lord's and all it contains, the world and those who dwell in it. For He has founded it upon the seas and established it upon the rivers." (Psalm 24:1-2) According to the Bible, every human on the planet belongs exclusively to God. Every plan, every possession, every action and every thought must conform to His purposes for us. We may not like it, but we are only the creation; He is the Creator. We must carry out His will for our lives.

And what is this purpose He has for humankind to perform? In the Bible, Jesus answered this clearly.

> One of them, a lawyer, asked Him a question, testing
> Him, "Teacher, which is the great commandment in

the Law?" and He said to him, "'You shall love the
Lord your God with all your heart and with all your
soul and with all your mind.' This is the great and
foremost commandment. The second is like it, 'You
shall love your neighbor as yourself.' On these two
commandments depend the whole Law and the
Prophets." (Matthew 22:35-40)

The first purpose is to love God and the second is to love our
neighbor. Everything else in life depends on fulfilling those two
commandments.

If you speak with tongues of men and of angels, but
do not love others, you are a noisy gong. If you have
enough faith to move mountains, but do not love others,
your faith is worthless. If you give everything you have
to feed the poor, but do not love others, it profits you
nothing (1 Corinthians 13:1-3).

God created you to love Him and others. If you ignore Him, you
are not fulfilling your purpose in life. If you ignore others, you are not
fulfilling your purpose in life, and anyone who does not fulfill his or
her purpose in life will be judged.

"That's not fair!" you may protest, but in the end, God is the One
who defines fairness, since He created all things, including you.
Yahweh will judge us not by our standards, but by His. God will
punish us not by the punishments we prefer, but with the consequences
He chooses to mete out. "For we know Him who said, 'Vengeance is
Mine, I will repay.' and again, 'The Lord will judge His people.' It is a
terrifying thing to fall into the hands of the living God." (Hebrews
10:30-31) As Yahweh said to Moses after Israel committed idolatry,

"Whoever has sinned against Me, I will blot him
out of My book. But go now, lead the people
where I told you. Behold, My angel shall go
before you; nevertheless in the day when I
punish, I will punish them for their sin."
(Exodus 32:33-34)

In the day God punishes sin, He will punish everyone who has ignored Him or turned against Him.

That judgment is going to be terrifying. Remember the horrors of the flood.

> "For the coming of the Son of Man will be just like
> the days of Noah. For as in those days before the
> flood they were eating and drinking, marrying
> and giving in marriage, until the day that Noah
> entered the ark and they did not understand until
> the flood came and took them all away; so will the
> coming of the Son of Man be. Then there will be
> two men in the field; one will be taken and one
> will be left. Two women will be grinding at the
> mill; one will be taken and one will be left."
> (Matthew 24:37-41)

In Noah's day, only those who trusted in the Promise given to Eve and then climbed aboard the ship were saved from God's judgment. Jesus warns us a new worldwide judgment is coming and warns that only those who believe in Him will be saved from God's wrath. "He who believes in the Son has eternal life; but he who does not obey the Son will not see life, but the wrath of God abides on him." (John 3:36)

God's plan for escaping that wrath centers on Christ. It begins with facing the fact you personally are committing terrible sins when you choose not to love God or your fellow humans. You must take responsibility for those sins and recognize God's perfect right as your Creator to punish you. In facing your personal rebellion, you must agree that this behavior has to change. Jesus describes this process as repentance. This was Jesus' message. "From that time Jesus began to preach and say, 'Repent, for the kingdom of heaven is at hand.'" (Matthew 4:17) When Peter preached an early message, he said the same thing. "Therefore repent and return, so that your sins may be wiped away, in order that times of refreshing may come from the presence of the Lord . . ." We read a later message preached by Paul, who urged the same response: "Therefore, having overlooked the time of ignorance, God is now declaring to men that all people should repent because He has fixed a day in which He will judge the world in righteousness through a Man whom He has appointed, having furnished proof to all men by raising Him from the dead." (Acts 17:30-31) Until you face up to your sinful acts against God, you will never have a reason to trust in Christ for deliverance from sin.

Once you have repented, you must do what Noah did—believe in the Son of the Promise, Jesus Christ and act on that belief. Noah's faith was not religious or intellectual, but involved both the Promise of God and stepping out in trust based upon that promise. Hebrews tells us, "By faith Noah, being warned by God about things not yet seen, in reverence prepared an ark for the salvation of his household, by which he condemned the world and became an heir of the righteousness which is according to faith." (Hebrews 11:7) Notice Noah by faith did something, i.e., he prepared an ark. Today we must do the same. For us, that means we face our sin, believe in Jesus as God's Promised Son and then follow Him. Following Him means hearing His teachings and doing them. "Truly, truly, I say to you, if anyone keeps My word he will never see death." (John 8:51)

Judgment is coming, a judgment far more severe and terrifying than the great flood of Noah's day. Everyone who ignores God's solution will encounter His wrath. Everyone who faces up to his or her own sin, believes in Jesus Christ and embraces and practices His teachings will escape the great judgment soon to fall upon the human race. As Jesus said:

> "Therefore everyone who hears these words of Mine
> and acts on them, may be compared to a wise man
> who built his house on the rock, and the rain fell and
> the floods came and the winds blew and slammed
> against that house; and yet it did not fall, for it had
> been founded on the rock. Everyone who hears
> these words of Mine and does not act on them, will
> be like a foolish man who built his house on the
> sand. The rain fell and the floods came and the
> winds blew and slammed against that house; and it
> fell—and great was its fall." (Matthew 7:24-27)

After reading this book, one reality should be clear: the God of the Bible will bring judgment upon all who sin, both those who passionately hate Him and those who passively ignore Him. The only pathway to salvation is the Promised Son, Jesus. The question you must ask yourself, then is this: Are you prepared for judgment?

Biblical References

Many of the biblical references listed below are inferences and not proof texts. Nevertheless, readers might be helped to see what Scriptures suggested various interpretations about life during Noah's days.

Note: Some may question why in this book almost all of Adam's descendants are ignorant of Yahweh and His work of creation. I am guessing no one beyond Seth's descendants worshiped Yahweh. This assumption is based on Genesis 4:26: "To Seth, to him also a son was born; and he called his name Enosh. Then men began to call upon the name of the Lord." (Genesis 4:26) Apparently soon after humans began multiplying, they forgot Yahweh. I do not believe, however, that humankind turned to idols at this point. Idolatry is the most visible form of animism, the belief that unseen spiritual power exists throughout the world and impacts everything we experience in one way or another. It seems as if animism fuels most religious activity around the globe. Yet surprisingly, God does not mention judging the earth for practicing either animism or idolatry. He judges instead the universal moral sinfulness of the race. "Then the Lord saw that the wickedness of man was great on the earth and that every intent of the thoughts of his heart was only evil continually." (Genesis 6:5). Idolatry is never mentioned until the tower of Babel. Therefore I suspect idolatry did not begin until after the flood. I have portrayed Canaan and Ham as animists after they leave the barge and will develop this theme throughout the series.

All of the following quotations are taken from the New American Standard Bible: 1995 update. 1995. LaHabra, CA: The Lockman Foundation.

Chapter 1: Year 1056

Entire Chapter: The Nephilim were on the earth in those days and also afterward, when the sons of God came in to the daughters of men and they bore children to them. Those were the mighty men who were of old, men of renown. (Genesis 6:4)

Page 24: "And I will put enmity Between you and the woman and between your seed and her seed; He shall bruise you on the head and you shall bruise him on the heel." (Genesis 3:15)

Page 25: Lamech lived one hundred and eighty-two years and became the father of a son. Now he called his name Noah, saying, "This one will give us rest from our work and from the toil of our hands arising from the ground which the Lord has cursed." (Genesis 5:28-29)

Chapter 2: Year 1066

Page 29: Behold now, Behemoth, which I made as well as you; He eats grass like an ox. Behold now, his strength in his loins and his power in the muscles of his belly. He bends his tail like a cedar; The sinews of his thighs are knit together. His bones are tubes of bronze; His limbs are like bars of iron. He is the first of the ways of God; Let his maker bring near his sword. Surely the mountains bring him food and all the beasts of the field play there. Under the lotus plants he lies down, In the covert of the reeds and the marsh. The lotus plants cover him with shade; The willows of the brook surround him. If a river rages, he is not alarmed; He is confident, though the Jordan rushes to his mouth. Can anyone capture him when he is on watch, With barbs can anyone pierce his nose? (Job 40:15-24)

Chapter 3: Year 1076

Page 49: Now to Enoch was born Irad and Irad became the father of Mehujael and Mehujael became the father of Methushael and Methushael became the father of Lamech. (Genesis 4:18)

Page 49: Now it came about, when men began to multiply on the face of the land and daughters were born to them, that the sons of God saw that the daughters of men were beautiful; and they took wives for themselves, whomever they chose. Then the Lord said, "My Spirit shall not strive with man forever, because he also is flesh; nevertheless his days shall be one hundred and twenty years." The Nephilim were on the earth in those days and also afterward, when the sons of God came in to the daughters of men and they bore children to them. Those were the mighty men who were of old, men of renown. (Genesis 6:1-4)

Page 49: As for Zillah, she also gave birth to Tubal-cain, the forger of all implements of bronze and iron; and the sister of Tubal-cain was Naamah. (Genesis 4:22)

Chapter 6: Year 1080

Page 124: Also the fountains of the deep and the floodgates of the sky were closed and the rain from the sky was restrained; (Genesis 8:2)

Chapter 7: Year 1441

Page 150: "Make for yourself an ark of gopher wood; you shall make the ark with rooms and shall cover it inside and out with pitch. (Genesis 6:14)

Page 155: In the beginning God created the heavens and the earth. (Genesis 1:1)

Page 156: Then the Lord God said to the woman, "What is this you have done?" and the woman said, "The serpent deceived me and I ate." (Genesis 3:13)

Page 156: When Adam had lived one hundred and thirty years, he became the father of a son in his own likeness, according to his image and named him Seth. Then the days of Adam after he became the father of Seth were eight hundred years and he had other sons and daughters. So all the days that Adam lived were nine hundred and thirty years and he died. Seth lived one hundred and five years and became the father of Enosh. Then Seth lived eight hundred and seven years after he became the father of Enosh and he had other sons and daughters. So all the days of Seth were nine hundred and twelve years and he died. Enosh lived ninety years and became the father of Kenan. Then Enosh lived eight hundred and fifteen years after he became the father of Kenan and he had other sons and daughters. So all the days of Enosh were nine hundred and five years and he died. Kenan lived seventy years and became the father of Mahalalel. Then Kenan lived eight hundred and forty years after he became the father of Mahalalel and he had other sons and daughters. So all the days of Kenan were nine hundred and ten years and he died. Mahalalel lived sixty-five years and became the father of Jared. Then Mahalalel lived eight hundred and thirty years after he became the father of Jared and he had other sons and daughters. So all the days of Mahalalel were eight hundred and ninety-five years and he died. Jared lived one hundred and sixty-two years and became the father of Enoch. Then Jared lived eight hundred years after he became the father of Enoch and he had other sons and daughters. So all the days of Jared were nine hundred and sixty-two years and he died. Enoch lived sixty-five years and became the father of Methuselah. Then Enoch walked with God three hundred years after he became the father of Methuselah and he had other sons and daughters. So all the days of Enoch were three hundred and sixty-five years. Enoch walked with God; and he was not, for God took him. Methuselah lived one hundred and eighty-seven years and became the father of Lamech. Then Methuselah lived seven hundred and eighty-two years after he became the father of Lamech and he had other sons and daughters. So all the days of Methuselah were nine hundred and sixty-nine years and he died. Lamech lived one hundred and eighty-two years and became the father of a son. Now he called his name Noah, saying, "This one will give us rest from our work and from the toil of our hands arising from the ground which the Lord has cursed." Then Lamech lived five hundred and ninety-five years after he became the father of Noah and he had other sons and daughters. So all the days of Lamech were seven hundred and seventy-seven years and he died. Noah was five hundred years old and Noah became the father of Shem, Ham and Japheth. (Genesis 5:3-32)

Page 157: For the creation was subjected to futility, not willingly, but because of Him who subjected it, in hope that the creation itself also will be set free from its slavery to corruption into the freedom of the glory of the children of God. (Romans 8:20-21)

Chapter 8: Year 1457

Page 176: Cain told Abel his brother, and it came about when they were in the field, that Cain rose up against Abel his brother and killed him. Then the Lord said to Cain, "Where is Abel your brother?" and he said, "I do not know. Am I my brother's keeper?" He said, "What have you done? The voice of your brother's blood is crying to Me from the ground. "Now you are cursed from the ground, which has opened its mouth to receive your brother's blood from your hand. (Genesis 4:8-11)

Page 170: For if God did not spare angels when they sinned, but cast them into hell and committed them to pits of darkness, reserved for judgment; and did not spare the ancient world, but preserved Noah, a preacher of righteousness, with seven others, when He brought a flood upon the world of the ungodly; (2 Peter 2:4-5)

Chapter 9: Year 1555

Page 183: Therefore God gave them over in the lusts of their hearts to impurity, so that their bodies would be dishonored among them. For they exchanged the truth of God for a lie and worshiped and served the creature rather than the Creator, who is blessed forever. Amen. For this reason God gave them over to degrading passions; for their women exchanged the natural function for that which is unnatural and in the same way also the men abandoned the natural function of the woman and burned in their desire toward one another, men with men committing indecent acts and receiving in their own persons the due penalty of their error, and just as they did not see fit to acknowledge God any longer, God gave them over to a depraved mind, to do those things which are not proper, being filled with all unrighteousness, wickedness, greed, evil; full of envy, murder, strife, deceit, malice; they are gossips, (Romans 1:24-29)

Page 183: Now it came about, when men began to multiply on the face of the land and daughters were born to them, that the sons of God saw that the daughters of men were beautiful; and they took wives for themselves, whomever they chose. Then the Lord said, "My Spirit shall not strive with man forever, because he also is flesh; nevertheless his days shall be one hundred and twenty years." (Genesis 6:1-3)

Chapter 10: Year 1556

Page 202: Know this first of all, that in the last days mockers will come with their mocking, following after their own lusts and saying, "Where is the promise of His coming? For ever since the fathers fell asleep, all continues just as it was from the beginning of creation." For when they maintain this, it escapes their notice that by the word of God the heavens existed long ago and the earth was formed out of water and by water, through which the world at that time was destroyed, being flooded with water. (2 Peter 3:3-6)

Page 207:So all the days of Lamech were seven hundred and seventy-seven years and he died. Noah was five hundred years old and Noah became the father of Shem, Ham and Japheth. (Genesis 5:31-32)

Page 208:Then God said to Noah, "The end of all flesh has come before Me; for the earth is filled with violence because of them; and behold, I am about to destroy them with the earth. "Make for yourself an ark of gopher wood; you shall make the ark with rooms and shall cover it inside and out with pitch. "This is how you shall make it: the length of the ark three hundred cubits, its breadth fifty cubits and its height thirty cubits. "You shall make a window for the ark and finish it to a cubit from the top; and set the door of the ark in the side of it; you shall make it with lower, second and third decks. "Behold, I, even I am bringing the flood of water upon the earth, to destroy all flesh in which is the breath of life, from under heaven; everything that is on the earth shall perish. "But I will establish My covenant with you; and you shall enter the ark—you and your sons and your wife and your sons' wives with you. And of every living thing of all flesh, you shall bring two of every kind into the ark, to keep them alive with you; they shall be male and female. Of the birds after their kind and of the animals after their kind, of every creeping thing of the ground after its kind, two of every kind will come to you to keep them alive. As for you, take for yourself some of all food which is edible and gather it to yourself; and it shall be for food for you and for them." Thus Noah did; according to all that God had commanded him, so he did. (Genesis 6:13-22)

Page 223: "As for you, take for yourself some of all food which is edible and gather it to yourself; and it shall be for food for you and for them." (Genesis 6:21)

Page 224: Methuselah lived one hundred and eighty-seven years and became the father of Lamech. Then Methuselah lived seven hundred and eighty-two years after he became the father of Lamech and he had other sons and daughters. So all the days of Methuselah were nine hundred and sixty-nine years and he died. (Genesis 5:25-27)

Chapter 11: Year 1655

Page 232: "Make for yourself an ark of gopher wood; you shall make the ark with rooms and shall cover it inside and out with pitch."(Genesis 6:14)

Page 233: "You shall make a window for the ark and finish it to a cubit from the top; and set the door of the ark in the side of it; you shall make it with lower, second and third decks." (Genesis 6:16)

Chapter 12: Year 1656–The Last Days

Page 239: "You shall take with you of every clean animal by sevens, a male and his female; and of the animals that are not clean two, a male and his female; also of the birds of the sky, by sevens, male and female, to keep offspring alive on the face of all the earth." (Genesis 7:2-3)

Page 254: Then the Lord said to Noah, "Enter the ark, you and all your household, for you alone I have seen to be righteous before Me in this time. You shall take with you of every clean animal by sevens, a male and his female; and of the animals that are not clean two, a male and his female; also of the birds of the sky, by sevens, male and female, to keep offspring alive on the face of all the earth. For after seven more days, I will send rain on the earth forty days and forty nights; and I will blot out from the face of the land every living thing that I have made." Noah did according to all that the Lord had commanded him. Now Noah was six hundred years old when the flood of water came upon the earth. Then Noah and his sons and his wife and his sons' wives with him entered the ark because of the water of the flood. Of clean animals and animals that are not clean and birds and everything that creeps on the ground, there went into the ark to Noah by twos, male and female, as God had commanded Noah. (Genesis 7:1-9)

Page 263: On the very same day Noah and Shem and Ham and Japheth, the sons of Noah and Noah's wife and the three wives of his sons with them, entered the ark, they and every beast after its kind and all the cattle after their kind and every creeping thing that creeps on the earth after its kind and every bird after its kind, all sorts of birds. So they went into the ark to Noah, by twos of all flesh in which was the breath of life. Those that entered, male and female of all flesh, entered as God had commanded him; and the Lord closed it behind him. (Genesis 7:13-16)

Page 263: (A description of how God's glory left the temple during those days when He judged Judah for her sin) Then the glory of the Lord departed from the threshold of the temple and stood over the cherubim. When the cherubim departed, they lifted their wings and rose up from the earth in my sight with the wheels beside them; and they stood still at the entrance of the east gate of the Lord's house and the glory of the God of Israel hovered over them. (Ezekiel 10:18-19) Then the cherubim lifted up their wings with the wheels beside them and the glory of the God of Israel hovered over them. The glory of the Lord went up from the midst of the city and stood over the mountain which is east of the city. (Ezekiel 11:22-23)

Chapter 13: Year 1656–The End of All Flesh

Page 256: In the six hundredth year of Noah's life, in the second month, on the seventeenth day of the month, on the same day all the fountains of the great deep burst open and the floodgates of the sky were opened. (Genesis 7:11)

Page 276: Then the flood came upon the earth for forty days and the water increased and lifted up the ark, so that it rose above the earth. The water prevailed and increased greatly upon the earth and the ark floated on the surface of the water. (Genesis 7:17-18)

Page 277: But God remembered Noah and all the beasts and all the cattle that were with him in the ark; and God caused a wind to pass over the earth and the water subsided. Also the fountains of the deep and the floodgates of the sky were closed and the rain from the sky was restrained; and the water receded steadily from the earth and at the end of one hundred and fifty days the water decreased. (Genesis 8:1-3)

Page 279: In the seventh month, on the seventeenth day of the month, the ark rested upon the mountains of Ararat. (Genesis 8:4)

Page 279: The water decreased steadily until the tenth month; in the tenth month, on the first day of the month, the tops of the mountains became visible. (Genesis 8:5)

Page 280: Then it came about at the end of forty days, that Noah opened the window of the ark which he had made; and he sent out a raven and it flew here and there until the water was dried up from the earth. Then he sent out a dove from him, to see if the water was abated from the face of the land; but the dove found no resting place for the sole of her foot, so she returned to him into the ark, for the water was on the surface of all the earth. Then he put out his hand and took her and brought her into the ark to himself. (Genesis 8:6-9)

Page 281: Now it came about in the six hundred and first year, in the first month, on the first of the month, the water was dried up from the earth. Then Noah removed the covering of the ark and looked and behold, the surface of the ground was dried up. (Genesis 8:13)

Page 282:In the second month, on the twenty-seventh day of the month, the earth was dry. Then God spoke to Noah, saying, "Go out of the ark, you and your wife and your sons and your sons' wives with you. Bring out with you every living thing of all flesh that is with you, birds and animals and every creeping thing that creeps on the earth, that they may breed abundantly on the earth and be fruitful and multiply on the earth." So Noah went out and his sons and his wife and his sons' wives with him. Every beast, every creeping thing and every bird, everything that moves on the earth, went out by their families from the ark. (Genesis 8:14-19)

Page 284: Then Noah built an altar to the Lord and took of every clean animal and of every clean bird and offered burnt offerings on the altar. (Genesis 8:20)

Page 285: The Lord smelled the soothing aroma; and the Lord said to Himself, "I will never again curse the ground on account of man, for the intent of man's heart is evil from his youth; and I will never again destroy every living thing, as I have done. While the earth remains, seedtime and harvest and cold and heat and summer and winter and day and night shall not cease." (Genesis 8:21-22)

Chapter 14: Year 1657

Page 294: These are the records of the generations of Shem. Shem was one hundred years old and became the father of Arpachshad two years after the flood; (Genesis 11:10)

Page 304: Then Noah began farming and planted a vineyard. He drank of the wine and became drunk and uncovered himself inside his tent. (Genesis 9:20-21)

Page 307: Then Noah began farming and planted a vineyard. He drank of the wine and became drunk and uncovered himself inside his tent. Ham, the father of Canaan, saw the nakedness of his father and told his two brothers outside. (Genesis 9:20-22)

Page 308: But Shem and Japheth took a garment and laid it upon both their shoulders and walked backward and covered the nakedness of their father; and their faces were turned away, so that they did not see their father's nakedness. (Genesis 9:23)

Page 309: When Noah awoke from his wine, he knew what his youngest son had done to him. So he said, "Cursed be Canaan; A servant of servants He shall be to his brothers." He also said, "Blessed be the Lord, The God of Shem; and let Canaan be his servant. "May God enlarge Japheth and let him dwell in the tents of Shem; and let Canaan be his servant." (Genesis 9:24-27)

About the Author

 Robert Wetmore pastored Bellevue Community Church in Nebraska from 1987 to 1995. He then served as Professor of Theology at Toccoa Falls College in Georgia until 2008. Currently Dr. Wetmore is Professor of Religious Studies and Dean of the Chapel at Forman Christian College in Lahore, Pakistan. He is married to his wife, Joyce, and they have three children and several grandchildren.

Books by Robert Wetmore

"The Promise Series"

The Two Trees
End of All Flesh
The Tower

The Revelation of the Christ

Principles of Evangelism

Worship the Way it Was Meant to Be

Robert Wetmore's books are available on line at
www.findingChristthroughfiction.com
www.findingChristBooks.com